# The Sleeping Knight

## A Novel

## Kristina Stangl

ISBN: 978-1-963232-19-6

Second Edition
Cover Art: BigValleyPress
Map: BigValleyPress
Library of Congress Registration Number: TXu002455546
Printed in the United States of America

# DEDICATION

In dedication to my loving family. Thanks for always being my rock.

And to those who might feel lost and in search of a life's purpose, may this tale bring you much joy, comfort and hope.

Lastly, to the hero in us all.

# Also by Kristina Stangl

**The Enchanted Forest Saga:**

The Curse of the Dark Horseman

The Sleeping Knight

The Emerald Prince

**A Villainous Ever After:**

The Heartless Villainess

**Silverheart:**

Cupid's Serenade

**Sex, Lies & Politics:**

The Ambassador's Wife

Wake Up, Darling

My Life is a Soap Opera

Kill Me, Kiss Me

**www.kristinastangl.com**

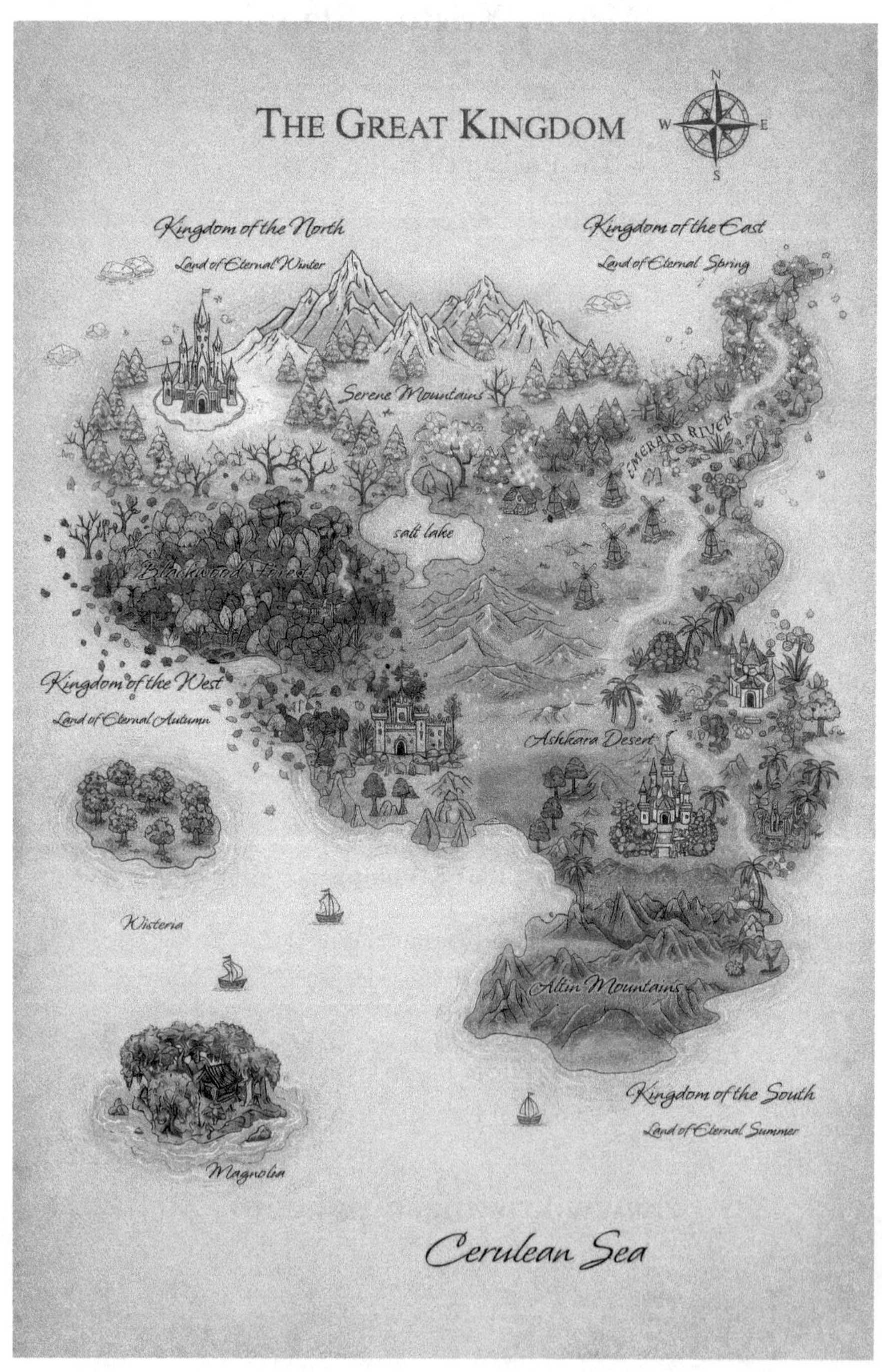
THE GREAT KINGDOM
N
W E
S
Kingdom of the North
Land of Eternal Winter
Kingdom of the East
Land of Eternal Spring
Serene Mountains
EMERALD RIVER
salt lake
Blackwood Forest
Kingdom of the West
Land of Eternal Autumn
Ashkara Desert
Wisteria
Altin Mountains
Magnolia
Kingdom of the South
Land of Eternal Summer
Cerulean Sea

# CONTENTS

# PROLOGUE

Long ago, a mother held her two young daughters closely within the tight grasp of her arms. On her right side, was her youngest daughter, whose hair was blonde and as bright as the sun; while on her left side, was her eldest daughter, whose hair was dark and as black as midnight.

While the mother loved her daughters equally, she also knew that they were two very unique girls, each exhibiting vastly distinctive and opposite styles of personalities. But regardless of their differences, the mother still loved and adored her daughters, endlessly. And even though she knew that their lives were predestined to wander off onto two separate paths, with one daughter destined for good and the other daughter fated for evil, the mother silently prayed that her daughters would remain steadfast in their overall faith and love for each other.

That in the end, no matter the outcomes of their individual fates, the mother remained hopeful that her daughters would one day, strive to overcome these unfortunate obstacles by recognizing the timeless power of their sisterly bond, regardless of the great misfortunes that lies ahead of them.

Although her daughters were two years apart, they were also ironically born on the same exact day: the first day of autumn, also known as the twenty-first of September. And today, was that special day. Today, was their birthday.

While her eldest daughter recently turned eight, her youngest daughter was now aged six. As birthday gifts, the mother presented her daughters with a matching set of jewelry, consisting of a necklace and a bracelet. Fashioned in the form of a golden chain, the necklace included a jewel pendant in the shape of a violet toned heart. A bright amethyst heart stone that shined and sparkled against the sunlight.

Meanwhile, the second pair of jewelry came in the form of a bracelet, that was also crafted using the same fine gold materials. Identical to the necklace, the bracelet also included an amethyst heart stone in the center. In the end, the bracelet was a matching replica to its sister necklace. A perfect pair.

According to their mother, the necklace and the bracelet served as a companion pair, in which both pieces of jewelry were needed in order to be deemed as a complete set. Carefully, the mother placed the necklace around the neck of her youngest daughter, and the bracelet onto the wrist of her eldest daughter. Smilingly, she cradled both of her daughters within her loving arms, as she began to tell them a story.

"No matter what happens in the future," the mother began, "Remember, your love for one another. The world might be a scary and a confusing place, but your sisterly bond will forever unite you both. Whenever either one of you grows angry or feels disappointed by the actions caused by the other, then simply gaze down upon these fine pieces of jewelry that I've gifted you all, here today. Think of these gifts as special keepsakes. A constant reminder to overlook each other's faults, as no one in this world is perfect. But most importantly, remember that love and forgiveness are the fundamental keys to everything that matters in this universe."

"My darling girls," their mother continued to say, "Kings may rise or fall, while kingdoms might flourish or crumble; worlds may begin or end, while honor and riches might come or go; but your sisterhood will outlast them all. While romantic love might be fickle in nature, sisterly love is the truest form of everlasting love. Unlike romantic love, this love is born not out of attraction or admiration or even, affection; but by blood. And blood, my dear girls, is thicker than anything."

* * *

# Several Years Later...

The bells rung across the land in the Kingdom of the West; chimes that were heard throughout all corners of the Great Kingdom. The Great Kingdom was comprised of four smaller principalities that were each governed by four separate kings. The Kingdom of the North was also known as the Land of Eternal Winter, while the Kingdom of the South was the Land of Eternal Summer. Meanwhile, the Kingdom of the East was the Land of Eternal Spring and the Kingdom of the West was the Land of Eternal Autumn. Each kingdom represented the four seasons found on Earth— another world that was connected to their realm through an enchanted forest that operated as a traveling portal.

It was a peculiar forest that was found in a small but sleepy secluded village, located in Northern England. The enchanted forest was not well known to many outsiders; however, for those who were blessed enough to accidentally stumble upon it, then they were ultimately, the only souls allowed to enter and explore it. While the enchanted forest had many great mysterious secrets and magical elements hidden away within its territory, it was also the one and only gateway that united the Great Kingdom to the lands of Earth.

Tragically, the late King of the West had recently died and today was his funeral. As the citizens eagerly gathered outside of the cathedral to usher in the burial ceremony, the new crown prince stood at the doorway to greet the arriving guests.

Out of respect, the neighboring kings and queens graciously traveled far and wide to personally deliver their heartfelt condolences to him, as well as the other royals and everyday ordinary citizens alike. Everyone who resided within their realm— young or old, female or male, rich or poor—they all came to pay their final respects to the late king. A man, whom many regarded as a fair, honorable and righteous monarch. A ruler, who was well admired, loved, cherished and adored by all of his many subjects.

Following tradition and duty, the newly appointed crown prince smilingly stood there at the door, in front of a grieving audience. Forcing a fake smile upon his handsome face and all the while, feeling nothing but utter anguish, all hidden away behind that insincere expression. That, along with another dose of tremendous sadness brewing high above within his chest. In his heart. Alas, he was *heartbroken*.

As much as he wished that this day had never came to be; in the end, he simply couldn't undue the past. Unfortunately, his brother's untimely death was a blow to his aching heart. His elder brother might have been the king to the rest of the kingdom, but to him, he was his loving older brother. A brother, whom he looked up to. A brother, whom he admired and adored. A brother, whom he loved with all of his heart.

Tragically, the late king had recently died from an unfortunate horseback riding accident gone wrong. But what was even more tragic than the accident itself, was the fact that Leopold was still in his prime years, no older than age forty. A newly appointed king placed onto the throne in his zenith, for a reign spanning less than three months. An inadequate amount of time reserved for anyone to claim a bride. Therefore, as a result of these unfortunate circumstances, Leopold died as an unmarried king, who most importantly, failed to produce any direct heirs of his own.

While the public accepted the late king's death as a devasting sporting event gone horribly wrong, many insiders within the palace suspected that his brother's so-called *accident* might have actually stemmed from something else far more sinister. A calculated plot that was secretly planned at hand. An untimely and tragic death resulting from foul play, executed in its finest and most unsuspecting of forms.

But, unfortunately, for the crown prince, there wasn't any substantial evidence to prove Leopold's death as a murder. As far as the public was concerned, such bold, cruel and devious claims were nothing more than an outlandish conspiracy theory. A false narrative that provided no successful leads to any specific suspect(s).

However, with that being said, the crown prince still remained ever suspicious about his brother's passing. After all, his elder brother was regarded to be a superior equestrian. In fact, Leopold wasn't the sort of person who ever made such poor, thoughtless or careless sporting errors. Not once, not ever. Truly, such mistakes were most unbecoming of his noble-like character. After all, Leopold was regarded to be a true *hero*. And heroes *never* made such foolish mistakes. That's why they were heroes. Unlike, himself…

As the second son and spare, the new crown prince didn't envision himself becoming the next future king. This was *never* his wish or plan. In fact, up until today, he was previously considered to be a reckless adventurer and a heartless vagabond. A foolish prince with a terrible reputation. A man, who gambled away every last penny in his pocket. A prince, who fought reckless battles, all for the sake of an adventure. A ruthless rake, who chased and pursued women as if they were prized possessions— albeit, only for the duration of a single but blissful night of pleasure. That, plus everything else that rebels were expected to do. Alas, everything that his late and honorable brother did, he did the exact *opposite*. And yet, in the end, here he was standing at his much beloved brother's funeral, as the next heir to the throne. An unwanted and unavoidable fate that he had somehow, still managed to circle back to.

Sadly, the crown prince was here today not only to mourn for the untimely passing of his brother, but to also attend his own coronation as well. A sacred and momentous ceremony that was also scheduled to take place shortly after the funeral procession. As much as it greatly pained the prince to be crowned as the new king on the *same day* that he buried his beloved brother, tradition held that this transfer of power had to be done. The sooner, the better.

Regardless of his own personal feelings about the whole matter, the kingdom still needed a new king. A monarch to protect the Kingdom of the West from any external threats and unwanted forces. And so, this is how the formal rebel became the new crown prince and ultimately, came to stand right here in this very cathedral.

Meanwhile, as the last guest arrived onto the scene, the prince was unpleasantly surprised to see this person dressed in all black, while also wearing a thick and dark black cloak over their body. As a sacred tradition of the Kingdom of the West, all mourners were expected to wear one of the late king's official colors: deep brown, forest green, amber, burgundy, scarlet or marigold— muted jewel tones that represented their western lands. However, unlike the other guests attending the late king's funeral, this unnamed person was clearly *not* abiding to the standard uniform. Already, a true and unforgivable offense.

"Who are you? Why are you dressed like this? Why have you come here not wearing the late king's colors?" asked the crown prince, angrily.

Being a rebel himself, the crown prince recognized trouble whenever he saw it. In fact, he could practically smell danger from a mile away. Whomever this stranger was, they obvious came here to bring forth bad news.

Reaching for his handy dagger located within his right-hand pocket, the crown prince kept his eyes directly affixed upon this dark stranger. However, before he had the opportunity to pull his dagger out, he suddenly heard screams coming from inside of the cathedral.

Immediately, the crown prince quickly spun around and to his horror, he saw a fire explode right in the center of the church. *A bomb.* A few seconds later, a host of enemy soldiers suddenly appeared, all dressed in black armors. They swiftly entered into the premise, with their swords in hand. *A barbaric invasion.* Ruthlessly, they began to mercilessly attack the invited guests, including torturing and slaughtering both royals and civilians alike.

Before his very own eyes, a brutal rebellion was unleashed and a bloody war was now upon them. As the frantic crowd of survivors fled outside through the back doors in panic, the crown prince returned his attention back and over to the dark stranger standing before him.

As the young prince stared at the dark stranger's shadowy face, the mysterious guest slowly pulled their hood down from off their head and shoulders to reveal their true form. And to his astonishment, the person standing before him was *not* a man but a *woman*. A female, who possessed a sinister face that was dark green in complexion. A color similar to poisonous ivy.

In shock, the crown prince quickly took a step back, as he watched the green faced woman with bright yellow eyes, approach him. While the prince was at a complete loss for words, the strange woman, on the other hand, was not.

"Step aside, dear prince," she spoke aloud, exhibiting a great sense of self-confidence.

"No!" cried the prince, with much determination.

The world might have come crashing into flames, but he absolutely refused to go down... at least not without a fight!

Pulling his dagger from out of his pocket, the crown prince was ready to attack this wicked witch. But suddenly, his hands quickly grew stiff and within the blink of an eye, he instantly collapsed down onto the stone floor. Alas, a spell was forcefully placed upon him. Instantly, he proceeded to kneel down against his will, as his body began to prostrate in front of her.

Triumphantly, the wicked witch stared down at the crown prince smilingly, foolishly believing that she had already won the battle before it even began.

Walking right past him, the witch gazed down upon his handsome but angered face and relished at the mere sight of it; all the while, taking great pleasure in witnessing the agony reflected within his silvery pair of eyes. While his body might have been frozen solid, his eyes, full of emotion, spoke a thousand words. Cries of anger. Of horror. Of injustice. Of pain. Of hate. Of *revenge.*

Meanwhile, as her own bright yellow eyes, with a hint of emerald green shining within the inner rims of her pupils, stared down at her enemy, the wicked witch slowly bent down and grabbed a hold of the prince's face. Now, with his chin safely resting within the palms of her dark green hands, she calmly addressed him.

"Fear not, my dear prince. I'm not here to kill you. But I am going to *steal* your kingdom away," she boldly declared with the most sinister and foul expression written across her wretchedly green face.

With great despair, the frozen prince watched as his brother's corpse burned into flames, turning into nothing more but burnt ashes. Meanwhile, the wicked witch proudly descended down the burning aisle and claimed the most valuable and honorable seat of their entire kingdom. A sacred seat, in which he was previously set to claim: the *throne*.

To his complete horror, the crown prince soon realized that the witch's promise to him that was made no more than a minute ago, was about to quickly come into fruition. Alas, for as he stood there motionless, the wicked witch had just managed to successfully snatch away his rightful throne and had treacherously crowned herself as the next queen.

And her name was Queen Vera, the new self-proclaimed ruler of the Kingdom of the West, also known as the former wicked witch and now the evil queen, who once lived in exile in the lands called Earth.

# CHAPTER 1

Today, was a special day for Lady Violet Galloway, for this day was her twenty-first birthday. The twenty-first of September in 1921, which also happened to be the first day of autumn.

As the eldest daughter of Lord Henry, the fifth Earl of Galloway and his wife, Lady Kassandra, the fifth Countess of Galloway, Violet was a blessed and privileged young lady. She, along with her two younger siblings, Daphne, her sister, aged sixteen, and her brother, Adrian, aged thirteen, all grew up in the grand ancestral estates of their parents. While their winters and autumns were spent at Wiltshire Hall—the seat of their maternal family— their springs and summers were spent exclusively at Galloway Manor— the seat of their father's line.

With Lord Galloway and Adrian currently touring London with the aim of enrolling her younger brother at an all-boys preparatory military academy, Violet remained at Wiltshire Hall, alongside her sister, Daphne, their mother, Kassie, and their great-grandmother, Maureen. While this milestone day marked her first birthday celebrated in the company of her family after many years spent away and alone at university, Violet's hard work and dedication to her studies, ultimately, paid off. In the end, she returned back home as a full-fledged university graduate. However, Violet's return home wasn't as exciting as she had initially hoped it would to be.

While she had previously lived an overall, rather modest life in London by primarily focusing solely on her studies and attending her classes religiously; but apart from academics, Violet did little else. Rather than visiting London's historic castles or famous landmarks, or even attending various balls and social gatherings, Violet instead, chose to keep quietly to herself in the hopes of graduating early.

By attending university, a full year ahead of schedule, Violet wanted to finish her studies as early as possible. For the sooner she started her studies, then the sooner she graduated. But why did Violet want to finish her academic studies so early? Well, in truth, she secretly had plans. Plans to study science and medicine. To even possibly become a doctor. Someone who *cured* things. Someone who *traveled* the world. Someone who experienced *adventures*. Someone who had a life's *purpose*.

While most young women in her time weren't allowed to take on such male dominated roles, Violet still wanted to challenge the norm and study in the field of science. While she was aware that her desire to pursue a career in medicine was a bold risk to take, especially for a young lady who was a member of the aristocracy; however, in the end, Violet was a true dreamer.

Even as the daughter of the famous Earl of Galloway, Violet still longed for a life of adventure. Listening to all of the numerous tall tales about curses, witches, magic, adventure and romantic love affairs as told by her mother and great-grandmother since the early days of her childhood, Violet longed for a life that brought her to different parts of the world. Places that she had only read about in books and nothing that she had actually ever seen before in real life. And by becoming a doctor or a scientist, then Violet would have the opportunity to freely travel and experience the world for herself, while also helping people along the way. In the end, it wasn't so much about her studying science and medicine; it really was just an excuse to leave her world behind and to discover her true self.

Growing up as a member of a British aristocratic family, who resided in a small, sleepy and secluded village located within the remote parts of the English countryside, Violet lived a rather sheltered and dare we say, a simple but boring life. While her parents might have experienced an adventurous life in the distant past— with her own father having been condemned to an unfortunate curse, previously cast by a wicked witch— by the time Violet was born, her father's curse had long been broken, and her parents and their children went on to live perfectly normal and ordinary lives, just like everyone else around them.

Although Violet was extremely grateful to have been born into a kind, wealthy and privileged family; however, her heart still longed for a different sort of existence. While her life might have appeared to be perfect; internally, Violet still wasn't satisfied. Instead, she longed for a life of adventure. A journey that brought her to far off places, including remote and exotic lands. A life that was anywhere else but *here...*

Ever since Violet returned back home from university, she felt a bit lost as she struggled to transition back into her old way of life. I suppose the wise old saying that once a person leaves home, then they can never truly return back the same way as before, was something that Violet kept near and dear to her heart.

While Violet didn't want to openly admit her melancholy feelings out loud to her family, she still silently struggled to adapt. At this point, Violet was at a crossroads in her life. Now, at aged twenty-one, she was expected to marry. Even though she wanted to return back to university to study science and medicine, she hadn't yet told her parents about her secret wishes. But even if she had, then would they still come to accept it?

After all, Violet was the eldest daughter of an earl. Therefore, she was expected to marry either a fellow aristocrat or at the very least, another wealthy suitor. Even though her parents never forced the subject of marriage onto her, Violet also knew what was expected of her as well. Unfortunately, upon her arrival into town, she had already heard the whispers spoken back at the village. Everyone in their community expected her to marry. And *soon.*

Of course, it was only natural for women of Violet's tender age to already be married or at the very least, engaged. In fact, it was rather rare for a young debutante, such as herself, to return back home after many years spent away, without a husband or even, a fiancé. Therefore, it was only a matter of time, before Violet eventually had to choose.

And so, by the arrival of her twenty-first birthday, Violet felt more sadness than joy. For with each passing day, Violet realized that she was going to have start to making decisions. Important choices about her impending future. Would she continue on with her studies, or marry a man of her family's choosing?

Alas, the pressures of society were starting to take a toll on her nerves. In truth, Violet was looking for a purpose in her life and because of these inner struggles, she wanted nothing more than to simply run away from it all.

"Violet, you do realize that they're planning a birthday party for you downstairs," Daphne delivered the news to her sister, as she unapologetically barged into Violet's bedroom, without so much as bothering to knock at her door in advance.

"Must you always come in unannounced?" Violet asked her, finding Daphne's unwelcomed entrance as plainly being just rude.

"You're my sister. Why ever should I knock?" asked Daphne, mockingly.

"Because unlike you, *I* choose to knock every time that I enter into your bedroom," Violet made sure to point this fact out. "It's called common curtesy."

"Well, that's on *you*," Daphne retorted.

As angry and annoyed as Violet was, she ultimately decided to let it go. Fighting with her younger sister on her birthday wasn't the answer. In the end, being upset on her special day just wasn't worth it. And if her family was planning a birthday celebration for her downstairs, then the last thing that she wanted was for them to hear their ongoing sisterly quarrels.

Giving into her sister's unwanted appearance, Violet sighed and simply asked, "Alright Daphne, why are you here?"

While Violet did her best to maintain her cool demeanor, she continued to watch her sister with a skeptical eye. If Daphne successfully managed to barge into her bedroom unannounced, then it generally served a greater purpose. And usually, it was to steal one of *her* treasured belongings.

"I need to borrow something of yours for the party," replied Daphne, as she went ahead and invited herself over towards Violet's vanity and began rummaging through her personal belongings, including her much beloved jewelry box.

"Don't take anything from inside of there!" Violet shouted, as she ran over and slammed the jewelry box shut.

"But it's not fair!" Daphne yelled in defiance. "You have all the pretty jewels, while I have none! And I do want to look pretty for your birthday party!"

For a moment, Violet almost felt sorry for her sister. However, the key word was *almost*. While it was true, as the eldest daughter, Violet did have more valuable jewelry than her younger sister. In truth, her jewels were technically considered to be priceless family heirlooms that were split between her mother and herself.

However, with that being said, Daphne was not entirely left without any special heirlooms of her own. While Violet might have owned most of the family's jewelry, Daphne had practically all of their family's collection of tiaras, including a few pieces of diamond brooches and a handful of other valuable hair accessories. So really, Daphne *wasn't* one to pity.

"Daphne, I might have all the jewels, but you've got the tiaras," Violet retorted. "I'd say that's more than a fair share on your part."

"Well, Violet, I may have the tiaras, but what good are they if I don't have any matching jewelry to go along with it!" shouted her teenage sister.

"Well, then you should have thought about that fact, before you asked Mother to make this arrangement," Violet reminded her sister.

It was true, it was originally Daphne's idea to take possession of their family's tiara collection, while Violet inherited all of the jewelry. But now, it seemed as if Daphne not only wanted to keep her cake but to eat it, too.

"I agreed to this arrangement years ago. Violet, you already know that. But now, I'm sixteen years old, and I don't want to look like a plain debutante at your birthday party!" Daphne pleaded.

"Why do you even care? Who's even expected to attend this party?" asked Violet, most curiously.

"No one really, apart from our family. But still, I want to look pretty, even for them," Daphne whined.

"Very well," sighed Violet. "I'll let you borrow my pearl ring. But whatever you do, please don't wear my new pearl earrings. Those were a graduation gift from Father. Plus, I'm saving them to wear on a special occasion."

"A special occasion?" asked Daphne, with widened eyes. "A special occasion, as in an upcoming engagement? Violet, are you secretly engaged? If that's the case, then why haven't you yet told me about this life-changing news?"

As Violet stared at her younger sister, she couldn't help but laugh. As different as they were personality wise on the inside, on the outside, they practically looked just like twins.

While they were only five years apart, they both still had the same pale skin and fiery red locks of hair that they inherited from their mother, along with the identical pair of emerald green eyes that they got from their father. It was only their younger brother, Adrian, who inherited their father's dark black hair. However, he, like his elder sisters, also had their similar emerald green eyes— a trait that was unique to the Galloway clan.

As much as Violet secretly wanted to lie to Daphne to stop her from asking more questions; in the end, she couldn't find it within her heart to avoid her.

"No, I'm not engaged," she answered truthfully. "But either way, I'd like to save those pearl earrings for another time and venue. In the meantime, you can borrow the pearl ring."

And just like that, Violet handed the pearl ring over to her sister. Although she was greatly disappointed by her sister's overall lack of sharing, Daphne reluctantly took the ring. Soon afterwards, she swiftly exited her sister's bedroom.

With her sister gone, Violet decided to change into a new lavender silk and lace gown. Given that today was her birthday and that her family was eager to celebrate it with her downstairs, Violet believed that the least she could do was to attend her own party looking her very best.

✳  ✳  ✳

Twenty minutes later, Violet descended down the staircase and walked into the grand salon. Given that this was the autumn season, the Galloway clan resided at their maternal family's estate, Wiltshire Hall. An estate that was also the permanent residence of their great-grandmother, Maureen Stanton.

Even though Violet personally preferred her father's mansion, Galloway Manor, due to its closer proximately to the forest, she politely and patiently held her tongue and followed her mother's wishes to spend her autumn and winter seasons in the company of her aging great-grandmother.

While the forest was in fact, actually an enchanted forest— the famous site, in which her parents had once met and fell madly in love— Violet, herself, had never witnessed nor experienced any real magic in there. Although most folks remained skeptical that the forest contained any true magic in the first place; in contrast to popular belief, Violet faithfully accepted in her heart that in all honesty, it most likely *did*.

After all, she, herself, was named Violet in honor of the magical flowers that blossomed within that very forest. If her parents hadn't believed in such enchanting notions, then they never would have named her Violet to begin with.

As Violet entered into the grand salon, she saw her great-grandmother, Maureen, already seated down on the sofa, while her mother, Kassie, was standing over near the window that overlooked the estate's scenic view of the luscious garden. Meanwhile, her younger sister, Daphne, was also seated nearby their great-grandmother. From the looks of it, they appeared to be enjoying their daily afternoon session of high tea.

Furthermore, as soon as Violet entered into the room, she couldn't help but notice a pair of sparkling white studs, shining around her sister's ears. It was a translucence white shine that was opaque in color and sparkly, just like... a *pearl*.

Alas, Violet quickly soon realized that her newly gifted pearl earrings were as of right now, currently worn around the ears of her highly annoying teenage sister! The very pearl earrings that Violet specifically asked her *not* to wear!

"DAPHNE!!!" she shouted angrily.

"Honestly, I don't care if it's my birthday or not, but I specifically asked you *not* to wear my new pearl earrings!!!" Violet yelled, once more. "Daphne, how could you do such a thing! Especially, after I lent you, my ring! How could you be so selfish! Why can't you respect my belongings! Must you always have everything of mine!"

Embarrassed by Violet's unexpected outburst, Daphne immediately flinched and instantly, broke into tears. A second later, she swiftly ran out of the room, slamming the door shut behind her. Although Daphne was technically wrong to have taken Violet's belongings without her permission; but as soon as Violet spoke her mind out loud, she quickly regretted her choice of words. While Daphne might have previously acted like a complete brat, Violet may have also been a bit too harsh on her younger sister as well.

Unfortunately, as soon as Daphne exited the premise, Violet stared at her mother's and great-grandmother's faces and instantly, she saw the looks of disappointment, reflected upon their expressions. At least, that was the case for her mother. In truth, her great-grandmother was usually quite difficult to read in general.

Even though Violet had her own personal reasons for yelling at Daphne; but now that she had, she actually felt guilty for doing so. Almost regretful. Truly, she never meant to make Daphne cry. Especially, not in front of their family. But now that she did, Violet was starting to feel embarrassed by her own actions and rude behavior.

"Really, Violet? Was that reaction at all necessary?" Kassie lashed out at her eldest daughter, angrily. "Honestly, Violet, you didn't need to embarrass her like that! Daphne might have been wrong to take your earrings, but she's still your sister. Truly, Violet, I expect more from you."

And then, without saying another word, Kassie quickly excused herself from the salon to chase after Daphne.

Meanwhile, as Violet stood there silently and motionless, she was about ready to turn around and flee back into the comfort and privacy of her bedroom. Unfortunately, this wasn't how she envisioned spending her twenty-first birthday. Really, this all was too much!

But to Violet's sheer surprise, after her mother left, her great-grandmother had an entirely different reaction. Unlike the blunt display of disappointment as expressed by her mother, her great-grandmother in contrast, appeared to have actually shared some surprising sympathy for her.

"Violet, don't leave," Maureen firmly spoke, with her first set of words sounding more like a commanding order, rather than a sincere plea.

"Don't worry about your mother or sister," she continued on. "They'll live. It's not the end of the world. Here, please come and take a seat beside me."

Following her request, Violet did just that. Taking the seat that her sister had previously occupied, Violet sat down and reverted her full attention over to Maureen.

"Would the birthday girl care for some tea? Tea with a dash of milk, correct?" she asked, with a bright smile.

Happily, Violet nodded in agreement. Already, she was starting to feel more comfortable and cheerful, once again.

"You know, sisters are one of the most complicated sorts of relationships," Maureen began, as she poured a fresh cup of tea for her great-granddaughter.

"Tell me about it," Violet sighed.

"Your mother and I might have grown up as only children, so I can't actually say that I completely understand as to how you must feel right now," Maureen admitted, as she handed the teacup and saucer over to her great-granddaughter. "But, at the same time, I do sympathize with you."

"I'll admit, I do love my sister," Violet remarked, as she took her first sip of tea. "However, nowadays, I feel like it's getting more and more difficult for us to get along. We really are total opposites."

"That's very true," Maureen agreed. "From what I can tell, you're both vastly different. She's a bit spoiled; whereas, you're more like me."

And *that* honest and bold statement certainly caught Violet's attention. No one else had ever dared to speak such a thing; let alone, to admit it openly out loud. In fact, no one else had ever recognized Daphne's recent spoiled streak, apart from herself. Honestly, it was a nice reassurance that someone else other than herself, could also see-through Daphne's childish and selfish cries.

"Your parents just love you girls way too much. Unfortunately, such love can also cause blindness to the faults found within their darling daughters," she added. "Not that I don't love you or your sister equally too, of course."

"I know," Violet sighed.

"But, as of lately, your sister has grown a bit spoiled, while you are blossoming into a fine young lady," complemented her great-grandmother, glowingly. "Whatever they say, pay little attention to them. You're stronger built, just like me. We may patiently endure the rough tide; but in the end, we *always* triumph over our adversities. Never forget that, too."

Her great-grandmother's encouraging words certainly brought a much-needed comfort to Violet's gloomy mood. It was overwhelmingly, refreshing to hear such heartfelt complements and recognition.

"Furthermore, ignore Daphne's tantrums, as well as your mother's harsh scolding. Plus, don't even think twice about those pearl earrings. Let Daphne have them. In fact, I have something that's far more special, just for you. A gift."

And then, reaching into her pocket, Maureen pulled out a purple velvet square box. Afterwards, she handed the box over to Violet, as she motioned for her to open it.

"Go ahead, my dear. Please, open it," she pleaded.

Excitingly, Violet popped open the box. Thus far, this was her only birthday present to date. Much to her delight, this gift certainly did not disappoint. Instead of another set of pearls, this gift was a violet jeweled pendant, presented in the shape of a heart and held together on a golden chain. A necklace.

As Violet stared down at the purple object, she was enchanted by its exquisite beauty. For as many pieces of fine jewelry that she owned in her private collection, this was by far, the rarest and most beautiful piece of all.

"Great-grandmother, this is so incredibly beautiful. Wherever did you acquire it?" asked Violet, as she held the necklace tightly within the grasp of her hands.

"It's an amethyst. It's meant to help guide you to your heart's greatest desire," replied Maureen, smilingly. "It will lead you to your destiny my dear, while always bringing you the best of luck. Just promise me, Violet, that from now on, you'll always wear it around your neck at all times."

"Oh, of course I shall!" Violet happily exclaimed, as she quickly placed the necklace safely around her neck.

"How does it look?" asked Violet with a beaming smile.

"Fit for a future queen," Maureen admitted, with much pride and joy.

"Great-grandmother, how did you come across such a fine piece of jewelry?" Violet curiously asked her. "I've never seen jewelry like this before. Is it another family heirloom? From the looks of it, this necklace seems rather old. Is it an antique?"

"Actually, you're right," agreed Maureen, as she took another sip of her tea.

Grabbing an almond scone from off the table, she took a bite of it and said, "It's an ancient piece of jewelry. In fact, this necklace once belonged to your own late grandmother, Sarah."

"My Grandmother Sarah? No wonder it's so elegant!" Violet happily exclaimed. "Based on the portraits that I've seen depicting my grandmother back at Galloway Manor, she was most certainly a refined, elegant and beautiful lady. Of course, she'd own a remarkably fine and rare antique necklace, such as this!"

"Yes, it's true. This particular necklace was gifted to Sarah by her own mother. While your grandmother was once the owner of this necklace, her sister also had the matching bracelet," Maureen revealed.

"A matching bracelet? Did it also share a similar design, too?"

And then, Violet realized that her grandmother had a sister and the fact that she wasn't privy about having a long-lost great aunt, up until now. Why hadn't she heard about Sarah's sister before?

"Wait, did my grandmother really have a sister? Why am I only learning of this now?"

"One question, at a time," Maureen happily laughed on. "But first, let's start with the bracelet. Yes, it was a matching pair to the necklace. It too, also shared an amethyst stone in the same heart shape. Both the necklace and the bracelet were gifted to them by your other great-grandmother on your paternal side."

"As for your second question," Maureen continued on, "Sarah did have a sister once. But unfortunately, not much is known about her. Truly, not much is actually known about Sarah's past, prior to her marriage to your late grandfather, Henrick, the fourth Earl of Galloway. Anything about your grandmother's life prior to her marriage to the earl is still a mystery to us all."

"That's such a shame," Violet sadly remarked.

"Yes, it is a shame," Maureen agreed. "Especially, since Sarah also shared a rather complicated relationship with own sister, too. Just like you. A relationship so complex, that in the end, both sisters eventually grew estranged from one another over time."

"How tragically sad," Violet reflected. "I wonder why the sisters grew apart? Do you know why that happened?"

"Over the years, I, too, have often wondered much of the same. But from what I do know, Sarah and her sister were opposite types of personalities. While Sarah chose love, her sister chose a very different route... a darkened path that led to much hatred, bitterness, sadness and self-destruction."

"Really? How so? Who was this sister? Have I ever met her before?" asked Violet, as she keenly listened to her great-grandmother's fascinating tale.

"No, I don't believe that you've ever had that unfortunate displeasure," Maureen remarked coldly. "But try not to think too much about the past. Let it stay buried away in there. Just promise me that from now on, you'll wear this necklace always. And whatever you do, please do not allow your anger to get the best of you. Your sister might be a spoiled brat, but remember Violet, she'll always be *your* spoiled brat. Love and forgiveness are virtues. Plus, my dear child, nothing is stronger than blood."

"So, you're saying that blood is thicker than water? Is that how you define sisterly love and affection? What about true love?" asked Violet, with a raised brow.

"Romantic love amongst lovers is a different sort of love. But a love shared amongst sisters, can outlast even the greatest of love affairs... centuries later," Maureen spoke, with much conviction. "In the end, your sister will *always* be your greatest admirer and supporter. Sometimes, my dear Violet, the person whom you hate the most might actually be the same person, whom you once loved more than life itself."

As strange as all of this was, Maureen was right. Daphne might have been a spoiled brat, but she was still *her* spoiled brat. And no matter their differences, Violet couldn't allow her anger to get the best of her. In truth, Violet needed to look past her sister's faults and to find it within her own heart to forgive her. After all, a loving heart is always the key to every obstacle, no matter how impossible or hopeless it seems.

# CHAPTER 2

Whenever Violet felt lost or troubled or in a desperate need of fresh air, she often found herself wandering off into the woods. A simple walk or ride through the outdoors generally improved her overall gloomy mood, because it allowed her the chance to have some much-needed time away from her overbearing and protective family. Ever since she was a young girl, Violet often rode on one of her family's horses— either her father's black stallion, Midnight, or her mother's white English thoroughbred, Faith— for a lap around the woods. In fact, equestrianism was one of her most beloved pastimes— a trait that she inherited from her father.

While the forest might have been the original setting of her parents' fateful encounter— a site, in which Henry and Kassie met and eventually, came to fall madly in love— it was also the location to where her father's original curse was cast. According to legend, a long time ago, her father was once cursed by a wicked witch named Vera. A woman, who ironically, also just-so-happened to be his own stepmother, too.

After murdering Henry's father, the late fourth Earl of Galloway, and alienating his half-brother, Phillip, Vera was determined to rid Henry altogether, in a sinister plot to steal his rightful inheritance, estate and most importantly, to confiscate his land— which also included this very forest. According to legend, this forest was no ordinary woods. As previously mentioned, this forest was *the* enchanted forest and as a result, this whimsical and magical site contained many mysterious and supernatural elements unknown to mankind.

Not only was Henry's mother, Sarah, buried within the grounds of this enchanted forest, but her own gravesite was the very seat to where an abundant supply of magical violets flourished over her final resting place. Being Sarah's most beloved and favorite flower of all time, violet seeds were planted at her gravesite in her honor. It was planted many years ago, by a young Henry and his caretaker; another wise woman named Maureen. A woman, who also just-so-happened to be Violet's own great-great grandmother on her maternal line, and the namesake to her great-grandmother, Maureen Stanton.

By pure happenstance, overnight, the violet seeds rapidly grew and magically transformed into a blossoming garden. Surprisingly, Violet's grandmother's final resting place was also a former religious shrine. Many years ago, it was a sacred site that the ancient druids previously worshipped. In fact, several centuries prior, these wandering druids valued this blessed territory due to its celestial alignment with the sky and its surrounding planetary galaxies and its constellation of stars.

But apart from its stunning beauty, the true reason as to why the violets were so incredibly special stemmed from its rare magical ability to heal all wounds and ailments, regardless of how minor or major the illness or injury might be.

Furthermore, as a result of her ongoing bitterness and jealousy towards the fourth Earl of Galloway's eternal love and dedication to his first wife, Vera had subsequently and ruthlessly removed Sarah's tombstone from off her grave. But in spite of this cruel act, the violets, in return, took on a magical shape of their very own.

In fact, without a proper tombstone to identify her grave, the field of violets were the only landmark that allowed Henry to track down his late mother's final resting place. In the end, the violets functioned more as Henry's unofficial map of the forest, which allowed him to locate his late mother's grave at all times, night or day.

And alas, it was during one of those fateful nights, when Henry was innocently riding on horseback through the forest to visit his late mother's grave, that he accidentally stumbled upon his stepmother, Vera, along the way. But unlike before, this time around, Vera didn't appear to him in her humanly form. Instead, she unexpectedly revealed herself to him in her ugly and witchy green shape.

And it was here, inside of the enchanted forest, that Vera, the newly exposed wicked witch, placed an evil spell upon Violet's father. A curse so devastating, that it lasted well over a hundred years. As a result, her father, Henry Galloway, became known as the legendary Dark Horseman— a man who never aged or died, nor ate or slept. A man, who was forever trapped in time, never to venture outside of the very forest that cursed him. Tragically fated to serve an utterly hopeless and lonesome eternal existence.

While it might have been Vera's original intent to murder Henry with that curse; his mother, Sarah, intervened on his behalf and traveled all the way down from heaven above to save him. Rather than allowing the spell to claim his mortal life, Sarah instead, managed to stop his death, altogether. But unfortunately, she could not undue the spell in its entirety. Sadly, a bargain was previously made with the forces of nature and subsequently, the damage was already done.

As a result of Vera's black magic, a debt was still owed to the forest. And so, while Henry's life might have been spared; in return, he was also cursed to remain as a servant to the enchanted forest for all eternity. And for one hundred years, Henry served as a faithful servant, as well as a prisoner of the land. In the course of a century, the world moved on and eventually, came to forget about his true name and famous manor; all the while, Henry remained stuck behind in his earthly prison, alone with only his trusted horse, Midnight.

And for exactly one hundred years, Henry upheld his sworn duties and accepted his fate of solitude. As the guardian of the enchanted forest, he stood as its watchman. Each day, helping the good souls who stumbled upon his forest to find their lost paths back to the village, while chasing the bad souls and frightening them to their doom.

For some, they regarded her father as a saint; and to others, he was believed to be the very devil, himself. And while it was presumed that the legendary Dark Horseman would forever remain as he was, a man who never truly lived nor ever died; her mother, Kassie, on the other hand, believed otherwise.

For years, after admiring his portrait displayed inside of her childhood home, Kassie believed wholeheartedly that there was a cure to Henry's unbreakable curse. Ever since she first laid eyes on his portrait as a young girl, Kassie not only believed in the legendary myth of the Dark Horseman, but she also had faith that he was real, too. Miraculously, her mother believed in true love and it was that same enduring belief in everlasting love, that Kassie ultimate came to break Henry's curse and restored him back into the man that he now currently was.

And ever since that fateful day when the curse of the Dark Horseman ended, her parents' lives gradually returned to normalcy. Shortly after the curse broke, Violet was born. In honor of the magical flowers that grew within the heart of the enchanted forest, along with the names of her ancestors, she was proclaimed as Lady Violet Sarah Maureen Galloway, the first child born to the fifth Earl and Countess of Galloway.

Even though Violet believed that her parents' legendary and epic fairy tale as foretold by her family to be true; she, herself, had never bore witness to such magic or splendor found within the forest. While these woods might have been known as the enchanted forest to her parents, but to Violet, it was simply the *forest* to her. A forest that wasn't so magical, but was nevertheless, still an adventure worth exploring.

Long ago, her parents told her that only a few selective souls were blessed to even venture into this forest; let alone to discover its mysterious location. According to her parents, only those who were specially chosen and blessed with a divine and predestined purpose, were allowed to journey into the woods. While Violet presumed that this unspoken rule might have been the case during her parents' time, she wasn't so sure if that same theory still applied to today.

Even though the forest rarely had any visitors apart from Violet and her younger siblings, she supposed that most villagers in this remote part of the English countryside just had no real interest to journey so far out into her secluded forest. In fact, given how scarcely populated their village already was in the first place, it was a real stretch of the imagination to think that others—

apart from her own family members— could actually care enough to travel and wander so far away from the town's square. Therefore, it was safe to conclude that whenever Violet journeyed into these woods, the chances were that she was almost always going to be left *alone*.

Alas, privacy and seclusion were welcomed most heartily to Violet. After a stressful day spent at home, she desperately needed some healthy time away from her family. Ever since she returned to Wiltshire Hall upon graduation, Violet struggled to fit back into her old way of life. While Daphne and Adrian were still relatively far too young to relate to her adolescent struggles; her parents, on the other hand, were also too preoccupied with their own busy lives to take notice of their eldest daughter's internal woes of transitioning from childhood into adulthood.

But fortunately for Violet, the forest was her friend. Indeed, ever since she was a young child, the forest was a reliable and comforting site that always helped to clear her stressful mind. Whenever she was troubled or worried about something, Violet would often secretly sneak away from home and wander deep into the heart of the forest. And almost immediately upon entrance, Violet's melancholy mood would instantly improve.

In truth, Kassie secretly believed that her daughter's love and fascination for the forest was something that came directly from Violet's own blood. A quality that she inherited from her father. After all, Henry previously lived within these woods for the greater part of the last century. Naturally, he'd be inclined to hold a special attachment to nature. And so, this admirable love and special bond with the enchanted forest was a unique Galloway family trait that was passed down from Henry to his children.

And so, as of right now, at this precise moment, Violet was seated underneath a willow tree and seriously contemplating about her impending future. Fortunately, everything around her was silently still and all-so-wonderfully peaceful. Truly, an ideal place to meditate.

Wanting to admire her new birthday gift, Violet proceeded to remove her necklace from around her neck. Afterwards, she held the necklace tightly within the palm of her hand. As the amethyst stone shined and sparkled against the sunlight, Violet looked on in amazement. Out of all of the precious jewels found within her private collection, this necklace was by far her most treasured possession.

While Daphne might have taken her pearl earrings, this amethyst heart-shaped stone necklace was certainly much more special in comparison between the two.  And to top it all off, her great-grandmother, Maureen, promised her that this necklace was destined to bring her luck. And currently, Violet could use all the luck in the world.

"Oh, what shall become of me," she whispered out loud.

Although Violet didn't think twice about uttering these curious set of words out in the middle of the enchanted forest; however, the forces of nature certainly caught wind of it. Even though her innocent speech stemmed straight from her heart, needless to say, they were chanted like a heartfelt prayer that couldn't easily be taken back. Instead, they were freely spoken out loud into the world; and therefore, they came into existence. Like a wish that couldn't be undone. Truly, just what was to become of Lady Violet Galloway?

After all, she was a young person, standing at the threshold of her future. Would she marry or return back to university? Would she become another wife to an aristocrat or pursue a career as a scientist or a doctor? To challenge society's norm and seek a life that was far less predictable. A life that was an adventure. A life that was like a fairy tale. A life like her parents once lived, so long ago.

Even though Violet wasn't so particularly interested on learning about all of the dirty details concerning curses; she was, on the other hand, fascinated by the notion of true love. The rare ability for love to be the cure to everything that's evil in this world. In reality, Violet knew that such love existed in real life. After all, she personally bore witness to the enchanting and loving relationship that was shared between her own parents.

Unlike most aristocratic marriages, Violet's parents genuinely loved each other. Their marriage was not a prearranged relationship; but instead, it was a true love match. Her parents had met, fell in love and chose to marry out of their own free wills. Their romance was the ultimate love story; a union that sparked the births of Daphne, Adrian and herself.

In truth, Violet was a secret hopeless romantic. Like her mother, she, too, believed in a happily ever after. After all, her own parents' fairy tale proved that true love was real in this challenging world. Although Violet hadn't yet discovered true love for herself; however, she still remained hopeful about its prospects. That eventually, one day in the near future, she'd also come to experience that same sort of whimsical romance, just like her parents did so long ago.

But alas, true love wasn't something that was guaranteed in twentieth century England. Unfortunately, not everyone had her parents' same good fortune. In fact, most of the parents of Violet's friends from school had mostly married for financial security and not necessarily, for love. Their marriages were primarily based upon titles, pedigrees or inheritance rights and not matters concerning the heart. Sadly, these types of loveless marriages were all too common in their era.

And so, as a result, Violet couldn't help but wonder that when the time came for her to marry (which really, was going to be much sooner rather than later) was she going to marry for love or for fortune? Truly, this question was really at the heart of it all. An all-important and consuming question that constantly lingered in the back of Violet's young and impressionable mind.

Luckily, Violet's parents never pressured her into marriage. Instead, they wanted their daughter to choose her own partner, whenever she was ready. Even as the daughter of aristocrats, Violet was gifted with the rare freedom to select her own life partner with the full blessing of her parents. While Violet was most grateful to her family for this rare and special opportunity, she also knew that not everyone else in her society was so equally understanding and sympathetic to her cause.

As it currently stood, Violet was well aware that most young ladies at her age and class often married for fortune and rarely for love. In the world of the upper class, marriage was more like a business transaction and not a union of the hearts. But, be that as it may, Violet still remained ever hopeful that one day, she'd avoid falling into this social trap and instead, marry the man of her dreams. A person, whom she respected, adored, cherished and most importantly, *loved*. And hopefully, when that time came, he'd magically come strolling into her life, just like her own personal knight in shining armor.

Once upon a time, as young girls, Violet and Daphne frequently used to masquerade as royal princesses and often pretended that they were stolen royals that were secretly hidden away in a prisoner's tower (aka, a tall oak tree). It was here within this very forest, that the young Galloway children used to partake in epic and grand playful adventures. With Violet and Daphne posing as young royal princesses, their brother, Adrian, arrived onto the scene as the heroic knight in shining armor, ready to rescue his older sisters and to slay the evil dragon or the wicked witch in the process.

While this was a harmless childhood fantasy that the Galloway children often played on an ongoing basis; however, as a result of this game, Violet secretly wished that one day in the future, she, too, would come across a real-life knight in shining armor of her very own. A knight, identical to the main character found within her beloved childhood fairy tale book called, *An Encyclopedia of Fairy Tales*. In fact, her favorite chapter in that book surrounded a heroic knight and his beloved princess.

Violet's most cherished fairy tale was called *The Traveling Knight*. The story was centered around a foreign knight, who had fallen madly in love with a princess from another kingdom, located in a far-off land. And because of his undying love and devotion to her, he traveled great lengths to find her. But along his journey, the knight underwent several challenges and hardships, while also battling an evil villain in the process. However, in the end, good triumphed over evil and eventually, the knight and the princess married and got their long awaited happily ever after.

And ever since that fateful day when her great-grandmother, Maureen, first introduced her to this beloved fairy tale, Violet frequently fantasized about that heroic knight in shining armor. All the while, secretly wishing that she could somehow, magically transport into that same fairy tale and become the famed princess, herself.

Therefore, from the age five and up, Violet often dreamed about her knight in shining armor. Although she seldom recalled most of her other dreams minus him; however, whenever it concerned the knight—or *her knight*—as she liked to call him, Violet could practically remember almost everything concerning him. While the dreams varied each time; however, the underlining theme always remained the same. Each time, Violet envisioned herself wandering alone, journeying deep into the dark woods. And as she traveled further down the road, she almost always managed to accidentally stumble upon a mysterious knight.

According to her dreams, at first glance, Violet usually presumed that her motionless knight was long dead. But as she slowly approached him, she'd eventually come to learn that he wasn't in fact dead... but rather, *sleeping*. With wild ivy vines and thorny crimson red roses wrapped around and encircling his stiff body, the sleeping knight was not an easy person to access. From afar, his coat of armor looked dated, worn and heavily rusted. Armor that was unique in design and appeared to be of ancient origin. A once shiny and silver suit, that was now glowing in rusted copper, stemming from several years (or decades) of deterioration and decay.

As fascinated as Violet was to stare at him directly, even within the realms of her own dreams, she always felt compelled to reach over and touch him. Even though Violet suspected that the knight was most likely cursed, she still didn't care. For some odd reason, Violet naturally felt drawn to him. Strangely enough, it was almost as if, she was meant to cross paths with this mysterious stranger, hidden underneath a suit of armor.

Whomever he was, this knight was someone connected to her. A soul that miraculously managed to capture her wandering attention, out in the middle of a secluded forest. And as Violet tried to reach over to grab a hold of his hand, she would abruptly awaken from her dreams and be thrusted back into reality. Meanwhile, as Violet closed her eyes once more, she tried her best to envision her sleeping knight, once again. All the while, hoping for a second chance to see what might have been, had she held onto his hand. Had she made contact with him, prior to waking up from her whimsical nightly dream.

And that was as far as her own dreams would take her. While Violet was well aware that such a person couldn't ever possibly exist within her own world; however, she still couldn't help but wonder as to who the identity of this mysterious knight might have been had he existed in the real world.

If only she had removed his helmet. For if she'd seen his face, then maybe she'd have gained some secret satisfaction. A face to a phantom that constantly haunted her dreams, ever since her childhood. Perhaps, by seeing his true face, then Violet would have some sort of closure. A chance to overcome her childhood fixation about knights in shining armor. To accept the fact, that the man that she'd eventually come to marry would most likely be another boring aristocratic gentleman and certainly, not a dashing and handsome knight. Ah, if only it could be...

Meanwhile, as Violet admired and played with her necklace, she noticed that its bright purple light flashed straight ahead and was shining against a tiny creature. Curiously, Violet followed that gleaming light and saw the figure of a small white bunny. Happily, it was hopping about in the woods, while chewing on a small piece of grass.

In all of her many years spent outside in the forest, Violet rarely saw any small creatures in her nearby vicinity. Normally, they were almost always hiding out somewhere else, or just avoiding her or her siblings completely. But today, this was a true first; because this marked the first time that Violet had ever witnessed another creature roaming so freely in front of her, out in the open field.

Determined to catch up with the small creature, Violet quickly placed her necklace back onto her neck and slowly, she began to tiptoe towards the bunny's direction. Eventually, she came about an inch or so away from the small critter. Carefully, Violet bent down and attempted to pick the animal up, when unexpectedly, the bunny suddenly jumped up high into the air. Without a moment's notice, the bunny started to quickly hop away.

Under most circumstances, Violet would have easily given up and allowed the animal to go on its merry way. However, given that today was Violet's birthday, she was surprisingly feeling a bit more adventurous than usual. And so, ultimately, her curiosity got the best of her. Therefore, as the white bunny fled the scene, so did Violet as well.

Meanwhile, the further out the bunny traveled to, the deeper Violet journeyed into the heart of the forest. Eventually, venturing off into places that were entirely unknown and mysterious, even to her. Although Violet had practically grown up inside of this forest, there were still certain areas that were completely unfamiliar to her.

However, given that there was still daylight outside, Violet was not at all concerned nor fearful about getting lost. Eventually, she'd come to find her way back home tonight before nightfall. After all, Violet always found her way back home, after exploring the forest on her own. In truth, the forest came second nature to her. They were one in the same. In all honesty, Violet was practically the daughter of the enchanted forest.

Eventually, the bunny came to a complete halt, near the edge of a hill. Carefully, Violet tiptoed across the dark brown and tangerine colored autumn field, until she arrived about a few short inches away from the tiny creature. With the bunny currently preoccupied with eating a small batch of blackberries, Violet slowly bent down and tried to scoop the furry creature up into her arms.

However, right as she was about to do so, an arrow suddenly flew by. The sharp arrow managed to bypass her and instead, struck a nearby tree. Startled by this unexpected commotion, the bunny quickly jumped up into the air and swiftly hopped away. Meanwhile, Violet turned around to inspect the scene.

"Who in the devil would dare to shoot an arrow right here, in the middle of the forest?" Violet asked out loud.

In all her many years spent wandering in this forest, Violet had never encountered an archer before. *This* was certainly news. Therefore, who else was secretly lurking out in these remote parts of the woods?

But then, before Violet had the opportunity to further ponder about this strange arrow and its archer, a second arrow was released. Seconds later, the arrow flew right by her, yet again. However, this time around, the arrow nearly struck her arm. While the first shot might have been accidental; however, a second arrow now seemed intentional. Was someone actually trying to harm her? And if so, whom? And why?

Fearful about a possible attacker, Violet instantly fled the scene. Unfortunately, for her, the archer had caught Violet so off guard, that she completely forgot that she was standing near the foot of a hill. And so, as Violet ran straight ahead, she accidentally managed to tumble down the edge and began rolling down the hill!

By the time Violet reached the bottom, not only did she survive her fall, but she was also now, covered from head-to-toe in dirt. With a combination of mud and dried leaves covering her dress, along with a few loose twigs and debris tangled within her red hair, Violet's birthday gown was all about ruined. But apart from a spoiled dress and a few small scratches to go along with it, she was otherwise, luckily, unharmed.

Dusting herself off, Violet proceeded to continue onwards with her journey. If there was someone out there looking to harm her, then she needed to get as far away as possible. And fast, too.

With daylight still available, Violet decided to continue walking straight ahead. Carefully, she tried her very best not to make a sound. Removing her shoes, Violet quietly tiptoed across the pathway as gently as she possibly could. If someone was still here and searching for her, then she didn't want them to hear her footsteps.

After walking about a mile out or so, Violet gradually regained her confidence again. Given how far and deep she now was in the woods, Violet was almost certain that whomever was following her before, that they must have lost her lead. Truly, this entire experience was so alarming and strange, too!

Never before, had Violet encountered another soul out here, in this forest. Apart from her own family, no one else had ever ventured out into this forest with her; let alone, a mysterious archer with a keen interest on shooting her!

Today might have been her milestone twenty-first birthday; but already, it was becoming one of her worst birthdays to date. And then, as Violet thought that nothing else could possibly get any stranger, she suddenly saw *him*…

Just like in her dreams, Violet saw a knight lying down above a bed of roses, out in the middle of the forest. Motionless, he silently lied above a large grey stone, right across from her. He was surrounded by what appeared to be an endless supply of thick emerald green vines of ivy and thorny crimson red roses. The vines and roses were so abundant in quantity, that they practically covered every inch of his armored body.

For a long moment, Violet silently stared at the knight in pure fascination. Alas, she was enchanted by the mere sight of him. Amazingly enough, he was lying peacefully there, just like in her dreams. Exactly as she had previously envisioned. Strangely, it was almost as if her childhood dreams had miraculously managed to come true in real life. But how… how… how… was *this fantasy*, even remotely possible?

Immediately, Violet rubbed her eyes and *hard*. Convinced that her tired eyes were foolishly playing tricks on her, Violet assumed that a good rubbing would automatically restore her natural sight back to reality. However, after blinking a few extra times, the knight was *still* there. Alas, he wasn't just a figment of her imagination! He was, in fact, *real*… just like in her dreams...

Swiftly, Violet ran towards him. Was he hurt? Or injured? Plus, how did he even get trapped underneath all of these thick layers of vines and blooming roses? Was he even... still... *alive?*

As Violet approached the mysterious knight, she soon realized that he really was in fact, the spitting image of the knight from her beloved fairy tale. And just like her dreams, rather than sporting a shiny and sparkling coat of armor; his armor, was instead, severely faded and rusted. In fact, his silver steel was no more. On the contrary, his suit was now replaced by deep shades of bronze and copper— colors reflecting extreme rust and decay.

Tragically, this knight was now surrounded by hundreds of rows of thick ivy vines and blooming crimson red roses. Additionally, he was also accompanied by sharp and prickly thorns that tragically, encircled his entire body from head-to-toe. Apart from his hands, helmet and feet, every other part of his armor was practically held prisoner by the wild vines and roses. Even if Violet wanted to help pull his body out and away from this messy site; she, alone, couldn't do it. At least, not without the help of a weapon to chop through this pesky nest.

Whomever this knight was, he must have been someone of importance. In all of her many years spent alone in this forest, Violet had never seen a knight venturing out here in the woods before. Furthermore, judging by the harsh condition of his rusted armor, along with the vast amounts and thickness of the vines and roses that surrounded him, this knight must have been ancient.

Logically, Violet naturally presumed that he must have died out here, in a battle from a long time ago. But why did her family fail to tell her about him? Or about his tragic story? Surely, her great-grandmother knew of him? Or her parents? Or, was she entirely wrong? Was it possible that no one else other than herself, had ever managed to accidentally stumble upon him before? Not until now?

Curiously, Violet kneeled down and took a seat on the ground. As she glanced at his helmet, she wondered how this knight might have looked like, back when he was still alive. Just like in her dreams, Violet remained ever-so curious. But of course, she was never going to get a proper answer to this riddle. Sadly, whomever this gentleman was, he must have been a skeleton by now. After all, this knight's corpse had to have been lying down here for quite some time. Centuries, even.

Compelled by her emotions, Violet genuinely felt sorry for this forgotten knight. Obviously, he must have died in a tragic manner. With his rotting corpse having never been recovered. Unlike the other soldiers who previously died in battle, this knight was denied a proper burial, along with an honorable grave. Instead, he was left alone to die and perish, with his armor eventually, becoming one with the forest. How shameful, lonely and tragic his life ending must have been!

And then, Violet gave herself permission to grieve for this mysterious stranger. Even though she didn't know a single thing about him, let alone his real name; Violet felt that at the very least, she could chant a short prayer for his lost soul. A small form of charity for an unknown knight, resting alone in an unmarked grave for all eternity. And so, out of the kindness of her heart, that is precisely what Violet did.

Peacefully, Violet closed her eyes shut and whispered a short prayer for him. Even though it was a such a small act of charity, Violet felt that it was the least that she could do. Afterwards, she stared down to look at him again. Strangely enough, in that moment, it almost appeared as if he wasn't actually dead. But rather, that he was instead, peacefully sleeping. Just waiting for someone to awaken him after a long period of slumber.

And as Violet continued staring at him, she couldn't help but admire as to just how lovely he appeared to be. Even in his rusted coat of armor, he was still beautiful. Mysterious. Enchanting. Ethereal. A real *sleeping beauty.*

Witnessing his left-hand freely dangling out in the open air right beside her, Violet was tempted to touch it. Just like in her dreams, one way or another, she always desired to reach out and grab a hold of his hand. Perhaps, that's what she ought to do here too, she thought to herself. If her mysterious and lonely knight had previously perished out here in this dark forest, then maybe a final handshake would free his soul. Help encourage him to graduate onwards to the next journey of life: the *hereafter.*

And so, Violet extended her bare hand and laid it against his armored gauntlet. At first, his armor felt extremely cold and dusty. However, a second later, it surprisingly warmed up by the mere touch of her hand.

"Go in peace, my dearest knight," she whispered aloud. And then, she added, "Your long sleep is over. It's time to finally go home."

And as Violet spoke these very words into existence, the most peculiar thing happened: his hand began to actually *move*!

After saying her final farewell to him, the knight's hand started to wiggle! Alas, he *wasn't* dead. Instead, he was very much… *alive*!

Miraculously, it was almost as if… he was *awakening*… after a long period of… *slumber*…

Out of fear, Violet instantly stood up and tried to pull her hand away from his. However, as she attempted to do so, his hand tightly gripped hers and actually *squeezed* her inner palm, all the while refusing to release her. It seemed that after a long period of seclusion and a lack of another humanly touch, this knight wasn't yet ready to let her go so easily.

And if Violet wasn't already surprised by such an unexpected act of affection, the knight suddenly spoke to her.

"Don't fret… my dearest… *Violet*," he softly whispered to her. "You're safe with me… and… I've been waiting a very long time *for you*."

# CHAPTER 3

## Two Hundred Years Ago...

Traveling down the grand hallway to the ruins of an ancient castle, Maximus felt as if he was journeying through an endless tunnel of darkness and despair. Walking with a great sense of urgency, he swiftly took his steps at incredible speed. Time was of the essence. But yet, it still failed to remain by his side. Recently, a war was unjustly unleashed. And now, if he failed to act quickly and efficiently, then his entire world would be lost forever. His palace. His land. His people. His kingdom. His identity. His place in history. Right now, *everything* that he cared for and believed in was all at stake.

Unfortunately, innocent lives were at a balance. Men, women and children alike; his citizens all depended upon the success of his fierce leadership. And as a result, his actions— either good or bad— would ultimately, come to seal their fates. Therefore, Maximus *needed* to do the right thing. Act strategically *and* intelligently. Exercise his best sound decisions. Align himself with whomever he needed to do so, in order to protect his people. *To save his stolen kingdom.* Because, at this very moment, everything that mattered to him in this world, all rested upon his inexperienced shoulders. A first, for the former rebel recently turned crown prince.

For once, Maximus couldn't afford to make another selfish and foolish mistake. In the past, God only knows that he made plenty of errors in his wild youth. A life built on being young, spoiled, rich, stupid and reckless. But alas, a twist of fate forced Maximus to journey down a new path in his life.

Within the blink of an eye, Maximus' entire world as he knew it, completely changed just overnight. Sadly, today marked a new and unpleasant chapter in his role as the crown prince. And so, instead of failing at another important task, Maximus desperately needed to step up and become what his people needed him to be: a *hero*.

Alas, Maximus was expected to act *heroic*. To *save* the day. To *rescue* his people from a misfortunate fate. But unfortunately, evil still found a way to sneak into their territory. And now, Maximus was determined to do everything in his power to get rid of it. To end the evil queen's reign of terror on his ancestral lands. To restore his rightful claim to the throne, as the one and only true legitimate ruler of the Kingdom of the West. To avenge his late brother, King Leopold's recent death. And that of his father's, too. After all, his father had been previously killed by a dagger plunged straight through his heart. Although the culprit was never caught; however, Maximus believed wholeheartedly that Vera was also responsible for his mysterious death, too.

But first, Maximus needed to pay a special visit to an elderly woman. A person, whom his late brother previously considered to be his most trusted and wisest advisor, as well as another mother-like figure.

"Welcome my dear, crown prince," Ruby greeted Maximus, as he arrived at the door. "Please, come in. I've been expecting you."

Staring directly at the old woman, Maximus couldn't help but feel a tad bit suspicious. With her grey hair tucked away into a tight bun, she was dressed in an oversized and long scarlet velvet gown, along with a black cape attached to her shoulders. At first glance, her face appeared ancient; covered in deep layers of wrinkles. But, unlike Vera, her flesh was not green in color. Instead, it was pale, just like his.

Furthermore, her eyes were a shade of emerald green. Overall, her physical appearance did not immediately alert him that she was a witch, for say. In fact, had he not been previously privy to the fact that she was indeed *one*, then Maximus would have mistaken her for another ordinary and perfectly sweet, innocent and harmless grandmother. A grandmother who just-so-happened to favor dark cloaks for fashion.

However, as Ruby patiently stood there focused on her latest concoction, while mixing her bubbling black caldron with the use of her handy wooden ladle, Maximus couldn't help but wonder if Ruby was indeed, trustworthy. After all, she was another witch, just like Vera. Therefore, was Ruby also treacherous and deceitful? Was she a person that he could blindly place his faith in for help?

"Please, have a seat," Ruby announced, as she motioned for Maximus to take the empty wooden chair beside her.

Glancing across her sacred lair, Maximus presumed that this space must have been Ruby's private laboratory. All around the stone walls were several bottles and figurines, which appeared to resemble a collection of magical potions. Conveniently enough, the bottles and figurines all ranged in various sizes, shapes and colors: from tall midnight blue crystal bottles to large emerald green clay jars, to circular crimson red marbled pots to squared honeysuckle yellow metal cannisters, to triangular candy purple decanters and miniature rosy pink wine glasses. Remarkably, it was almost as if a rainbow had crash-landed straight through this very room and thus, leaving a trail of bright lights that were forever memorialized in the many objects found residing above her plentiful rows of shelves.

But apart from Ruby's potions, there was also an endless array of books. No doubt, these must have been spell books. And if Ruby was a witch, then Maximus sought to approach her using extreme caution.

"If you don't mind, I'd personally, rather not sit," Maximus boldly proclaimed, as he decided to stand in place.

Meanwhile, he slowly rested his hand slightly above the handle to his sword, which was conveniently attached to his hip.

"My dear prince, you don't need to worry about me. Certainly, I'm *not* your enemy," Ruby retorted, refusing to hide her displeasure caused by his stiff attitude.

"Enemy or not, I simply don't have the time nor luxury to get too comfortable. Time isn't on my side and—"

"Time is *never* on anyone's side," Ruby interrupted him to make this valid point.

"Be that as it may, I've still got to at least try and fight," Maximus proudly declared. "Time is ticking away, as we speak. And if I don't take any swift action right now, then more blood will be shed. Innocent lives will be lost."

"Sadly, I know," Ruby sighed. "It's why I've agreed to help you."

"And why precisely did you agree to do so?" he asked, with a skeptical raised brow. "Why are *you*, of all people, choosing to help *me* and not Vera? After all, you're both witches, are you not?"

"Contrary to popular belief," Ruby quickly responded, "Just because we're witches doesn't mean that I owe her any special allegiance."

"No, my prince," she continued on, "Vera and I are two very *different* kinds of people. She likes to dabble in black magic, while I work with white magic."

"Is there a difference?" asked Maximus, now intrigued by her statement.

"A huge difference," she answered. "Black magic kills, while white saves. Whatever little goodness that Vera once had in her, is now, all but gone."

"That may be the case," he acknowledged. "But apart from Vera's past history, why do you really want to help me? What's in it for you?"

"Because you're our only hope to defeat her," Ruby replied, truthfully. "Even if you find my answer too difficult to believe, but it's still the truth. The fact remains that I've always been on your team. That's why I chose to remain as a loyal servant to your brother and became his most trusted advisor while he was on the throne."

"Yes, I do recall. Although I never really understood as to why that was," Maximus plainly admitted, as he finally gave in and took a seat on the empty wooden chair. And thus, leaving a satisfied smile painted across Ruby's delighted face.

"A long time ago, Vera was a good witch," Ruby began to explain, "But over the years, heartbreak and corruption slowly destroyed what little humanity was left in her heart. Gradually, overtime, Vera ventured down a darkened path. A path of loneliness, misery and despair. A place of no return."

"Right now, as we speak, she's not only slaughtering your people alone, but of mine as well," Ruby passionately declared. "Already, she's imprisoned thousands of other witches and sorcerers alike, all in an effort to monopolize their magical abilities. If she's not stealing their powers, then she's suppressing their supernatural talents in prison. And for the ones not already rotting inside of a darkened cell, then sadly, she's most likely, executed them. Unfortunately, Vera will not risk having anyone more powerful than herself to remain alive. No matter what, she will never allow another soul to rise up and seek to challenge her tyrannical authority. As far as I'm concerned, Vera is committing mass genocide against *our people*, both yours and mine. But worst of all, she's getting away with it. And if we don't act together as allies, then her reign of terror will be the end of our world as we know it."

"Do you really believe this to be true? The end of our world?"

"Yes, I do," replied Ruby, in earnest. "I honestly believe that it's only a matter of time, before Vera eventually, conquers the rest of the continent. Our homeland is only but the first territory that she's chosen to invade. However, I refuse to turn a blind eye. I swear, my crown prince, with all of my heart, that I vow to do everything in my power to stop her at all costs. Even if I must sacrifice my own life to accomplish this goal. This much I can promise you."

Her passionate and heartfelt words certainly struck a chord with Maximus. For the longest time, he curiously wondered as to why Ruby wanted to become his partner so badly. And now, he finally understood why. As it currently stood, Ruby had just as much to lose as he did. Thus far, they were true equals.

Tragically, *all* of their lives were in danger. Sadly, if neither of them did anything to stop Vera's current reign of terror, then alas, they really were doomed.

"But why start at my kingdom? Why the Kingdom of the West? From what I've heard, she's not even a native to our land."

"Not true," Ruby corrected him. "Actually, Vera *is* a native of this country. Although, a long time ago, she was once in exile and forced to live in a foreign land."

"Exiled? Really? Care to explain?" Maximus asked her, as he reclined back into his chair and leaned his left leg against a small stool located nearby.

"From the looks of it, I can see that you're finally getting more comfortable," Ruby happily acknowledged. "Which is a good sign, because we've got much work to do."

"Where shall we start?" he proceeded to ask her. "My men are currently stationed inside of an underground tunnel and waiting for my direct orders. Shall we combine your magical talents with my army to launch a mass invasion? How shall we attack and reclaim the palace? Any specific strategies for war?"

"Not so fast, my dear prince," Ruby was quick to scold him, as she waved her wooden ladle towards his direction, just like a grandmother would have done with her own grandson.

"I have another task for you, instead. Call it a rescue mission," she said with a warm smile.

"A rescue mission? Who needs saving? Another royal?" he curiously asked.

"Sort of," she hinted. "I know that you're most eager to attack now and to think later, but I beg of you to first listen to what I'm about to tell you."

As Ruby lifted up her chin to meet his, she was pleased to see that at long last, she captured his full attention. Alas, he was finally ready to listen to her bold plan-in-action.

"Go on," Maximus commanded, as he focused on her with keen and impressionable ears.

"Right now, I think we've already established that more bloodshed will not stop her. Unfortunately, with all of that stolen magic, Vera is far too powerful," Ruby pointed out.

"In fact, it's already a real stretch of the imagination that you're even standing right here in front of me, as I currently speak," Ruby acknowledged. "The very fact alone, that you survived today's assault at the cathedral is a true miracle. Especially, after fleeing from that burning building that Vera practically decimated into ashes."

Remembering that painful event that took place only but a few hours ago, really was difficult to bear. Just earlier this morning, Maximus was previously mourning the loss of his late brother at his state funeral. Afterwards, he was supposed to be crowned as the next king. But of course, that didn't happen. Absolutely nothing went according to plan.

Instead, not only did Vera stop the funeral and the coronation, but she also violently attacked them. Unleashed an unjustly and unholy war. Stole his crown and kingdom. Cast a wicked spell that kept him frozen in place. And thus, inadvertently forcing Maximus to silently watch on, as his beloved brother's corpse burned into ashes. Unwillingly bearing witness to his own people frantically fleeing from that horrid and bloodshed scene, all desperately trying to save their own innocent lives. All the while, observing the martyrs' blood spilled across the stained floor. Alas, he cringed at the devastating remembrance.

Sadly, it was so incredibly *painful* to relive it all. And now, the urgency to punish such heinous crimes remained his highest priority. Regardless of his own fears and self-doubts, Maximus needed to remain brave and face this new looming threat upfront. To deal with this crisis head-on. The sooner, the better.

"Okay, Ruby. I get it. So, what exactly are you suggesting?" he bluntly asked her, getting straight down to the point.

"There is a prophecy about a savior," she revealed.

"A savior?" asked Maximus, in surprise. Suddenly, this unexpected news got a lot more *interesting.*

"What kind of savior?" he pressed on.

"The savior comes from a far-off land," Ruby replied. "And they, and only they, can stop Vera."

"Why them? Can't we slay the damn witch ourselves?"

"It's not that easy to kill a witch," she emphasized. "You might be able to slay them, but unless they're willing to die based on their own free wills, then they'll just reanimate into another form."

"I see," Maximus sighed, with great disappointment. "So only this so-called savior can succeed in killing her?"

"The savior can stop her," Ruby clarified. "And stopping her is just as effective as killing."

"At this point, I'll take anything," Maximus sighed once again, as he ran his rough hands through his thick chestnut brown head of hair. "Okay, so, pray tell, where precisely is this savior? Tell me now, and I vow to make it my personal mission to go out and retrieve them."

"Not so fast, my dear prince," Ruby warned. "I'm afraid that it won't be so easy to simply run out and abduct her. Especially, right now."

"*Her*? That's rather intriguing. So, she's a *woman*?" asked Maximus, with a beaming smile that stretched from ear-to-ear.

For some strange reason, the notion that the savior was a *female* brought an unexpected devilish grin across his roguish face. Perhaps, there was *more* to this story, after all.

"Don't get any special ideas about this one," Ruby promptly forewarned. "To be fair, I've already heard about the scandalous rumors surrounding your playboy behavior, my dear prince. After all, you weren't called Maximus, the Brute, for nothing."

"I might have had my share of lovers here and there—"

"More than enough," Ruby scolded him. "Prince Maximus, you've broken more hearts than even I dare to count. Please, I beg of you, whatever you do, please refrain from exerting your usual roguish allure with her. Particularly, this girl. After all, she's incredibly special. And most importantly, we need her. Plus, I can't afford to deal with a savior who's suffering from a broken heart. Especially, after you've had your rakish ways with her."

"Who's to say that I'll break her heart? Maybe, she'll actually end up liking me?" he playfully suggested, accompanied by a deep grin and a sweet twinkle that glimmered and shined across his silvery pair of eyes.

"They *all* end up liking you, that's the problem," Ruby retorted, in great annoyance. "Except, the *real* problem is that *you* never end up liking any of them!"

"Touché, Ruby. Point taken," Maximus was reluctantly forced to agree.

Leaning against his seat, with his legs stretched across the stool, he finally said, "Fine, as the crown prince and future king, I give you my word of honor that no matter what happens, I won't use my dashing charms on her. Regardless of how tempting it might be. I swear. Furthermore, I promise that not only will I *not* beguile her, but I vow to *never* fall in love with this precious savior, either. As far as I'm concerned, she's off limits."

"Now, I didn't mention anything about *you not* falling in love with her," Ruby contradicted him, with a sly and sinister smile of her own. "After all, I merely stated that you must refrain from exerting your infamous boyish games on her. But, if by chance, your heart is somehow later drawn to hers, then who am I to deny true love?"

"True love?" asked Maximus in surprise.

Apart from everything else that recently occurred within the past twenty-four hours, Maximus never once contemplated about the possibility of discovering his one true love in the midst of an ongoing crisis. But rather than questioning Ruby any further about this wild topic, he decided to just let it go and move onto more pressing matters: business.

"For the time being, I'll let this conversation go. In the meantime, just tell me what I need to do. Either way, I promise to behave myself."

"Excellent," Ruby replied, feeling highly satisfied with his positive response.

"Her name is Violet Galloway," she began, "And she's not from our world. In fact, she hasn't yet been born."

"Not yet born?" asked Maximus, in pure astonishment. At this point, he practically fell out of his chair by hearing such surprising news.

"If that's the case, then how can she possibly be the savior?"

"Time works differently between her world and ours," Ruby explained. "A day in our world is equal to a hundred years in hers."

"I don't understand," Maximus admitted. "How can this stretch of time possibly work to our benefit?"

"First, hear me out," spoke Ruby. "By the time you retrieve Violet and bring her back to our world, only but a day or two will have passed."

"So, according to your calculations, this journey will take me about two days to achieve?"

"Two days in *our* world," Ruby emphasized. "Mind you, your absence will buy us some extra time to prepare. But I should also remind you that it will still be a two hundred years wait on her end."

"Two hundred years???!!!"

And this time around, a surprised Maximus really did come to fall out of his chair and thereby, slammed straight down onto the floor by this startling revelation. Given as to just how tall and muscular his physique was, Maximus managed to make a large thump as he crash-landed onto the cobble stone floor.

"Rest assured, my dear prince, I've already prepared everything that you'll need for this upcoming journey," Ruby stated in a calm and directive tone, all the while, hoping that her confident response was enough to help ease his dwindling nerves.

"Are you honestly suggesting that I travel to her world, only to wait for another two hundred years to pass by before I can bring her home? To our world? If that's the case, then can't you work your magic to speed up time? Or even, have me stay and wait here in my own kingdom?"

"Unfortunately, I can't alter time... at least not *yet*," Ruby reluctantly confessed.

"What do you mean by not *yet*?"

"Unfortunately, when Vera entered into our world, she disrupted the natural order of time."

"How so?"

"Let's just say that she might have tricked *death*, but she failed to do the same with *time*. And as a result, her return inadvertently caused a time loop shared between our two worlds."

"But can't you still try to fix it?"

"I've tried, but I can't," Ruby admitted in defeat. "Vera is an anomaly. Her return has disrupted everything. Including time. Plus, Vera has spies almost everywhere. Even if I were to attempt to meddle with specific time frames, she'd know and then, our war would have already been lost, before we even stepped foot onto the battlefield."

"Plus," she added, "We can't risk you remaining here without Violet. It's already a true miracle that you're still alive."

"Okay, so time is something that we definitely cannot change and neither is it a safe option for me to stay behind, either," Maximus acknowledged. "But why the two hundred years wait? Why must I wait so long for the savior?"

"Because Violet hasn't yet been born, but she will be. It's already been foretold," Ruby reassured him.

"Are you certain that she's really the savior? What if the prophecy is wrong?"

"Prophecies are never wrong, for they are written by time, herself," Ruby revealed. "The prophecy speaks of a savior, who will rise above during our darkest of times. And it will be her heart that will save us all from doom."

"And that savior is Violet?"

"Yes," Ruby answered. "She'll have fiery red hair, emerald green eyes, and she will come from the lands of Earth."

"Earth? That sounds so familiar," he remarked. "Isn't that a realm that's connected to our world?"

"Yes, it's located in another dimension. Now, Prince Maximus, if you don't mind, please look straight ahead."

And then, Ruby pointed to an oversized mirror that was located on the far end of her laboratory. It was adorned with a golden brass frame. Based upon his first glimpse and impression of the object, the mirror appeared rather ancient and mysterious.

"That mirror serves as a gateway... a portal, you might say," she explained. "In fact, I believe all of the royal households have an identical mirror of their own.”

Upon closer inspection, Maximus really did recognize the mirror, after all. It was true, his late father had a similar mirror of that style, hidden away inside of his study. However, Maximus never thought anything more of it. Prior to today, a mirror was always just a mirror. But apparently, he was wrong. Some mirrors weren’t just ordinary objections of reflection. Instead, they were enchanted.

“Come to think of it, you’re right,” he agreed. “I’ve seen a similar mirror to this before at the palace. But I’ll admit, I’ve never considered them to be modes of interdimensional travel.”

“Ah, but they are,” Ruby smiled on. “And now, whenever you’re ready, you will walk through that very mirror. *A magic mirror.* Afterwards, you’ll arrive into Violet’s world. The journey will lead you straight through a cave located inside of an enchanted forest; a blessed site that links our two worlds together. Space and time operate differently between our realms.”

“I see,” Maximus sighed.

As strange as all of this really was, Maximus was still willing to give it a try. For a man who never once cared for magic and instead, preferred the use of his sword to that of a potion bottle; the new crown prince was willing to sacrifice his own personal beliefs for the safety of his people.

“Very well, I agree. I’ll do it.”

“I knew that you would!” Ruby joyfully exclaimed, as she happily clasped her hands together.

Alas, her huge smile beaming across her face was a genuine reflection that as of now, she truly believed that victory was as good as theirs.

Reclining back in his chair, Maximus addressed her, “So, Ruby, how do you suggest I go about this task? What am I expected to do for the next two hundred years?”

Recognizing the important shift in their conversion, Ruby instantly stopped stirring her caldron altogether. Focusing her attention over to their new joint mission, Ruby placed her wooden ladle down onto the table and walked over to the front of an armoire. Without saying another word, she proceeded to open its door.

Quietly, Maximus watched on, as he observed her open its mysterious door. To his surprise, it revealed a shiny and sparkling suit of armor made of pure silver, along with a matching helmet. It was a knight's uniform.

"A knight's coat of armor?" he inquired, with a raised brow. "Ruby, I'm not sure if you're already well aware, but I've got plenty of those back at the fort. At least an extra dozen pairs or so."

"Ah, but you don't have this one," she replied with a sweet twinkle that shined across her emerald green eyes. "And this particular *one* is extremely special."

Curiously enough, Ruby looked almost proud to showcase this prized possession to him. To be perfectly honest, Maximus was rather impressed. Even though he had plenty of spare knights' uniforms back at his station, this particular set of armor looked special.

With its pristine craftsmanship, along with its high-quality metals, anyone with a visible pair of eyes could easily recognize the superiority of its design. Plus, judging by Ruby's behavior and her overall, joyful expression, she must have been the creator to such an impressive set of steel.

"Apart from its stellar appearance, may I ask as to what's so special about this specific set?" One way or another, Maximus was highly intrigued.

"Two hundred years from now... *Earth time*," she made it a bold point to highlight this important fact to him. "Violet will be born. And once she comes of age, she'll be gifted a special necklace containing an amethyst heart-shaped stone. However, Violet will remain ignorant about the gem's true extraordinary gifts."

"What do you mean?" Maximus curiously inquired.

"The stone is derived from our world. And this coat of armor that you're staring at right now, will be attracted to her stone."

"How so?" he asked.

"The stone and armor are forged from the same caves found in our southern kingdom," Ruby revealed. "While her stone will be attracted to your armor;

your armor, in return, will also be attracted to her stone. And vice versa. Hence, you'll *both* be attracted to one another."

"How interesting," Maximus acknowledged in fascination.

An enchanted stone necklace and a pristine knight's uniform attracted to one another. Linked. Bonded. What could this unique connection mean to the wearers of such magical objects?

"Congratulations Ruby, you've officially succeeded on capturing my sole attention," Maximus laughed on.

"Thank you," she proudly replied. "I take it that such honors must be rare?"

"Yes, indeed it is," he answered in earnest.

It was true that capturing the wandering attention of a former rebel now turned into a responsible crown prince, wasn't a particularly easy task to achieve. But alas, Ruby had certainly accomplished the most impossible deed.

"But please, do go on," he said, as he carelessly waved his hand in the air and thus, signaling for Ruby to continue on with her instructions.

"When the time draws near for you to awake, Violet will be wearing the necklace. Once worn, she'll be instantly drawn to you. Wherever she is in her world, her necklace will guide her back to you. Like I said before, the gem and the armor are forever linked to one another. Eventually, when that fateful day comes, you'll awake to find her by your side. And then, from there, you must convince her to come away with you and journey back into our world."

"Wait, Ruby, you said the word *awake*. What does that mean exactly? Will I be in some sort of unconscious state or something?" he asked, out of concern.

"Given that two hundred years is a long wait and the mere fact alone that you're mortal, I've prepared a special sleeping spell that's specifically designed just for you," Ruby told him, as she then, used her eyes to bring forth attention to her bubbling hot caldron.

"Ah, so that's what you've been brewing here," Maximum remarked.

Suddenly, everything was starting to make a little more sense in the end.

"Precisely. And with one sip of my potion, the spell will be enacted."

"So, this potion of yours will place me in a deep slumber? A sleeping curse? Never to be awakened by any external forces? Including nature?"

"Yes," replied Ruby. "No matter what happens, you'll remain in your unconscious state. You will not age, not by a single day. And might I add, no one else in the enchanted forest — man or creature— will be able to find or see you. You'll be hidden through an invisible veil. You'll only reappear to the human eye, once Violet stumbles upon you later on in the future. And by then, the veil will have been lifted."

"But how will I be released from this deep sleep? Is this some sort of a spell pertaining to true love's kiss?"

As intriguing and serious as all of this was, Maximus couldn't help but allow his boyish curiosity about Violet to get the best of him. If this sleeping spell was indeed cured by true love's kiss, then Maximus was looking forward to locking lips with this fated female savior.

"Prince Maximus, I do hate to disappoint you, but it doesn't quite work that way," replied Ruby, laughingly. "No, this spell is *not* designed to be lifted by true love's first kiss."

"Well, I can't say that I'm not disappointed," replied Maximus, as he folded his arms against his chest. "But I do get it."

However, just one look at him and instantly, Ruby could already see the high level of disappointment in his melancholy expression. After all, it was practically written across his handsome face.

"Don't worry, my dear prince, I'm not such a heartless romantic," she encouraged him. "A kiss might not wake you, but the mere touch of her hand will."

"Her hand? But why? Couldn't you have at least made your spell a bit more romantic?" he playfully asked, in a half joking, half truthful manner.

"A true knight is the epitome of gentleness," Ruby boldly proclaimed. "And a proper gentleman *never* kisses a lady upon their first chance encounter. Instead, they'll offer them their hand, as a sign of true affection. Thus, in your case, she'll offer you *her* hand, instead."

"Okay, a hand… but who's not to say, that she won't want to reach out and grab me there?" he asked, skeptical about that presumption.

Truth be told, had the roles been in reverse, then Maximus highly doubted that he, himself, would have done much of the same.

"Trust me, she will. The stone will guide her to do it. Plus, her heart will want to do it as well."

"Her heart? What does her heart have anything to do with this?" he asked, surprised by her bold prediction.

"Her heart has *everything* to do with it… that's why she's going to be the savior," she revealed.

"Whatever you say," remarked a skeptical Maximus. "And once I wake up from this spell, then how will I be able to convince her to come away with me?"

"Ah, well that's where we're going to need your suave and persuasive skills to woo her over," Ruby replied, with a beaming smile. "Don't think I haven't heard about the ladies of our court, referring to you as the charming roguish prince."

For a moment, Maximus almost wanted to blush out of embarrassment. Even though he was well aware of his rakish reputation, he was genuinely surprised to learn that his romantic liaisons still found a way to reach the ears of the palace courtiers, including their advisors.

"Now, I might have previously warned you about not breaking her heart earlier," Ruby clarified, "But at the same time, try not to be so dry with her, either. You'll need to use some of that special charm of yours to help convince her to fulfill her destiny."

And then, in all seriousness, she told him, "Maximus, we're all counting on you. Please don't let us down. Be the hero that I know you are."

And there it was again, the word *hero*. For most of his life, Maximus constantly fled from this role. But in the end, he still circled back to it. As much as he had his own reservations and self-doubts, Maximus couldn't afford to allow his lack of confidence to get the better of him. Unfortunately, the consequences of war forced him to step into that role of a hero. A *hero* with a *purpose.*

"Okay, I'll find a way to do it," he vowed.

Rising up from his chair, he stood up, looked over at Ruby and asked, "When shall I leave?"

"As soon as you change into that knight's uniform," she instructed.

And then, without a further delay, Maximus, the new crown prince, followed Ruby's lead and quickly changed into his new coat of armor. With the sleeping spell safely tucked away within his hand, Maximus walked straight through the magic mirror. And just like the traveling knight from Violet's favorite fairy tale, he journeyed straight into her world.

And for the next two hundred years and counting, he patiently slept, waiting for Violet's arrival…

# CHAPTER 4

## Two Hundred Years Later...

Shock was a complete understatement, as to how Violet felt right now. Never in a million years, did she ever imagine for a knight... *this* sleeping knight... to be awakened from his deep slumber and cry out to her.  But... how... how was this at all remotely *possible*? And most importantly... how... did he even know... *her name*? Who was *he* exactly?

"Oh my God!" Violet exclaimed, as she collapsed down onto the ground.

With her hands gripping the dirt and her dress brushing against the dried foliage scattered across the muddy meadow, Violet attempted to crawl away. Desperately, her mind instructed her to flee; however, her heart told her to remain. Running away from this whimsical scene was probably the wisest decision to take right now. To simply run and forget about this entire incident, altogether. But alas, Violet was a true adventurer. And so, in the end, she chose to face this strange and mysterious knight head-on and thus, she stayed put in place.

Acknowledging her own curious nature, Violet already knew well-in-advance that had she chosen to flee without getting any real or solid answers to this riddle, then her mind would forever obsess about this mysterious stranger. Just how did this knight know her name? She had never met him before until now. Why, she wasn't even aware that knights had previously visited her part of the world. Let alone, in the forest that she grew up in.

But apart from crying out her name, his voice sounded as if he actually *knew* her. Surprisingly enough, the tone in his voice was so incredibly soft, kind, sincere and almost... *loving*. But how could that be? How could he care for her? She, a total stranger? After all, they hadn't met before. Was it possible for someone to truly care for another soul, without previously laying eyes on them? Love at first sight?

Again, her mind told her to flee. It practically screamed for her to run. But alas, Violet possessed a stubborn heart. After all, it wasn't each day that a knight in shining armor magically appeared, out in the middle of the enchanted forest.

But most ironic of all, was that this mysterious stranger was exactly how Violet had always envisioned her special knight to be. Just like in her dreams, he was resting on a bed of roses. Miraculously, he was the spitting image to the very same knight in shining armor found within her favorite fairy tale. Except this time around, he was *real*.

"Don't be afraid...Violet," he softly whispered.

Perhaps, it was the kind reassurance that she heard spoken within his sweet voice, that ultimately prevented her from fleeing. Whomever he was, his voice sounded like a true friend. Someone who not only knew her, but also cared about her, too.

Slowly, Violet turned back around to face him. As she caught a glimpse of him for a second time, she noticed that he was still lying there, motionless. Tragically, he was trapped inside of a thorny fortress, consisting of wild ivy vines and blooming red roses that encircled his entire body. While his hands and feet might have been dangling outside freely within the open air; his body, however, appeared entirely sealed. A beautiful yet deadly cage, built entirely out of crimson red roses, prickly green thorns and poisonous ivy. Nature's deadliest tomb.

"Are you alright?" Violet asked him, as she swiftly ran back and over to his side.

Pushing her fears aside, Violet's natural instincts to rescue him took hold. Obviously, he was still very much alive. And now, he was trapped inside of this pesky nest. Regardless of her initial reaction before, this man desperately needed her help.

Furthermore, Violet couldn't bear the thought of leaving him alone to face what would surely be, his imminent doom. Had she not chosen to stay, then this man was destined to die out here in this forest, due to this godforsaken entrapment. One way or another, she just had to save him. To become *his hero*, even though she felt so far removed from being considered as such.

"I promise to find a way to save you," she yelled at him, in the event that he failed to hear her spoken words due to the thick layers of his steel helmet.

Frantically, Violet searched around her vicinity, hoping to find something that she could use to help free him. Anything that might be considered as a useful tool that possessed the ability to cut through these deadly vines and stubborn roses. But unfortunately, all that Violet found was a long and thick stick that had recently fallen down from a nearby oak tree.

Being that she was limited with options, Violet decided to take her chance and swiftly, she picked up the weapon. Without thinking any further, Violet started swinging away. Back and forth, she began slamming against the nest; hitting it as hard as she possibly could. All the while, hoping that her blind efforts would eventually come to break it and in the process, free some of the enclosed areas that entrapped him.

At first, all seemed well. Miraculously, her rescue mission seemed to be actually working. However, the stick was only strong enough to cut through the initial layers of the vines, but not of the rose bush. Unfortunately, the rose bush was too great in size and its thorns were quite prickly, that even Violet managed to garner a few minor cuts from it, along the way.

"It's not working," she shouted over to him. "The rose bush is too thick for me to cut through on my own."

And then, for a brief moment, Violet could swear that she heard him *laugh*. Even in the midst of this ongoing chaos, he remained ever calm, confident and unaffected by this deadly predicament. It was almost as if, even in this hopeless situation, he was *hopeful. Trusting* and *believing* in *her* ability to do the *impossible.*

"Use the sword," he advised her.

"A sword?" she asked in confusion.

And then, it dawned on her that he was indeed, a knight. A member of the military. Naturally, he'd have advised her to use a sword to do the deed.

"I'm afraid that I don't have one," Violet answered him back.

He might have been a knight accustomed to the convenient access to such weapons; but unfortunately, they were in the remote English countryside. Not in Medieval Europe. Such requests were truly impossible to achieve.

"Use *my* sword," he clarified.

Glancing back at him, Violet scanned his entire body again and sure enough, she saw his sword. It was attached to the right side of his hip, near the very hand that she had recently embraced. Meanwhile, his sword was also covered by a thick layer of vines. But luckily, it wasn't underneath another rose bush. If Violet could somehow make use of her stick once more, then she'd most likely have a chance to break through this barrier. And if she managed to do so, then she could hopefully make an opening large enough to grab a hold of his sword. Either way, it was worth a try.

Retrieving her stick back from off the ground, Violet said, "Okay, I'm going to try to break through this next layer of vines, so I can get to your sword. But if I should hurt you along the way, then please forgive me ahead of time."

And then, he said the magic words that made her heart skip a beat, "Violet, you could never hurt me. *I trust you.*"

For a brief moment, Violet ceased moving. Truly, she was frozen in mid-air. How could this stranger place so much trust in her? Even if he miraculously knew her somehow, she certainly didn't know him. Plus, no one else in her life had ever trusted her so deeply. To have relentless faith in her ability to accomplish an important task, all on her own. And yet, here was this perfect stranger, who practically entrusted her with his entire livelihood. But why?

"I will try my best to go gentle," Violet announced, hoping to prepare him for any potential accidental injuries. "But if my stick somehow manages to hit your armor in the process, then I apologize in advance. Truly, I am sorry."

"Violet, whatever you do, it can't hurt me anymore than how I already feel right now."

Instantly, his words caught her attention. He was *in pain*. Indeed, he was *suffering*, while trapped underneath this wretched nest. Unfortunately, Violet finally understood that his cage was far more uncomfortable and unpleasant than what she had originally anticipated. The urgency to rescue him was even more critical than ever before.

"Don't worry," she reassured him.

"No matter what happens," Violet swore to him, with much conviction, "I'm going to do whatever it takes to get you out of there."

Recognizing that she was his only hope for survival, Violet vowed to save him. Therefore, with one strong and powerful smack, Violet miraculously managed to break through the first layer. However, this new opening still wasn't enough space for her to reach in and retrieve the sword.

Taking a deep breath, Violet swung away once more. And this time around, she successfully broke through another inch or so. Again, she swung away for a third and a fourth time. By the time Violet reached her fifth swing, she finally managed to break through the barrier and made a hole large enough to reach in and pull out his sword.

"You've done it!" he proudly exclaimed, while acknowledging her remarkable accomplishment.

"I'm almost there," she reassured him, once again.

Carefully, Violet reached in and tried to pull his sword from off his suit. However, her first attempt failed. Apparently, it seemed that after several centuries of rust and decay, his sword was currently stuck in-place.

"Your sword, it seems to be stuck, alongside your hip," Violet shouted to him, hoping that he could hear her.

"Try wiggling it," he suggested.

Following his suggestion, Violet did just that. But again, she didn't have much luck. No matter how much she tried to remove it, the sword still refused to budge. Already, it felt like a hopeless situation.

"It doesn't seem like its working," Violet admitted in defeat.

"Don't give up, Violet," he encouraged her. "Please, give it another try. I know that *you* can do it."

Again, why did he have so much faith in her? Was it because she truly was his last and only hope? After all, there wasn't anyone else around in their vicinity other than herself.

Or, was it possible that this mysterious knight in shining armor really did believe in her? Her ability to accomplish the impossible? To become an unlikely hero?

"Okay, I'll try it again," she shouted back to him.

Taking another deep breath, Violet closed her eyes shut and recited a short prayer. Hoping to accomplish the impossible, she prayed for the strength of a lion, while maintaining the courage of an eagle. Quietly, Violet prayed to save this knight and make him proud. Even though she hardly knew him, deep down inside, she already felt a special connection to him. He, a perfect stranger.

Determined to rescue him once and for all, Violet quickly reached over to his side. Again, she gave another tug at his sword. Even though Violet had failed before, this time around, she *believed* in herself. Either way, she was *going* to do it!

In truth, without Violet's help, then this knight was sure to die out here alone, inside of this abandoned forest. After all, nightfall was soon approaching. And once darkness arrived into the woods, then the wolves were eventually going to descend down onto their land. No doubt, her knight in shining armor was destined to be their next meal, if she failed to release him!

The fear of losing her knight to the wolves, sent an ominous chill down Violet's spine. Once upon a time, in their youth, her own parents previously fought a pack of hungry wolves within this very forest. Luckily, they survived to tell their tale. And because of this mere fact alone, Violet didn't want history to repeat itself again.

And so, with much determination, Violet stretched her arms as far as she possibly could. Using all of her inner strength, she tried her very best to reach for his sword. And much to her relief, this time around, it actually worked! At long last, the sword was finally within the grasp of her hand!

"I've got it!" she happily exclaimed.

"Violet, I knew you could do it," he proudly complemented her, while also sounding equally relieved by the positive outcome.

"Okay, I'm going to chop off these roses now and then, I'll free you from this horrid nest."

And then, without a further delay, Violet swung away and proceeded to chop the remaining vines and roses that encircled his body. As Violet worked her magic, a million or so crimson rose petals broke apart and scattered across the open sky. It was accompanied by the addition of tan, scarlet and tangerine leaves and hunter green vines, that descended down onto the ground. Just like a swirling tornado, its bold and rich colors reflected a mix of brown, red, orange and green hues, that magically surrounded the pair of them in real-time.

Truly, it was a rather remarkable sight to behold. A fair and young maiden, swinging her heavy steel sword to help rescue her knight in distress. It was epic. It was whimsical. It was honorable. It was heroic. It was oh so utterly... *romantic*. A sweeping romance fit for an enchanting fairy tale, in which the princess was the hero and not the other way around.

After a few long minutes, Violet succeeded on destroying a good portion of the nest. Even though her dress was now covered in head-to-toe with rose petals, leaves, twigs and vines, Violet still remained fully concentrated on the condition of her knight. At this point, she could finally see the full outline to his set of armor.

To her surprise, up-close, the knight was far larger than what she originally anticipated. At first glance, his chest appeared broad and powerful, as it laid against his steel coat of armor. Furthermore, judging by his long length, Violet concluded that he must have been a tall man. A man, who was probably well over six feet tall. A person, who was significantly taller than her medium sized self. And just like the knight in shining armor from her dreams, he certainly was... well... dreamy...

"Thank you, Violet," he told her. "I'll take it from here."

And then to her amazement, he actually began to rise up. Even with a significant number of vines wrapped around his torso and legs, the knight somehow still managed to overcome them. As he fought to regain his posture, he succeeded in freeing his arms on both sides of his body. And then, using his free arms, he ripped off the remaining plants that surrounded him. Afterwards, he quickly disregarded the mess down onto the dirty ground. And before Violet knew it, the knight was completely freed from his entrapment and was now, standing right before her.

For a second, Violet just stared at him in awe. In that blissful moment, she was entirely at a loss for words. Just like the knight from her favorite fairy tale, he was everything that she had ever imagined a knight in shining armor to be. Dashing, courageous, heroic and... devastatingly *handsome.*

But truth be told, he was actually far *more* handsome than what she previously imagined. Even with his rusted coat of armor, he was still quite stunning. And now, after seeing him in real life, he was absolutely without a doubt, *perfect...*

Suddenly, he grabbed a hold of her shoulders and began to speak, "Violet—"

But before he could say another word, Violet beat him straight to the punch.

"Wait, how do you know my name?" she asked him directly, as she gazed at his helmet. Desperately, she was trying to catch a glimpse of his eyes.

"Have we met before? Sometime, in the distant past?"

Although Violet couldn't see much of him through the thick layers of his steel helmet, she did manage to catch sight of his eyes that were peeking through the opening of his visor. From what she could see, his eyes were a unique shade of grey, almost silver like... a color that ironically, was almost identical to his original suit of armor. Meanwhile, his eyelashes were a soft shade of chestnut brown. Based on these observations alone, Violet concluded that he must have possessed a natural shade of chestnut brown hair, along with fair skin and silver eyes.

"Violet, I don't have much time," he replied, with great urgency. "But I have traveled a very long way to find you."

"A long way?" she asked in amazement.

It was almost as if her childhood fairy tale had truly come to life. Except, unlike her beloved tale, Violet wasn't the same princess from that story.

"Yes. And I've been waiting a long time for you, too. You're our only hope."

He continued, "And the long wait, most certainly paid off. Not only did you prove your worth, but I honestly believe that I can entrust my life, along with the lives of my entire kingdom within your caring hands."

"Kingdom?" Violet echoed, in sheer surprise.

A kingdom seemed surreal. Honestly, it felt more like a whimsical place that belonged to a far-off fantasy tale, instead of real life. Why, the only kings and queens in this country nowadays belonged to the British royal family. And even they resided back in London, and not anywhere near here. Plus, even *that* was a far cry from a traditional medieval kingdom that still employed actual knights. Just where exactly did this traveling knight come from?

"Violet," he tenderly spoke her name out loud, while sounding just like a typical knight in shining armor plucked straight out of a medieval fairy tale.

And upon reciting her name, he gently grabbed a hold of her hand. Softly and delicately, he held onto her, just like the gentleman that he was. Instantly, Violet's heart melted into butter.

"As you'll soon come to learn, trusting others isn't easy for someone like me," he admitted. "But I do trust you. Violet, you're special. And if you're willing to give me a chance, then I'm sure you'll also come to trust and lean on me, too."

His enchanting words sounded like poetry to her ears. Oh, where oh where did this mysterious stranger come from?

"Who... who are you?" Violet blurted out.

"I promise to explain everything, once we safely reach our destination," he promised her. "But right now, Violet, I need you to trust and follow me. Whatever happens, I vow to protect you, at all costs. Even, if I must sacrifice my own life to protect yours."

It was almost as if she was in a dream and it was, *she*, who was actually waking up from a long sleeping spell and certainly *not him*...

"Now, is the time for you to honor your destiny and become a hero," he continued on. "For both of *us* to become heroes. To fulfill our true purposes. You and I are in this together. We're forever linked."

That was *it*. Suddenly, everything became so abundantly clear. Without even knowing, he said *the* magical word: *purpose*. All this time, Violet was desperately struggling to adapt back into her old way of life, mainly because she was searching for a purpose. Her life's purpose. A reason or a cause to belong to. It's why she considered studying medicine and science in the first place. It's why she contemplated being a doctor and traveling to far off lands. In the end, Violet was searching for both an adventure, as well as a place to belong to. A mission. A cause. A *purpose*.

Amazingly enough, this man... this mysterious knight... was offering her everything that she secretly wished for. A rare and golden opportunity to find herself. An offer for a thrilling adventure. An opportunity to become a hero. A chance to have a happily ever after.

One way or another, Violet was almost ready to accept his offer. While he might have waited a long time for her; she, on the other hand, still had her affairs to straighten out first. Mainly, she was obligated to tell her family about her new plans. After all, Violet couldn't bear the thought of them thinking that she had abandoned them and subsequently, ran away from their family's home. Especially, after her most recent fallout with her sister, Daphne.

"I'll come," she promised him. "But first, I need to tell—"

But before Violet could even finish her sentence, an arrow flew right by them. And then, another... followed by another... and then… another...

A moment later, about a dozen more arrows came flying down towards their direction!

Immediately, Violet recalled the main reason as to why she arrived down here in the first place: the archer. Previously, she was fleeing from *a* mysterious archer. And now, judging by the increased number of flying arrows, there must have been several more men. *Archers.* And whomever they were, they obviously were hunting them down. Apparently, they wanted them *dead.*

"It's Vera's men. They've found us. We're not safe here."

Without a proper chance to react, the knight swiftly lifted Violet from off the ground and carried her tightly within his arms. Before she knew it, he was running straight ahead, moving as fast as his two feet could take them.

As Violet glanced back behind them, she saw an army of at least ten or so archers. They were chasing after them, while shooting several arrows aimed at their direction.

But where did they come from? In all of her many years spent wandering this forest, Violet never saw any archers before… or better yet, soldiers out here. And now, there was an entire army fleet of them! But why was that? Why were they hunting them? Did they really want them dead? And if so, then why?

"Who are they?" Violet asked him, as she wrapped her arms tightly around his shoulders. Holding onto him for dear life.

"I don't have much time to explain, but we've got to get out of here as soon as possible," he warned.

"If we need a place to hide, then my home is further up the hill—"

But before Violet could finish her sentence, they wandered off deep into a darkened cave. And then, there was a sudden and bright flash of light. Before she knew it, they arrived to a place that Violet did not at all recognize…

# CHAPTER 5

"'Welcome back, my prince," spoke the strange old woman.

And then, to Violet's surprise, the old woman reverted her full attention over to her and said, "But it's an even greater honor to finally meet you, my dearest... *Violet.*"

If Violet was shocked before, then now, she was truly at a loss for words. Who was this strange woman? How did she know her name? How did everyone else around her, seemingly know about her identity? People, whom she had never met before until now? Was Violet really this popular?

Furthermore, where were they precisely? This place didn't look like the village. Heck, it didn't even resemble England at all!

Plus, did she just hear her say *my prince*? Was her mysterious knight in shining armor really an *actual prince*?

"Ruby, I'd like the honor of formally introducing you to the one and only Lady Violet Galloway," Maximus proudly announced, as he walked past the magic mirror, accompanied by Violet safely at his side.

And then, at long last, Maximus finally removed his helmet to reveal his face. Just as she envisioned, Violet's knight in shining armor was indeed handsome. Breathtakingly so. He had perhaps, one of the loveliest, if not, *the* most beautiful face that she had ever laid eyes upon before.

Silently, Violet observed him. Just as she suspected, his thick head of hair was indeed chestnut brown. A color that also matched his heavy eyelashes and thick brows. Additionally, his face was muscular, exhibiting a strong jawline and a chin that was both angular and sharp. Furthermore, his nose was straight and long, while his lips were full and colored in the shade of rosy red. Meanwhile, his almond shape eyes were sparkling in silver, along with a unique hint of violet found within the inner rims of his irises.

And now, standing beside him, Violet personally acknowledged just how remarkably tall he was. While she had initially presumed him to be at least six feet tall back in the enchanted forest; however, now, side by side, he was closer to six feet and five inches! If not, then possibly even taller! In truth, he was a mountain! A real life giant!

Furthermore, while Maximus might have been blessed with the face of an ancient god, but he also possessed the stature of a fierce warrior. Ladies across this land must have frequently vied for his constant attention; for seriously, he really was that incredibly sexy and gorgeous!

Overall, if Violet had to guess, then she'd presume that her knight in shining armor must have been a man at around thirty years of age or so. And apart from being ridiculously handsome, Maximus also maintained a certain suave debonair about him. It was a sort of sexy and devilish-like charm that transcended not only in the form of his physical appearance, but in his personality as well.

"Violet, this is Ruby," Maximus introduced them. "She's my part time advisor, part time witch."

"Wait, did you just say that she's a *witch?*" asked Violet in surprise.

Apparently, everything that she had previously read from the pages of her favorite storybook had magically come... well... *true...*

"Not to worry," Maximus reassured her, as he leaned in and gently whispered into her ear, "She's a good one."

"A good one? Do you mean there are also *bad* ones out here, too?"

And then, both Maximus and Ruby laughed on. Although they didn't fault her for asking such an honest question; however, anyone residing within their kingdom already well knew the answer to this riddle. Indeed, there were bad witches residing here. After all, Vera alone, had proven this fact all-so-incredibly well.

"My dear Violet," Ruby began, as she pulled out a wooden chair, "Please take a seat and make yourself more comfortable. We've got much to discuss."

Following her direction, Violet promptly sat down.

"Now, that we're finally face-to-face, I'd like to properly introduce myself," she continued on, "I'm Ruby, the Wise. Also, sometimes known as Ruby, the Elder. But everyone here calls me Ruby. Although, I'd personally prefer that you call me Granny."

Considering that Violet had only just met her, calling her *granny* seemed a bit too personal and intimate. Therefore, she decided to keep it formal and went with her proper given name, instead.

"Ruby," Violet addressed her. "Isn't that name similar to the stone currently found around your necklace?"

Indeed, Violet was correct. Even while seated across from her, the old woman's ruby red gem still managed to sparkle and shine against the light. And strangely enough, the stone was also similar to the shape of Violet's own necklace: a heart. Had the stone not been in the color red, then their necklaces would have been virtually identical to each other.

"Yes, just like my stone," Ruby happily confirmed.

And then, she further added, "But it seems that you also have a necklace that's similar to mine, too. A purple gem fit for a Violet."

Instantly, the women smiled at each other, while recognizing that they both shared similar taste in jewelry. Thus far, they shared some common ground. And even though Violet had only just met Ruby, already she felt at ease with her. She might have been a witch, but according to her knight in shining armor, Ruby was a good one.

Afterwards, Violet curiously glanced around the room. From the looks of it, they appeared to be seated inside of a laboratory or even, a kitchen of some sort. All around them, were numerous bottles that were out on display. Bottles, that came in a variety of shapes, sizes and colors. In truth, they almost resembled perfume bottles. Judging by the mere fact alone that Ruby was a witch, Violet presumed that these bottles must have been magical potions.

But apart from these whimsical ornaments, there was also a collection of books that were organized and placed upon several shelves made out of stone. Furthermore, the building itself, appeared to have been built using that same grey stone material as the shelves. Cold stones that stretched from the walls and upwards to the ceiling and then, traveling all the way down onto the floors.

At first glance, it seemed as if they were all congregated together, inside of a wing that was located within an ancient castle. Furthermore, in the center of the room, was a large black caldron. It was placed within a stone fireplace, which was currently lit by a warm and blazing fire.

But on the far left-hand corner of the space, was a gigantic mirror. It, just like everything else around them in this foreign dwelling, also appeared to be of ancient origin. An antique of some sort. As Violet gazed at the object, she noticed that the mirror was tall and shiny, while its frame was made from a bronze metallic-like material that projected a bright and golden shade.

Recalling their recent arrival, Violet soon realized that *this* was the very mirror in which they traveled through. But unlike the mirrors back at home, this particular one was truly special. A whimsical magic mirror that housed a connecting portal, which surpassed logic and defied both time and space. An enchanted object that possessed an interwoven wormhole, which led them directly into this new realm; a foreign land that Violet did not at all recognize. Not even from the maps or the many books that she had previously studied back in her university's library.

"Where I am?" she finally asked the million-dollar question.

"I suppose that's a valid question to ask," Ruby acknowledged. "I guess it's finally time to fill you in on the truth."

And then, Ruby and Maximus pulled themselves each a chair and took a seat by the fire.

"A long time ago," Ruby spoke, her tone ever-so-serious now, "Your father was cursed by a wicked witch. As you might recall from this tale, her name was Vera."

"Yes, I am well aware about her, as well as the famous tale concerning my family in great details," Violet stated. "I've heard their story told a hundred times over. Once upon a time, Vera was my father's evil stepmother. A wicked witch, who also murdered my grandfather and then went on to curse my father, too. But after the curse, my father sought his revenge and killed her."

"Or so, the story goes," Maximus chimed in.

"What do mean by that statement?" she asked him, point blank.

"Just that, perhaps, your assumptions about Vera's fate might have been… well… what's the proper word… *premature?*"

Clearly, he was hinting that her presumptions about Vera's death was most unfortunately, entirely *wrong*. Was she missing an unknown chapter pertaining to the famous legend about her own father?

"Wait, are you suggesting that my father *didn't* actually murder Vera?" asked Violet in astonishment.

Never before, did Violet ever consider the remote possibility that her father's version to this legendary story might not have been entirely accurate. Apparently, there was another alternative ending to the infamous tale surrounding the Dark Horseman and the wicked witch who cursed him.

"Yes *and* no," Ruby answered, in earnest. "Your father did indeed slay her. However, it's important to understand that killing a witch isn't so simple. In order for a witch to remain dead, then she must willingly accept her fate at the time of her death. Otherwise…"

"She'll just reanimate into another form," Maximus interjected.

"Reanimate? Do you mean that Vera is somehow… *still alive?*"

Suddenly, Violet's shock grew into concern. If Vera was indeed, alive and well, then she was a living threat to the welfare of her family. What if Vera wanted to return back to England? Reclaim Galloway Manor and its land for herself? Seek revenge against her own darling father? No, Violet couldn't allow for any of this to happen!

"Vera is *still* very much alive," Ruby informed her. "In fact, she's not only alive and well, but she's also managed to invade our kingdom. Just recently, Vera unjustly stole the throne from our very own prince. Sadly, she's already crowned herself as the new queen."

And then, Violet recalled that when they first arrived here, Ruby had previously referenced her knight in shining armor as a prince.

"Wait, are you really a prince?" Violet asked him directly, as she stared at the young man seated right next to her.

"My dearest Violet, he's not just a prince," Ruby interrupted. "He's our *crown prince*. And as soon as we defeat Vera, he'll be crowned as our next king."

"But you can just call me Maximus," he playfully smiled and then winked at her.

Instantly, Violet blushed. She wasn't used to so much attention from the male sex. Especially, coming from a charming prince. However, given how closely they were seated together by the fireplace, Violet hoped that her recent flush of redness found on her face could easily be blamed on the heat stemming from the flaming fire. Hopefully, that fact alone, would conceal her excitement. Alas, not only was her handsome knight a prince, but he was also a soon-to-be king!

"But before he becomes our next king," Ruby warned, "We must first deal with Vera."

Curiously, Violet silently listened on in fasciation, as the old witch continued with her tale.

"Years ago, Vera was once a citizen of our world," she explained. "However, she had a fall out with Maximus' father, the late King Elryk. Due to their bad blood, Vera was banished from our land and sent to Earth through my magic mirror. The very same mirror that you and Maximus recently traveled through. From what you might have already gathered, that mirror is a portal that links your world to ours via a pathway through the enchanted forest."

"So, it really *is* an enchanted forest, after all?" asked Violet in amazement.

In the end, her parents' claims to the forest being enchanted really was *true*.

"Yes, it very much is," Ruby told her.

"So, where am I exactly?" Violet inquired.

"You're currently in the Kingdom of the West," Ruby answered. "The Land of Eternal Autumn. However, this kingdom is only but one of three others. There's also the Kingdom of the East, the Land of Eternal Spring; the Kingdom of the North, the Land of Eternal Winter; and the Kingdom of the South, the Land of Eternal Summer. All four kingdoms are ruled by four separate kings. Together, they encompass the Great Kingdom."

"That's fascinating," Violet remarked. "It's like a whole another universe."

Based on what Violet had already seen, their world was incredibly enchanting. Truly, everything in this realm was identical to something plucked right out of a fairy tale.

"Yes, I think so, too," Ruby agreed, with a warm smile.

"But why was Vera exiled in the first place?" asked Violet. "And how did she return here, after my father supposedly killed her?"

"The reason concerning Vera's exile isn't important," Ruby stated. "However, it's her death on Earth, that ultimately, served as the catalyst that brought her back into our world."

"Really? How so?"

"As punishment to her fallout with the late king, Vera was banned from returning to our world for the remainder of her lifetime."

"So, I see," Violet acknowledged.

"And so," Ruby continued on, "Vera needed to be slayed."

"To die?"

"Yes, to die," replied Ruby. "Personally, I believe Vera's exile was the real reason, as to why she cursed your father. Ultimately, Vera needed a means to escape her sentence. She knew the power of the forest. She understood why the ancient druids worshiped its land. It's because the enchanted forest is a portal that connects our shared worlds. That is the truth."

"Wait, Vera cursed my father, so that he could *murder her*?" Violet interrupted. "But how did she know that he'd even do that, in the first place?"

"By murdering Henry's father, alienating his brother and then cursing him, Vera calculated that these unjustly actions would eventually, force him over the edge. But more than anything, she just needed to push Henry so far enough that he'd come to resent her. To hate her so much, that he'd have no other choice but to finally give into his spiteful desires and claim his revenge. Which, mind you, is precisely what she wanted to happen, too."

"But I thought that my grandmother saved my father from the brink of death?" asked Violet, in confusion. "I was led to believe that Vera originally sought to kill my father, in order to steal his inheritance. Her supposed intent was to murder him, not to curse him as the Dark Horseman. That part of the curse was an accidental consequence of his life having been spared."

"The problem was that Vera knew Sarah all too well," Ruby sighed. "To outsiders, it might have appeared as if Vera desired to kill your father, but that isn't entirely true. In fact, Vera predicted that Sarah's loving spirit would descend down onto Earth to save Henry. And so, Vera calculated well. She gambled that Henry would succumb to the Dark Horseman curse, as a means for Sarah to preserve the life of her only son."

"It's starting to make a little more sense now, right?" asked Maximus, as he glanced over towards Violet's direction.

Silently, Violet nodded in agreement. And so, Ruby continued on with her story.

"The moment your father plunged his dagger straight through Vera's heart, her death set her free. As you can imagine, her death on Earth also meant her rebirth back into our world," Ruby revealed. "And so, this is how Vera ventured back into our kingdom. However, her past resentment with King

Elryk still laid claims to her blackened heart. Unfortunately, her forced exile wasn't something that she could easily forgive nor forget. And so, as a result, Vera sought her revenge against him."

"What did she do precisely?" asked Violet, now growing more nervous and concerned by each passing minute.

"She murdered my father, my brother and now, she's recently crowned herself as the new queen of my land," Maximus answered, this time. "Right now, she's executing thousands of our people. As I speak, please know that not only has she destroyed my kingdom, but her men have also brutally slaughtered, raped and tortured our innocent citizens. Vera's reign of terror only worsens by each passing day. Even death is a more honorable fate than for most. And unless we do everything in our power to stop her, then it's only a matter of time before she conquers not only our world but of yours as well."

"Violet, what the prince speaks is true," Ruby concurred. "Unless, we work together to end her reign, then I'm afraid that we're all doomed."

"Of course, I'm eager to help aid in this fight," Violet bravely spoke up. "I'm willing to do whatever it takes to stop the reign of an evil villain and protect innocent peoples' lives, including the lives of my own family in the process. But at the same time, how can I help you? What can I, myself, do? After all, I'm just a young woman, who's freshly out of university. I know nothing of the world. Especially, yours. What could you ever possibly need my help with?"

Impressed by her vivid emotions, both Ruby and Maximus happily smiled at her with great admiration.

"Violet, do you know the real reason, as to why your parents chose that lovely name of yours?" Ruby asked her.

"Why yes, I do," replied Violet. "I'm named after a magical flower that grows deep inside of the enchanted forest. In fact, violets were once considered to be the favorites of my late grandmothers, too."

"But do you know as to why they're even considered to be magical at all?" Ruby pressed on.

"Well, my mother once told me that the violets found within the enchanted forest, possess the rare ability to cure all ailments," Violet answered. "But what does any of this have to do with my name?"

"It has *everything* to do with your name," Ruby boldly revealed. "Just like the flower's unique ability to cure, you've also got that same enchantment imbedded within your own heart, too. Truly, your name is most suiting. For you see, my dearest Violet, you're *our savior.* You're *our cure.* It's already been promised. You, and only you alone, can defeat her."

If Ruby's message wasn't enough to convince Violet to stay, then Maximus had a few more words of his own to help encourage her.

Extending his hand over to meet hers, he gently said, "Well Violet, are you ready to join me in this battle and become a hero?"

Without thinking another second thought, Violet stared straight into his moonlit silver eyes and found her answer. One way or another, he needed her help. Plus, she wanted to help him, too. To protect both his people and hers.

And so, without a further delay, Violet found herself shaking hands with the young prince and agreeing to his proposal. And thus, in the process, making the single most important deal of her entire life— an alliance that would forever alter not only her own destiny but of their combined worlds, too.

# CHAPTER 6

Later on, that evening, Violet found herself upstairs in what appeared to be her new bedchamber for the next foreseeable future. How long was she expected to stay in this foreign realm? Honestly, Violet didn't have a clue.

But for however long or little she was destined to remain here in this new world, one thing was for sure: she couldn't return back home as of yet. At least, not until she helped her new friends to defeat the evil queen, once and for all. Plus, not only did she want to help them, but she also *needed* to as well.

Previously, in the distant past, Vera unjustly cursed her father and left him for dead. And as a result of her heartless actions, for one hundred years, the Earl of Galloway was forced to wander the enchanted forest as the legendary Dark Horseman. Tragically, Vera's cruel actions single-handedly caused so much pain, suffering and anguish for Violet's family, especially for her parents. And because of her father's past history with his estranged stepmother, Violet simply refused to idly stand by and watch as the evil queen caused more havoc. She couldn't risk allowing Vera to have the opportunity to hurt her family ever again. Not now, or in the future.

And so, Violet had no other choice but to stay behind. To become the savior that her new friends believed her to be. To become a hero, just like Maximus, the crown prince.

According to Ruby, time moved differently in their world. A day in theirs was equal to a hundred years in hers. It's why she accidentally stumbled upon Maximus as he previously slept in the enchanted forest; it was because he was placed under a sleeping curse. An enchanted spell that enabled him to sleep for the past two hundred years. Exactly a hundred years prior, before her own father became cursed as the infamous Dark Horseman.

But why hadn't anyone else discovered Maximus, the sleeping knight, prior to Violet's arrival on that fateful day, out in the middle of the woods? Well, apart from the many mysteries lurking within the magical enchanted forest, Maximus' sleeping curse was designed to conceal him.

Not only did his sleeping curse place him in a deep slumber, but it also operated as a protective shield. An invisible veil that prevented any external forces from seeing or interacting with him. All except for Violet. She, and she alone, was the only person, who was immune to the protective restrictions placed upon this powerful sleeping curse.

In fact, Maximus' sleeping curse was personally brewed especially for him, by none-other-than Ruby, herself. Not only did this curse place him in a deep slumber as he patiently waited for Violet's arrival; but it also kept him safely hidden away, unseen by other potential external threats.

According to Ruby, Violet's necklace and Maximus' armor were interlinked. Two enchanted objects that were attracted to one another and therefore, bonded. As a result, regardless of which realm(s) either one of them traveled to, they'd always be linked together through fate. Even from afar, they'd be drawn to each other, just like magnets. An invisible red thread of destiny that forever united them. And so, this is why *and* how, Violet ultimately came to stumble upon Maximus on that fateful day, as he peaceful slept.

But now, two centuries later, Maximus had finally awakened. And as a result, Violet found herself whisked away to a brand-new world that included an unexpected adventure. Although Violet remained ignorant about this new world and its surroundings, but already, she could tell that this was quite literally, a fairy tale realm that was comprised of kings, queens, princes, princesses, knights, witches, wizards and other magical beings. Characters that all lived amongst one another, as if they were regular everyday neighbors. Truly, this was a stark contrast in comparison to her own world back in twentieth century England!

While time remained stretched between their two worlds, Ruby did assure her that once their mission was complete, then the clocks would revert back to their original settings. And as a result, Violet would be able to return home within the same time frame, in which she previously left.

According to Ruby's explanation, under Queen Vera's recent reign of terror, exercising magic was a newly forbidden and unlawful practice in their kingdom. In fact, the penalty for practicing any form of magic was a guaranteed death sentence. Sadly, as a result, many witches and magicians were persecuted and subsequently, executed. The mere fact alone that Ruby used her sleeping curse to protect Maximus on his journey, was already a great risk on her part. Furthermore, Ruby also explained that she was a practitioner of white magic; whereas, Vera delved into the dark arts using black magic.

Although both forms were essentially still magic; however, there was a significant difference between the two. Apparently, white magic was innocent and pure and born out of love; while black magic arose from anger and hate and always resulted in nothing more than anguish and sorrow for its practitioner. Additionally, the type of magic one practiced directly stemmed from their internal emotions. Thus, in the end, one's personal feelings ultimately determined which type of magic one associated with.

However, apart from all of this, Violet was supposedly a prophesied savior. And more specifically, *their* savior. But what did that even mean exactly in the first place?

In truth, Violet had absolutely no clue. She'd never been a savior before, let alone a leader. For most of her life, she assumed the roles of a daughter, an elder sister, a student and a maiden. But most importantly, she was the first-born daughter of the Earl of Galloway. A refined lady.

From the time she was born and placed inside of her crib, Violet was expected to grow up to become a bride and marry well off. Unfortunately, as the daughter of an earl, that was all that society expected of her. Sadly, Violet wasn't designed to be anything more than that of another rich aristocrat's wife. Even though Violet never faulted her family for these limited options concerning her future; tragically, society, along with its ongoing pressures, dictated otherwise. Looking back at it all, she wasn't made to be a savior. Let alone, a *hero*.

But for the first time in her life, someone else thought to question her predictable future. To actually challenge it, for a refreshing change. And ironically, it was these two perfect strangers who actually believed in her the most. Convinced in the bold notion that she was destined for a different sort of future. That Violet was capable of having an honorable role, that wasn't limited to just being a student or another rich man's wife. But instead, a role that was deemed heroic. A role that was generally reserved for a man. Plus, they genuinely seemed to *believe in her*. Trusted in her. Placed their utmost faith in a perfect stranger, such as she.

Even though Violet secretly confessed her own self-doubts about the whole matter over to Ruby, the old witch reassured her otherwise. Confidently, Ruby advised her to believe in herself. That eventually, in time, Violet would have all the answers that she needed. Furthermore, she also explained that it was her heart— and her heart alone— that was ultimately, destined to save them.

And so, in the end, Violet found herself agreeing to the crown prince's terms and conditions, without question. As foolish as it was to align herself with a perfect stranger for a war that she knew very little about, she decided to follow her instincts. To take a leap of faith. To follow her heart.

Once their meeting concluded, Maximus excused himself to check on his men, while Violet stayed behind with Ruby. Afterwards, the old witch gave her a guided tour of the property. Based on her observations, Ruby's castle, ironically named Castle Hope, appeared to be an ancient fortress of sorts. A site that resembled more of a forgotten ruin, rather than a functioning and habitable castle.

According to Ruby, after Vera's invasion, Maximus and his court were forced to flee the royal palace and its surrounding territory. As sanctuary, Ruby graciously offered to host the crown prince and his companions at her castle. As a result, these new guests (or refugees) were all secretly hiding at

Ruby's private estate, under her watchful protection. And so, as of now, the castle served as their new headquarters and fortress. A training camp built almost entirely out of grey stone blocks, that covered all the floors, walls, doors, ceiling and roof.

Meanwhile, the castle, itself, was rather small in comparison to the other grand European palaces that Violet had previously visited back in her homeland. In truth, Castle Hope was more like a medium sized castle, rather than a formal palace meant to host a large gathering, including the royal family and their entire court.

But apart from its overall limited size, Castle Hope still contained three levels, with approximately fifty rooms allocated per floor. The ground level included a large and spacious ballroom and a generous sized banquet hall that was also accompanied with a kitchen, a salon, a study, a laboratory and a grand foyer. Meanwhile, all of the bedchambers were situated on the upper levels.

Furthermore, as a sign of its own old age, several sections of the castle were missing a significant amount of stone blocks. As a result, these missing sections left many openings and holes found in-between the walls. And because of this, Violet found the castle to be closer to a ruin, instead of a typical medieval or fairy tale like palace. Additionally, on the outside, the castle was hidden by a vast forest that consisted of several tall oak trees that encircled the entire premise. Another forest that reminded Violet of her own enchanted forest from back at home.

Upon touring Castle Hope, Violet was then escorted upstairs to the top third floor to visit her new bedchamber. To her surprise, Violet's room was quite elegant and regal. Unlike the other rooms found at the castle, her bedchamber looked more up-to-date by its infrastructure and showed no visible signs of embellishments. Fortunately, in this particular room, there were no holes, no broken knobs, no missing pieces of stone, or anything else that was deemed questionable. Nothing run-down. Nothing that signaled a *ruin*.

Instead, Violet's bedchamber was modern, pristine and decorated with the loveliest style of furniture and décor. While the other rooms might have been more minimal with its overall decoration and furniture (mainly consisting of a single bed and if lucky, a wash basin and no more); Violet's bedchamber, on the other hand, was the exception to this general rule.

To her amazement, Violet's bedchamber was not only filled with several pieces of hand-crafted furniture built using rich and solid materials, but the entire premise was also decorated in the theme of purple. From top to bottom, her namesake, violet, was spread all around. A whimsical shade that also ironically, represented the same traditional color that was historically worn by royalty.

Glancing across her new bedchamber, Violet saw various purple-toned shades proudly out on display. From violet lace curtains to a silk magenta ruffled and ribboned bedding, to golden and lilac colored furniture, the many variations of purple dominated the entire space. Furthermore, the room also included: a vanity, a matching pair of nightstands, an armoire, a matching set of a velvet sofa and two velvet chairs, a chest and a headboard. In the end, Violet's new bedchamber was truly fit for a typical fairy tale inspired royal princess, to say the least.

Innocently, Violet smiled proudly to herself. Secretly, she was delighted and pleased by this sight. Never before in her young adult life, had she been surrounded by such lovely, enchanting and feminine things. Even back in her own home, most of her belongings were primarily dark colored pieces. Items that she had previously inherited from past family members, descending from her long family tree.

In reality, most of Violet's possessions were antiques that belonged to her ancestors. Priceless heirlooms that were most certainly, not custom made especially for her. And even though she was only but a temporary guest residing at this castle, somehow, Violet also got the impression that this bedroom was specifically designed and tailored *just for her*. It was almost as if this magical and luxurious space was just waiting for her arrival, even after all these long years.

Suddenly, Violet heard chimes ringing. Alas, the clock stroke five o'clock in the evening. In exactly one hour from now, Violet was expected to arrive downstairs for supper. With the recent arrival of Maximus and herself, a special banquet ceremony was going to be held tonight in their honors.

Without a further delay, Violet hurried to wash herself up in time for tonight's festivities. Ironically, tonight was still technically, Violet's twenty-first birthday. After starting her morning back on Earth, she spent the remainder of her day fleeing from a shooting archer, rescuing a sleeping knight, traveling to an unknown foreign realm, learning the truth about her father's past curse, discovering that she was a prophesied savior and to top it all off, she was about to celebrate tonight with a real-life prince! And a crown prince, at that!

Oh, my, what a whirlwind adventure and spectacular birthday this had certainly turned out to be!

* * *

At the stroke of six o'clock in the evening, Violet arrived to the foot of the staircase, which led down to the castle's ground level. Standing at the top, she took in a moment to observe a bird's eye view from high above. In the past, Violet had previously attended her fair share of balls and celebrative parties. Grand events, in which the ladies in attendance wore their finest gowns, while the gentleman showcased their best suits. But tonight, the scene at this particular event was entirely different from the other parties thrown back in her homeland.

Instead, Violet witnessed a field of armor. The colors of silver, bronze, copper and gold, which overwhelmingly, overtook the entire view. All throughout the castle, the men were dressed in their traditional knights' uniforms. Armors that were specially crafted using the highest quality of pristine metals. Shining and sparkling coats of armor that signaled only the utmost best for the Kingdom of the West.

As for the other remaining men not sporting a knight's uniform, then they were dressed in either a plain white, cream, brown or burgundy long-sleeved ruffled tunic, and accompanied by a selection of red, black or green trousers. Meanwhile, if their hairs were long, then they were pulled back and placed into a sleek and tightened ponytail, with the use of a satin chocolate brown or crimson red bow. However, if their hairs were cut short, then they wore a green or burgundy round velvet bure, adorned with a white or brown feather to cover their heads. In addition, they all possessed leather boots, worn in the colors of either jet black or dark brown. Overall, the scene resembled more of a medieval kingdom than anything else.

But apart from the men, there were also a fair share of women in attendance, too. No doubt, these ladies must have been the knights' accompanying wives, daughters, sisters or other familiar family relations.

Just like the pretty debutantes attending the fancy balls held in Violet's world, these ladies were also equally elegantly dressed, wearing their finest gowns out in public. Many of these ladies of the court's gowns were made in either silk or velvet and came in a variety of shades, including crimson red, pale pink, chocolate brown, golden orange and mossy green. From what Violet could gather, these tones must have been the traditional colors that represented their local culture. Regional shades that symbolized their western kingdom.

But apart from their vivid gowns, their hairstyles and makeup were just as equally lovely.  In fact, most of their hair coloring reflected shades of either golden yellow or chestnut brown, with an exceptional few sporting a rare form of midnight black or icy blonde hair. However, to Violet's surprise, there wasn't a single redhead around. It seemed that, at least at this party, Violet was the only one sporting a fiery red mane.

Moving on, Violet noticed that the ladies of the court either wore their hairs styled in a single thick and long braid, or they were left freely down to graciously flow behind their backs. Furthermore, their hairs were either adorned with a jeweled hair clip, such as a ruby or an amber stone, which were clipped to the center of their hairs, or they opted for a transparent and sheer lace veil that hung over their backs to cover the lengths of their long hairs.

As for their jewelries, most ladies wore a variety of metallic objects, such as rings, bracelets, necklaces or earrings. Similarly, these accessories also appeared to match their accompanying husbands' or chaperones' coats of armors, too. Additionally, if their accessories included a jewel, then they were mainly oval or square cut and were either a ruby, an amber or an emerald stone— traditional shades that again, seemed consistent with the Kingdom of the West's regional colors.

Based upon her keen observations, Violet could already tell that she stood out from amongst the crowd. Apart from her own physical appearance, with her bright red hair and emerald green eyes, her choice of attire certainly didn't blend in with the rest of these guests. Not only did Violet not match with this court, but she was also the only woman wearing a crystal beaded lilac and ruffled mermaid silk gown. A dress that she had recently discovered hidden inside of her new armoire, which just-so-happened to match her own amethyst heart stone necklace, too.

But apart from her lilac gown, Violet's wavy red hair was let loose and wildly floating down her slender back. Additionally, her hair was adorned with a bright amethyst bejeweled hair clip that was currently attached to her side and resting above her ear.

As Violet finally descended down the staircase, she suddenly grew nervous. In a sea filled with an endless crowd of people, Violet came to the realization that all of these guests were essentially, total strangers to her. Not only was she in a strange and foreign land, but apart from Ruby and Maximus, she didn't know anyone else. Plus, she was completely ignorant about their local culture and traditions. But unfortunately, this new fear of hers was only further heightened by the mere fact that her attire alone, failed to blend in with the rest of the gowns worn by the other ladies of the court. As it currently stood, Violet was literally blind folded and walking directly into an unchartered future, all by her lonesome self.

Taking a deep breath in, Violet proceeded to take her first step off the staircase and onto the ground floor. It was funny how much her life had changed, all within the span of a single afternoon. From fighting with Daphne over a pair of pearl earrings to fleeing from an army of archers and escaping to a faraway land, Violet was venturing off into unknown territory. While the future still remained a total mystery to her, she was still, none-the-less, open to experiencing new adventures. In the end, no matter what became of her, Violet just hoped that she'd come to discover her true self and what she really wanted out of life, along this journey.

And then, suddenly, she saw *him*. There standing tall and proud in the center of the grand foyer, he, like her, stood out from amongst the crowd. Alas, it was Maximus, aka, her knight in shining armor. The man, whom she had recently rescued. The man, whom she had miraculously set free from his previous sleeping curse, all by the mere touch of her hand. The man, who was identical to the same knight in shining armor found from her beloved fairy tale and dreams. The man, whom she considered to be the epitome of the ideal gentleman. In reality, Maximus was everything that Violet had always envisioned her knight in shining armor to be: charming, courageous and most importantly, deathly handsome.

For years, Violet always wondered as to how her knight in shining armor would look like underneath his helmet. Ever since she could remember, Violet curiously pondered as to whether or not he was a blonde or a brunette? Tall or short? Blue or green eyed? In fact, for every male face that she saw over the years, Violet couldn't help but daydream as to whether or not one of those faces was his.

Now, several years later, Violet finally got her answer. And today, on her birthday, of all days. Alas, Violet received her long-awaited birthday wish. For today, she finally bore witness to the true identity of her beloved knight in shining armor. And much to her delight, his reveal certainly did not disappoint. In fact, Maximus was far handsomer than how she had originally anticipated him to look like. Ten times folded. His beauty extended far beyond the reaches of her wild imagination. In truth, he was absolutely *perfect*.

Just like a dashing and charming prince plucked straight out of a fairy tale, Maximus was criminally handsome and deathly attractive. His shiny chestnut colored hair looked so soft and velvet-like. Meanwhile, as Violet glanced at him from across the room, she couldn't help but curiously wonder as to how it would actually feel like to freely run her hands right through his silky head of hair. The very thought of it excited her!

But apart from all of that, Maximus also possessed a lovely face. His features were soft and elegant, yet bold and refined. Meanwhile, his body was firm and muscular. Plus, he was tall, to be sure. But his eyes... oh… his eyes were so incredibly stunning and beautiful. In fact, for all of Violet's many years spent on Earth, she had never seen such a fine and rare pair of silvery set of eyes like his before. He might have been the crown prince, but to Violet, Maximus was equivalent to a Greek God in human form.

Meanwhile, as Violet smiled at his direction, she suddenly noticed a new crowd of women suddenly emerge from out-of-nowhere and quickly surrounded him. It was like watching a pack of hungry wolves, all gathered together in search of their next prey. Obviously, they, like she, were all admirers of the crown prince.

But to be fair, it made perfect sense, Violet thought to herself. After all, Maximus was *the* crown prince. Furthermore, he was attractive, handsome and single, too. Plus, he was the heir to the throne. The future king-in-waiting. Therefore, it was only natural for him to draw plenty of attention. It was to be expected, after all.

However, with that being said, while it was normal for the single ladies of the court to practically throw themselves at his direction, Violet wasn't expecting for Maximus to actually *enjoy* and *participate* in their advances, in return. No, she certainly did not!

Standing perfectly still, Violet squinted her eyes and watched on in frustration. To her complete disgust, she witnessed as Maximus beamingly smiled and flirted with at least a half a dozen or so debutantes. A flock of determined young ladies, each hovering at both sides of his arms.

In particular, on his left side, there was one young and attractive blonde, who was practically pressed up against his body. With her bare breasts exposed in a scandalously low plunging neckline, she shamelessly rubbed her cleavage against his chest. And if that wasn't enough, afterwards, she placed a wet kiss alongside his left cheek!

Meanwhile, on his right side, was another young female. A brunette, this time. Not only was this fair maiden dangling from off the side of his right arm, but she was also leaning against him and actually licking his ear, too! But if that wasn't enough to shock Violet, then it was the fact that the maiden also had the audacity to swing herself around, push him down onto a nearby open chair and then, she leaped straight onto his lap. And at that point, the brunette moved to kiss him, right smack on his bare lips!

Horrified by such a repulsive and devastating sight, Violet tried to look away. But unfortunately, for her, Violet's foolish curiosity got the best of her. As much as she didn't want to spy on him; in the end, she couldn't help herself. Alas, Violet just had to know the truth!

And so, Violet returned her gaze back over to Maximus' direction. To her great disappointment, she saw him engage in another kiss with the maiden. Or, perhaps, it was still the same kiss; either way, she didn't care to know. But for the longest time, that kiss of theirs lingered on. It was a long, passionate and oh so incredibly revolting sight!

Instead of politely declining her advances, Maximus actually seemed to *welcome it*. From what Violet could tell already, Maximus appeared to relish in this tasteless display of public affection as another form of pleasure and entertainment. But if this brunette's kiss wasn't enough to sustain him, then there were several more ladies lined up to replace her. Shockingly enough, it appeared that there was an actual *line* of women, just waiting for their turn to kiss the crown prince afterwards…

Dear God, how could this be! The man, whom Violet had foolishly placed on a high pedestal, was nothing more than a heartless and spineless rake! This person wasn't the same gentle, faithful and caring knight in shining armor that she had previously envisioned! He wasn't at all charming, polite or gentlemanly like! No, in fact, he was the exact *opposite* of it!

Alas, he was a scoundrel… a player… a wicked prince without a respectful conscience nor did he hold an appreciation to a lady's self-worth! No, he was clearly, a *heartbreaker*! Sadly, her so-called knight in shining armor was nothing more than a wretched and spineless womanizer!

A womanizer, who at this precise moment, could care less about Violet or her feelings. Instead, Maximus was clearly more interested on having a one-night stand with a random debutante, rather than investing his precious time with her. Meaningful time dedicated on getting to properly know her. To court her, just like any true gentleman would have done!

Angrily, Violet huffed in rage. In defiance, she frowned and then, she proceeded to fold her arms tightly against her chest. Needless to say, she was gravely *disappointed and crushed* by his flamboyant behavior. How stupidly foolish she was to blindly presume that just because he was a knight *and* a prince, that somehow, it automatically made him a saint! For clearly, he wasn't! No, he was the very devil, himself!

As far as Violet was concerned, her admiration and affections for him were officially *over*. After all, a man who was willing to kiss just about every other walking female in the room that practically threw themselves at him, wasn't worth her attention. No, that sort of man wasn't worthy of ever being considered as a possible suitor for her— regardless, if that man was a prince or a knight. Alas, he was most certainly, *not her* knight in shining armor! No, not at all!

Feeling almost ashamed and embarrassed for having foolishly mistaken Maximus for someone else whom he clearly wasn't, Violet suddenly felt compelled to leave. To simply turn around and return back into the comfort and safety of her bedchamber. To forget about everything that had recently happened. To undo what she had recently witnessed with own pair of eyes.

Furthermore, given that no one else at this party even knew her name, Violet doubted that anyone else would have missed her presence had she left. At least by fleeing this scene, then she could cry her heart out within the privacy of her own bedchamber. To avoid having to see Maximus flirt and kiss with more ladies, while she silently sat and watched away. Honestly, it felt like an invisible dagger had been plunged deep into her already shattered heart.

Unfortunately, as much as Violet wanted not to care; in the end, she still *did*. Sadly, regardless of his rakish behavior, she still *liked* him. She couldn't help it. Her mind might have told herself not to care, but her own foolish heart betrayed her!

Determined to get away from it all, Violet quickly spun around. However, by doing so, she accidentally bumped into another guest. Another man. Looking up, Violet noticed that he was a young man. Perhaps, even the same age as her.

With wavy blonde hair, crystal blue eyes and a sweet and youthful face, he was dressed in a cream-colored tunic, along with burgundy trousers. Meanwhile, his long hair was swept away from his face and pulled back into a tightened and sleek ponytail. Feeling almost shy and embarrassed for having collided with Violet, the young man kindly sought to apologize to her.

"I'm so sorry about that, my lady," he spoke, nervously. "My sincerest apologies for running into you like that. It was most unbecoming of me."

"That's quite alright," she reassured him. "It's partially my fault, too. I should have been more careful."

Sensing his friendly demeanor, Violet decided to take this opportunity to introduce herself. At least, this way, she'd make one new friend.

"My name's Violet, by the way," she informed him.

"Yes, I know," he replied, much to her surprise.

"You do?" Violet asked, with a raised brow.

"It's the red hair," he smiled on.

"Oh, I see," she gushed.

Once again, Violet was reminded that she was the only foreigner and redhead for miles on end.

"It's good to finally meet you at long last, Lady Violet. My name's Garreth. Sir Garreth Blackstone," he proudly announced.

And then, much to her astonishment, Garreth kindly offered her his hand, as a sincere and gentleman-like gesture.

"Lady Violet, if you might grant me this rare opportunity, then I'd like to escort you into the banquet hall," he inquired. "Of course, that's if you don't have any objections to my request, nor have any other prior commitments?"

Even though she had only just met him, Violet liked Garreth already. He was kind, thoughtful and considerate. He might not have been as handsome as Maximus, but he certainly made up for it by his good manners.

Besides, Garreth was the first person who welcomed her at this damn party. She might as well take advantage of his unexpected offer and accept his open invitation. Plus, any new friend was well worth acquiring in this new foreign land. After all, it was far better to have plenty of friends and allies, instead of more enemies.

"Thank you, Garreth, for your offer. I gladly accept," Violet replied, with a beaming smile.

Afterwards, she linked her arm around his and together, they took their first steps forward into the crowd.

Along the way, Garreth gently leaned into Violet's ear and casually gave her a brief overview to some of the night's attendees. Naturally, there were of course, the crown prince's knights, who were faithful members to the royal army. Along with these men, there were also their respective wives, daughters, mothers and sisters in attendance.

But apart from these folks, there were also several key palace advisors, along with their families also present. And if these guests weren't either knights or palace advisers and their clans, then there were also former palace courtiers and ordinary everyday citizens here as well. All of them, regardless of their titles or classes, resided at Caste Hope. Together united. A safe haven offered to all of the many citizens of this kingdom.

According to Garreth, after Vera unleashed her bloody rebellion, she slaughtered anyone who refused to bow down and accept her status as their rightful new queen. And all of these people standing right here tonight, each and every single one of them refused to bend the knee. All of them rebelled against her. All of them remained loyal to the true bearer of the crown. All of them were Maximus' followers. All of them risked their lives, as well as the safety of their own families for the sake of the crown prince. To remain steadfast by his side through these darkened, unpredictable and scary times.

Although Violet might have had her own personal opinions about the rakish prince, she couldn't help but admire his remarkable ability to unite a mass group of people under the banner of freedom. To inspire a large sea of people, such as this huge crowd to stand behind him. To be fair, this fact alone concerning the crown prince's charm and charisma, deserved some ounce of recognition and respect on her part as well.

A few minutes later, they arrived to the banquet hall. Once they passed through the threshold, Garreth proceeded to escort Violet to the far side of the room, towards the end of the table. Much to Violet's dismay, there was only one table. A single long wooden bench designed to host several hundreds of guests on both sides.

Assuming that the head of the table was reserved especially for Maximus, Violet was relieved when Garreth helped her to sit down at the very end. Several feet away from the crown prince. At least this way, she'd have the freedom to avoid Maximus, all thanks to this healthy and most welcomed distance.

After taking their seats on the bench, Garreth poured them some wine and then offered her some bread. Graciously, she accepted.

Glancing across the room, Violet observed that the banquet hall was just like every other room in the castle. Ancient, cobble stone and spacious. Plus, decorated with minimal furniture, apart from the basics.

However, minimal was not the appropriate word to describe the entertainment; because in the center of the hall, was a band of merry musicians. Currently, they were playing a cheerful and jolly melody, using various instruments including the harp, flute, drum and bagpipe.

And beside the band, was a court jester. He was dressed in a red, white and black polka dot uniform, along with a black and red double pointed cap with silver bells attached to its ends. The jester was currently performing a juggling number using three red balls, as a form of their nightly entertainment.

Meanwhile, there must have been about a hundred or so guests congregating at the entrance, all making their ways into the party. Judging by the appearance of the space, this banquet hall must have maintained the capacity to host at least a few hundred or so people together in one group setting.

"Is every night like this? Or is tonight's crowd solely due to the prince's arrival?" asked Violet.

"Every night is pretty much like this," Garreth admitted.  "But in honor of the prince *and* yourself, extra wine has been brewed."

"So, do people really know who I am?"

"Most, but not all," Garreth replied, in earnest. "At least, all of the key and important figures know about you. But the rest, not so much. However, to be truthfully honest, most folks have been left in the dark about a whole lot of things. For their sakes, ignorance is bliss. The less they know, the better they can sleep at night."

"I can't blame them. I do understand," Violet sympathized.

After all the loss and bloodshed that they recently experienced as a community, it was a true miracle that they still continued to show up each night for dinner, while putting on a brave smile.

"Milady, don't look so gloomy," Garreth tried his best to cheer her saddened mood. "We're all alive and well. That's all that matters, right now. Here, let me fix you a plate."

Before Violet knew it, Garreth handed her a full dinner plate. At first glance, it appeared to be some sort of a roasted meat, accompanied by a handful of boiled potatoes and carrots.

"What's this?" Violet asked him, as she poked at the food found around on her plate, while using her wooden spoon to do so.

"It's roasted rabbit with vegetables. It's one of my favorites."

Suddenly, Violet lost what little appetite she had left. After chasing that innocent white bunny back in the enchanted forest earlier this afternoon, she no longer had the heart to eat another furry friend.

"Do you mind if I give you my rabbit to eat, instead?" she asked. "Personally, I rather just stick to eating my vegetables."

Without saying another word, Garreth swiftly swooped in and stole the meat right off from Violet's plate. Within a handful of bites, he devoured the entire animal with his hungry mouth. For a young man, he most certainly had a huge appetite!

Meanwhile, as Garreth was busy eating his supper, Violet took a bite of her potatoes and decided to scan the room once more. Just like Garreth, everyone else at the banquet appeared to be famish. Unlike Violet, every guest was practically gobbling up their dinners like wild birds.

However, there was, at least, one other exception to this rule. Unfortunately, it seemed that the crown prince wasn't too keen on consuming his nutritious meal. Instead, he was busy locking lips with *yet* another lady of the court! This time, a new pretty blonde maiden!

"He really can't control himself," Violet angrily uttered underneath her breath.

However, her comment didn't go unnoticed. Much to her annoyance, Violet's spoken words caught the attention of her neighbor, Garreth.

"Lady Violet, don't think too much about it. It will only aggravate you even more," he told her. "Prince Maximus is known to be this… er… *special way.*"

"Special way?" she repeated.

Sadly, deep down inside, Violet already knew the answer.

"Unfortunately, it's his reputation," Garreth replied. "Before all of this, he was known as the rebel and rogue prince. While his elder brother might have been Leopold, the Great; up until recently, our new crown prince over here, used to be known as Maximus, the Brute. Although, as of lately, we don't call him by that title anymore."

"Maximus, the Brute? What a terrible nickname! Why in God's name would people call him by that?"

However, as soon as Violet asked this very question, she instantly came to regret it. For at that precise moment, it immediately became abundant clear as to *why* Maximus was called by that ridiculous title. Just witnessing with her own two eyes on how much he flirted *and* kissed random women at this party, it only became that much clearer.

How stupid Violet was to ever think that Maximus was a chivalrous and gentleman-like knight! Truly, he was a snake at best!

"Judging by your expression, I take it that you've probably admired or liked him at some point before," added Garreth, with a sigh. "But please don't be ashamed. Honestly, I don't judge you. Had I been born a lady like you, then perhaps, I, too, might have also felt the same wild emotions as you do, right now."

"I'll admit, when I first met him, I didn't expect him to turn out this way," Violet revealed, with a heavy heart.

"Really?" asked a surprised Garreth. "What, pray tell, did you expect of him, then?"

"To be a knight in shining armor," she sighed.

"A knight in shining armor? What does that mean, exactly?" asked Garreth, in confusion.

"It just means someone who's faithful, romantic and a true gentleman. That's all."

"Ah, now, I understand why you look so gravely disappointed," Garreth acknowledged. "Because, I hate to be the one to break this to you milady, but

Maximus is definitely *not* any of those sorts of things."

"Sadly, yes, I can see that now. Most *clearly*," Violet reflected with great disappointment.

"He may be our future king, but Maximus is also a notorious scoundrel."

Suddenly, Garreth spoke the heart-wrenching words that would eventually, come to haunt Violet's mind for the remainder of her evening.

*"He breaks more hearts than he sheds tears. Don't be fooled by his uniform nor his crown."*

While her heart might have felt otherwise, her mind told her to forget about him. Even though they were forced to remain as allies, under no circumstances was Violet ever going to allow herself to fall for such a man! Not now, not ever!

But as Violet stared out towards his direction, for a split second, she accidentally caught sight of his gaze from afar. After freeing himself from the clutches of his latest admirer, Violet could swear that in a room filled with a hundred other faces, it was her face and her face alone, that she saw reflected within his silverly pair of eyes.

And for that brief second, Violet felt as if she had somehow, miraculously captured the sole attention of the future king.

# CHAPTER 7

As Maximus watched Violet from afar, she suddenly grew anxious. Even though she was absolutely determined to avoid his unwanted attention; alas, his unwelcomed stares became too difficult to ignore. For if Violet had any prior doubts about him actually gazing at her, then Garreth only further confirmed this obvious truth.

"It appears that our prince has taken a fancy to you," Garreth acknowledged with a beaming smile, as he took another bite of his meat and then, gulped down the rest of his wine.

"Nonsense," Violet huffed in annoyance, trying her best to deny his unfavorable attention.

In an effort to avoid making any direct eye contact with the crown prince, Violet quickly turned her back away. Rather than foolishly flirting with him from afar like the rest of the young ladies of the court, Violet made the bold decision to shift both her body and attention over to Garreth.

"Enjoying your meal?" she asked him, hoping to change the subject.

"I was—"

But before Garreth had the opportunity to finish his sentence, the lights suddenly dimmed low and the band began to play another tune. But this time around, the melody was fast, upbeat and a bit more dramatic.

With the music playing in the background, several guests quickly flocked over to the dance floor. Men, women and children alike, all took center stage. As Violet watched them gather in pairs, she realized that tonight's festivities weren't just limited to food, music or entertainment performed by a court fool. No, dancing was equally incorporated into the itinerary as well.

"I thought we were invited here only for the meal," she whispered over to Garreth.

"Food *and* dance. That's how we celebrate in our land," he answered her back, as he took another bite of his meal.

"I see," replied Violet, wryly.

Although Violet half expected for there to be some form of dancing; however, she never expected it to happen so early in the evening— at least, not until dessert was served.

Meanwhile, as Violet watched the happy dancers take to the stage, she silently observed their dancing techniques. While Violet was never an enthusiast for the art of dancing, just like her mother before her; she was, however, familiar with it.

As the daughter of a respected earl, her father paid for Violet's weekly dance lessons from the moment she took her first walking steps. From the Viennese Waltz to the Argentinian Tango, to the Spanish Salsa to the Foxtrot, Violet was well versed in a variety of dances. Although she much preferred to sit and watch other dancers glide across the ballroom from afar; however, when presented with the opportunity to take to the floor, Violet could indeed dance well and gracefully, too.

However, this style of live dancing happening right now, was unfamiliar and entirely brand-new to her. Foreign steps that most certainly weren't the waltz or the tango... or even the foxtrot. In truth, Violet didn't recognize any of these dance steps at all. In fact, Violet had never seen these moves performed before out in public. Perhaps, this performance was considered as a local folk dance?

With a fast-paced and upbeat melody playing out loud, Violet keenly watched on as the happy couples danced away in the center of the room. As the men assumed their leads, their female partners followed in suit. Raising their arms high and above their chests, the men guided their respective ladies, as their feet quickly glided across the dance floor.

Although uncustomed to this local dance, Violet was a quick learner. Therefore, if given a chance to dance here tonight, then she predicted that she could simply follow her leading male partner on stage with great ease. However, if given a choice, then Violet preferred to remain seated with her feet safely tucked underneath the dinner table.

However, at the same time, she also believed that dancing might be her only means to an escape. For at this precise moment, Violet noticed from the corner of her eye, that Maximus had recently arisen up from his seat and was currently heading over towards her direction! Unfortunately, for her, if Violet continued to remain seated as is, then she was going to be forced to cross paths with Maximus much sooner than what she had initially hoped for!

Desperately wanting to avoid another close encounter with the rakish crown prince, Violet decided to quickly flee the scene.

"Garreth, do you mind if we take a turn about the room?" she asked him.

Amused by her sudden request, Garreth graciously accepted her offer. As much as Violet tried her best to conceal her true reasons for claiming a dance with her neighbor, Garreth was quick to acknowledge that his lady companion most likely, secretly desired to avoid the attention of a certain prince.

"Very well, let's dance," he humored her, as he quickly rose-up from his chair and took a hold of her hand.

And just like that, they were off to the dance floor. Thus, leaving Maximus, the crown prince, standing right behind them, all alone and most importantly, *ignored.*

Eventually, once they reached the stage, Garreth leaned into Violet's ear and whispered, "Aren't you afraid that he'll return back again to reclaim your hand afterwards? In my opinion, he seems most eager."

Sure enough, Garreth glanced across the hall and saw Maximus. He was standing there, looking tall and proud as ever. Resembling a confident peacock or a determined alpha wolf, rather than an innocent and lovelorn youth.

"I do believe he's set on conquering you," Garreth playfully smiled on.

"I'm not one to be conquered," Violet huffed in annoyance. "Besides, if I must dance with you all night long just to avoid him, then so be it!"

"Now, *that* would certainly be entertaining," Garreth laughed on.

Although Garreth wasn't the sort of person who ever dared to cause anger or distress for the crown prince; however, when presented with the rare opportunity to admire the irritated expression currently resting upon the young prince's face for a refreshing change, it truly was *priceless*.

Not wanting to think a single thought more concerning Maximus, Violet decided to fully immerse herself in her current dance with Garreth. Allowing him to take total control of the situation, Violet followed his lead and spun away at his command. Step by step, the couple danced away against the backdrop of a candlelit room.

Currently, the stage was remarkably dark and overwhelmingly crowded. Apart from the main table and enclosed stone walls, Violet really couldn't see anything else with regards to her surroundings. If Garreth hadn't escorted her onto the stage, then she'd have sworn that she was now dancing with someone else. A brand-new partner. A partner with a peculiar set of silverly eyes. Eyes that shimmered and sparkled, just like the moonlight. Eyes that were currently, solely focused on her and staring directly into her own emerald green eyes.

Suddenly, her dance partner gave her another spin around and then, he brought her body closer to his chest. As they stood face-to-face, Violet finally realized that somehow in-between her turns around the dance floor, Garreth had abandoned her and left her in the care of another. Within the blink of an eye, he secretly managed to replaced himself altogether with an entirely new partner. A man, who was none other than Maximus, himself!

"Maximus! What are you doing here? Where's Garreth?" she hissed at him, sounding half surprised and the other half in utter annoyance.

"Well, a hello to you too, Violet," Maximus playfully replied, with the most dashing of smiles. "Why, aren't you happy to see me? Pray tell, why have you been avoiding me all evening?"

Truly, he really was the very wretched devil, himself!

"I avoid you?" Violet huffed in anger. "Why would I ever give you that sort of satisfaction? I was merely trying to enjoy my dance with Garreth. Or at least, I *was* enjoying my dance with him, up until *you* came along."

"At the last minute, Garreth decided to sit this dance out," Maximus bluntly admitted.

"To sit down in the middle of a dance? Or did you *order* him to do so, my dear prince?" she asked in a sarcastic and mocking manner.

"Just because I'm the crown prince, that doesn't mean that I dictate as to whether or not a person should dance or not. He, like everyone else in this kingdom, are free to choose as they will," he spoke, with a devious smirk gleaming across his handsome face. "And in your case, Garreth asked me to take his place."

Clearly, that response was a blatant *lie*. And Violet knew it, too. But then, Maximus told her something that made her heart beat at an unexpected and accelerated rate.

"Just as Garreth chose to sit this dance midway, *I* choose not to leave you standing here, all alone. Out of my own good heart, I made the effort to be by your side," Maximus made sure to point this fact out.

"You didn't want me to be alone?" Violet asked, in surprise. "But why is that? Why did you take it upon yourself to appoint yours truly as my new dance partner? Why personally seek me out, when you're already busy chasing the other young ladies of this court?"

"I wasn't chasing them, *they* were chasing me," he corrected her.

"Excuse me, but was it or was it not your lips locked in with theirs?" she challenged him. "From what I saw, I highly doubt that any one of them dared to hold your lips hostage for a ransom. Honestly, I don't think it took so much effort for them to convince you to gift them all with such heartfelt and passionate kisses!"

Suddenly, he laughed. Which in return, made Violet flare red with anger. Really, this wicked prince found *yet* another way to strike at her nerves! And she barely even knew the man!

"You managed to see all of that? In the course of a single evening?" he innocently asked her.

"Just because we kissed, that doesn't mean that I care for them," he explained. "A kiss is merely a kiss. Just like another innocent peck on the cheek. Except, this time around, it was on my mouth. What's the big deal?"

"You know," she began, with her voice raised high, "Where I come from, a kiss means *something*. People don't just randomly kiss others, unless they care about that person. It's what *honorable* knights do. They only kiss women, whom they *love*."

"Are you saying that in your eyes, I'm *not* an honorable knight?" Maximus asked her point blank. After such a bold, heartfelt and profound statement, he was now greatly intrigued.

"Absolutely. You're *far* from it," she proudly proclaimed.

"In that case, by your definition," he began, "If I'm not honorable, then should I just go ahead and kiss you, too? Be entirely *dishonorable*?"

"What???" she choked.

"Hmm, maybe, if I did that, then you might change your so obvious poor opinion of me," he teased her.

"Perhaps, we could even clear the air? You never know, Violet, you may actually enjoy a kiss from me. It might do us both some good. Release this growing tension brewing between us, right now," he suggested, hoping that she'd give into his curious demands.

"Maximus... or Prince Maximus... or whichever title you prefer—"

"Maximus will be fine," he interrupted her. "Others may call me by any other name, but you can call me Maximus."

"Fine," she uttered underneath her breath in annoyance.

"Maximus, you might be able to charm the other young ladies here, but you certainly can't fool me," Violet asserted. "Personally, I know how honorable gentlemen and knights are *supposed* to behave like. And you, Maximus, are far from it!"

Her words were too enticing for him. For the first time in his life, Maximus finally met a woman, whom he considered to be a true challenge. Unlike all the rest before her, Violet stood out and painstakingly so, too. Apart from everyone else in his acquaintance, she was the first and only person who truly didn't care about him nor his title.

Apparently, him being the heir to the throne and the future King of the West, meant absolutely nothing to her. His title, wealth, fame and kingdom, weren't enough to captivate her. Judging by her cold attitude towards him, Violet hardly seemed interested in him at all. In fact, she actually appeared appalled by him. Annoyed. Even disguised.

And yet, that didn't stop *his* curiosity about her. In contrast to Violet's poor opinion about him, Maximus surprisingly found himself *greatly* intrigued *by her*. Perhaps, even more than he initially thought possible.

Yes, Violet was the savior. She was the very same woman, whom he previously traveled multiple realms to find. Relentlessly, waiting two hundred years for her arrival. And even though it had only been but two days in his world; but regardless, he still waited for her. Patiently. Albeit, courtesy of a sleeping spell.

Somehow, this truth alone should have counted for something in the eyes of her affection. After all, what act could be more daring, heroic and romantic, than a man willing to travel hundreds of years into the distant past? All for the sake of a single woman?

Alas, Maximus was truly at a loss for words. Even though he very well knew that he wasn't at all a saint, he still maintained the small glimmer of hope that she, at the very least, would take a little liking to him. Especially, after all of the sacrifices that he made for her. Not to mention, his generosity by hosting a banquet in their joint honors and by bestowing her with one of the best bedchambers in the entire castle.

But now, standing here and gazing at her, Maximus realized just how little she cared for him. How much she *disliked* him. But why was that? Heck, everyone else in the kingdom liked him. Respected him. Admired him. So, why couldn't she?

Maximus might not have been as honorable as his late brother, Leopold, but he was still a prince. Certainly, that counted for something, right? Granted, he lived most of his wild youth as a rebellious prince in the past, but his adventurous spirit always captured the attentions of young ladies everywhere. Regardless, of their statuses. But apparently, his charms weren't welcomed by all. In the end, there seemed to be at least one debutante immune to his dashing good looks and charisma: *Violet.*

Prior to today, Violet knew absolutely nothing about him or his world. In fact, had it not been for her, then he'd probably still be lying out there in the enchanted forest. Trapped underneath that pesky nest of prickly thorns, blooming red roses and overgrown vines of ivy, had she failed to break his sleeping curse and rescue him from that unfortunate fate.

But instead of welcoming him with open arms, Violet was desperately trying to avoid him. While Maximus was far from being an angel, he still hoped that they could at least be friends and not enemies. After all, they were supposed to be allies. Standing together, unified as a team. But if they couldn't even be civil or cordial with one another on the dance floor, then how could they ever defeat Vera, together?

"Relax, Violet," he whispered softly into her ear. "I'm your friend, not your enemy. Remember?"

"We might be allies, but I can't yet call you, my friend. I mean, I don't even know you," she hissed back at him.

To be fair, he couldn't entirely blame her. She really didn't know him. If he had been a woman, then perhaps, he too would have been annoyed by his rakish behavior. Displeased by watching him flirt with the other young ladies of the court. Ladies who weren't *her.*

In reflection, he probably should have behaved better tonight. Especially, with Violet around. However, at the same time, Maximus couldn't help it. It was always his nature to flirt. It simply came natural to him. Even if he didn't mean to do it. After all, he was single *and* a prince. Why, he'd flirt with anyone, even with his eyes closed. It's what he *always* did. That's why he never thought to question it before. At least, not until *now*.

Unlike before, this time around, he actually felt a brand-new emotion lingering within his chest: *regret*. He *almost* came to *regret* his flirtatious behavior and advances tonight with the young ladies of the court. A sense of *guilt* on his part.

But why was that? Why did Maximus suddenly care about Violet's feelings? About her personal thoughts concerning him? Since when did her poor opinion of him start to bother him? It's not like he wanted to impress her. He never wanted to impress her. Never cared to.

Previously, all that Maximus desired was to find Violet and then, to bring her safely back into his world to fulfill the prophecy and save his kingdom. That was all. Nothing more. Just as simple as that. And yet, her lack of affection towards him still bothered him. In fact, it bothered him *greatly*.

Perhaps, this shouldn't have been such a strange surprise to him. After all, today was already dedicated to endless surprises. After awakening from his two-hundred-year slumber, Maximus awoke to find Violet there, by his side and ready to rescue him. Even though he already knew her identity from long ago, he was still surprised when he finally locked eyes with her. Saw her for the woman that she really was in real life.

Even though he spent the last two centuries suspended in a deep sleep, he wasn't entirely in a blank comatose state, either. He did dream. While he seldom recalled the specific details surrounding most of his past dreams; however, whenever they pertained specifically to her, then he could always remember them. Recount them all, in such vivid and full details.

For the past two-hundred years, while mentally sequestered within his eternal dream-like state, Maximus subconsciously wondered about Violet. How she would be, well before she existed in the physical world, prior to her birth. Before her own parents had even met and married.

In his dreams, he often wondered if she'd be pretty or average looking. Kind or cruel. Happy or melancholy. Blonde or brunette. Tall or short. Blue-eyed or brown-eyed. And instead, she was *nothing* of the sort.

Everything that Maximus had ever previously considered her to be, was all wildly incorrect in every possible aspect.

In fact, she was the complete *opposite* in everything. But to be perfectly honest, the real Violet was *far better* than what he previously imagined. In the end, she was practically *perfect*.

For starters, Violet was far braver and stronger than what he originally expected her to be. Never before, did Maximus calculate that it would be *her* rescuing him and not the other way around. For her to be the *true hero* and most certainly, *not him*.

While he knew ahead of time that Violet was always predestined to awaken him from his sleeping curse by the mere touch of her hand; however, he never expected for her to courageously use his sword to free him from that nasty nest. No, he certainly didn't expect that twist of fate!

But apart from her relentless courage and bravery, Maximus took quick note on how trustworthy and honorable she truly was. Barely a single day had passed, and already she had agreed to help fight this ongoing war alongside with him. Granted, this was also her ticket back to home, too. After all, Vera's reign of terror not only threatened his world, but of hers as well. But still, Violet agreed to help him, and her promise did not go unappreciated by him, either.

While Maximus remained unfamiliar with her unique personality, he was still nevertheless, intrigued by her. For a young lady such as she, Violet certainly was fearless. Unlike everyone else in his inner circle, she wasn't afraid to share her opinion about him— albeit, a poor one. Regardless, Violet was outspoken. With her wild and fiery locks, her spirit was equivalent to fire itself.

Apart from everything else, Maximus never anticipated Violet being so incredibly beautiful. Breathtakingly so. With her porcelain-like face and perfect hourglass figure, Violet was a stunning and rare beauty to behold. How foolish he was to have imagined her being a blonde or a brunette! She was, in fact, the most exquisite redhead that he had ever laid eyes upon before!

Just like her bold personality, Violet also possessed the most unique shade of hair color, too. In truth, her red hair was more amber-like. In fact, it was almost as if a blazing fire was burning right above her. Honestly, it was absolutely magnificent.

But if that all wasn't enough to captivate him, then, it was ultimately, her eyes that did him in. It was there within her emerald green eyes, that Maximus found himself entirely bewitched. Even seated from afar in a room filled with a hundred other faces, her emerald green eyes miraculously stole his sole attention. And this unpredictable act alone, was certainly a true first!

Unfortunately, the lady at the dinner table vying for his attention was no match for her. In truth, no one else could ever be a match to Violet, the Savior. Everyone else dimmed in comparison. It's why Maximus made the initial effort to approach her side at the table tonight. He *wanted* to dance with her. That is, before Garreth stole his opportunity to ask for her hand. An act that was entirely unforgiveable!

But unbeknownst to Violet, Garreth was also one of his closest and dearest childhood friends. Garreth might have been several years younger than him, but that didn't stop them from playing with each other on the playground as children. It certainly didn't prevent them from fighting alongside in the military. Garreth and him were both friends and fellow warriors. And so, when Maximus made his move to steal Violet away, Garreth was only too happy to lend his dance partner over to the care of his dear old friend.

Of course, Violet wasn't aware about any of this. After all, she was ignorant about his life and of his past. However, he didn't want this to always remain the same case in the near future. Now, that he finally found her, Maximus wanted to use this extra time to personally get to know her better. One dancing step at a time.

Even if Violet greatly disliked him right now, then Maximus was more determined than ever to change that poor opinion. For the longer he stared at her, the more he desired to be by her side. In fact, she was even lovelier than the last time he saw her, as she silently stood there underneath the dimmed candlelight. Ethereal. Heavenly. Majestic.

Suddenly, Maximus felt an unexpected urge to kiss her, right there and then. Against his own better judgment. Even though he knew it was ungentlemanly-like to do so, he couldn't help but feel this way. For some reason, Violet brought out his inner beast. If Violet was the forbidden fruit, then he was ready to sell his wretched soul to taste her!

As the music began to slow down, Maximus gave Violet one last turnabout. As she spun right back towards him, he caught a glimpse of her sweet lips. Much to his delight, they were soft, pink, plump… and oh… so mouthwatering. Alas, her being so incredibly close to him was beyond tempting! It was both sinful and cruel! But either way, he needed to kiss her. For the sake of his own sanity, he just had to!

Even if she'd come to hate him later on, he still needed to do it. After dreaming about her for so long, Maximus wanted to finally give into his desires. To discover what it felt like to kiss her in real life.

And so, without a second guess, Maximus leaned in and kissed Violet straight on her bare lips.

Although their first kiss felt right to him, the same could not be equally said with regards to Violet. Much to his great disappointment, her reaction was not at all what he had hoped for. Rather than joyfully smiling back at him; she, instead, gasped and stared directly at him in pure shock. Shamefully, in disgust!

"Maximus, you're certainly *not* a gentleman," she coldly declared. "And I'm definitely *not* one to have my heart broken, either."

Within the blink of an eye, she was *gone*. Abandoning him right there and then, on the stage. Fleeing the scene, without so much as a farewell. While Maximus didn't fault Violet for leaving; however, he still couldn't help but feel sad and disappointed in the outcome.

Although he didn't regret his decision to kiss her, because if given a second chance, he'd make the same choice again in a heartbeat; however, her choice of words negatively struck him. What did she mean by *breaking her heart*? Why did she say that to him? Think that? Those words certainly stuck in his mind.

If Violet was fearful of him breaking her heart, then he'd just have to prove her otherwise. Because right now, at this very moment, all he could think about was *her*. How brave and courageous she was. How strong willed and determined her personality was. How incredibly green and lovely her eyes were. How now, he wanted nothing more than to see his own reflection mirrored within those enchanting pair of emerald green eyes…

# CHAPTER 8

"A raving lunatic! A scandalous rake! A complete and total madman!" Violet shouted to herself, as she angrily stomped up the staircase, making her way back to her *greatly missed* bedchamber.

Thankfully, no one else was around to listen to her ungodly swears. Or, best yet, witness her very *un*-lady-like departure. Especially, after escaping from the clutches of the most insufferable, rudest and wicked man, while still miraculously surviving in one solid piece!

"Imagine, the nerve of that hateful and spiteful man! That wretched rakish prince!" Violet huffed in rage, as she clenched her hands into a perfect pair of fists that dangled against the sides of her now wrinkled dress.

"How could he kiss me like that? Publicly humiliate me, in front of all those people? Like I was one of those silly debutantes? Another pathetic and foolish lady of the court! Besides, that so-called-kiss of his wasn't even *that good!*"

But unfortunately, that statement wasn't entirely true. In all honesty, Violet did secretly enjoy their kiss... *shamefully*. Much to her own disappointment, she actually *liked it*. Which made it all the more devastating! And to top it all off, it was also her very first kiss, too!

Either way, he'd never know the truth. She'd never reveal it to him. Even if kidnapped or cornered against a brick wall, and her very own livelihood depended upon her truthful confession regarding her feelings surrounding their latest kiss, then she'd *still never* admit the whole truth! That she *didn't* mind it all too much. No, not in a million years! After all, her own dignity and pride were at stake!

Eventually, by the time Violet finally arrived upstairs and retired off into her bedchamber, she was determined to forget all about Maximus. Along with everything else that recently took place downstairs tonight. But unfortunately, once Violet lied herself down to bed and closed her eyes shut, that night, all she dreamt about was *him...*

* * *

The next morning, Violet decided that the best way to erase her unwanted memories surrounding the events from last night— including that infamous *kiss* with a certain crown prince— was to redirect her focus back onto her next challenge-at-hand: *training*. After all, being the promised savior wasn't going to be an easy task. Like everything else in life, it required practice.

If Violet was destined to save this kingdom from the paths of destruction and ruin, then she needed to begin her job as their savior by first learning a few new tricks of the trade. Valuable skills to squash her powerful enemies. And so, because of these reasons, Violet was determined to stay focused, agile and adapt to her new surroundings. And the first stop towards defeating Vera and her dark army was to visit Ruby's laboratory in time for today's grand lesson: *magic*.

"Good morning, Ruby, I'm here," Violet happily announced, as she entered into the laboratory.

"Just in time," Ruby acknowledged Violet's arrival.

"Just-so-you-know, I'm never late to anything," Violet proudly proclaimed. "Whatever I do, I can assure you that I always do it with my full heart and dedication."

"And I'm very relieved to hear that, too," Ruby noted.

"So, what are we planning on doing here, today?" asked Violet, most curiously. "Are we going to practice turning a slimy green toad into a charming prince? Or perhaps, alter the color of my hair? Or, maybe, I can transform my enemies into spiders? Certainly, that'd make everything so much easier and smoother for us. Just one step using the bottom of my shoe and then, the job will be done. Instantly, the war would be over in no time."

Ever since breakfast, Violet was anxious about her first lesson. She wondered how magic worked in-action and the sorts of spells that Ruby intended to teach her. In truth, Violet never previously thought about learning the art of magic before. But now, given this new opportunity, Violet gladly welcomed it. After all, studying topics that were outside of her comfort zone, excited her tremendously.

"Not so fast, my dear Violet," Ruby informed her with a sly grin, showcased across her old and wrinkled face. "Since today is your first day on the job, we're going to start with the basics."

"The basics?" she echoed.

"Yes, the basics," Ruby confirmed.

"Now, Violet," she continued on, "Pick up my wooden spoon over there, and start by stirring this boiling hot cauldron. You mix and stir, while I'll pour in the ingredients."

Disappointment was a complete understatement, as to how Violet felt right now. Here she was, foolishly believing that today was going to be her first enchanted lesson on the art of magic, when instead, she was expected to stir a regular old pot of boiling hot water. Another typical *cooking lesson*. And in truth, Violet never cared to cook. Was this really all the excitement reserved just for today?

"Violet, don't act too displeased," Ruby remarked, as she gathered a few bottles from off her shelves.

"First of all," she explained, "If you're going to start dabbling in magic, then you've got to understand which sorts of ingredients go best together. The elements of nature. Learning the working and inner knowledge of what complements or discourages an active ingredient is key. Master this aspect, then the rest will come naturally to you. Magic, at best, is instinct."

And as Violet proceeded to stir the boiling hot cauldron, Ruby poured in several colorful liquids into the pot from out of a few potion bottles.

"A hint of lavender for calming one's nerves," Ruby spoke, as she threw in a few dried petals.

"Sage for clarity of the mind," she continued on, "Chamomile to help diffuse an angry spirit. Rose petals for love."

After sprinkling in these ingredients into the boiling hot water, Ruby beamingly smiled at Violet and said, "And last, but certainly not in the least, a hint of violet to cure a broken heart."

"Wait, violets can cure a broken heart?" asked Violet, in astonishment. "I've never heard about that before."

While Violet knew that her name was associated with a great many things, hearing that her namesake flower also possessed the ability to cure even a broken heart was a true first.

"Oh, you'd be surprised to learn as to just how powerful violets really are."

Meanwhile, Violet curiously wondered what it was that they were brewing. Prior to this lesson, Violet always presumed that magic meant smoke or fire. Instant transformation. Snap your fingers and boom, there it was… *magic*. But apparently, she was mistaken. Magic wasn't instantaneous. In the end, it required effort. Just like everything else in life.

Overall, today's lesson felt more like a science experiment than anything deemed magical. Just silently standing still and mixing a boiling hot black cauldron, felt like Violet was back at school. Once again, studying at the science laboratory of her old university. Not to mention, Ruby also felt more like a wise and experienced professor, than that of an old witch.

"You know Ruby," Violet began, "If this assignment is considered to be a form of magic, then it's almost like a science. Another method of applied medicine, used to cure various ailments. I, myself, have always been a fan of science. It's why I previously considered taking up medicine as a possible future profession."

"Oh, is that so?" asked Ruby, glowingly. "Perhaps, you'll make a perfect candidate to serve as my next apprentice, after all."

Judging by Ruby's joyful expression, she was delighted by Violet's enthusiasm. Apparently, today's lesson was turning out to be a real success, after all.

Suddenly, an unexpected knock came at the door. Within the blink of an eye, a knight was standing right before them. Except this time, he wasn't wearing a helmet. Furthermore, the expression reflected upon his face looked serious. It was almost as if this knight had some urgent news to deliver to them.

"Pardon the intrusion," he apologized in advance. "But Lady Violet is needed in the garden."

"Oh, I see," replied Ruby, with great disappointment.

As surprised and confused as Violet was about this unexpected request, Ruby didn't at all seem taken aback by this sudden summons.

Turning her attention over to Violet, she said, "My dearest Violet, I'm afraid that we'll just have to continue with our lessons at another time."

"Must I really go?" she asked. "Can't I just stay here a little longer with you?"

"I'm afraid not," Ruby answered, in earnest. "But here, please take this with you."

And then, Ruby handed over to Violet an oversized, thick and dusty emerald book. Its binding was worn and molded, and its pages were slightly torn due to old age. Whatever this mysterious book was, it appeared to be ancient and foreign.

"Take this and be sure to study it religiously," she told her. "As you might have already guessed, this is a spell book. It has everything that you'll need to learn, while you're here with us. Keep it with you, at all times."

Carefully, Violet took possession of the strange and mystical book. Afterwards, she promised Ruby that she'd do just that. Somewhere, hidden within the pages of this mysterious spell book, was the answer to their problems. A solution on how to defeat the evil queen. Had circumstances been different, then Violet would have much rather have stayed behind to study this book alongside Ruby, instead of departing solo over to the garden.

Suddenly, Violet got the courage to ask the knight directly about her early departure. Just why was she needed out in the garden, right now? What was the real reason behind this unexpected request? Was her attendance really this important? Urgent? Didn't the palace courtiers know that she was already busy training with Ruby at this hour?

"I'm sorry, sir," Violet addressed the knight, "But is there a reason as to why I'm being summoned, right now? Can't my attendance at the garden wait, until at least after my lessons have concluded?"

"Of course, my lady," replied the knight, most graciously. "You've been summoned by our crown prince. He specifically requests for your immediate presence at the garden. At once."

Maximus! Damn him to hell! So, *he* was the one responsible for this intrusion! He was to blame for her lessons being cut so damn short!

But this didn't make any sense, at all. In fact, Maximus was the very one, who was solely responsible for arranging today's training session with Ruby. He, alone, was in charge of her overall schedule, along with her general care in this land. *His kingdom.* Therefore, why the sudden change of heart?

And then, to her horror, she recalled their last kiss from the night before. The very thought of seeing him again so soon afterwards, brought a chill down her spine. Sadly, Maximus was the *last* person in the entire world, whom she wanted to see. Prince or no prince, Violet simply wasn't interested to face the man, who so rudely kissed her, like she was another one of his many mistresses that he could so easily conquer. No, she certainly wasn't that sort of female!

"Please kindly inform the crown prince that I have no intention of leaving my lessons so early today," Violet boldly declared, in defiance. "I have no interest on entertaining *anyone* outside in the garden. Especially, at this hour."

"Violet, I'm not so sure that's a wise decision," Ruby warned her. "Please, reconsider."

However, the knight appeared completely unaffected by Violet's harsh choice of words. Like the true professional that he was, his facial expression remained unchanged: stern and determined. Judging by his stiff reaction, his mission was clear: one way or another, the knight was here to carry out the crown prince's order. To the death.

"The crown prince expected you to say as much," he revealed.

"He what???!!!" exclaimed both ladies simultaneously.

"Yes, he did," the knight confirmed. "Which is why, the crown prince has also included in his order, that should Lady Violet refuse to comply with his request at this time, then he intends to personally come and collect her himself."

"Collect her himself?" asked Ruby, now most amused.

Over the years, she witnessed first-hand, Maximus engaging in a lot of crazy and questionable acts in his wild and rebellious past. However, Ruby never heard or saw him going so far as to practically kidnaping a damsel *not* in distress. Certainly, this was a true first!

"Yes," answered the knight.

He further added, "And if the crown prince should be forced to come, then he intends to throw Lady Violet straight into the dungeon. Afterwards, he stated that he plans on locking her up indefinitely and disregarding the key into a hot blazing fire— should the lady, of course, decide to decline his most generous invitation."

And then, looking straight over to Violet, he warned, "Again, my fair lady, the choice is all yours. But, please take gentle note, that the crown prince *highly* suggests that you choose *wisely*."

"Well, when you put it like *that*, do I really have *a choice?*" asked Violet, sarcastically.

Truly, Violet never expected for Maximus to behave like this. Was he really this stubborn and demanding? A constant pesky thorn to her side?

"My darling girl, I'm afraid that answer is only too obvious," Ruby sighed. "Clearly, you don't. But as strange as all of this really is, it appears that you've somehow managed to capture the sole attention of our dear prince. I honestly never thought that I'd live to see the very day."

As much as Violet hated defeat, she knew that she was cornered. Unfortunately, she had no other choice but to face him. Oh, the absolute horror of it all!

And so, with her new spell book in hand, Violet bid Ruby farewell and reluctantly followed the knight out into the garden. While Violet might have been a new student in the art of magic, come night fall, she was determined to study that new spell book of hers with all her might. One way or another, there just had to be a spell designed to divert the unwanted attention away from a certain rogue prince!

# CHAPTER 9

As Maximus silently stood outside in the garden, he impatiently waited for Violet's arrival. Unfortunately, for him, he already well knew that she'd hate him for summoning her like he did. Forcefully. Without logic or reason. Abruptly ending her morning lessons, without any consideration to her own personal feelings about the matter. But either way, Maximus simply didn't care. If she'd come to later resent him, then so be it. So long as he saw her again, right now at this precise moment, then that's all that mattered to him.

In truth, Maximus acknowledged that Violet was most likely, still mad at him from the night before. Especially, after kissing her. And yet, again, he still didn't care. The reality was that he *longed* to see her. Even if she *disliked* him... *resented* him... *despised* him... it was all *irrelevant*. As far as Maximus was concerned, even if she *hated* him, then it also meant that she *felt something* for him. And feeling *something* was far better than feeling *nothing*, at all.

Ultimately, in the end, Maximus recognized that hate was also the sister to love. Its fair companion. And if one could hate, then they also maintained the equal capacity to love... and *love* is what he *wanted*. Or at least, the physical aspect of love. Possibly, in the form of another kiss. After all, after their last kiss, she was all that he thought about ever since.

Impatiently, Maximus marched back and forth, up and down the lawn, while bypassing all of the perfectly manicured bushes and romantic floral scenery along the way. And instead of looking like the soon-to-be-king that he was; instead, Maximus resembled more of a knight in a game of chess, frantically pacing through a complicated maze in search of his lost queen. Reflecting a desperate and lonesome knight, rather than a proud and confident crown prince. A future monarch, who was simply waiting for the arrival of one of his many subjects.

Except, Violet really wasn't one of his subjects. In fact, she was the golden exception to this rule. Instead of being another common chess piece in the form of a regular pawn; she was, in fact, the savior. The true queen to this political game. As well as a foreigner to his kingdom, too.

And then, right before he lost his mind and fell into a state of pure madness, Violet finally appeared. With her long and dark shadow cast right in front of him, as reflected below the mossy green lawn; Maximus quickly turned around to face her. And once he did, he saw her standing there across from him, looking as proud and as confident as ever. She was magnificent. Breathtakingly beautiful. With her fierce and wild hair freely flowing across the howling wind, and the bright sunlight shining against the golden highlights found within her reddish hair, Maximus was at a loss for words. At first sight, he was simply enchanted by her. Truly, Violet was a rare and unique beauty.

In all of his many adventures and travels across this grand kingdom, never had Maximus seen such a beautiful creature such as she. And then, much to his own amusement, he smiled at her.

But unfortunately, for him, *his* happiness was *not* equally matched by *hers*. For as he smiled, she frowned. Alas, Maximus might have tricked her to come but despite her ill reaction, he still had no regrets. Absolutely, none.

"You came," Maximus beamingly smiled, as he welcomed her to his side.

"Did I really have much of a choice?" Violet sarcastically asked him.

Much to his own surprise and delight, Maximus unexpectedly burst into laughter.

"No, I suppose that you most certainly didn't," he laughed on. "But now that you've come, aren't you glad that you did?"

"Not really," Violet replied in earnest, as she folded her arms against her chest, just like an angered youth.

Suddenly, Maximus found himself laughing, once more. Never before had he met someone so incredibly *uninterested* in him— especially, coming from someone on the opposite sex. Apart from her stunning beauty, Violet's wild and sassy attitude not only intrigued him, but he was also *greatly* attracted to it, too. Alas, she truly was a real challenge and that made things *so* much more *interesting*.

"My love, you do realize that as I speak, several young ladies at my court would simply die just to take *your place*, right now. Consider yourself more than lucky to have been blessed with this rare honor," Maximus told her, as he flashed his princely good smile, that just-so-happened to showcase his perfectly sparkling and pearly white pair of teeth. It was both seductive and intoxicating.

"With all due respect, *all of them* can gladly take my place," Violet proudly declared. "Personally, I'd much rather return back to the laboratory to continue on with my lessons, instead of wasting more precious time out here with *you*."

"If that's the case, then consider *this* meeting to be a further extension of your lessons," he pointed out to her.

"Magic," Maximus continued on, "Isn't everything in our world. To win this war, then you must also train for battle, too."

"What do you mean?" Violet cried.

Was she really expected to actually fight? As in a real battle? Violet had never participated in combat before. This was certainly news to her!

"Dare to find out?" he taunted her. "If you really want to succeed in this mission, then you might want to start by putting down that damn spell book of yours and instead, pick up one of those swords over there."

Following his gaze, Violet noticed that right next to them was a tall oak tree. And underneath that large shaded tree, were several shiny metallic weapons. Curiously, Violet's eyes stared at those glimmering silvery objects. Dropping her spell book down onto the grassy lawn, she proceeded to walk over towards them.

As Violet inspected the site, she noticed that the weapons were all swords, just as Maximus declared. But they were not all uniform. Instead, the swords came in a range of designs, shapes and colors. Some were long, skinny and pointy, while others were short, thick and sharp. A few were made from silver, while others were crafted out of either bronze, copper, steel or gold. Each were constructed using a collection of diverse metals and materials. Additionally, their handles all varied, too. Some had a soft cushioned grip, while others were metallic and adorned with various jewels, just like a relic.

However, the one that caught Violet's immediate attention was a long silver sword. It was medium in size, width and thickness. It also possessed a peculiar amethyst jewel in the front of its handle— a similar violet stone that also ironically matched her necklace. If Violet was expected to claim a sword for herself, then this sword was *it*.

"I'll take this one," Violet happily announced, as she quickly grabbed her chosen sword from off the ground.

"Nice choice," Maximus complemented her with a warm smile, not at all surprised by her somewhat predictable choice.

Following her lead, Maximus walked over to her side and picked up a sword for himself. Like Violet, he also chose another silver steel sword that was also long, thick and sturdy. But instead of selecting another fancy and decorative weapon; he, instead, opted for a sword with a plain black soft cushion for its handle.

"Are you ready for battle?" he asked her, with the most seductive grin beaming across his handsome face.

"Wait," she cried, with her new sword in hand. "Are you honestly expecting me to fight you? Here? Right now?"

"Less talk Violet and more action," Maximus replied, with a devilish smile. Meanwhile, his silvery eyes sparkled against the bright sunlight. Just like a shiny pair of diamonds.

"Come on, I promise to stand still," he told her. "You can try to hit me first."

"This is absolutely absurd!" Violet exclaimed, in outrage. "I mean, we aren't even wearing any helmets or protective gears. What if you get hurt?"

"Ah, so you do care about *me*, after all," he playfully joked. "It's good to finally know that I can invoke some ounce of concern from out of you. That only means that I'm making great progress."

"Don't give yourself too much credit," she interjected. "I'm only looking out for your welfare for the sake of your people. After all, you're their crown prince. If anything should happen to you, then what shall become of them?"

"They'll just have to find a new king to replace me, that's all," he shrugged, nonchalant.

"But right now," he spoke, as he took two steps forward to face her. "All that matters is just *you and me*."

And then, staring directly into her eyes, he told her, "Come on Violet, I'm waiting. Show me what you've got."

Alas, Violet finally recognized that the only way to escape him, was to accept his challenge. To fight him, through and through. And so, with the desperate determination to end this godforsaken meeting of theirs, while holding her sword tightly within her hands, Violet closed her eyes shut and swung straight away.

"Not too bad," Maximus observed, as his sword came crashing down to meet hers.

Instantly, Violet reopened her eyes wide and saw him standing there in front of her. Much to her disappointment, he was staring at her with an approving smile.

"You're a feisty one," he acknowledged. "But swinging with passion isn't going to win you any points, from here on out. Instead, you've got to focus on your opponent. Which, my love, means that you must keep both eyes wide open and directly affixed on your target at all times. No matter how devastatingly handsome they might be."

And then, much to Violet's horror, he actually *winked* at her. Imagine, the nerve of that ridiculous man!

"Fine, I'll keep my eyes open," she said, in defiance. "But I have *yet* to see a handsome face."

Obviously, that was a *lie*. But none-the-less, it still felt so incredibly good to say that comment out loud. Anything to wound his super inflated ego was well worth the effort!

"Really? Do you not find me that handsome?" asked Maximus, with a hint of disappointment found within his voice. "Funny, I found you to be rather pretty. I'd even go so far as to say that we'd probably make a fantastic looking pair, don't you think?"

And *that* was *it*! The nerve of this ridiculous man to actually insist that they'd make such a lovely couple. Especially, given the fact that he probably already had his way with half… no… most likely, *all* the ladies at this damn court! No, they'd *never* be a couple. Violet would rather die a thousand deaths than to ever be caught in a relationship with him! Not now, not ever!

"Take that!" Violet passionately yelled, as she forcefully swung her sword against his.

For a moment, Maximus genuinely appeared startled by her sheer strength and dominating force. However, her bold determination only intrigued him *even more*.

"Hmm, I say, I rather like that," he told her. "You've got a relentless spirit. You'll need that in the battlefield."

And then, his sword came crashing down to meet hers, for a second time in a row.

"But an angry expression doesn't suit you, my love," he teased her. "Better to smile, it causes less wrinkles."

And then, he winked at her *yet again* and *that act* alone, was entirely unforgiveable! Good grief, the nerve of that man, Violet thought to herself. Not only was he such a pain-in-her-ass, but he also had the audacity to ridicule her, too. Really this was all too much!

"You know," she began, "I almost *regret* rescuing you back in the enchanted forest. In hindsight, I probably should have just left you there alone to rot."

"Ouch, Violet," he laughed on. "That one actually stung."

"Good," she smiled victoriously, which in return, made his heart unexpectedly soar with excitement.

"Let's make this match more interesting, shall we?" Maximus suggested to her.

"If you can beat me, fair and square," he proposed, "Then, we'll end this lesson of ours immediately, and you won't have to endure my presence for the remainder of today."

"That sounds excellent," she remarked aloud.

"Not so fast," Maximus informed her. "I haven't even mentioned my part of the bargain yet. Should I win, of course."

"Okay… so what is it? What's in it for you?" Violet asked, with a raised brow.

"First off," he began, "If I win, then you'll have to accompany me to our nightly banquet dinners for the remainder of your stay."

"Accompany you to our dinners? But I already did that last night. We sat at the same table," she was quick to point out.

"That doesn't count," he replied in a serious tone. "Last night, I sat at the head of the table, while you were seated at the far end. No, that will not do."

"What exactly are you suggesting, then?" she asked him.

"My love, you'll just have to remain by my side at all times," Maximus informed her.

"Starting tonight, you'll be seated next to me," he explained. "Plus, *all* dances will be reserved for me and *only me*. No exceptions."

"But what if someone else asks for my hand to dance?" Violet innocently asked him.

"If you're seated next to me, then no one will ever dare to ask."

"Very well. If I lose, then we can sit together. However, I refuse to be obligated to engage in any meaningful or polite conversations with you at the table. After all, I'll most likely be too preoccupied with eating my supper in blissful silence."

Overall, Violet's relentless refusal to entertain Maximus was a childish tactic to slice at his ego. A poor attempt on her part to annoy his overconfident self. But, much to her frustration, Maximus didn't at all appear to be disappointed by her honest response. In fact, he actually seemed to be *pleased* and dare we say, *amused* with her answer.

"And," he further added.

"And? Wait, there's more?" she asked, in surprise.

Suddenly, Violet began to feel both confused and nervous. If being his nightly companion wasn't enough, then what more could Maximus possibly want from her?

"Second, if I win, then you'll have to kiss me again. Today, right here, in this very garden," Maximus revealed, with a huge smirk showcased across his handsome face, stretching from ear-to-ear.

"Haven't you already kissed me enough?" Violet asked, trying her best efforts to convince him to forgo this silly request.

"No, I don't believe I have," he admitted, with all honesty.

"Why me?" Violet asked him, most curiously.

"Maximus, you could kiss any other lady at this court," she reminded him. "Therefore, why the sudden interest in me? Besides, I don't even like you. And I'm pretty sure that you don't like me, either."

"Whoever said that I don't like you, Violet?" Maximus was quick to confront her. The sound of his voice as serious and as sharp as ever.

"Oh," she gasped, in surprise. "I just assumed that naturally..."

"I do *like you*, Violet," Maximus corrected her. "I like you very much. In fact, with each passing minute, I find myself liking you *even more*. Perhaps, more than I initially thought possible."

For a moment, Violet actually believed him. Meanwhile, as she stared directly at him, she watched as his silvery eyes sparkled against the bright sunlight. And for a second time in a row, Violet saw her reflection shine from within his dreamy pair of eyes, just like staring right through a mirror. An inner reflection to his very soul. Of *his heart.*

"Unlike the others, it was *you* who saved me out there in that forest," he explained to her.

"Because of the prophecy, I always knew that you'd be the one destined to free me from my sleeping curse. But at the same time, I never anticipated you actually *rescuing me*, either," he revealed, speaking straight from his heart.

"In my experience, most villagers would have been afraid. Fearful. Especially, with those rogue archers out on the loose. Many folks would have simply abandoned my rescue efforts and run off. To leave me behind to fend for myself, out in that dark and gloomy forest. But no, not you, Violet. You didn't do that. Already, from the start, you were the exception to the rule," Maximus informed her. "Even in the face of danger, you remained by my side. Violet, you were so brave and courageous. Absolutely fearless. That's why you're not only a savior, but a hero. *My hero.*"

"You might be the savior, but you didn't know that when you saved me," he continued on. "Violet, I need someone like you by my side. Someone that I can both respect and trust. It's not easy to be in my shoes. There are very few people that I can truly trust. And even though we hardly know each other; but already, I feel like I can trust you. Furthermore, ever since we arrived to my kingdom, I haven't had the proper chance to personally thank you."

Taking a step forward, he took in a deep breath and said, "So, here it goes… *thank you… Violet.* From the bottom of my heart, thank you for rescuing me. Thank you, for saving me when you didn't have to. I am forever grateful and indebted to your service."

Suddenly, Violet felt her knees go weak. She was at a complete loss for words. For a future king to be indebted to another person, just what did that mean precisely?

And to be *his hero?* A hero to the crown prince and the future king. Violet had never been a hero before; let alone to anyone else. A second ago, she hated him. And now, a second later, she kind of admired him. *Liked him.* Surprisingly, Maximus was actually starting to act like a true gentleman, once again.

This version of Maximus… *this* was the side that Violet always envisioned him to be. Just like in her dreams. Her childhood knight in shining armor. This was the person, whom she wanted to know. Not the version she met last night.

"Okay, if I agree to this wager, then starting now, you must promise to be faithful to me. Which means, no kissing other girls. Especially, while I'm around," she firmly set the boundaries straight. "Do you hear me? Because, I really do mean it. I can't risk my reputation being publicly tarnished, if I'm to remain by your constant side."

"A fair trade," he agreed with a playful smile. "So, is it safe to say, that seeing me kiss other girls makes you feel somehow… well… what's the word… *jealous?*"

"Me jealous? Ha! Such a ridiculous statement," Violet huffed.

Unfortunately, for Violet's pride, her bluff was quickly called. For at that precise moment, she turned a bright shade of red, due to sheer embarrassment and guilt. A curious reaction that Maximus quickly took note of, much to his own personal satisfaction and delight. Indeed, she really was *jealous.*

"Very well, I agree to your terms. Let the battle continue," Maximus declared, as he took a step forward, ready to proceed with their fight.

Without saying another word, their swords came crashing down, swinging back and forth against each other. Left to right, front to back, the duo battled against one another, as if their very lives depended upon it. In truth, it was their prides that laid at stake the most, out on the forefront.

Meanwhile, as Violet swung away at him, she dove two steps forward. One way or another, she was attempting to knock Maximus down and force him to lose his tight grip around his sword. However, much to her surprise, Maximus didn't look at all bothered by her tactics. Instead, he happily took a gracious step back and allowed her to fully dominate their sparring match.

But then, suddenly, Violet missed a step and tripped. Tumbling sideways and downwards, she dropped her sword and landed right onto the lawn. With her sword located a foot away, Violet stared up ahead and saw her opponent hovering right above her. Much to her fear, he had a victorious smile painted across his handsome face. But worst of all, the pointy end of his sword was now directly aimed at her exposed neck.

"I believe I've won," Maximus proudly announced.

"And now, rise so that I can claim my prize," he ordered her, as he released his weapon down onto the ground.

Afterwards, he offered her a helping hand to get back up.

Nervously, Violet arose to meet her challenger. Alas, she lost. Her pride wounded. And now, she was forced to face the consequences of losing a fierce battle.

But before Violet even had the chance to take a step back, Maximus already whisked her right into his arms. A second later, she was trapped in a tight embrace.

"I'm not letting you go. Not until I kiss you. A deal is a deal."

Damn it, he had her. She was cornered. As much as Violet wanted nothing more than to run away, she was trapped. Plus, technically, he was right. After all, one way or another, she did lose in the end. Fair was fair.

Rather than arguing with him, Violet decided to comply. The sooner she kissed him, then the better off she'd be. And so, much to her displeasure, she closed her eyes shut and leaned in forward.

Even with her eyes closed, Violet could still feel him around her. Instantly, his grip tightened around her waist. A few seconds later, she discovered his lips pressed against hers, just like the night before. But this time around, their second kiss was different. It wasn't short. Instead, it lingered on. Too long. Far longer than what she originally anticipated.

Violet was about ready to open her eyes, when suddenly, she felt his tongue push through the opening of her mouth. A second later, their tongues were gliding against each other. This was so intrusive! This *wasn't* at all what she signed up for!

However, with that being said, rather than pushing him away, she found herself *actually participating* in their latest kiss. Against her own better judgment, Violet allowed her tongue to plunge forward to meet his. Welcomingly. Believe it or not, but she was actually kissing him back and quite possibly, liking it! Maybe, even enjoying it!

"I can't," Violet admitted, as she slowly moved away and reopened her eyes to meet his.

And then, she saw *him*. With his silvery eyes meeting hers and wanting more. If Violet didn't know any better, then she'd have sworn that he was actually staring at her with loving eyes. But how was this possible? Did he really harbor genuine feelings for her? When he said he *liked* her, did he truly mean it?

Regardless, even if he did, she wasn't yet ready to accept him. No, she couldn't continue kissing him so openly out here in public. She wasn't like those other women. Ladies who chased him, every chance they got.

"Are we done now?" Violet finally blurted out, as she quickly pulled away from him.

Gazing at her with a deep and maddening expression reflected upon his face, Maximus resembled a wolf who had recently discovered his new prey.

"Far from it," he told her. "We've only just begun."

"You are just *too* much!" she cried, out of great frustration.

Without saying another word and before he had a chance to stop her, Violet slammed her fists hard against his chest and forcefully shoved herself away from him. Afterwards, she darted right by him, as she ran as far away as she possibly could. And thus, leaving the crown prince standing behind, all alone, with nothing more than the recent memory of their latest kiss.

A kiss that was most certainly, *not* going to be their last. No, not by a long shot.

✳  ✳  ✳

# A Few Hours Later...

After abandoning the crown prince and angrily storming away from the garden, Violet was determined to lock herself up inside of her bedchamber and try her best to forget about that horrid kiss. To erase the unwanted memory of Maximus' lips pressed against hers. But unlike the night before, this time around, his latest kiss felt more damaging.

Rather than a simple peck on her bare lips, she instead felt his tongue brush against hers... and to be perfectly honest... *her* tongue was an active player, too. Much to her great disappointment, not only had he kissed her, but she had also been an equal participant! This kiss... this was *fierce... passionate... long...* but most importantly, it was so *incredibly wrong*! Oh, how she hated herself! But more than anything, oh, how she hated him so much more than ever before!

Oh, what was to become of her now? More likely, Violet was probably just another one of his many female conquests to add onto his very long and never-ending list of lovers. In fact, he probably didn't even care that she was the savior. To him, she was just another debutante. Another maiden to seduce and conquer. A woman, whom evidentially, he not only liked and was attracted to, but also enjoyed her kisses. But unlike Maximus, she wasn't interested in him at all. Regardless, if he was a prince!

If she was back home in her world, then Violet would have run away or hid herself inside the comfort of her childhood bedroom. Anything to avoid dealing with someone like Maximus. But unfortunately, for her, she wasn't in her world. Instead, she was in *his*.

And so, Violet wanted distance. Time away from him. But unfortunately, she also knew that eventually, sooner or later, they'd cross paths again. They were destined to.

One way or another, he'd either summon her back to the garden or crash her next training session with Ruby. Or worse, invade her private bedchamber. Dear God, if that should ever happen... then, what *really* would become of her?

And then, Violet recalled their wager and the fact that she lost their match, fair and square. Now, as a result, she was going to be forced to smile, dine and dance with him for the remainder of her stay. No, if she was going to beat Maximus at his own game, then she needed to understand him. Learn about his wild past. Discover the real man, hidden underneath that suit of armor. The prince behind the crown.

To tame him, Violet needed to learn everything about him. Starting from his likes to his dislikes, to his past and present, and everything else in-between. And so, this is why Violet came to invite Ruby for an afternoon cup of tea. If there was anyone in this kingdom who knew the truth about Maximus and of his past, then it was most certainly her.

Flash forward to two hours later after their latest kiss in the garden, Violet returned back to the infamous scene of the crime. But this time, however, she was comfortably seated at a table, alongside with Ruby. Together, they were admiring the rose garden, which was located in the castle's back courtyard.

"Don't worry about Prince Maximus," Ruby advised her, as she took a sip of her rosebud herbal tea, followed by a small bite of her almond biscuit.

Even though Ruby wasn't a blood relation to Violet, she still felt a strong connection to her. In many ways, she reminded her a great deal of her own great-grandmother, Maureen. Although Ruby didn't have any grandchildren of her own, she did tell Violet that she considered her to be a *spiritual granddaughter.* And having an elderly and wise grandmother-like figure in a foreign land, brought much comfort and ease to her. She, a young lady, who at times, still experienced an occasional dose of homesickness.

"Just so you know, you can always call me granny," she told her, followed by a smile and then a wink.

Happily, Violet smiled back at her in return, as she added a dash of milk to her tea. Afterwards, she took a generous sip, while she listened to her mentor. It was nice to know that she had Ruby to lean on for both guidance and support.

"Maximus is a difficult man to understand, let alone love," Ruby sighed. "He's been a warrior for years and sadly, as a result, he lacks any of the diplomatic skills that his late brother previously mastered. Leopold was regarded to be the perfect son, while Maximus was always cast aside to hide in the shadows."

"He wasn't ever supposed to be king," she continued on, "As a second son, he wasn't expected to inherit the throne. That's why he never trained for it. In truth, Maximus never really fit into our world. For many years, he always seemed lost. Wildly embarking on endless adventures, all in the pursuit of finding himself and his place in this world. A journey of self-discovery. A purpose."

Suddenly, Violet's ears instantly caught the word *purpose*. Was it possible that Maximus' wild and rebellious past was all due to his quest to discover his true destiny? Surprisingly, Violet could also relate to him. After all, she, too, was in search of hers, as well.

"Ruby, are you telling me that Maximus has lived most of his life, desperately searching for his life's purpose? A true meaning behind his existence?"

"Yes. Honestly, it's probably the real reason as to why he used to live such a bold and reckless life in the past. It's why he was previously known as Maximus, the Brute. But whatever you do, please don't tell him that I told you that. I do believe that he wants to make a better impression on you," she said with a warm smile.

"It's starting to make a bit more sense, now," Violet admitted. "He's lived a wild and reckless life in his youth, all because he's been trying to find his way out in this world."

"Exactly," Ruby agreed. "Which, I suspect, might be the same case for you, too. Albeit, you're not as wild and reckless as he was. Or, still is."

And then, the two ladies laughed on, as they took another sip of their herbal tea.

An afternoon tea session with Ruby was probably the grandest idea that she had since her arrival. Granted, it was far too late in the afternoon to continue with their magic lessons together. However, a nice tea break, along with some much-needed fresh air, was well worth the indulgence.

Upon listening to Ruby's tale, Violet realized that she had much more in common with Maximus than what she originally thought. Her knight in shining armor might have been the crown prince and the next future king, but according to Ruby that wasn't always the case.

Once upon a time, Maximus was just another young man, hoping to find his place in this great wide world. Like her, he was lost and searching for a fitted role to belong to in society. As much as Violet hated to admit it, but she unfortunately, understood him only all too well. She, too, knew what it felt like to be young and lost. To desire more than the paths laid available to them. A journey to discover their destinies. To achieve their true purposes.

Meanwhile, as Ruby poured herself another cup of tea, Violet caught sight of the prince, just a few feet away. Across from her, he was standing in the middle of the courtyard and chatting with his fellow knights on horseback. For once, it seemed that Maximus was too preoccupied to even notice her on the opposite end of the courtyard.

But as Violet stared at him from afar, she began to look at him with a fresh pair of eyes. Perhaps, this heartless rebel and spineless rogue prince just needed someone like her to be his friend, after all. Maybe, just maybe, she'd make a tiny bit more of an effort to be nicer to him. That is, if he stopped trying to endlessly kiss her!

# CHAPTER 10

Crown Prince Maximus of the West was never meant to be a hero. Instead, at birth, that was a role reserved for his elder brother, Leopold. In fact, it's why his late brother was known throughout the Great Kingdom as Leopold, the Great, while he was simply Maximus, the Brute— aka, the rebel and rogue prince. The rakish younger prince, who was notorious for getting himself into an endless amount of trouble. A mischievous scoundrel, who always brought forth much grief and despair to his frustrated father.

As the second son to the late King Elryk, Maximus' role was never established or enshrined like Leopold's. Unlike him, Leopold was born as the automatic heir apparent. And so, without a clearly defined designation of a proper or a fitted role, Maximus spent the majority of his youth trying to figure out *who* and *what* he should *and* wanted to *be*.

A brave, courageous and honorable prince? Or a fierce villainous barbaric warrior and a wretched heartthrob? Really, Maximus could have easily chosen either path by the simple toss of a coin. In hindsight, both paths were laid available to him. He just had to simply choose.

Unlike their father, all of their previous ancestors historically had all but one son. A sole heir to inherit the throne of their western kingdom, along with several daughters. In fact, it was rare for a King of the West to have sired two sons, born within the same generation. However, in their father's case, Maximus was the first second son born to a western king in more than a century.

And so, because of these reasons, both King Elryk and the palace really didn't know what to do with him. Let alone, what to train and groom him to become. Unlike daughters who could easily be married off to another prince or a duke in a neighboring kingdom, a second son proved to be much more challenging and difficult to mold. A son, who at the time of his birth, was already a prickly thorn at his father's side. That, along with a constant question mark looming over his head.

For starters, a second son could never be crowned as the next king. But yet, he was also overqualified to serve as another commander or a knight in the king's army. Technically, by law, all military officers reported directly to a royal, including a younger prince. Naturally, by default, Maximus would always outrank anyone in the military, including his superiors and the Great General, himself.

To complicate matters even further, it was also deemed inappropriate for Maximus to assume the role of a lesser nobleman or a lord of a grand estate, either. According to his father, the late snobbish King Elryk felt that *any son of his* serving as a lower-class nobleman, such as a duke or an earl, was absolutely *beneath* him.

In fact, a blood royal prince serving in the capacity of a lesser nobleman would not only be scandalous in his eyes, but at the same time, it would also cheapen the integrity of the crown. Especially, for a prince directly descended from the ruling monarch. According to his late father, such actions would place both shame and disgrace to his pristine legacy. And so, because of King Elryk's displeasure, the opportunity to serve as a lesser nobleman was denied to him.

Furthermore, if Maximus rebelled against his father's wishes and joined the military and eventually, rose-up in the ranks to become a fierce and respected warrior, then would the younger prince go on to later challenge the existing ruling authority, one day in the future? Was it possible for the brutish prince to wage a potential violent and brutal war? A war against his own family? To threaten the foundation of the monarchy by leading a possible rebellious army to usurp the crown? Could the forgotten and ignored second son eventually transform into a villainous foe, determined to destroy the very livelihood of his naturally assumed enemy and brother, the rightful heir, aka the crown prince? Be the flame that sparks a mass civil war? A black sheep in disguised, pushed completely over the edge, with nothing else to lose but to seek his revenge and reclaim the throne? That, along with innocent spilled blood on his dirty hands in the process?

Ah, yes, these questions were *always* at the forefront. Was Maximus trustworthy? Was he loyal? Would he one day unleash a deadly war against his own brother? To betray his kingdom? Behind his charming and dashing smile, was Maximus secretly the evil, corrupt and villainous younger prince hidden underneath?

Furthermore, if Maximus appeared too trustworthy, then he'd also be deemed as a dumb, foolish and weakly prince. A jokester. But at the same time, if he acted too cunning or wicked, then he'd be viewed as a traitor. Really, it was always a failing battle... for all paths led to his eventual demise and doom. A real damned if he did or damned if he didn't. Truly, Maximus was already ruined at sunrise. Before he even bothered to step one foot out of his front door to start his morning, he was already proclaimed as the villain.

Luckily, for Maximus, his elder brother, Leopold, always protected him. Unlike their father, Leopold trusted him wholeheartedly. Maximus might have been a great many useless things to most folks at the palace, but Leopold was the exception. Unlike everyone else around him, Crown Prince Leopold could always look beyond Maximus' woes and see through his younger brother's thick exterior walls. Behind that barrier, he knew that there was a kind hearted boy and an adventurous spirit hiding in there.

In truth, Leopold was more than just a brother to him. Even after the death of their mother, Leopold helped to raise him. They might have been ten years apart in age, but Leopold still took care of his much younger brother's welfare none-the-less. Meanwhile, as the world turned their backs on Maximus, Leopold frequently stepped in to fill that missing void of a loving, caring and dedicated parent.

In the end, Leopold was the only person that ever had his back. Crown Prince Leopold wasn't only an honorable and respectful royal, but he was also the perfect older brother. The prime example of a brother, who not only protected and advocated for him, but most importantly, loved him unconditionally and taught him right from wrong. Thanks to him, Leopold set the ideal standards on how an honorable, respected and dignified prince was supposed to behave like. That's why, Leopold was not only a well-respected older brother, but he was also his one true hero.

While the palace, along with their own father, often questioned Maximus' allegiance growing up, Leopold never once doubted his loyalty. In fact, he often defended his younger brother out in public. Regardless of court whispers, Leopold stood firm in his beliefs. He knew his brother's heart and most importantly, he trusted him, too. And so, Maximus was ultimately spared the unwarranted daily accusations of treason by the palace advisors and courtiers... all thanks to his one and only ally: *his beloved brother.*

Since being a hero was a role reserved for his elder brother, Maximus decided at an early age to become the wild and rebellious prince that everyone else expected him to be. To act and behave as the complete opposite of his heroic brother. If Leopold was deemed the hero, then he'd take the lesser place of the villain.

And so, while the public viewed Leopold to be kind, proper, elegant and good mannered, Maximus instead, chose to establish himself as the complete opposite: a wild, rebellious and brutish prince.

After all, what was the point of being so damn good and honorable, when the rest of the entire world saw him as anything but? Just having been born as the second son, no one else at the palace, let alone in the entire kingdom plus his own father, ever expected much from him, anyways. Therefore, why bother trying to be so damn good? If the world wanted a bastard, then Maximus was all in for the show!

But at the same time, no matter how Maximus behaved in public, he still continued to secretly love, respect and admire his elder brother tremendously. Leopold was everything that he aspired to be and yet, he could never be like him. In truth, Leopold was perfection. He literally put *perfect* in the very word *perfection.*

And so, over the years, Maximus earned his reputation as the younger rebellious prince. While his brother was busy studying literature at the palace and attending various balls and diplomatic conferences, Maximus was frequently traveling outdoors and exploring the woods, stealing treasures from other thieves and wandering vagabonds, drinking himself crazy at local rundown taverns, wrestling with brutish thugs for fun and breaking as many unsuspecting female hearts as he possibly could, along the way.

Everything that a wicked prince was *expected* to do, he did it. And thus, rightfully earning his nickname Maximus, the Brute, for a reason. Truth be told, he might have been born a prince, but he certainly grew up to become a brute. A brute of the worst possible kind!

In the end, Maximus decided to defy his father's wishes and joined the military. He didn't care about rank or title, being a regular knight was good enough for him. Since he was never going to become king, he'd figure that he might as well learn to fight well. At least this way, if Leopold ever needed his help to fight in the future, then he'd be ready to lend a helping hand. Should an unforeseeable war ever break out, then Maximus planned on defending his brother's kingdom and legacy out on the battlefields, where he belonged. Anything to serve, protect and honor his brother, along with their kingdom's innocent civilians.

Furthermore, even though their father wasn't at all pleased by his defying act to join the military, by this point, Maximus no longer cared. Regardless of King Elryk's opinions, Maximus desperately needed to do *something meaningful* with his life. He simply refused to idly sit by at the palace and be reduced to nothing more than a pretty statue. A handsome face. He was *more* than just that. He *had* to be.

But after his father's and brother's untimely passings, Maximus became the unlikely heir to the throne. A prince who was never meant to be king. Never trained to be. And yet, here he was as the new heir apparent. A king-in-waiting. Ultimately, being forced to walk down a path to become something that he wasn't... a *hero*. A surprising role that he avoided almost all of his entire life.

How could a wretched brute like him ever be worthy of such an honorable role? What did it mean exactly to be a hero? To have everyone in the land depend solely upon him, he a single person? A prince who spent most of his time exploring the kingdom outside, rather than staying inside and learning how to rule it from within? To not only become the next king, but a righteous one at that?

And even when they eventually defeated Vera, which he no doubt believed full heartily they would, what then? How was he going to rule? How was he going to follow in his elder brother's shadows and become a righteous king that his kingdom desperately needed? Truly, the Kingdom of the West deserved better than him. They deserved a king like Leopold.

If only Leopold had lived. If only he survived his accident, then *everything* would have been so much different. *He* would have been different. Instead of fighting in this godforsaken war, he'd be out and chasing countless quests to buy his time, partake in grand sword fighting adventures for the sake of having fun, drinking alcohol all day and night until he couldn't see anymore and sleeping with as many beautiful women as he possibly could. But at the same time, if he was back to his old ways, then he'd never have met *her*....

Ah, Violet.... she *complicated* things. Especially, his feelings. Never before, had Maximus thought so much about one single woman. In fact, as of lately, she was always on his mind. In his every passing thought. Even when he slept, he dreamed of her. But was this normal? After all, she was the savior. Violet was destined to help him to fight in this fierce war to reclaim his throne and save his land and people. Therefore, thinking and dreaming about her was perfectly normal, right?

But sadly, Maximus knew that it was more than just that. Thinking of her was one thing, but fantasizing about kissing her was another. And if he was being completely truthful to himself, then just kissing her wasn't entirely accurate. No, kissing her wasn't within the limited scope of his fantasies.

Instead, Maximus wanted nothing more than to strip her down bare and conquer her entire body, from head-to-toe. To taste every inch of her. To enter himself inside of her and claim her as his own, over and over again. He desired her and yet, Violet claimed that she felt nothing for him. But he was no fool. He very well knew that when his lips last locked in with hers in the garden, she kissed him back. She wanted him, just as much as he wanted her... even though she was reluctant to admit it.

The very thought of her brought an unexpected smile to Maximus' face. For the first time in his life, he wanted one woman. Not another princess or a barmaid, or a duchess or anyone else for that matter... just *her*. Someone he couldn't easily conquer. Someone who denied him. Someone who most likely, hated and despised him. A person, whom his mind told him to stand ten feet away from... and yet, his heart said otherwise. Someone he couldn't have. A real challenge.

While Maximus spent most of his life uncertain about himself or his future, the one and only thing that he now felt certain about was the fact that he wanted Violet. She might have been the savior to everyone else, but to him, she was *his hero*. She saved him, when she didn't have to. She was very much his hero, just like his elder brother had been. In truth, Violet reminded him so much of Leopold.

Throughout his life, Maximus was accustomed to disappointment. He was used to people abandoning him and leaving him alone to fight his endless battles all on his own. Apart from Leopold, no one else had ever willingly came to his aid for anything before. Not even, his own father, the late king. Heck, if it was up to his father, then Maximus would have probably been left for dead on numerous occasions. In the end, whenever Maximus was in trouble, he learned to take care of himself. To fend for himself. To fight for himself. To survive.

But for once, Maximus felt like he had a true partner. Someone, who had his back. A real friend. Although Violet might have had her own personal reasons for helping him, but still, she didn't have to rescue him back in the enchanted forest. When she first discovered him, she could have easily run away to get help. But instead, Violet stayed behind and fought for him. Even though she probably never picked up a sword in her entire life, but regardless, Violet still courageously swung away and freed him from that nest. If it wasn't for her, then he might still be trapped in there. And because of these reasons, he trusted her with his life, even if she didn't trust him in return. At least, not yet.

One way or another, Maximus was determined to make it right with her. After their latest kiss, he decided to do whatever it took to win her heart. If he needed to become a better man in order to win her over, then so be it. Whatever these feelings meant, Maximus wanted to pursue them. He had to. Because as it currently stood, whenever he closed his eyes, he saw nothing else but her. With her long and bright fiery red hair gracefully floating down her gentle back, and her shimmering emerald green eyes staring directly at him. Whenever he envisioned her, he felt lost. Even within his own dreams.

Love was always dangerous territory; Maximus was well aware of that.

Meanwhile, as the rest of his future remained uncertain, the one and only thing he knew with absolute certainty was that if his future didn't include Violet, then none of this mattered. Not the war. Not the throne. Not the wealth. Not the honor or prestige. When it was all said and done, she was all that he cared about. All he wanted, in the end.

Violet was the treasure. The gold at the end of the rainbow. Alas, for the man who never had any real desire or strive to accomplish anything in his past, at long last, he unexpectedly discovered his motivation. She was his happily ever after, and he intended to fight for her... even if he had to battle his way right into her stubborn heart. After a lifetime of searching, he finally realized that she was *his purpose*.

# CHAPTER 11

While seated above her golden throne, Queen Vera glanced at her empty throne room and sighed. Wanting to distract her depressing view of *nothingness*, she chose to instead, redirect her attention over to the recently delivered fresh bouquet of violets. Currently, they were out on display above a wooden table, located by an open window that was positioned right across from her throne. Apart from herself, these freshly picked violets were the only other living thing that was thriving inside of this dreary and suffocating room. Suddenly, a gust of autumn wind swooped in and carried it's fresh sweet and floral scent and dispersed its intoxicating fragrance throughout the open space.

As Vera closed her eyes shut, she was once again reminded of someone, whom she desperately longed to forget. A person, who haunted her for many, many years. A person, whom she once loved most in the entire world. *Her sister.*

It was in this very empty and lonesome throne room, that Vera couldn't help but sigh. Of course, her throne room would be empty. After all, everyone in the land, including her own royal guards and palace courtiers, were completely scared of her… and rightly so. She deserved it. One way or another, Vera justly earned her terrifying reputation as the wicked witch and the villainous evil queen.

After *everything* that she endured over the years, Vera finally made it to the throne... even though she had to plot, steal and kill for it. But wasn't that what all great conquerors did? Fight, murder and take without any restraints nor thoughts pertaining to fear or consequences? Isn't that what distinguished great rulers from all the rest? Wasn't that the making of a *great* queen? A *powerful* and *respected* queen? A queen to be *feared?* A queen to be *remembered* in the history books of the future?

Tragically, as of right now, the future meant *absolutely nothing* to Vera. She might have sat on a golden throne and controlled dominion over the entire Kingdom of the West at her feet, but it came at a *great cost.* In the end, she was *lonely.* All so incredibly lonely. And bitter, too. Had she known the end game from the very beginning, then maybe, Vera would have abandoned her lust for power and revenge long ago. In the end, her quest for vengeance cost her dearly.

If only she had known about the sad future ahead of time, then perhaps, Vera would have done so many things differently. Made alternative decisions concerning her own life. Chosen the opposite walking path towards her final destiny. If only she had owned a crystal ball in her youth!

But history always taught children at an early age to seek power and to do whatever means necessary to hold on to it. While the libraries were often filled with endless books dedicated to the strategies on the art of war and the detailed instructions on how to defeat one's adversaries out on the gruesome battlefields; however, there were seldom any books written discussing on how to cope *afterwards.* How it *felt* emotionally to live *after* the war. Once the battle was fought and won.

Apart from governing, Vera had no issues on ruling her stolen kingdom with an iron fist. If need be, she'd easily outright slaughter any and all of her opponents within the blink of an eye. That is, if they should ever dare to threaten her crown or authority. *Her reign.*

But apart from the tactics of warfare, there weren't any other books dedicated to the subject concerning on how a ruler could peacefully sleep at night. How a ruling queen could still achieve peace and solace, well after a brutal and bloody conquest. No, nothing of that sort existed on the many shelves found within their palace library. Or in any other western library, for that matter.

Tragically, no one else previously bothered to write about the internal struggles of a monarch post-war. Only the glory of conquest, the golden age of enlightenment or the expansion of more land. And more land. And more land. *An empire.*

Unfortunately, no authors or historians of the past, ever dared to recognize the emotional sufferings associated with the consequences of war from within the palace court; let alone, transcribe these melancholy feelings down onto paper. And thus, becoming a tangible record of *history.*

Long ago, Vera wasn't a heartless, soulless and wretched evil queen. Once upon a time, she was just another innocent peasant girl. A young maiden who grew up in a small cottage located on the outskirts of the Kingdom of the West. It was there in a modest but humble hovel near the edge of the forest, where a young Vera was raised by her single mother, along with her younger sister, Sarah. It might have been ages ago, but to Vera, it felt only like yesterday.

Before Vera became the evil queen, she was an adolescent witch-in-training. She, along with Sarah, were trained by the greatest of all teachers: *their mother.* As the daughters of a powerful sorceress, Vera and Sarah were trained in the art of magic. Back then, Vera was considered to be a good witch; in which she manifested only white magic, just like her younger sister and mother did.

During the day, the girls were taught magic by their mother, while their nanny, Maureen, took care of them, along with their daily household affairs in the evenings. As a widow, their mother was often busy teaching them and the other children of the land on the art of magic. As a result of their mother's hectic schedule, her best friend, Maureen, was appointed to serve as the girls' caretaker.

Unlike Sarah, Vera never cared for Maureen. It's why, even as young children, Maureen always favored Sarah over Vera. But that never bothered Vera. In truth, she was never jealous of Maureen's affections, for Vera loved Sarah dearly. In fact, she loved her sister more than anyone else in the entire world. It's why what happened to them in the bitter end, became one of the most heartbreaking and painful parts of her past.

As the girls grew and blossomed into fair maidens, Vera and Sarah both encountered important crossroads in their young adult lives. Even though Sarah mastered their lessons best; however, unlike Vera, she wasn't interested on pursuing a career in magic.

Instead, much to her dismay, Vera discovered that her one and only precious sister was secretly sneaking off into a distant land behind her back. The land beyond the magic mirror; a mirror that their mother had hidden inside of a closet found within their cottage. And in the process of aimlessly wandering through an enchanted forest, Sarah managed to fall hopelessly in love with a young man. A wealthy aristocrat and a foreigner named Lord Henrick, the fourth Earl of Galloway. And after weeks of secretly meeting with each other in private, the young earl was most eager to marry her sister at once.

At first, Vera laughed at the news, while foolishly thinking that it was all fate's cruel joke played on them. That her own sister would voluntarily give up her magical world, in exchange for a magic*less* life spent on Earth. A lonesome land that was so far removed from their own family and ancestral roots. To forsake becoming a mighty and powerful sorceress and instead, opt to live a quiet life as a noble woman... a countess, at that. A life of servitude. A life as a *wife*.

But Sarah was a free spirit. One way or another, her heart was devoted entirely to Henrick, the Earl of Galloway. Her first and only love. Within a heartbeat, Sarah confessed the earl's proposal to their mother. And much to Vera's own surprise, their mother had no objections to Sarah's wishes. In the end, their mother supported her youngest daughter's decision to marry, without any questions or objections. Happily, she accepted her daughter's God given free will to follow her own heart and marry her beloved earl.

And so, on Sarah's nineteenth and Vera's twenty first birthday, her younger sister bid her and their mother a final farewell. However, as a caveat to Sarah's departure, their mother sent Maureen to serve as Sarah's chaperone and her lady-in-waiting. It was one thing to allow her youngest daughter to marry a foreign man on Earth, but it was another to permit her to leave without a protector. And so, this is how her sister, Sarah, came to marry the fourth Earl of Galloway (Henry's father and Violet's grandfather), and relocated to Earth with Maureen (Kassie's great-great-grandmother and Violet's great-great-great-grandmother) by her side.

After her sister's departure, Vera slowly fell into a state of depression. Practically, come overnight, she lost her one and only true friend: *her sister.* And now, with Sarah gone, there was an empty void left inside of her grieving heart.

But rather than confessing her sorrow to her mother, Vera decided to take her frustrations out on her magic. Indeed, she was angry that Sarah abandoned her. She was upset that her younger sister picked someone else over her, out of her own free will. In the end, Sarah didn't choose *her.*

No, she, instead, chose the love of a man, in spite of her sister's affections. No matter how much Vera pleaded with her to stay, Sarah still left. Abandoning her behind to become Henrick's wife. And because of these reasons, Vera's white magic gradually darkened over time, due to the bitterness and negative energy stirring from within her.

If love was what drove Sarah away, then Vera also wanted to experience true love, too. Perhaps, love was the answer to the sorrow and emptiness that she now felt within her aching heart. A *broken heart.*

But luckily, for Vera, her broken heart was short lived. For now, there was a new frequent visitor trespassing in her part of the woods. A young man and royal: Prince Elryk of the West.

One day, the prince was hunting outdoors by her cottage. Out of the blue, he accidentally tripped over a pebble and fell down into a nearby ditch. Luckily for him, Vera had just-so-happened to be traveling in the forest to gather some berries, when she heard his cries. Instantly, a concerned Vera followed the prince's troubled voice. Within a few short paces, she found him. Using her magic, she lifted him up from the ditch and back onto solid ground.

Grateful for her rescue efforts, the prince was instantly smitten by Vera. Unlike the other fair princesses at his court, Vera was a rare and wild beauty. With her dark locks, pale skin and emerald green eyes, she was an enchanting sight to behold. While Sarah might have been the sister with the cheerful disposition, along with her bright and sunshine glowing hair; Vera's beauty, in contrast, was far more exotic, as reflected by her dark hair and ravishing features.

But not only was he smitten by her physical appearance, but he also admired her bravery and courage, too. Her heroic willingness to save him. Had it been any other maiden in their land, then Elryk was sure that they would have abandoned him down there, out of fear. Prince or no prince. However, that wasn't the case with Vera. Unlike every other female of his acquaintance, she was fearless. And so, once the prince was back on solid ground, at first sight, Elryk fell madly in love with Vera and she of him…

After that fateful day, Vera and Elryk instantly became lovers. For an entire year, he visited her daily, out in the forest. And with each visit, he brought her many gifts. Mostly jewelry. But even with the endless supply of gold, silver, pearls, emeralds and rubies that he bequeathed her, Vera only wore her amethyst stone bracelet. A companion piece to Sarah's necklace. At least by wearing her bracelet, it felt like her sister was still with her… in spirit… if not in the flesh.

Sadly, Vera's happy romance was destined to be short lived. After a year of joy and bliss, Elryk delivered her the most shocking revelation and heartbreakingly painful news: *his engagement.* It was there outside in the forest, as Vera lied within his loving arms, that Elryk broke the news of his engagement… to *someone else.*

As the heir to the throne, he was forbidden to marry anyone who wasn't a blood born royal. Even though Elryk wished to marry Vera, their local customs and laws forbid him from marrying her. She, a simple and poor peasant girl. And so, this is how a young Prince Elryk came to marry Princess Yesinia from the Kingdom of the North… leaving Vera's aching heart crushed into a million tiny pieces in the process…

On the day of Elryk's and Yesinia's wedding, Vera was about ready to die from a broken heart. For a second time in a row, she was left devastated. Her sister was gone and never heard from again. Her one true love was about to marry another princess. Meanwhile, her mother was focused on building her own career as a teacher and had little time left over to spend with her already grown daughter. Plus, Vera was now aged twenty-two… without a sister… a friend… a mother… a lover… a husband… without anyone… other than a broken heart…

That day, Vera contemplated taking her own life. End her sad and pitiful existence. Destroy her aching heart.

But on that very desperate night, to her surprise, she unexpectedly received a visitor: Elryk. With her mother busy away on her travels, Vera faced Elryk in-person, alone inside of her childhood home. On what should have been his honeymoon with his new bride, Elryk instead, spent the entire night in Vera's bed, making endless love to her into the late hours of the evening.

While Vera was never one to steal another woman's man; but technically speaking, Elryk was *hers first*. And so, as he passionately kissed her away until kingdom come, Vera surrendered herself to a man... who really didn't belong to her... but she still wanted anyways...

The next morning, Elryk made her a bold proposition. While he was forced to marry Princess Yesinia, he'd take Vera as his mistress. Even though the role of a palace mistress was greatly frowned upon by polite society and wasn't nearly as respectable as that of an honorable role as a wife, Vera was willing to sacrifice it all. Her honor, reputation, dignity… *everything*, so long as it meant her being together with Elryk. Her one true love.

In the end, Vera finally understood her sister, Sarah. At long last, Vera recognized what it meant to sacrifice one's livelihood for the sake a great love. For in all reality, she *loved* Elryk. Even if she couldn't be his wife, she'd accept the lesser role of his mistress, as long as she could be with him.

Although her mother wasn't entirely pleased by this fickle arrangement; however, to be fair, she accepted Vera's choice, just as she had accepted Sarah's decision to marry the earl. And so, this is how Vera came to move into the palace and became Prince Elryk's mistress.

Over the years, Elryk and his wife were crowned as the king and queen. In due time, Queen Yesinia bore him two sons, Leopold and Maximus. While his sons knew nothing about her existence, Vera silently watched them grow up from behind the palace's curtains.

For many years, their secret arrangement became a standard routine. Vera spent her palace days practicing magic in the comfort of her private laboratory, while Elryk ruled on his golden throne beside his wife, the queen. But come night fall, Elryk's time was dedicated solely to her.

Each night, he made love to her like it was the end of the world. Their passion, chemistry and attraction were unlike any other. Even after all their years spent together, Elryk still desired her. In fact, apart from Vera, he never took another mistress. Furthermore, after bearing his two sons, Elryk had all but abandoned Yesinia's bedside. According to Elryk, he did his lawful duty to produce an heir and a spare and as a result, he was done with her... his queen.

Yesinia, to her credit, accepted Elryk's bitter coldness and did not interfere between him and Vera's relationship. Their marriage was based upon a *mutual understanding*. However, given what little choice Yesinia had on the matter, Vera suspected it was more of Elryk's doing than hers.

In the end, Yesinia knew that Elryk never married her for love, nor did she ever try to force her affections upon him. Yesinia might have been a great many things, but above all else, she was practical.

As a born royal, Yesinia knew how the palace operated... both the good and the bad parts of the family business. Whatever happened behind closed doors, she still publicly presented herself to the court as the graceful, humble and beloved queen. Regardless of her unhappy marriage, Queen Yesinia knew her place in the palace and in the history books. No matter her husband's lack of affections towards her, she'd still go down in history as the honorable and loving Queen Consort to King Elryk and the mother to the future King Leopold and his descendants. Meanwhile, history would hardly take notice of the king's unnamed mistress. A poor peasant girl, who was nothing more than a dirty seductive whore and an evil wicked witch...

In all reality, Vera could care less about history. She'd been born into poverty, and she never aimed for power. She just wanted love. If not the love of her sister, who practically disappeared upon her marriage and never once bothered to write to her afterwards, then at least she'd have the love of a great king. But unfortunately, for Vera, that very love would one day be called into question.

By the time Elryk's youngest son reached the ripe age ready for grade school, Vera discovered that was pregnant. Indeed, she was carrying the bastard child of the king.

But being the mother of the king's bastard wasn't something that

Vera was proud of. However, at the same time, she wouldn't be the first woman in history to be one, either.

Naturally, as the illegitimate child of the current ruling monarch, Vera's unborn child wasn't eligible to inherit the throne. Therefore, she believed that her baby wasn't a threat. As the king's bastard, her child at birth wouldn't have a legitimate claim to the western throne. Therefore, her pregnancy *shouldn't* have been an issue. While Vera was unexpectedly pleased with the new promise of motherhood; Elryk, in contrast, didn't take it all so well.

Surprisingly enough, Yesinia, of all people, actually wished her well and even went so far, as to write her a formal letter of congratulations. She, the very female who was notorious for being the *other woman* that stood in the center of her loveless marriage. A marriage of three. The very infamous woman who claimed her husband's heart within the palm of her hands. *His lover.*

But regardless of their differences, Yesinia bore no ill will towards Vera nor her unborn child. Like Vera, she, too, was a victim to court politics. Their fates permanently sealed for better or for worse, all due to the business of the crown. However, Yesinia's warm wishes could not also be equally applied towards King Elryk's personal feelings concerning the matter of Vera's unexpected pregnancy.

Apparently, being his mistress was one thing, but being the mother of his bastard child was another. Regardless of all of Elryk's previous heartfelt promises and proclamations of true love… in the end, he was *ashamed of her.* Of their so-called eternal love. A mockery of the heart!

Vera's and Elryk's love might have been nothing more than a prolonged and passionate affair, but a bastard born from their lustful union was an inconvenient blemish to his legacy. Especially, as a poke to his honorable and respected reputation and role as a faithful king to the beloved queen. Given that most of the public were entirely unaware about his true relationship with Vera, only a handful of high-ranking palace officials and courtiers knew the truth about her real status as his mistress.

And now, with Vera pregnant, King Elryk was ready to finally put an end to their union. To not only abandon her, but to destroy her honor and reputation in the process. To disregard and bury their love, like it was a shameful act. Erasing the happy and blissful years that they once shared together as star-crossed lovers.

Vera's fate as the fallen mistress was a tragic one. For in their kingdom, what else could be viewed as the worst possible outcome for an unmarried spinster in the eyes of the public? To be viewed as a disgraced woman, who recently bore the bastard child of the king? Society would be quick to fault her for seducing Elryk and then, cruelly cast her aside to be devoured by the wolves. All the while, the kingdom would portray their beloved king as the innocent victim in this scandal. Either way, he'd be forgiven… *unlike her.*

But worst of all, she could always be stoned to death, like many before her. One bloody stone at a time. A painful death. However, as much as Vera braced herself for her unknown future, her real fate was far more tragic than what she had originally anticipated it to be.

And so, after confessing her pregnancy to him in private, Elryk called in a very public meeting with his royal counselors. It was there in the presence of his high court, which was comprised of his team of palace advisors, including various knights, dukes, earls and other royals, that the great King Elryk came to seal her fate.

In a surprising move, the king accused his own mistress of going *rogue* and secretly plotting to assassinate him. According to Elryk, not only was his former mistress a traitor to their kingdom, but she was also a heartless and ambitious wicked witch who deceived him. A femme-fatale who desired nothing more than to steal his crown by using her wicked *black* magic against him. Indeed, like a coward, Elryk claimed victimhood and then blamed their long-lasting extramarital affair as a result of Vera's enchanting seduction. A devious witch and a lustful whore who blinded him with dirty sex.

Caught entirely off guard, Vera was both shocked and horrified by his brutal accusations. It was untrue and hurtful. However, what could she say? How could she challenge such a false narrative? How could she ever defend herself against her king?

After all, Vera was entirely at *his mercy.* She was his mistress. His so-called love of his life. Plus, she was carrying *his child.* And yet, here they were.

Standing in front of the royal high court, accusing her of treason and above all else, ready to hang her… or worse… burn her alive at the stake. A damning public mockery of her so-called virtue and honor. And judging by their gruesome stares, Vera was as good a scum. A devious witch and wicked whore, who apparently, was secretly plotting to murder the great King of the West.

Fortunately, by the king's surprise mercy and direct order of decree, Vera, along with her bastard unborn child, were spared death. However, as a direct result of her so-called alleged crimes, they were sent into exile to the lands of Earth. Both mother and child.

After her shamefully public, disgraceful and embarrassing verdict, Vera was forcefully removed out of the palace. Afterwards, she was personally escorted by the king's guards and transported to Earth. Without so much as having the decency to bid farewell to her mother or even to Elryk himself… not that she ever wanted to see him again. But still, even a final goodbye was denied to her. It was both cruel and painful. An unforgiveable betrayal.

And so, this is how Vera came to live on Earth. As punishment for her accused crimes, she was sentenced to spend the remainder of her life on Earth and never again, to return to the Great Kingdom so long as she lived. As much as it pained her to accept her sad fate, Vera was a fighter. A survivor. Furthermore, given the fact that she was forced to live on Earth against her own will, Vera decided to use this rare opportunity to pay a visit to her estranged sister, Sarah.

But the most shocking of revelations were still to come. As Vera searched for her sister, she came to discover that Sarah had tragically died a few years back during childbirth. As a result, her surviving young son, Henry Galloway, was being subsequently raised by Maureen, along with the widowed earl, at Galloway Manor.

The news of Sarah's unexpected death was a crushing blow to her already troubled soul. Losing Elryk and being forced into exile was one thing, but at least Elryk was still alive and well. However, in Sarah's case, Vera was never going to see her sister, ever again. Sadly, it had been years since she last spoke to her. Saw her. Touched her. And now, after everything, Sarah was truly gone, forever. Her beloved sister was no longer of flesh and bone, existing within this earthly realm. All thanks to the Earl of Galloway and his precious heir, Henry.

Although Vera knew in her heart that she should have instantly loved Henry at first sight, for at the end of the day, he was Sarah's only son and her nephew; but tragically, she couldn't. Sadly, Vera couldn't find it within herself to accept and love him. After all, Henry was the true cause of Sarah's death. It was because of him, that Sarah died young, while giving birth. Henry was to blame for Sarah's early departure. The Earl of Galloway was to blame for impregnating her. Had Sarah never been pregnant, then maybe she'd still be around to live and see her. Maybe.

Men like the earl and Elryk, they used women like Sarah and her. They simply took and took and took, until there was nothing left for them to take. They used their bodies, while foolishly claiming ownership of their hearts. However, once they were done, they discarded them like a piece of trash. Her so-called love of her life, abandoned her in the middle of the enchanted forest, alone and pregnant. Whether she lived or died, it didn't matter to him. In the end, Vera could only depend on herself. And now, with this child growing within her belly, she was obligated to step up and save them both.

And so, acting upon vengeance, Vera's heart blackened overnight. And whatever little white magic she still had left in her, all but died on that fateful day out in the enchanted forest. Following the Earl of Galloway on his trip back east, she found and seduced him. Afterwards, she forced his hand into marriage. Even though he wasn't the biological father of her unborn child, she convinced him and his son, Henry, otherwise. And while Henry and Phillip grew up believing that they were half-brothers; they were in fact, actually first cousins. Meanwhile, as Henry came to accept Vera as his wicked stepmother, he remained entirely ignorant to the fact that she was also his maternal aunt, too. Ah, how little they knew of the actual truth…

There were many times when Vera seriously contemplated loving Henry. But in the end, she couldn't find it within her aching heart to forgive him. He might have been her beloved sister's only child and her nephew, but Henry was also the cause of Sarah's untimely death. And that fact alone, was entirely *unforgiveable*.

Apart from Elryk and the earl, Henry was her sworn *enemy*. She could *never* love or accept him... let alone show any real affection or compassion towards her nephew. Even if he was a young and innocent boy…

But the one and only time that she showed compassion for him, he'd been left entirely in the dark. It happened on one fateful day, when Vera secretly followed a young Henry and Maureen out into the woods as they visited Sarah's gravesite. Although Henry and Maureen presumed that Vera ordered Sarah's tombstone removal due to her evil jealousy over his late mother, the reality was that it couldn't have been any further from the actual truth.

No, Vera did not remove Sarah's tombstone out of jealousy due to the earl's affections for his first wife. In truth, Vera could care less about the earl's opinion or sentimental feelings for her. No, she did not remove Sarah's tombstone out of *hate*… but out of *love*. In the end, Vera removed it, because it was a constant and painful reminder of what *she alone, lost*. Her sister. Her best friend.

Losing her sister was one thing, but having it plastered in front of her face for all eternity was a whole another struggle. Seeing Sarah's name… her death date… her status as a loving wife and mother… with no mention of either herself or their mother… it fucking *killed her*. It *killed her* each and every time she looked at it. And so, Vera decided not look at it any longer. Therefore, it was removed by her command. A direct order of decree by the former Mistress of Galloway Manor.

But as she watched a young Henry kneel down and cry, something tugged away at her icy heart. She might have hated the boy, but clearly, he, like her, loved Sarah dearly. Their love for Sarah might have been the one and only thing that united them.

And so, as Vera silently watched Henry and Maureen plant their seeds of violets, Sarah's favorite flower, into the dirt ground, she unexpectedly smiled. For the first time in years, she was surprisingly happy to see something of familiarity. Even as young girls back in their childhood cottage, Sarah used to tease that Vera should have been named Violet. That unfortunately, she was bestowed with the wrong letter "V" name.

Meanwhile, as young Henry and Maureen departed Sarah's gravesite, Vera stayed behind and whispered a silent prayer in honor of her late sister's memory. And instead of having her sister lay in an unmarked grave, Vera decided to use her magic... for good... one last and final time.

Closing her eyes, she unleashed her last bit of white magic out freely into the air and with the flick of her hand, the newly planted seeds instantly grew overnight and blossomed into an enchanting field of magical violets, that stretched from one end of the meadow and to the other.

As a gift to her late sister, Vera blessed the field in memory of Sarah. And so, this is how Sarah's final resting place became enchanted with an endless supply of magical wild violets that grew along her borders in her honor. Furthermore, this is why our heroine, Violet Galloway, came to bear her name. It was all because of Vera's love for Sarah.

Years later, after her role in the earl's demise and with Phillip grown and gone from the nest, Vera was now ready to enact her quest for revenge. After a long period of waiting, she was finally eager to return back home to the Kingdom of the West. To at long last, see Elryk once again. The man who broke her heart and darkened her soul. But in order to do so, Vera needed to do one last and final act: enact the curse of the Dark Horseman.

Although Elryk's verdict ruled that Vera was obligated to remain as a prisoner on Earth for the remainder of her lifetime; however, had she died, then she'd have technically fulfilled her punishment. In the past, she previously contemplated taking her own life many times over. But, had Vera chosen the path of suicide, then her magic would have also died alongside with her.

Therefore, killing herself wasn't the correct answer. Instead, she required an alternative. Another person to claim her life. She needed a secondary person to murder her. And fortunately, for her, Henry was just going to have to be the lucky one to do it...

And so, Vera secretly conspired and plotted away. The enchanted forest needed a guardian and so, Vera gambled Henry's livelihood in exchange for her free passage back to her native realm. In the meantime, she gradually needed to make Henry resent her. To despise her. To hate her. To push him so far over the edge, that he'd have no other choice but to finish her off, once and for all.

To accomplish this, she shunned and alienated him from *everything*. From the time he was a young child, Vera consistently ignored and belittled him. She purposely drove a wedge between him and Phillip. By the time Henry grew up and left home, Vera made sure to claim the life of his father. It was only too easy. A simple horseback riding accident, followed by a generous dose of poison afterwards... and shortly thereafter, the Earl of Galloway was a goner.

Meanwhile, as Henry was off touring the continent, she made sure to rule Galloway Manor with an iron fist... using the same ruthless tactics that she now applied to the Kingdom of the West. Furthermore, Vera also used her own son, Phillip, as a pawn to steal Henry's fiancé, Julia, away from him.

Ah, yes, Vera was the most wicked of stepmothers. A horrible and ruthless aunt. A woman who wanted nothing more than for Henry to plunge his trusted dagger right through her blackened heart.

Eventually, when Henry returned back home to Galloway Manor on the eve of his wedding, Vera made sure to enact her curse. While he mistakenly took her attack as a means to kill him, nothing could have been further from the actual truth. In reality, Vera never desired to claim his life. Instead, she just wanted to push him over the edge. Press his buttons so hard, that he'd want nothing more than to murder her... out of his own free will....

In truth, Vera always calculated that her sister, Sarah, would eventually come to Henry's rescue on that fateful night of his curse. After all, she was his mother. Plus, Sarah possessed the purest of hearts. She'd save her son, even in the brinks of death.

In fact, its why she pleaded with her son not to kill Vera. It wasn't because Sarah feared about Henry not discovering a cure to his curse. In reality, Sarah always knew that one day in the future, Henry would eventually break his curse through the act of enduring true love. Sparing Vera's life had nothing to do with finding a cure to his curse, even though he was told otherwise. Saving Vera was to *protect her sister*. In the end, Sarah loved Vera unconditionally, just as much as she loved her, in return.

And so, Vera made a bargain with great mother nature, herself. In exchange for Henry to serve as the cursed Dark Horseman, she'd be allowed to return back to the Kingdom of the West. However, to do so, it required Henry's sacrifice. In the end, he needed to kill her.

Only upon her death, would Vera be permitted to return back to her homeland in a reanimated form. After all, it was never that simple to kill a witch. At least, a witch *not* willing to accept her fate and die out of her own *free will*. Only a witch *willing* to die could actually die.

As Vera predicted, a month later after his curse, Henry showed up right on time to her front door. The wheels were in motion and the trap was set. And as Henry plunged his dagger straight into her heart, Vera was finally freed... at long last...

Shortly afterwards, her spirit journeyed back to the Kingdom of the West, the very place where she had once called home. Upon reclaiming her physical form, Vera plotted her revenge. By then, her magic completely darkened, and she was now a full practitioner of black magic. But more than anything else, after dying and resurrecting back to life, Vera also became more powerful than ever before.

And so, this is how Vera rose to power: by stealing the magic of other witches and sorcerers along her journey to the top. To her credit, she gave her fellow magicians an option: surrender their magical powers freely and join her dark army, or refuse and die. Many opted for option two, but for those opting to stand by her, she granted them and their families' full sanctuary and protection, in exchange for stealing their magical powers.

Was it the correct thing to do? No, of course, not. It was absolutely dishonorable and morally corrupt. It was *pure evil*. But after everything that she endured over the years, Vera no longer cared. There was no turning back. Elryk, along with his kingdom, already painted her as the evil villainess long ago and so, she decided that she might as well live up to their poor expectations of her and not to leave them disappointed.

No longer was she the former exiled mistress and the mother to the king's bastard son. After years of plotting, she was now, a real and dangerous threat to Elryk's reign and all those who were considered nearest and dearest to him. From his lover to his enemy.

After forming her own rebellious dark army, Vera led a mass invasion straight into the heart of the royal palace. But to her surprise, when she finally came face-to-face with Elryk after all these long years, the old king stared at her... with *longing*... in his eyes. After *everything* that had transpired between them, he still *cared* for her. *Missed* her. *Loved* her.

He *ruined* her and yet, he still *loved* her. He *banished* her and yet, he still *missed* her. He *condemned* her and yet, he still *longed* for her. It was twisted, cruel and so incredibly *painful*. It was love in the sickest and ugliest of forms. Total corruption of the heart. A love so sour and bitter... and yet... she couldn't turn away from it... she couldn't escape from him...

For a brief moment, Vera almost considered abandoning her mission and reclaiming her undying love for him. But alas, she couldn't. He threw her away like she less than dirt, with no disregard to her or *their son*. In fact, in all her years spent away in exile, not once did he ever seek her out. Not once, did he apologize for his cruel actions towards her. Not once, did he care to inquire about *their* son. A son, whom he never bothered to meet. No, the damage was done. There was no returning back to their innocent lives before his betrayal. *His betrayal.* Not hers.

Over the years, Elryk had so many chances to make amends and yet, he did absolutely nothing. And now, it was too late. The damage was done. They were over. He was over... and so was his reign...

But before, Vera could end him, she gave herself to him, one last and final time. In memory of their forgotten love, she gave her body freely to him. And as Elryk passionately entered into her body and claimed her as his own, with each strong thrust in-between her thighs as she lay spread out within his golden bed, Vera discretely reached for her dagger from behind her back.

Meanwhile, as Elryk climaxed inside of her, Vera plunged her dagger deep into his unsuspecting heart. After everything that transpired between them in the past, she desperately wanted him to experience the same devastating pain of a broken heart. She wanted his heart to shatter into a million tiny pieces, just like he had broken hers all those many years ago.

And as he stared down at her in complete shock and horror, instead of fighting with her in his last moments of his life, Elryk instead, gave her the most startling of confessions. As he lied above her naked body with her bloody dagger plunged inside of his bleeding heart, he gathered his last bit of inner strength to finally confess the truth to her.

In his last final moments, Elryk apologized to her and their son. With a heavy heart, he told her that he never wished to send her away all those many years ago. That he regretted it each and every passing day, ever since.

That he'd been forced to against his will. Secretly, he was delighted when he first discovered that she was pregnant. He relished in the fact that he shared a child with her. She, the woman, whom he loved with all of his heart. A child born out of their true love.

But tragically, he was also the king. And a king with another child, regardless if they were born legitimate or a bastard, would always be a threat to the crown and his heir, Leopold. It was bad enough that he already struggled with the future of his second son, Maximus. However, a child born from the love of his life, mistress or not, then that child was always going to be destined for a life of danger.

What if that favored son grew up to be more loved and cherished by the king, instead of his other two sons? What if he desired to appoint Phillip, his preferred love child, over to the throne, instead of Leopold, his rightful heir? Or what if Phillip grew to become more popular amongst the people? What if the kingdom wanted Phillip as their next king, instead of Leopold or Maximus? What then? Unfortunately, too many possibilities often led to too much confusion and chaos. And historically, too much confusion and chaos generally led to brutal and savage civil wars.

According to Elryk, his high court voted to execute Vera, while she was still pregnant with Phillip. Elryk's decision to send her into exile wasn't as a form of punishment. Rather, it was a means to *save her* and their unborn child. In the end, Elryk sacrificed his own happiness for the safety of Vera and Phillip. No matter what, he *still* loved her. He *never stopped* loving her. He had *always loved her...*

Afterwards, Elryk peacefully died within her arms. For a long time, Vera just lied there, underneath him and cried. She cried and cried and cried. And when she was done crying, she cried some more. She cried to make up for all the lost years that she didn't cry. Alas, there was no point in hiding her tears or pain anymore. She allowed herself to continue to weep, until there were no more tears left in her dry eyes. And if her heart was broken before, then it was completely decimated by now.

While her plans always intended killing him, Vera never expected Elryk to apologize and admit all of these shocking revelations to her. To actually confess that he still loved her. That he loved her unconditionally... even as she plunged a dagger straight through his heart and watched him bleed to death, with his cock still buried inside of her.

Oh, how cruel fate had been to her! To them! His so-called betrayal was to protect her and their son! It was all for the sake of the goddamn crown! The pride of the crown! The integrity of the crown! Damn the fucking crown!

Since the crown *robbed* them of their happily ever after, then damn it all to hell! Let the kingdom all burn down! Let it all fall into ruin! Let them all pay for what the entire kingdom did to her! To them!

With Elryk now dead within her arms, Vera angrily vowed to steal the crown and bring all havoc into the kingdom... the land that *stole* their happiness. If she couldn't have a happily ever after, then neither could anyone else...

After Elryk's death, Vera, along with her dark army, quickly retreated from the palace and went into hiding. If she was going to steal the throne, then she needed to execute her plans very carefully. And so, this is why Vera came to murder Elryk's heir, Leopold, the former King of the West with a staged horseback riding accident. Furthermore, Vera could have also easily killed Elryk's younger son, Maximus, too, during the siege of the cathedral, but instead, she ultimately decided to let him go.

By then, Vera already stole his throne and crowned herself as the new queen. So long as Maximus behaved himself, then she'd have no further need to murder the son of her former lover. A harmless prince, who spent most of his life venturing outside the walls of the palace, rather than staying inside and learning how to actually rule it from within.

Just like her, they both had been unjustly painted as unworthy members of the palace. Once upon a time, Vera was the scandalous mistress, while Maximus was the forgotten prince... the unwanted legitimate son. Forget about Phillip, Maximus was practically raised a bastard, himself. She might have been known as the wicked witch and the evil queen, but he, too, was previously regarded to be a brute. Thus far, they were equals. They both embodied what the kingdom *wanted* them to be, but not necessarily, what they *chose* to be.

Suddenly, a knock came at the door. Two of her knights entered into the throne room, while dragging a third knight tightly by his neck. To Vera's surprise, the two men moved to throw the third man into the center of the room, faced down on the ground. Afterwards, they disgracefully removed his helmet. From the looks of it, their harsh actions spoke louder than their lack of words. A *traitor.* That's what he *must* have been.

"Your Highness, we've caught this one writing a letter addressed to the rebel prince," announced the standing knight to her right.

"Ah, I see," she replied with a devious smile. "It seems we've had a mole in our palace, after all."

"Yes," answered the second guard to her left.

"Apparently, all this time, Maximus and his army have been hiding in Ruby's castle," replied the knight.

"Ruby," Vera huffed in utter annoyance. "I see that she's *still* stirring up trouble for us."

"Very well," she began, with a careless wave of her hand, "Send the troops over to sack them all and be done with it."

"But," she interrupted, "Before you do, let's be sure to send a message first."

With a smirk across her wicked face, Vera's previous pale face now turned into a sinister shade of green. By now, her emerald eyes had completely transformed into the color yellow, as she unleashed her dark magic right into the open air.

"If they want an evil queen, then let's not disappoint them. It's showtime," she announced.

As much as Vera preferred to spend the remainder of her afternoon alone in peaceful silence; but instead, she was forced to perform on queue. After all, she had a reputation to protect and uphold. They wanted an evil queen and so, an evil queen was what they were going to get!

And so, with the twist of her hand, she released a flaming spark directly towards the fallen knight... leaving behind nothing but black smoke and a trail of ashes...

"Take these ashes and deliver them to the rebel prince. Let it serve as a warning to those who dare to threaten my crown and supreme authority," she ordered.

Finally, after the two knights exited the premise, Vera reclined back into her throne and adjusted her heavy golden crown above her head. Ah, it wasn't easy to be the queen.

Meanwhile, as she stared away at her bouquet of violets, she sighed to herself. Anything that reminded her of Sarah made her interiors soft, much to her great disappointment. One day, those violets really were going to be the death of her.

# CHAPTER 12

The atmosphere might have been lovely and the music serene, but for Violet, neither atmosphere nor music was enough to satisfy her intense desire to flee from this dreadfully jolly scene. For at this precise moment, she found herself at the head of the banquet table and seated right next to the infamous crown prince and soon-to-be-king, Maximus.

Their bargain was simple: she lost their sword fight and now, she was forced to suffer the consequences of their wager. A seat beside him each night was more than enough to poke fun at both her patience and pride. But to be actually forced to spend every passing night as his chaperone, now that really was too much to bear!

After he last kissed her, Violet desperately tried her best to keep her distance away from him. It was bad enough that she was forced to serve as his constant companion to their nightly banquets. However, wherever she traveled to within the castle's grounds, his presence was all around her. Like a constant shadow that never failed to disappear, no matter how much light was shined upon it.

One way or another, Maximus was always there, just waiting for her. Standing tall and proud, wherever she happened to be. Either that, or leaning against something that was close by to her. A wall. A tree. Even a horse. Anything that surrounded her, he was always there beside it. That, along with his stupidly wicked but handsome grin. A smile that could trap and enslave a thousand women at first glance. All the while, desperately striving to gain a reaction from her. To provoke her. To wait for her impending attack. To hit him. To punch him. To do *anything* really…

So long as she touched him, then he'd have a motive to wrestle back with her. A reason to kiss her... *yet again.* And for Violet's sake, she couldn't risk kissing him anymore. After all, she had too much pride for that. Kissing him meant defeat, and Violet wasn't yet ready to surrender her heart to the brutish prince. No matter how dashingly handsome and charming he might have been.

Ah yes, the sly crown prince always just-so-happened to be around, wherever Violet traveled to. From the second floor to the first, to the garden and courtyard, and even to Ruby's laboratory, Maximus was all around. Although he claimed that his appearance was nothing more than purely *accidental,* Violet knew better. After all, his nickname was Maximus, the Brute. Obviously, he earned it, for better or for worse. Mainly, for *worse.*

Her troubles all began one day, while Violet was visiting the garden to get some much-needed fresh air. It was there, outside, where she saw Maximus already standing and waiting for her. Determined, he leaned against a tall oak tree with his arms folded against his chest, while sporting a devilish grin painted across his charming face. And as he cornered her, Maximus challenged her to another duel. A chance to win back her freedom. To end their nightly companionship.

Naturally, Violet accepted his challenge. And so, as Violet swung away using her sword, not only did she lose their second match, but she also managed to learn some new fighting moves from him, along the way. Eventually, once her sword fell crashing down in defeat, instead of kissing her again; this time around, Maximus offered her his hand and summoned her to return back the following day for a rematch.

And so, on that day forward, Violet became Maximus' official new sparring partner. As a result, Violet's daily sparring matches with the crown prince not only allowed her to strengthen her own swordsmanship skills and techniques, but it also helped her to better train and prepare for any potential future combats as well.

But their time spent together didn't just stop there. No, instead, Maximus also cornered Violet at the horse stables, too. Although she was already an excellent equestrian, he convinced her that her leisure riding style wasn't a match for a real battle. Horseback riding through the park was an entirely different sport rooted in recreational activities, as opposed to riding war horses used to fight in fierce battles.

And so, much to her dismay, Violet reluctantly accepted yet another round of Maximus' training. Alas, apart from their daily sparring matches, she now, was forced to add horsemanship practice to their ever-growing list of shared activities, too.

Now, one might presume that between Ruby's daily magic lessons and Maximus' sparring and horseback training, that Violet's schedule was already overbooked. But sadly, no, Maximum didn't think that same way. If anything, according to him, her schedule was *too underwhelming*. Instead, he wanted her trained on *everything*. But most importantly, he wanted to *personally* train her, himself. After all, she was the savior. And so, came forth more lessons concerning...

*Wrestling...*

*Archery....*

*Hunting...*

*Knife throwing...*

*First Aid...*

*Running...*

*Kick boxing...*

*Strategies on war and conquest...*

*And not to mention...*

*Dancing...*

Ah, yes, apparently, Violet's dancing skills were less than ideal. Even as the daughter of an earl, Violet might have been an exceptional dancer in twentieth century British society; however, that form of dancing was no match for Maximus' world. Dancing in the Kingdom of the West was a foreign art. Plus, being a foreigner in this strange realm, Violet needed to quickly adapt to her new environment. Thus, she needed to learn both their local customs and dances to fit in.

If she had been a doll, then she was *his* doll. His playful experiment. His personal solider. And in truth, Violet never played with dolls before. In fact, she never liked them. Nor, her younger brother's toy soldiers, too, for that matter.

But as much as Violet tried to hide her annoyance concerning Maximus, gradually, those repressed feelings began to evolve. Each time they met across at the field, she felt a little less troubled by his overall presence. Slowly, but surely, Violet was slightly growing more tolerable of him. Dare she admit it, even accustomed to him?

From their daily sparring matches to their practice laps ridden around the horse track, to their rehearsed dances and even, down to their wrestling tournaments, each time, Maximus was growing less of an annoyance and more like... a... real... *friend...*

He might have been her trainer, but she also confided in him, too. After all, as long as she spoke and carried on with any real conversations with him, then it also helped to serve as a distraction from him kissing her. And God only knows he tried! On *many, many* occasions, too!

But early on, Violet understood that as long as she spoke, he listened. Truly listened. From her childhood adventures to her stories about her crazy younger siblings and her family, to her experiences spent away at university, to her hopes, dreams and aspirations about her future. As long as Violet spoke, Maximus carefully took his time to listen to her. And for that alone, she was truly grateful.

And so, this is how Violet avoided Maximus' kisses, but along the way, she might have also risked losing her heart in the process, too...

The day that finally changed her feelings about him magically happened out of the blue. One afternoon, they were wrestling outside in the meadow, when she managed to throw a punch to his stomach. Mistakenly, Violet missed and accidentally fell forward towards him. Unfortunately, they were standing near the foot of a small hill. And so, as Violet fell, Maximus caught her in his arms and together, they tumbled down the hill.

By the time they crash-landed down at the bottom of the hill, Violet found herself entangled around him in an embrace. Surprisingly, she was lying right above him and he, underneath her. And as she stared down into his silvery grey eyes, for the first time since their initial meeting, her heart suddenly skipped a beat.

Alas, no longer did she dread his embrace, but she actually took pleasure in it! It felt *good* to have his arms wrapped around hers. It felt *nice*. *Pleasant. Comforting.* And she didn't want this warm feeling to go away. She didn't want him to stop holding her. Touching her. Possibly kissing her. Really, they were so incredibly close, that had she so much as moved just one inch forward, then she'd have landed right onto his bare lips. But then...

Suddenly, he pulled them back up, dusted her off and once again, they were back to wrestling. It was one of the most *unromantic* experiences that she had ever had the displeasure to endure! Here she was, inches away from actually kissing him; but instead, she was back to square one. Being his toy solider.

But then, came the most startling revelation of all: she really *wanted* to kiss him! Unlike before, she wasn't forced to accidentally kiss him. This time around, Violet truly wanted to kiss him, out of her own free will. But at the same time, if she tried to kiss him now, then wouldn't he get the wrong idea? After all, it's not like she wanted to be with him, right?

Flash forward to weeks later, Violet was now seated beside Maximus at the banquet table. Even with the lovely atmosphere and serene music, Violet felt anything but peaceful. She was nervous. After hating Maximus for so long, she no longer knew how to conduct herself around him. Especially, once she started to... well... *like him...*

Because that's how she felt now. She *liked* Maximus. She *liked* him a whole *lot*. He might have started out as her knight in shining armor and then, turned into the detestable and brutish heartbreaker; but afterwards, he became her trainer, then her friend... and now... well... she didn't really know who he was to her anymore…

He might have been the crown prince to the rest of the guests at this banquet, but Violet wasn't a part of his world. Of his kingdom. She was supposed to be a stranger to him, and he to her. But somewhere, along the way, he became so much more. He became someone, whom her heart secretly clung to.

And then, it was time to dance. As Maximus escorted Violet onto the dance floor, she took in a deep breath and smiled.

"You look lovely night," he whispered into her ear, as he took her hand and got into position, ready to start the next dance.

"Thank you. It's your dress, by the way. According to Ruby, you picked out this emerald gown for me to wear. A gown to match my eyes and complement my necklace," she whispered right back to him.

"Ah, yes, that's right. And I'm glad you wore it, too. Sometimes, I forget how lovely you are, when dressed as a proper lady. Nowadays, I think I'm more accustomed to seeing you wearing a coat of armor with your hair braided. That, along with a generous amount of mud splashed across your face," he laughed on.

"Mud or no mud, I can still kick your ass outside or indoors," she hissed.

And then, he laughed once more.

"Yes, I do believe you can," he agreed, with a warm smile.

And then, from across the room, Violet saw another pretty blonde wink at him, to which, Maximus graciously smiled back at her in return. Ever since she made him vow not to disrespect her by flirting with other women in her presence, to Maximus' credit, he surprisingly kept his word. But at the same time, he was also most unfortunately, the crown prince, too.

Naturally, there were always going to be women vying for his attention and practically, throwing themselves at his direction. Even though Violet preferred to slap that blonde maiden right across her face, but at the same time, she also couldn't fault Maximus, either. For him to ignore her would also be rude. After all, she was one of his future subjects. Plus, he was single, too. It's not like Violet meant anything more to him, other than serving as his key partner in defeating Vera, right?

As the music played on, the couple started to dance. As they twirled around the floor, Violet accidentally brushed up against his face. But instead of backing away, she took an extra step closer.

"Careful Violet," he warned. "Any closer and I'll be forced to kiss you."

"Actually, this time, I don't think that I'd mind... *so much*," she admitted and then, blushed.

With that honest admission, plus the redness found on her complexion, her choice of words certainly caught his attention. In fact, as a result of that surprise confession, his heart nearly stopped beating altogether.

But rather than second guessing her spoken words; Maximus seized this rare opportunity. Instantly, he pulled her closer to him. Slowly, he bent down, with the full intention of kissing her. Meanwhile, Violet closed her eyes shut and waited for his magical kiss. But unfortunately, for her, that kiss simply couldn't be... at least, not for now...

Suddenly, the doors flew open and several knights entered into the premise. A second later, the crowd began to make noise and chatter from amongst themselves. Violet concluded that if the knights managed to arrive unannounced to disrupt their nightly celebration, then it must have been urgent news.

Quickly, Maximus brought Violet safely over to his side, while his attention shifted to his knight now standing in front of him. Whatever happened, it was crucial to hear.

"Your Highness," he spoke, as he kneeled down to bow before the prince.

"Yes, Sir Drake. What is it?" asked Maximus.

His knight looked concerned. Whatever the message was, it certainly made Maximus nervous.

As the knight rose back up to his feet, he presented Maximus with a black ceramic jar. At first glance, Violet wasn't sure what it was. However, her initial impression was that it might have been some sort of an urn.

"Sir Thomas has been executed," he announced, in despair.

Almost immediately, the entire audience gasped in both surprise and fear.

"Sir Drake, what do you mean? Who's responsible for his death?" asked Maximus, angrily.

"Queen Vera. She discovered that he was one of our spies, and she killed him for it. Burned him alive. Turning his mutilated body into nothing more but ashes."

And then, Sir Drake took another step forward and presented Maximus with the urn.

"Here lies his remains. The queen sends this to serve as a warning to those who dare to challenge her supreme authority and regime," he conveyed.

"Damn her to hell!" Maximus yelled, in rage.

This was the first time that Violet had ever seen him look so incredibly upset. Enraged. And rightfully so, too. Queen Vera might have stolen his throne, but now, she also just proved herself to be a heartless and cold-blooded killer, too. Sir Thomas' ashes only proved that point exactly.

But before Maximus could take hold of the urn, another knight appeared at the door. He was out of breath. Clearly, he had been running.

"Your Highness, I'm afraid that I've got some bad news," he announced.

"More?" asked Maximus, in frustration.

"Queen Vera's army has arrived. They've just broken through the gates."

And then to everyone's horror, he added, "We're under attack."

Without so much as a flinch or a bat of the eyelash, Maximus turned his attention over to Violet and with a warm smile, he said, "I guess it's time to finally put your new sword skills to the test, after all, huh Violet? For both our sakes, I hope you're ready."

And so, begins the epic battle fought between good v. evil...

# CHAPTER 13

"**L**ive, so you can kiss me again," he told her.

A ridiculous promise for the future, but a promise either way. A reason to survive. Motivation. To fight. Anything to stay alive.

"Same goes for you, too," she said right back to him, in return.

"Deal," he vowed.

"Deal," she vowed.

And then, they shook each other's hands in agreement. Afterwards, they each grabbed their respective swords nearby and prepared to exit the banquet hall together.

Unfortunately, for Violet, wearing a formal emerald silk evening gown was less than ideal for fighting. Oh, how she wished she wore her armor suit tonight, instead! Or at the very least, some trousers underneath this damn dress!

Suddenly, the room fell silent, once again. Promptly, Maximus turned his attention over to his commanding knight, standing in front of him.

"Sir Rowan, please gather as many civilians as you can. Escort them down into the tunnels for safe passage," Maximus quickly ordered.

Instantly, Sir Rowan took off running. Afterwards, Maximus addressed his second knight in command.

"Derek, take Violet and follow Plan B," is all he said.

"Wait," cried Violet, upon hearing her name.

"What precisely are your plans concerning *me*?" she demanded.

"We're going to escort you and everyone else down safely into the tunnels, while my knights and I stay behind to fight off Vera's army."

"Are you honestly telling me that you're intending to stay? To personally fight alongside with your men? But you're the crown prince! You shouldn't be here by yourself!" she passionately advised him.

"Come with me, instead," Violet pleaded, as she quickly grabbed a hold of his hand.

"I can't," Maximus breathed, as he pulled his hand away from her tight grip.

"No matter my fate, either way, my place is with my men," he declared.

And then, Violet finally acknowledged that although Maximus might have been a man of many things; however, in the end, he was by far, a man deeply rooted in his honor. A chivalrous knight, if ever she saw one. Regardless of the dire circumstances lay out before them, Maximus would never abandon his men, despite the outcome. Even if it meant risking his own life to protect them. No matter how hard Maximus tried to desensitize himself to their cause, he really was a *hero*.

"But follow Derek," he ordered. "He'll take you down with the rest. Please, whatever you do Violet, be safe."

"No," she boldly replied.

"What?" Maximus asked in surprise.

"If you fight, then I'll fight alongside with you!" she informed him.

Her words felt like an arrow piercing right through his very soul. Alas, he was absolutely stunned. Speechless, even.

"It's not safe," he finally got the courage to say. "You're the savior. It's my sworn duty to protect you. To keep you safe, at all costs."

"If I'm the savior, then *I* should be the one doing the *saving*. Not just you," she pointed out.

"Besides, I'm not going to leave my sparring partner behind to fight our battles alone," she retorted. "Especially, when I've recently kicked his ass and won the last two matches."

But the reminder of their last two matches completely bypassed Maximus' attention. Instead, he focused solely on her mere mention of their battles.

"*Our* battles?" he blinked.

"Yes, *our* battles," she clarified.

Never before, did he have someone choose to *stay* by his side. To actually *willingly* help him to fight. Heck, forget about his battles, he never had a real partner to help in on *anything* before. Not even at the royal palace, during his youth. Apart from his elder brother, Violet was the only other person who genuinely had his back. To care about his general welfare. To be his one and only true friend.

And then, to his surprise, Violet placed her sword down onto the floor. Without any warning, she grabbed the bottom left hem of her gown and began ripping off the edges, pulling the torn fabric moving upwards. Once done, she repeated the same process on her right side, too. Afterwards, there were two slits made to each side of her now tattered gown, exposing her two naked bare thighs and legs.

"For better mobility," she winked at him.

Slowly, as Maximus was coming to discover, Violet was full of surprises. And for once, he rather liked being surprised for a happy change.

"Are you sure that you really want to do this with me?" he hesitated to ask her again.

"Yes," she confidently replied.

Although Maximus wasn't pleased by her decision to stay behind to fight in this upcoming battle; however, watching a feisty female knight fight alongside him was such a rare and enchanting sight to behold. Truly, it was a real dream come true for him.

"Fine," he sighed. "But we don't have time to gather any extra supplies or armors. We'll just have to make do with what we've already got. Stay close to my side, at all times. One way or another, we'll have to fight, together. It's the only way we'll be able to make it through, safely."

"Agreed," Violet answered.

And together, they finally exited the banquet and made their way over to the front entrance gates of the castle.

As they reached the outside grounds, they saw the once lively and enchanting garden replaced by a sea of knights, fighting on both sides. Silver metallic uniforms on Maximus' side v. black knights on Vera's. Silver v. Black. Good v. Evil. Already, it was a bloody and gruesome battlefield. A new unholy war unleashed. And the fate of the entire kingdom, all rested upon their shoulders.

"Stay close," he whispered to her, as they stood back-to-back. "And if anyone comes near you, then don't be afraid to swing away. Exactly, as I taught you."

"I promise," Violet vowed.

And then, it was showtime.

❊　❊　❊

With all her might, Violet swung her heart away. After weeks of practice, it was finally time to put her swordsmanship skills into action. As she battled the black knight before her, Violet swung her sword forward, while simultaneously studying her opponent's footsteps. If she could somehow track his pace, then hopefully, she'd be able to make her moves to corner him.

Unfortunately, for Violet, her opponent was far too fast to keep up with. Before she knew it, she accidentally lost her balance and tumbled straight down. And as she lied there motionless on the ground, Violet watched as her enemy aimed his sword towards her, ready to strike at her neck. However, following the swift moves that Maximus had previously taught her, Violet stretched her legs and kicked at his feet, tripping him down almost immediately. And thus, giving Violet enough time to run away.

But as she ran, Violet saw an arrow fly right by her. Miraculously, it managed to miss her arm. However, it inadvertently struck her opponent, instead; which in return, brought him falling back down, right onto the ground for a second time.

However, her good luck was only temporary. Soon after, a second arrow flew by... and then a third... and afterwards, a fourth. Fortunately, they all managed to miss her. However, by the time a fifth arrow was released into the air, Violet saw that this time, it was headed towards Maximus! Currently, he was standing and fighting right next to her.

"Look out!" she screamed.

But unfortunately, he did not hear her. And so, Violet had no other choice, but to reach for his hand and pull him aside.

As soon as she moved them, the arrow struck Maximus' opponent, instead. Immediately, he fell straight down onto the ground, with the arrow piercing right through his heart. Killing him, instantly.

"You saved my life," he breathed in amazement.

"Yes, I did. And now, we've got to keep on moving," she insisted.

"There's too many of Vera's men. Most of our knights are already underground in the tunnels. We don't have enough people up here to take them all out," he admitted in defeat.

"Then, we go. We flee. We can't stay here in this sinking ship. Think of your people."

"You're right. And I've got to—"

But before Maximus could finish his words, another black knight suddenly appeared. Within the blink of an eye, Violet was gone. Abducted. And now, she and her captor were fleeing the scene, with Violet trapped within his arms.

"Help! Maximus!" Violet cried, as she tried to kick and scream.

Witnessing Violet in danger, made Maximus see all red. A rage, so violent and fierce, it grew deep within his soul. It was as if his inner beast had finally been released. All hell was about ready to break loose!

Instantly, Maximus ran like the wind and chased them down. Like a hunter, he cornered them against an oak tree and swiftly yanked Violet out from his enemy's arms. Once her feet were safely back down onto solid ground, Maximus cursed all that was holy, as he punched the living daylight out of that black knight. And thus, leaving his helmet smashed with several dents, along with a trail of blood dripping down the back of his head. Alas, he was out cold on the ground, if he wasn't already dead.

"We need to go," she cried.

Without saying so much as another word, Maximus scooped up Violet straight into his arms and threw her face forward behind him, placing her entire body over his shoulder. Even though Violet did not expect such treatment, she was nevertheless, grateful to him. After all, he did save her. And God only knows what would have become of Violet had Maximus not rescued her.

However, to her surprise, instead of running alongside with him, he actually carried her away! But after her most recent attack, Violet no longer cared to question anything that Maximus felt compelled to do. Instead, she trusted his actions. After everything that they had recently endured today, Violet decided to place her faith and overall welfare into his care.

And so, with Violet safely tucked away within his arms, the couple fled straight ahead into the forest. And as he ran, he carried her as if she was the most precious thing in the entire world.

# CHAPTER 14

"**M**aximus, I think it's safe to put me back down, now," Violet pointed out.

And yet, he chose to ignore her request. *Again.*

They had walked about a mile away from Castle Hope... no... correction, *he walked*; whereas, *she was carried*. Held tightly by his strong and sturdy arms, as they wandered deep into the woods. Cradling her so carefully against his chest, as if she were a fragile doll. Like she was the world's most precious jewel. Ah, if only he had treated her more like his toy solider again. At least that way, she'd have the freedom to travel using her own two feet!

"Maximus...," she sighed.

"Not until the path is clear," he answered her. "I'm not taking any more chances. I... I... almost lost you back there."

His words struck a chord with her. He sounded so utterly heartbroken. It was almost as if the very thought of something happening to her... actually... well... *crushed him.*

"It's okay. I'm okay. You're okay. We're both okay," she reminded him.

"Not yet," he insisted. "There could still be enemy soldiers hiding in these trees."

"Then, we'll fight them off together. Both you and I."

"For once, can't you allow me to be the charming and courageous prince? Maybe, *I* actually *want* to be your knight in shining armor. Perhaps, that's my purpose."

"Wait, what? Are you serious?" Violet asked him, in confusion.

Was he really interested on courting her? Romancing her? Charming her?

"A knight in shining armor? Isn't that a role reserved to woo a princess? The last I noticed, I wasn't a princess," she pointed out.

"Perhaps, for now. But maybe, that won't always be the case. Maybe, you'll one day capture the heart of a prince."

"Let me guess, he'll marry me and therefore, make me his princess? Is that what you're implying?"

"There are worse fates," he shrugged.

And then, he added, "But wouldn't you want to be a princess? Isn't that every young girl's dream? Their hopes and aspirations? To grow up and marry a real-life royal prince?"

"Well, unless the other royals in the Kingdoms of the East, North or South are available, then I don't think I'm going to have much luck. Apart from you, I don't know any other prince. Especially, back in England."

"But back to your original question about my dreams," she continued, "Actually, I don't really know what I aspire to be or do."

"Really?" he asked, in surprise. "And pray tell, what did you imagine yourself being or doing?"

And *that* was *the* million-dollar question. Up until now, Violet's purpose in her young adult life was unclear. It's why she struggled back at home. But a chance to be a savior, well that certainly felt like a legitimate purpose. However, once this war ended and she was forced to return back home, Violet wasn't really sure about her next step. What else lay out before her, at the end of this road? What did she really want out of life? Or whom, did she want to share the rest of her own life with?

"Honestly, I'm not really sure," she admitted.

Her sincere words struck a chord with him. Maximus, like her, also previously struggled to find his rightful place in the world. Except now, once this war was fought and won, he'd be forced to become the one thing that he never imagined himself becoming: the king.

"You know, up until now, that's how I felt, too," he also admitted. "In the past, I never knew where I fit in, exactly."

"But you're a royal prince. *The* crown prince. Your place is at your court. Alongside, with your people," she pointed out.

"Yes, my people *now*. But they weren't always my people," he revealed. "Once upon a time, I was a second born son to a king. From birth, I was an unwanted son, without a role... without a proper function. But everything changed, once my father and brother died. And then, come overnight, I went from a brute to a crown prince and the accidental heir to the throne. That's when *I belonged* to them. That's when I was *given* a purpose. Officially designated as their hero and not a moment before. A hero and soon-to-be-king by default."

"And how do you feel about that?" she asked softly.

"Nothing, apart that it's my duty. But..."

"But what?" Violet asked curiously.

"I'm just afraid that once I reach that golden throne, then I'm going to discover something that I've long suspected..."

"Which is?" she hesitated to ask.

"That it's going to be a lonely seat. And I think..."

"You think...," she repeated.

"I think that when that day comes…"

"Yes…"

"I'm going to miss *my Violet* by my side."

And then, her heart practically stopped beating altogether. Did he really just say what she thought he said? That he'd miss her? That he wanted her by his side? That she was *his Violet*. Could that mean…

"You stopped talking," he reminded her. And thus, killing their prolonged moment of blissful silence.

"I… I… you just took me by surprise, that's all," she blushed.

"I meant what I said," he confirmed. "When this is all over and done, I'm going to miss you."

"I'm going to miss you, too," she blurted out.

"I'm going to miss our sparring matches… our horseback ridings… our dance rehearsals… our dinners… our chats… I'm going to miss it *all*."

"I think I'm going to miss it all, too."

"And that's why I can't put you back down," he admitted. "I almost lost you back there. And Violet, if you were truly gone, then there wouldn't be any more sparring matches or dancing or wrestling…"

"Or everything else in-between," she finished his sentence.

"And I don't want to lose you, like my brother. He was all I had in this wretched world, before you came along."

"Okay, if you want to be my knight in shining armor, then you should at least start by wearing a proper suit of armor," Violet teased him, as she finally gave into his demands and decided to humor him for a refreshing change.

Obviously, when they fled the banquet at last notice, Maximus had no time to change into his knight's uniform. And neither did she, either.

"Next time," he promised her, with a beaming smile.

"But Maximus...."

"Yes?" he asked.

"If you insist on carrying me, then how will we ever share that kiss? I believe I was promised one, so long as we survived the siege."

"Ah, so you remembered," he replied, impressed by her dedicated memory.

"But tell me," Maximus said, "Do you see a lake straight up ahead?"

"Actually, yes I do," she answered.

"Good, then the path is clear."

Instantly, he dropped her back down onto the ground. But before she had a chance to even regain her balance, he already had her wrapped up within his arms. Slowly he bent down and as Violet closed her eyes shut, she found herself lost in the moment.

Unlike their previous kisses, this kiss was soft and tender. Sweet and gentle. It was a kiss not born out of passion, but of affection. It was a kiss rooted in something deep and meaningful. If he was showing her his heart, then he was proving it by his latest kiss. It was, without a doubt, the best kiss of her entire life.

"Ahem," spoke a female voice.

Instantly, Violet reopened her eyes and to her surprise, she saw Ruby standing right in front of them. Conveniently, she was leaning against a wooden door to what looked to be a small cottage out in the woods. Funny, Violet hadn't even bothered to have noticed the cottage being there before. Either way, Ruby didn't seem too pleased by the sight of Violet wrapped tightly around Maximus' arms. Judging by the looks of it, Ruby appeared impatiently annoyed.

"You two are late," she scolded them, with her arms crossed against her chest.

# CHAPTER 15

"Late? We hardly escaped alive!" cried Violet.

"Relax, Violet, I was always going to get you out of there," Maximus interrupted her, hoping to calm her nerves.

"Violet, welcome to Plan C," added Ruby.

"Plan C? What, this cottage?" asked Violet, with a raised brow.

"Why don't you two come inside, so we can talk," Ruby advised them, as she led the way into a small thatched roof hovel, located on the outskirts of the forest.

* * *

An hour later, Violet found herself sitting at a wooden table, located in the far corner of what appeared to be a dusty old home. This tiny cottage was situated in the heart of the forest... in quite frankly... out in the middle of nowhere...

From the outside view, the cottage appeared to be a simple and humble abode.  A perfect place fit for the setting of a classical fairy tale. The structure was made from blocks of grey stone, along with a thatched straw roof. In addition, the property also maintained a medium sized yard at the front. The yard included a full cabbage patch, plus a small garden consisting of freshly grown mint, lemons, rosemary, sage, thyme and other essential herbs.

Furthermore, the property was surrounded by hundreds of trees on all of its four corners, encircling it like an island. Overall, it was a simple, old-fashioned and modest cottage. Nothing too luxurious or glamorous, to be sure. Most certainly, it wasn't another grand castle or a palace-like estate fit for a future king. But regardless of its appearance, it was shelter. A place to camp out. And in the end, that's all that really mattered. Somewhere safe to stay, along with a roof over their heads.

But apart from its humble outer appearance, the cottage's interiors were just as equally plain and simple, too. For the most part, it was *bare*. It was a one level darkened flat, with two miniature windows: one located in the main living quarters and the other, at the back of the house.

Furthermore, apart from the wooden table situated in the far corner of the flat, the rest of the furniture in the main living quarters consisted of no more than four chairs and a single black cauldron that was kept inside the center of the fireplace. From what Violet could tell, there also seemed to be only a single bedroom at the property, which appeared to house three separate beds in one room. So much for privacy!

"Here's your cup of tea," Ruby announced, as she handed a warm mug over to Violet and then took a seat across from her at the table.

"Drink up and enjoy," she said. "Starting tomorrow, we're going to have much longer days ahead of us."

Graciously, Violet took a sip of her tea. It was warm and comforting. Mint tea, with a slice of lemon. In the past, she seldom drank herbal tea. Back in England, it was primarily Earl Grey with a dash of milk. But mint with lemon was a refreshing change that Violet welcomed wholeheartedly. After all, she was grateful to be here. Sitting down, peacefully drinking tea with Maximus and Ruby. *Alive.*

"Thank you for the tea," Violet spoke. "But do you think it's safe for us to remain here? To calmly sit and not keep on moving? Surely, someone will find us soon enough?"

"Not quite," Maximus remarked, as he took a seat beside her.

The thing about this cottage was that not only was the property ghastly small, but so was its furniture. Including the chairs. While the chairs might have been a decent size for Violet and Ruby, the same could not be equally said with regards to the crown prince.

Therefore, when six-foot-tall plus Maximus decided to sit down on a chair that was truly designed for an adolescence, he looked entirely out of place. In fact, his legs overstretched outwards awkwardly and dangled forward onto the floor. Meanwhile, the back of the chair was limited to only supporting his rear behind. As it currently stood, if Maximus were to make another unexpected move, then the legs to his chair was surely going to collapse and snap broken into pieces!

"Damn chair," Maximus huffed in annoyance, as he struggled to get more comfortable.

"Your Majesty, you know, you could always sit on the floor, instead," Ruby laughed on.

To which, Violet couldn't help but giggle, too.

"Very funny, Ruby," he sighed. "But after today's excitement, I'll take my chances."

And then, he reached over and took a sip of his tea.

"Suit yourself, your grace," said Ruby.

"Anyways," Maximus continued on, "Not to worry, Violet. I promise, we're safe here."

"But how can you be so certain?" she pressed on. "Surely, Vera's army will discover our location? And when she does, it's only a matter of time before she captures us!"

"No, she won't," Ruby interrupted her. "And even if she wanted to, she *can't*."

"Can't? But how?" asked Violet in surprise.

"Because this cottage is enchanted," Ruby revealed. "It's a blessed home that is completely immune to any of Vera's dark spells. One hundred percent."

"It's protected by an ancient sort of magic that Vera wouldn't dare to challenge," she continued on, "As long as we're here, then we are all perfectly safe. Think of this place as a sanctuary located deep inside of the remote woods. And besides, even if Vera wanted to come, she wouldn't have the heart to step a foot in here, either. Neither her, nor her men. I promise, you are safe."

"But Ruby, how can you be so convinced that Vera wouldn't challenge this rule? Nothing has ever stopped her before," Violet pointed out.

"I know for certain, because once, a long time ago, I was her teacher. And a teacher never forgets about her student," Ruby confessed.

"Her teacher?" Violet repeated in amazement.

She was stunned, just absolutely astonished by this shocking confession. Ruby was such a nice old witch. A *good* witch. But how could a good witch, also be the former teacher to someone... who was so... so... *evil?*

"Ruby is the best sorceress in all the land," Maximus explained. "She's a well-respected professor in her field. Over the years, she's taught many students, and I assure you, Violet, that none of her former or current students have ever gone rogue. Vera is simply the exception."

"So, what made her become so evil? What snapped?" asked Violet, most curiously.

"A lot of things, but none of which should concern you at the present," said Ruby.

"Moving forward, we need to refocus on your training," she continued on.

"Starting tomorrow, we're going full fledge with your lessons. The mornings will be reserved with me, while your afternoons will be spent with him. Maximus and I have already discussed about your schedule thoroughly."

"My afternoons with Maximus? But I thought that my combat training with him was already done?"

And then, Violet turned her attention over to him and said, "No disrespect, Maximus, but I believe we've already had a fair share of matches. Don't you agree?"

But Maximus was unmoved by her suggestion. Especially, after today's siege. No, after their latest battle, he was more convinced than ever that their training was still essential. More was yet to come.

"I'm sorry Violet, but I cannot agree with your suggestion," he stated, most seriously.

"Like it or not, as long as Vera sits on my throne, then your life will always be in danger," he told her. "While I vow to protect you at all costs; but at the same time, I'd also be a damned fool, if I actually believed that there won't come another time when I won't be around to personally save you. And if you were to ever face a real threat on your own, then I need to be absolutely certain, without a shadow of a doubt, that you'll be ready to face these unforeseeable challenges. Therefore, I must do everything in my power to ensure that you can defend yourself, in my absence. Remember, like I said before, magic isn't everything."

"His Highness is right," Ruby interjected. "Violet, my dear, you're going to need all of the training that you can possibly get and more, while you still can. Think of it as a mini holiday. As we hide out here for a bit, it will also give you the blessed opportunity to sharpen your skills. Strengthen all of *our* skills, too."

"But what about the others? Are they also safe, too? What about the remaining knights and ordinary citizens back at Castle Hope? What of them?" asked Violet, out of concern.

"The survivors should have already relocated to our hidden underground tunnels. With my men by their side, they will be looked after and cared for," he answered confidently.

"That was Plan A, by the way," added Ruby.

"So, what was Plan B?" asked Violet.

"Us joining them," replied Maximus.

"Which brings us to Plan C, the cottage," Ruby chimed in.

"Ah, I see," Violet acknowledged. Slowly, it was starting to all piece together.

And then, Maximus gazed into her emerald green eyes and asked, "Are you satisfied, now?"

"What can I say, I suppose I am," replied Violet, in all honesty. "If this is going to be home for the next foreseeable future, then I'll..."

"*We'll* make the best of it," he finished her sentence, followed by a warm smile.

"We're a team, aren't we?" she asked him, with a smile of her own.

And as Maximus gazed into Violet's emerald green eyes, he reached over and placed his hand over hers. Truly, it was a heartfelt moment. And had they been anywhere else, then Violet was most certain that he would have kissed her on the spot. But alas, they weren't alone. And with Ruby intensely staring at them, she was quick to kill their romantic moment.

"Enough of that you two," Ruby huffed in annoyance, as she rose-up from her chair. "It's almost supper time, and I'm going to need Violet's help to prepare."

"Oh, and pray tell, what's on tonight's menu?" asked Maximus, most curiously.

It had been hours since he last ate a real meal and after today's hectic activities, he was quite famished.

"Why, my dear prince, it's mint soup of course," replied Ruby, as a simple matter-of-fact.

"Mint soup? But we just drank mint tea!" he cried, out of great disappointment.

"Right now, at this hour, fresh mint is what's easily available in the garden. Therefore, mint soup is what we shall have tonight. Unless, you prefer to eat raw cabbage, instead?" she asked, with her hands resting alongside her hips.

And as Ruby and Violet prepared their supper, Maximus vowed that no matter what happened next, either rain or shine, there was one thing that he was going to do with absolute certainty come tomorrow morning: hunting!

# CHAPTER 16

Later on, that evening after supper, as Ruby, Maximus and Violet were ready to retire for the night, they encountered an impossible new dilemma: the bedding arrangements. While our heroes previously acknowledged their inevitable fates of sharing a single bedroom together; however, none of them foresaw that the next real adventure was going to be solely directed towards their respective beds. Even though there were technically, three separate beds located within the room; they were, however, all gravely *disproportionate* from each other.

For starters, the beds all *greatly* varied in size. For example, the first bed was the largest. Overall, it was grand in scale and it could easily fit two grown-sized adults inside of it at the same time. Meanwhile, the second bed was less than half the size of the first one. In truth, the second bed was really designed to host no more than a single teenager at one time. Not even a full-sized adult could comfortably fit inside of it!

Lastly, there was the issue concerning the third bed. Sadly, the last bed was as small as a child's toy chest. Plus, judging by its tiny outward appearance, the third miniature bed looked to have been specifically built for a toddler. As it currently stood, their sleeping arrangements for tonight was going to be a real challenge!

"These beds look straight out of a classical fairy tale," Violet observed. "It's like they're from the tale, *Goldilocks and the Three Bears*."

"I'm afraid you're right," Ruby sighed. "It's been several years… no… maybe even decades, since I last slept overnight in this cottage. Sadly, I'll admit, I'm afraid that I completely overlooked the fact that these beds are really out-of-date. Whatever, shall we do?"

A second later, both Ruby and Violet reverted their full attentions over to Prince Maximus and patiently waited for his advice. After all, he was the future king, was he not? Shouldn't *he* be the final decision maker in this most impossible entanglement? An unfortunate challenge that they all now faced, together, as new roommates for the next short-term future?

Unfortunately, Maximus could already foresee that tonight was *not* going to end in his favor. Given that the two other beds were far too small to host either Violet or Ruby; out of respect, he was going to have to make a sacrifice: his own comfort in exchange for their needs. In the end, Maximus was just going to have to offer them the larger bed, so that both ladies could share and sleep in it together.

Unfortunately, as a true gentleman, it was entirely improper for him to selfishly claim the larger bed as his own, while Violet and Ruby suffered sleeping in the smaller beds. Plus, he very well couldn't share the largest bed with either one of them. It'd be too scandalous. Therefore, Maximus, was just going to have to make do with the two smaller beds and perhaps, try to combine them together, so that he'd have enough room to fit into *something* to sleep in. Ah, the sacrifices we make for those we love...

"You two take the first bed, and I'll make do with the others," he acknowledged with much defeat.

Meanwhile, Ruby happily smiled on, while Violet looked absolutely horrified by this new prospect.

"But Maximus," Violet cried, "Surely, you can't possibly fit..."

"Don't trouble yourself, Violet. I'll make do," he sighed.

And that was that. Afterwards, Ruby and Violet went off to bed in the grand first bed, while Maximus pulled the two smaller beds together and tried to make the best out of it. Or at least, he *hoped* for the best...

* * *

An hour later, Maximus struggled to fall asleep. As it currently stood, combining the two smaller beds together proved to be absolutely useless. Instead of lying comfortably in one large bed, half of Maximus' body was overstretched onto the second bed; which sadly, hardly covered the entire span of his legs. In fact, starting from his knees and all the way down below past his ankles, his bottom half of his body was left to dangle out into the open air. Meanwhile, his upper body could seldom fit into the width of the larger bed at all. God forbid, if Maximus was to accidentally turn to his side in his sleep, then he'd most likely roll off of the bed altogether!

"This is hopeless," he sighed to himself.

As a respectable gentleman, Maximus wanted to do the right thing. He wanted to be generous and act as the perfect knight in shining armor that Violet so longed for. He wanted to do the honorable deed. To make Violet proud. To prove himself worthy of her affections. For once, he wanted to be *her hero*.

"Are you still awake?" she whispered over to him.

"I thought you were sleeping," he whispered right back to her.

"I can't," she admitted.

And then, to their surprise, they suddenly heard Ruby snoring. Apparently, *she* was comfortable enough to fall fast asleep tonight!

"Unlike your sleeping partner over there, I don't think that I'm going to be able to doze off anytime soon. Especially, that easily," he admitted.

"Uncomfortable, eh?" she playfully asked him.

"Very," he laughed on.

"In that case, Maximus, shall I recite to you a bedtime story? When I was a young girl, listening to an adventurous tale used to always help me to fall fast asleep. No matter the location."

"Hmm... a bedtime story," he reflected. "That sounds intriguing. Which kind?"

"Any kind," Violet answered. "Let's see, I know epic tales about dragons, princes and witches—"

"Perhaps, we skip the witches. At least, for tonight," he interrupted her, seeking to avoid any wild stories involving Vera-like impersonators.

"Fair enough," she agreed.

After all, they were in this messy predicament all due to a witch. Albeit, a wicked witch. Had it not been for Vera, then they'd most likely still be sleeping safe and sound within the comfort of their own beds back at Castle Hope.

"Then, what else shall I tell you?" she asked.

"How about you tell me your favorite tale? I think I'd like to hear that best of all," he said, hoping to use this rare opportunity to gain more insight into her private life.

"My favorite tale? Really? Do you truly want to listen to my favorite childhood fairy tale?" Violet sincerely asked him, with a hint of excitement found within her cheerful voice. A charming trait of hers, that Maximus found completely sweet and endearing.

"Of course," he replied, with a warm smile.

Luckily, for Maximus, inside of this darkened room, Violet couldn't bear witness to see how excited he really was to listen to her grand tale. Ignorance was certainly blissful.

"Alright, here it goes," she began, "This tale is called *The Traveling Knight*."

"Once upon a time, there a brave knight who fell madly in love with a princess from a faraway kingdom. Just one look at her through the wishing well and instantly, he was smitten by her. But unfortunately, she lived on the opposite side of the well. However, distance did not stop the knight from pursuing her. And so, one day, he traveled down the wishing well and ended up on the other side... into the princesses' realm. At the time, all hope seemed to be lost; for you see, the princess was already engaged to a villainous cruel prince. But regardless of this unfortunate predicament, the brave knight was still determined. After all, he had traveled across their realms to find her. Therefore, he wasn't going to give up so easily and let her go. In the end, he challenged the villainous prince to a duel. Needless to say, he won."

"And so, just because he won the duel, the princess accepted his hand in marriage?" asked Maximus, tuned to her every passing word.

"Not quite," Violet admitted. "Along their journey, the knight wooed his princess. But ultimately, it was his kindness, generosity and gentleman-like spirit that captured her heart. Apart from being a brave knight, he was also her knight in shining armor, too. Her hero."

"Hero," Maximus repeated. "And pray tell, which specific traits made him such? Why is this tale in particular, your favorite above all else?"

"His relentless determination to make her happy. To unselfishly devote himself to her every passing need, while sacrificing his own. True love is not all about beauty and charm, just so you know," she pointed out.

"It isn't?" he asked, wanting to learn more.

"No, it certainly isn't," she confirmed. "True love is beyond that. It's acts of consistent kindness. Of respect. Of devotion. Beauty comes and goes, but a loving heart... that lasts forever. It exceeds all time and space."

"And *this is the reason* as to why you love this tale so much? *The Traveling Knight?*" asked Maximus, in all seriousness. "Because you admire an honorable knight, who's willing to love, cherish and treat his fair lady with the utmost honor and respect, come all obstacles?"

"Yes," she admitted, while blushing in the shade of bright red.

Good thing she was still in the dark, for had he seen her face right now, then she was quite ready to die from pure embarrassment! Really, Violet hadn't anticipated admitting all of this personal information about herself to him!

"Thank you for sharing your favorite fairy tale with me. I am truly honored," Maximus admitted.

"Really?" asked Violet, in surprise. "You're welcome, I guess?"

"Violet, I promise to make all of your dreams come true," he told her. "I vow to be your knight in shining armor."

By that confession alone, Violet's heart skipped a whole beat. And for a split second, she could swear that he silently sighed the words *I love you…*

But instead of freely confessing his true feelings to her directly, Maximus instead, did something entirely unexpected. To Violet's surprise, he extended his arm over towards her and offered her his hand.

"What's this about?" she asked in astonishment.

"Obviously, I can't kiss you, right now," he answered underneath his breath, while sounding a bit irritated and annoyed by the mere fact that Ruby was inconveniently in the same room as them.

"Trust me, if I could, I would. So, I'm doing the next best thing," he concluded.

"By offering me your hand?"

"Yes," he admitted. "For as long as you'll have me."

And then, she extended her hand over and reached for his. At long last, their hands were finally intertwined. Locked together in a heartfelt link.

"What if I decide to hold your hand all night long?" she asked him with a raised brow, sounding as if she was challenging him to another duel.

"I can only hope," he replied with a beaming smile.

"And what if you should grow tired of holding my hand?"

"I won't. I'll simply fall asleep with our hands embraced."

"Ah—"

"Please, Violet," he interrupted her. "Just let me court you. Right now, I'm trying *really hard* to be the perfect gentleman for you. For once, allow me to be your knight in shining armor."

At long last, he finally dozed off to sleep and thereupon, she gazed at him and quietly whispered:

"You already are."

And then, she joined her sleeping knight's lead and fell fast asleep.

# CHAPTER 17

The next morning, Violet, once again, participated in Ruby's rigorous magic lessons. By now, she already learned many valuable remedies, including brewing several notable potions concerning the following: cures for headaches, stomach cramps, sore throats and swollen muscles. Plus, not to mention her favorite concoction above all else… love potions!

But alas, even with this newfound knowledge, magic alone didn't seem to be *the solution* to Violet's growing list of problems. Somehow, stemming from her own heart, Violet had the inclination that stopping Vera had little to do with magic. Or even, pursuing a full-scale war against her nemesis, too.

No, ending the evil queen's reign of terror was going to require something else all entirely. Something different. Something clever. Something fresh and brand new. But what that was precisely, Violet still didn't quite yet have her finger on it. In truth, this ongoing puzzle was far trickier than what she had originally predicted.

Apart from concocting a few potions and brewing some remedies here and there, Violet's magic was still limited. She certainly didn't possess any telekinetic or supernatural abilities. If she was indeed, the savior, then beating

Vera solely based on magic alone wasn't going to suffice. At this rate, Violet was still an amateur student at best. Therefore, there had to be another solution. Either way, Violet just needed to concentrate and study even harder, until she finally discovered the correct path to set things right.

"I think that's quite enough for today," Ruby instructed her.

"But Ruby," Violet interjected, "All this time, we've primarily focused on creating potions. While I've very much enjoyed this part of our lessons; however, shouldn't I also be learning more about physical magic? You know, the combating sort of kind?"

"What do you mean?" she asked.

"You know, the kind where I wave my hand in the air and send things crashing down. *That* sort of magic," Violet clarified.

"Ah, yes, *that* sort of magic," Ruby answered, smilingly. "And do you believe that kind of magic will stop Vera? Particularly, concerning her ongoing quest for vengeance?"

"Perhaps..."

"Or perhaps *not*," Ruby remarked. "Perhaps, Vera requires something *else* entirely. Something that even *I*, myself, as your instructor cannot teach you."

"What do you mean?" asked Violet, in confusion.

"My dear, I believe that when that time comes, you'll have already discovered that very answer for yourself," replied Ruby.

"But for now," she continued on, "I want you to study this spell book. Unfortunately, due to the last battle fought at Castle Hope, I understand that you weren't able to travel with the spell book that I previously gifted to you with. However, I think you'll come to find this version more useful than the first. Especially, while I'm away."

And then, Ruby handed over to Violet a bright and shiny golden book that was as thick and as heavy as an encyclopedia.

"Are you going to be traveling somewhere soon?" she asked her instructor.

"Eventually, I will. I always do," replied Ruby. "But for now, Violet, please promise me that you'll review this spell book each and every day. Promise?"

"Yes, I promise."

"Good," said Ruby, with a warm smile. "Now, go. It's time to continue on with the rest of your lessons outdoors. Plus, I'm sure that our crown prince has been most patiently waiting for your arrival, too."

"I'm sure he is," Violet laughed on.

One way or another, he was *always* waiting for her.

* * *

Outside in the forest, while seated above an oversized tree stump, Maximus attended to his most recent catch of the morning. After eating another round of mint soup for breakfast, he was determined to break this endless cycle of plant-based brothy liquids and instead, replace it with a hearty and nutritious solid meal. After all, men like him needed a stronger serving of protein to successfully carry them out onto the battlefields. And so, as soon as dawn arrived, Maximus exited the cottage with the sole determination to hunt for game.

Luckily, for him, the cottage was well equipped with a host of weapons. Hidden within the fireplace and underneath the cauldron, was a secret storage compartment that contained the following: three hunting rifles, four silver swords, three sharpened daggers and a chopping axe. A sufficient supply of weaponry to hopefully carry them over onto their next destination. While the cottage might have been severely deficient in a great many things; it did, however, provide them with needed shelter, supplies and most importantly, *time* enough to prepare for their next move.

And so, with much effort, Maximus managed to catch three rabbits and two wild pheasants. Plenty enough meat to cover both today's lunch and dinner. And maybe, even a third round of a meal, come tomorrow.

After skinning the rabbits' fur, Maximus was now currently preoccupied with plucking the feathers off from the pheasants. In contrast to the adolescence chairs found back at the cottage, this tree stump was rather large in stature and was surprisingly, comfortable, too. And to be fair, after spending last night sleeping in the world's tiniest of beds, Maximus was extremely grateful to have some extra space to stretch out his long legs!

"Do you need any help?" asked Violet, as she approached him.

Lifting his chin up to meet her face, Maximus was suddenly struck by the arrow of love. Even out in the middle of the remote forest and wearing nothing more but a modest brown cloak and a simple white linen dress, Violet was already breathtakingly gorgeous. With her bold red hair shining against the bright sunlight, and her sparkling emerald green eyes identical to the same leaves found within this very forest, Violet was the ultimate enchantress. She was by the far, the most beautiful woman that he had ever had the pleasure to catch sight upon.

And even though Maximus wanted nothing more than to kiss her, right here and now, his duty and honor prevented him from doing so. After all, our heroes still had much work ahead of them; including, a kingdom to save, too.

"Here," he tossed the second pair of the wild pheasant over to her. "You can clean this one up."

Almost instantly, Maximus quickly observed the dreaded look of disgust on her face. However, to Violet's credit, her dislike for this gruesome task didn't deter nor discourage her in anyway. Instead, she took a deep breath in and then, she quietly sat down on the ground to join him and simply carried on.

"Would you prefer to sit on this stump, instead?" he asked her. Again, trying his very hardest to act like a true gentleman. A proper knight in shining armor.

"No, it's alright" she replied. "As it is, you've already had a rough night. At least, I got to sleep in the larger bed. No, you go on ahead and enjoy your seat."

As the two of them continued plucking the feathers from off the pheasants, Violet decided to use this opportunity to have a heart-to-heart conversation with him.

"Since we're out here alone, I was hoping to talk to you in private," she told him.

For a second, Maximus hesitated. Just what exactly did she want to tell him?

"Go on," he encouraged her.

"I've been doing some thinking. Especially, after our last kiss and..."

"And...," he echoed.

"When this is all over and done, I want us to be... to be..."

"To be..."

Slowly, Violet took in another deep breath. And then, she finally told him, "I want us to be... a... *couple.*"

Instantly, he dropped his pheasant straight down onto the dirt ground. Suddenly, his heart skipped a beat. Did she really just admit to what his own desperate heart so longed to hear?

"I'll admit," she began, "I don't have much experience with matters of the heart.  But if I were ever to give it a try... then I'd like it to be with *you.*"

Her spoken words tugged at his very soul.

While Maximus had his fair share of lovers over the years, none of them were ever serious. Never before, did he desire to be in a real, meaningful and lasting relationship. But with Violet, it was different.

Not only was he extremely attracted to her, but he also admired her from afar, too. From her bravery to her sense of adventure, all the way down to her dedication to her studies and her relentless participation in their rigorous trainings, Maximus admired her for the woman that she was. Plus, in many ways, Violet reminded him of himself, too. Really, they were like two peas in a pod, even though they came from very different worlds. Allies. Friends. And now... *lovers*.

"Alright, I agree," he promptly answered her question, in a calm and assertive manner.

"You do?" she asked him, entirely surprised that he agreed to her proposal so quickly.

"Yes, *but*," he added as a condition.

"But?" she repeated.

"We don't have to wait for this war to end, in order to be together," he pointed out. "Life is already short as it is. Violet, as you know, there's no promise of tomorrow. If you want to be with me, then *be with me*. Right here, right *now*. There's no need to wait for another passing day. It's *now or never*."

"Maximus, are you certain? Do you really want to be with *me*?" she whispered.

"Yes," he said. "Now, come over here."

Instantly, he tossed his remaining game down onto the ground and quickly pulled her over to his side. Afterwards, he sat her down onto his lap and with his arms wrapped around her waist, he held onto her ever-so tightly.

"After knowing you, Lady Violet Galloway, I don't think my life will ever be quite the same again," he sighed.

"Neither will mine, too," she agreed with him.

Happily, he laughed, as he squeezed her body and buried her face into his warm chest. Against his beating heart. Thump, thump, thump... his heart rapidly beat.

"Hmm... you smell so good," Maximus confessed, as he leaned down to place a tender kiss upon the top of her head. Quickly, sending a chill down her back.

"There's so much I can show you... teach you...," he whispered into her ear.

"I'd like that," she answered. "I want to learn... everything there is to know... with you."

And then, Maximus lifted her chin up to face him and in return, she closed her eyes shut. At long last, they were finally going to kiss. But to her surprise, instead of kissing her lips, he instead, bent down, lifted her hand up to his lips and then, he placed a soft and gentle kiss against her knuckles.

"What's this?" Violet asked in surprise.

"I'm trying to be a gentleman, right now," Maximus admitted.

"But what if..."

"Shush... this is me courting you," he told her, as he placed a second kiss onto her other hand. "Plus, we have our whole lives ahead of us," he proudly proclaimed.

And she, in return, smiled and said, "So, I see, my chivalrous knight."

Suddenly, a large *ahem* was uttered nearby. Instantly, both Maximus and Violet shifted their attentions over to the person standing in front of them. Naturally, it was Ruby there, of course.

Wearing a black cape and carrying a medium-sized straw basket, Ruby was fully dressed and ready for business. Based on her appearance, it seemed that Ruby was ready to soon depart and travel to some mysterious location.

"I've got some business to attend to," she announced. "I'll be gone for the next few days. In the meantime, please feel free to use the cottage to your likings. And remember Violet, continue to keep up with your studies. Review the spell book every day."

"Yes, I promise," Violet vowed.

"Good," replied Ruby, content with her pupil's answer. "As for you, my dear crown prince, I'd say to take good care of our savior. However, you and I both know that's entirely unnecessary. I can see that you need no reminder."

Afterwards, Ruby laughed on, while Maximus and Violet both blushed out of embarrassment.

Needless to say, Maximus still said, "I will guard and protect her with my life."

And those very words felt like a match lit against her burning heart.

Regaining her composure, Violet asked her mentor out of concern, "But where will you be traveling to?"

"I need to gather some special ingredients. But do not fear, I shall be alright," Ruby promised her. "Besides, Vera wouldn't dare to mess with the likes of me."

And then, within the blink of an eye, Ruby was gone. She simply vanished into thin air, without a trace.

Meanwhile, Violet was left all alone in the arms of Maximus. While she enjoyed his company and the feel of his body against hers, she suddenly grew fearful. One way or another, she was now all alone in a secluded cottage, out in the middle of the remote forest. Away from both civilization and the rest of the world. Just her and Maximus. The only two people in this part of the dark woods.

Suddenly, Violet gulped. Come nightfall, the physical temptation between them was going to be too great. If there was anything scary lurking within these dark woods, then it wasn't found on the outside... but instead, it resided within their own four walls.

Just how was Violet going to survive spending the entire night alone, with no one else but herself and Maximus?

# CHAPTER 18

Much to her satisfaction, Violet quickly soon realized that she had absolutely nothing to fear. Especially, when left in the care of Maximus' sole company. In fact, during their entire time spent together, he behaved like the ideal gentleman. A real knight in shining armor.

Keeping true to his word, Maximus attended to all of Violet's every need. For starters, not only did he pluck all of the dirty and sticky feathers from off the two pheasants, but he actually cooked them, too! In fact, Maximus even went so far as to order Violet to remain seated and focused on her studies, while he personally took it upon himself to cook an entire feast just for her!

Consisting of baked pheasants, roasted potatoes, boiled cabbage and mint tea, Maximus prepared a gourmet meal fit for a queen. Meanwhile, as Violet comfortably sat in her chair and read from her golden spell book, Maximus assumed the role of a chef and oversaw the kitchen's affairs. By the time they finished eating their nightly supper, they spent the remainder of their evening chatting and roasting chestnuts by the fireplace.

Underneath the warm and toasty fire, Maximus shared tales with

Violet concerning his past adventures and travels, while also discussing about the reality of everyday life in his kingdom. With much enthusiasm, he described to her in great details about the beauty and thrills of this magical land, including their local customs and traditions.

As the Land of Eternal Autumn, the Kingdom of the West was famous for their bright tangerine hued and oversized plump pumpkins, which were commonly used to make just about every sort of dish imaginable. From pumpkin pies to sweet tarts, to tasty jams and salty pickles, to roasted stews and creamy ice creams, to crisp crackers and custard puddings— pumpkins were a staple ingredient to western food culture.

But apart from pumpkins, corn, cranberries and chestnuts were also highly cherished and frequently used ingredients found within western dishes as well. As for their favorite pastimes, most westerners took up archery, the violin, horseback riding, hunting, painting, sparring, harvesting, cooking or farming as their chosen hobbies. Furthermore, visiting all year-round local pumpkin patches, while also eating caramel-covered green apples and drinking warm cinnamon spiced red apple cider were some of the most popular food choices and outdoor activities that the majority of native westerners participated in.

While most of the aristocrats in the kingdom were land owners, there were also many independent farmers who owned their separate plots of land as well. According to Maximus, most of his peoples' chosen professions were roles pertaining to farmers, bakers, entrepreneurs, merchants or officers in the military— especially, amongst the men. Meanwhile, most western women were primarily school teachers, seamstresses, doctors, housewives and even a select few actually served as knights within his royal imperial army.

As for their clothing attires, most westerners wore garments in the colors consisting of deep brown, forest green, amber, burgundy, scarlet and marigold. According to Maximus, these shades represented the unique colors of his nation, with each hue symbolizing some sort of physical aspect found within their land. From the rolling brown hills to the forest green shrubs, to the amber and burgundy colored foliage, to the scarlet and marigold bright sunsets— each color was a special trait associated with the Land of Eternal Autumn.

But apart from these autumn inspired colors, most citizens in this region primarily wore shawls, woolen sweaters and thick coats, along with knitted scarves and long leather boots. While the men primarily opted for an outfit consisting of tights, black buckled belts and loose oversized burgundy ruffled blouses, the women usually wore long dresses in dark colors. Furthermore, while some men occasional wore velvet feathered circular bures or triangular shaped hats in the shade of hunter green, most women generally wore their hairs down. In fact, most ladies of the west generally grew their hairs long and styled them using an elegant hair clip that were usually shaped in the form of a pumpkin, an apple, a rose or a marigold flower.

Additionally, Maximus shared stories about his childhood. From his past days spent wandering through the forest and aimlessly chasing bandits on horseback, to shooting blank arrows out into the blue sky from his bow, Maximus was a true adventurer at heart. A man similar to her own father. In fact, it was rather difficult to swallow that this wandering soul really was in fact a royal prince. A crown prince, at that; aka, the rightful heir to the throne. The future king.

But according to Maximus, that wasn't always the case. Once upon a time, he wasn't the heir but the spare. The second son to the former king. And as such, Maximus grew up with less restrictions in comparison to his elder brother, Leopold, the first heir to the throne. As a result, Maximus was not constrained to a life hidden away behind the shadows of the palace. Within the royal and golden gilded cage.

And so, because of these reasons, he had the full freedom to travel and to do as he pleased. Which is why, Maximus grew up to be a different sort of prince. A prince of his people. Someone, whom Violet greatly came to admire and love.

Unlike the other wealthy aristocrats that Violet grew up alongside with in merry old England, Maximus was a breath of fresh air. He wasn't the typical stiff, snobbish and uptight sort of fellow. Instead, he was down to earth and highly approachable. Warm, kind, charming and thoughtful. Someone, who was genuinely fun to be around with. Really, he was the perfect gentleman. In the end, Maximus truly was Violet's special knight in shining armor. Just like her favorite childhood fairy tale. Except this time around, her childhood dream actually came true.

And so, as they ate their roasted chestnuts cozy by the fire, Maximus gave a history lecture to Violet about the three other neighboring kingdoms: the East, the North and the South. According to the prince, each kingdom had their own special customs and traditions, just like theirs. For example, in the deserts of the south, camel riding was a famous outdoor activity in their region; while the snowy north favored reindeer-based sporting events. And for the floral east, annual garden parties were all the rage. Especially, during their famous Midsummer Night's Dream Galas. Overall, each kingdom had their own specialized cultures and values, respective to their specific regions.

Meanwhile, as Maximus enchanted her with stories about these foreign lands, Violet found herself entirely immersed within his gifted storytelling. Story by story, Maximus told her about the delicious kebabs of the south or the yummy hot chocolate drinks of the north, or even the tasty lavender rose flavored sugar cookies of the east, all the while, Violet secretly longed to visit each of these magical kingdoms for herself. For each land sounded like a dream. A brand-new adventure that she so longed to venture to. If only one day, it could be...

Sensing her excitement by her joyful expression, Maximus vowed to personally take her to all of these great lands himself. Hopefully, one day near in the future. As far as he was concerned, as soon as the war was over and he was crowned as the next king, Maximus was determined to appoint Violet as his official traveling companion. And as Violet happily accepted his proposal, Maximus stood up and asked for her hand to dance.

"Do you really want to dance with me right now, here in this cottage?" Violet asked in surprise.

Surely, this tiny cottage was not fit to use as a dance hall. Plus, there wasn't even an audience around to watch them here, too.

"Why not?" he playfully asked her, in return. "It's just you and me. We don't need a castle to dance. Besides, I haven't taught you about all of our customed western dances just yet. So, while we're here, I might as well take advantage of this time and teach you. After all, my leading lady needs to know about these sorts of things."

And then, Maximus gave her a wink, as he extended his hand over to meet hers. Considering, as of lately, just how kind and thoughtful he had been to her, Violet decided to humor him. Besides, learning another new western dance couldn't hurt, right?

"Very Well," Violet replied, as she stood up to face him. "What shall I be learning tonight?" she asked him, as she took a hold of his hand.

"The Lover's Knot," Maximus replied.

"Come again?" she asked, surprised by the unique name.

"The name of the dance," he informed her.

"The Lover's Knot," Violet repeated. "But why is it called that?"

"You'll see," Maximus answered, with a devious grin.

And then, before she knew it, he swiftly positioned them. With his right-hand tucked around her waist and his left-hand intertwined with hers, Maximus swiftly took the lead.

"Now, my love, just follow me like we're dancing to another waltz," he explained.

And to her credit, Violet did just that. As he moved, she moved. As he stepped to his right, she also stepped to her right. As he turned, she turned. And as he twirled her around the room, she willingly followed his strict guidance. Together, they danced in perfect harmony.

Meanwhile, as they danced away, he hummed a sweet melody. Even though the cottage was absent of any musical instruments, Maximus instead, used his lips to improvise music to their moving steps. And so, as they continued dancing, Violet gazed right into his sparkling silvery eyes and thick brown lashes and smiled to herself. Slowly but surely, she was falling in love with the crown prince. And even though they came from two different worlds, she couldn't help but wonder that once this war was fought and won, would she still have her happy ending? Would she and he be destined to end up together? A couple fated for a happily ever after?

Suddenly, they came to a stance and Maximus came to a complete halt. Before Violet knew it, they were standing face-to-face, with their foreheads and noses touching each other. Meanwhile, their arms were high-up in the air, stretched above their heads. Alas, they were truly interlocked with one another. A real *lover's knot.*

Without saying another word, Violet stared at him. They were both breathing hard. This attraction shared between them was only intensifying with each passing moment. After all of their endless battles and will-they-or-won't-they flirtation, this escalating tension was finally coming to an abrupt end.

Right now, they were mere inches away from sharing another kiss. And not just any kiss. Not another simple peck on their lips, but a real and passionate one. And at long last, Violet was ready. Indeed, she welcomed his kisses... and his hugs... and everything else... in-between. Everything that lovers were meant to do...

But unfortunately, to her surprise *and* great disappointment, Maximus did not kiss her. Instead, he gently pulled himself away and walked over to the far corner of the room. Alas, he *rejected her.*

With his back turned against her, he finally spoke, "We should probably head off to bed, now. We've got a long day ahead us, come tomorrow."

And then, he abruptly exited the room. Meanwhile, Violet was left standing by herself, with her hand held tightly over her chest. Over her rapidly *beating heart.* Why didn't he kiss her? Was it possible that he didn't care about her anymore? That, he no longer wanted her, now?

❋ ❋ ❋

Later on, that evening, Violet found herself lying alone in her oversized and spacious bed, while Maximus lied in the smaller beds next over. With Ruby gone, Violet had the entire grand bed all to her lonesome self. To be fair, it seemed a bit selfish on her part to have all of this luxury, while Maximus struggled to even fit into his. But after their last dance, he stormed out of their living quarters and quickly headed off to bed. So much as failing to even wish her a proper goodnight!

"Maximus, are you still awake?" she whispered over to him.

Silence.

"Maximus...," Violet spoke, once more. "Are you awake?"

Again, total and complete utter silence.

"Maximus..."

"Yes, Violet," he sighed. "What is it?"

"Maximus, why don't you come over and sleep here with me?" Violet suggested. "With Ruby gone, there's plenty of extra room in my bed for the both of us. You shouldn't have to suffer another night in that child's bed of yours."

"Violet, are you honestly inviting me, a grown man, into your bed in the dead of night?" he asked, with a sense of hesitation in his voice.

"Yes, I am," she answered, confidently. "Besides, I trust you. I know you won't hurt me."

"Violet, I fear that you've given me way too much credit," he admitted. "Really, I'm the *last* person you should *trust*. Especially, when it comes to sharing your bed."

And then, Maximus closed his eyes shut and finally said, "Good night, Violet. Sleep tight."

And that, was it. All except...

Violet didn't want their evening to end. At least, not just yet. After all, they were alone in a cottage. In the middle of the forest. Plus, they were *supposedly* a couple, now. Didn't new couples sleep together in the same bed? Also, if she was being perfectly honest with herself, Violet also wanted to take their relationship to the next level. They were already friends... best friends really... and now... Violet wanted them to become more. She wanted them to graduate from being just friends into... well... lovers...

"Maximus," Violet spoke, once more. But this time around, her words were spoken in a more high-pitched, forceful and demanding voice. A tone that he couldn't so easily ignore.

"What is it, Violet? I'm trying to sleep," he answered.

"I want you in my bed," she demanded. "And I want us to spend the night together."

Instantly, his heart skipped a beat. Did she even know what *spending the night together* meant precisely? Especially, a night shared between a man and a woman?

"Violet, you know that I'd do anything for you," Maximus told her. "But as a man, even I have my own limits. If I sleep in your bed, then I can't make any promises to refrain myself. It'll be too much temptation. Please, I beg of you, just try to forget about this entire conversation and go to sleep."

"But Maximus—"

"Violet, *please*, I'm trying *really hard* to be a gentleman, right now," he interrupted her. "Trust me, it's *not* easy."

"Well, did you ever bother trying to ask *me* as to what *I want*, exactly?" she cried. "Maybe, tonight, I *don't* want a gentleman!"

"What do you mean?" he asked, nervously.

"Maybe, tonight, I want someone else. Maybe, I want a *brute*."

"A brute? Ha! Do you even know what that means?" he questioned her.

"Yes, I know precisely what a brute means," she responded right back. Challenging him. Daring him.

"And tonight," she added, "I want a brute, *not* a gentleman. I'd like to finally get acquainted with Maximus, the Brute. Not Maximus, the Gentleman."

"Take that back," he ordered.

"No," Violet spoke up, with much determination.

"Maximus," she continued on, "If you can be a brute with dozens of other ladies, then why can't you do the same with me? Why can't you kiss me and love me, like the others?"

"Because you're different."

"But why?"

"Because you're special... and I..."

"You..."

"Never mind."

In truth, he was *almost* ready to confess his true feelings to her. If she pressed him any further, then he'd have no other choice but to admit that he had actually fallen for her. That in all honesty, he *loved her*. Yes, Maximus loved Violet. Not only did he fall madly in love with her, but he loved her with all of his heart.

"Listen," he began, "I promised Ruby that I'd be honorable, when it came to you. We might be a couple right now, but I want us to take our time. To do things the proper way. Just like the knight from your story."

"The knight from my story?" she asked in surprise. "Is this why you're holding back?"

"Part of it," he admitted.

Actually, that was the *truth*. In its entirety. If Violet's ideal dream hero was the knight in shining armor from her favorite fairy tale, then that's who he aimed to be. For both their sakes. For once, this brute wanted to be a hero. *Her hero.*

"Or is it... because you don't find me attractive... like the others...," she whispered.

Did he honestly just hear her comparing herself to his past lovers? Was she crazy? *None of them* could ever compare to her. Everyone else paled in comparison. To Maximus, Violet was God sent. She was a miracle. A savior. A saint. Not only was she breathtakingly gorgeous, but she had the purest of hearts. Heck, even he wasn't worthy of her. And yet, she still wanted him.

"Not at all," he clarified, hoping to set the record straight.

And then, Maximus rose-up from his bed and walked over to her. As he leaned against the side of her bed in the dark, Violet took in a deep breath. Her choice of words had certainly moved him.

"You don't think that I want to be with you?" he asked her, in the most serious of tones.

And then, to her surprise, Maximus brought Violet's hand up and over to his beating heart.

"Can you feel *it*?" he asked her. "Violet, can you feel how *fast* my heart is beating, right now? It beats this rapidly fast, whenever I'm near you. It's so intense. Like a race that doesn't end. And I've never felt this way before. Not until, *you*."

"I...," she stuttered.

He might have held out before, but *now* was the time to finally come clean.

"Violet, I love you," he admitted in defeat.

"Maximus... I... I… I love you, too...," she confessed.

Before a second thought, Violet got up from her bed and embraced him. As they held onto each other tightly in the dark, she leaned down and placed a soft kiss alongside his lips. But before she could pull away, his lips came crashing back down onto hers. Instantly, their soft and gentle kiss grew into a more passionate one. And before either one of them knew it, they both crash-landed down onto her spacious bed...

# CHAPTER 19

"Are you sure you're ready?" Maximus asked Violet.

"Yes, I'm sure. I want my first time to be with you," she answered.

This might have been Violet's first time sleeping with a man, but without a shadow of a doubt, she wanted to experience this milestone event with Maximus. After all, she loved him and he loved her. They were in love. They were a couple. And if they were going to face a war within the next foreseeable future, then she wanted to spend this precious limited time safely tucked away within his loving and caring arms. Surrendering both her body and soul over to his custody.

"In that case, don't fret, my love," he said with a warm smile. "I promise to go gentle. You have my word."

And so, with the moonlight shining inside of their bedroom, Violet and Maximus quickly undressed themselves, stripping down all of their garments in great haste. Afterwards, they turned to face each other. Alas, they were both completely stark naked.

"Beautiful," he acknowledged in amazement. "Absolutely, breathtaking."

And she really was, too. After dreaming and fantasizing about her for so long, Maximus finally saw Violet's physical beauty in full, underneath all of those endless piles of fabric. And in-person, she, and her hourglass figure, certainly didn't disappoint.

In fact, Violet was far lovelier and more ravishing, than what he had previously imagined her to be. From her soft skin to her slender curves and tiny waist, to her full and plump breasts to her long and flowing fiery red hair streaming down her slender back, Violet was equivalent to a famed goddess from ancient mythology. She was, without a doubt, perfection at its finest.

"I don't deserve you," he whispered to her in shame.

Maximus might have been the crown prince and the heir to the western throne, but that still didn't make him feel worthy of her. After all, this former brute spent most of his life doing all the *wrong* things. *Unspeakable* things. *Wicked* things. *Rakish* things. Really, he shouldn't be rewarded with an angel, like Violet. After all, he was equivalent to the damned devil, himself. Truly, she was too good for his wretched soul!

"Maximus, please don't go there," she warned. And then, to his surprise, she told him, "We *both* deserve each other."

Afterwards, Violet slowly walked over to his side, calmly leaned her body against his warm chest and then, she softly placed a tender kiss alongside his lips. And that was that. Before Violet knew it, Maximus quickly wrapped his arms around her body and lifted her up into the air. Within seconds, he whisked her off and gently placed her down onto the bed.

As she silently lied there, Violet looked up and stared at Maximus' naked body for the very first time. Just as she suspected, after years of rigorous training, her knight in shining armor's body was godly shaped just like Zeus, himself. From his chest and all the way down to his ankles, Maximus was covered in pure muscles. It was almost as if his entire body had been chiseled by none-other than the greatest sculpturer of all of history: Michelangelo. For in truth, every inch of him was reflected in endless curvatures. Just like the famous statue of David in Florence, he was, without a doubt, perfection at its finest.

And then, she saw.... *him*. Behold, Violet finally caught sight of his long, thick, and glorious cock. It was *hard...* and *enormous*. Dear goodness, just how was he ever going to fit into her petite self?

Instantly, Violet gulped out of nervousness and quickly, looked away out of shyness. But really, this was so silly of her, wasn't it? After all, at this point, what else was there to be shy about? By now, she had kissed him about a dozen or so times. Plus, he already saw her naked. Now, this was just the next gradual step to the natural progression of their romantic relationship.

In the meantime, Violet's nervous reaction certainly didn't go unnoticed. Without saying a word, Maximus instantly saw her glow in the shade of bright red, stemming from her embarrassment. And to his credit, Maximus knew why, too.

"Don't worry my love," he said with a beaming smile. "Like I said before, I promise to go gentle with you."

His reassuring words brought much comfort to her. In truth, Violet trusted Maximus wholeheartedly. In fact, she trusted him with her very own life. He earned it, too. After all this time that they spent together, he genuinely took great care of her. Plus, he did save her back at the castle, too. Therefore, if Maximus promised to go gentle with her for their first time, then she was ready to believe in him.

Without saying a word, she nodded to him in agreement. And with that reassurance, he knew exactly what to do next.

Slowly, Maximus crawled onto their bed and covered his entire body over hers. At long last, they were finally alone and together. Instantly, he lowered his mouth over hers and began to kiss her with such longing and desire. As his tongue glided against her teeth and lips, Violet joined his lead and did the same. First, she licked his lower lip... then his upper lip... then his teeth... and then... his tongue... and before she knew it... their mouths came crashing down together passionately... and were rapidly dancing the night away...

Meanwhile, Maximus let his hands roam free against her naked body. As they kissed, his wandering hands explored the rest of her. From her petite waist to her perfectly sculpted abdomen, to her plump breasts to her slender legs and inner thighs... Maximus made his formal introduction to her.

Carefully, he pulled himself away from her lips and then, he moved himself down towards her chest. With her eyes closed shut in pure ecstasy, Maximus brought her breast into his mouth and began licking at her, one stroke at a time. Instantly, she arched her chest upwards towards him, which in return, made him even more excited. After tasting her soft breast against his bare lips, Maximus brought his mouth lower down to her chest and began to suck on her nipple. *Hard.*

Almost immediately, Violet moaned out of pure pleasure, as Maximus continued to have his way with her. As his mouth sucked on her hardened and pink nipple, his hands continued to explore the rest of her body. Tenderly, his hands stroked her stomach, slowly making its way down to her thighs. By the time his hands reached her inner thighs, Maximus reached over and began to touch and play with her folds. Instantly, she flinched.

"Shush," he commanded. "Just relax. Don't be afraid."

Following his lead, she did just that. Again, closing her eyes shut, Violet surrendered her body over to her new lover. The time to unite with him was growing ever near.

Using his fingers, he explored her most private of parts. Touching her slowly and gently, he continued to play and fondle with her folds. A moment later, he bent down in-between her thighs, while placing both of her legs above his shoulders. And then, with one long sweep, he licked her womb and began to suck her hard.

"Aaaahhhh…," Violet happily moaned, as she tossed her head backwards.

Pleasuring her brought tremendous joy to Maximus. Her cries of ecstasy were like music to his ears. And as she moaned, he continued to feast upon her moist cunt. Afterwards, he pulled his face away and replaced his tongue with his forefinger. To which, she shuddered upon his contact.

Much to his delight, Violet was already wet and ready for his invasion. One way or another, Maximus was determined to make this a night that she'd never forget. Because as far as he was concerned, he was going to remember this night for all eternity.

"Now, Violet," he began to instruct, "I need you to listen to me very carefully."

Silently, she nodded in agreement and proceeded to listen to his every passing word.

"My darling Violet, I'm going to *fuck you* now," he declared.

Instantly, she moaned at the mere mention of his glorious but wicked plan. To be *fucked.* How exciting and strange this new experience was for her. *For them.*

"I'm going to start by going in very slowly," he explained. "It might hurt at first, but I promise, you will get used to it as we go. In fact, I'm quite convinced that you'll come to enjoy it, as much as I will."

"Are you certain?" she asked.

"With my life," he answered. "Now, do you trust me?"

Again, she nodded in agreement.

"Good," he said, pleased by her positive reaction. "Now, let's get on with this, shall we?"

Upon his words, Violet threw her arms around Maximus' neck and pulled him down even closer to her. With their noses and foreheads pressed against each other, she said with full confidence, "I'm ready."

With her permission, Maximus quickly got into position. Carefully, he stretched her thighs wide and as far apart as he possibly could, while he climbed himself on top of her. As she took in a deep breath, Maximus nudged the tip of his cock inside of her, smashing through her inner walls.

Instantly, Violet flinched, as she dug her nails into his back. Leaning forward, he pushed another inch in. And then, another. And then, another. And before Violet knew it, Maximus was completely inside of her... stretching her… filling her up whole… and it felt... well... rather... *amazing. Fantastic,* really. Truly, there were no proper words to describe as to just how *wonderous* this all really felt...

"Are you okay?" he asked her, hesitantly. All the while, hoping that his initial entrance into her womb didn't hurt her.

"I'll admit, at first, it felt a bit strange, but..."

"But what?"

"Well… I kind of *liked it*…," she admitted, bashfully.

Her reaction pleased him, immensely. And if she enjoyed it, then he was ready to deliver her more waves of pleasure. Ecstasy. Yes, *fucking her* was going to be the ultimate *undoing of him*. God save him.

"Alright, my love, it's time," he said eagerly.

And then, this time around, he finally let himself go.

Giving into his carnal desires, Maximus lost himself within Violet's arms. At first, he thrusted into her as gently as possible. But afterwards, as she quickly got used to his slow rhythm, Maximus gradually picked up speed. Before he knew it, he was rapidly thrusting back and forth into her, stretching her thighs further and further apart, as his hands ingrained his fingerprints onto her skin.

Meanwhile, as he moved, she moved, too. Scratching away at his back, in the process. Marking her own marks onto his skin. Together, they danced the night away within the comfort of their bed. As he pushed, she welcomed him in. And as he fiercely pounded repeatedly into her body, she kissed him as if her entire life depended upon it.

While this might have been their first-time having sex together; it also strangely felt all so familiar, too. It was almost as if they had been lovers in another lifetime. They were perfectly aligned and comfortable with one another. If ever there was an ideal partner fated for her, then Maximus was her soul mate. Already, he knew her body and how to set it alive, too.

Forward, he plunged himself into her wet body, as he thrusted deeper into her womb. *Faster. Harder.* He entered her. Claiming her as his own. *Fucking her* over and *over*… and *over again*. Wave after wave of pure pleasure. *Fucking her harder* and *deeper*, as she screamed his name out loud and inadvertently, flaming his ever-consuming desire for her. With each of her screams, setting him on fire.

Once again, Maximus thrusted and slammed into her body… *savagely pounding over*… and *over*… and *over again*… until she felt like melted butter. With his erect cock filling her up inside of her stretched womb, as she desperately begged for more.

Finally, at long last, he pushed one last and final time, as they both climaxed together at the same time. Afterwards, Maximus collapsed on top of her and then, he rolled over to her side.

Out of breath, he pulled her and buried her in his chest. With his arms wrapped around her waist, Violet sighed a happy moan. So, *this* was *pleasure. This* was *love* making at its finest. *This* is what it felt like *to be* with Maximus. *Both body and soul.*

Really, it was all wonderful. Magical. Memorable.

"Are we done already?" she innocently turned to asked him.

Instantly, he laughed with utter amusement.

"For now, my love," he whispered into her ear. "After all, it's our first time together. I don't want to push you *too hard.*"

But unfortunately, Violet couldn't help but feel a tad bit disappointed. And of course, Maximus noticed her reaction. By now, he could practically read her every passing thought, just by staring at her. Really, he knew her that well, inside and out.

"Don't fret, Violet," he reassured her. "There's always tomorrow. Besides, I've got plenty more to teach you, too."

And *that* was a promise Violet was determined to make sure he kept!

# CHAPTER 20

"Aim straight ahead and release," Maximus instructed her.

But before Violet bothered to respond to his advice, she had already released her arrow from off her bow. And lo and behold, she struck something on her first try!

"Looks like we'll be eating dinner tonight, after all," she proudly declared, with a beaming smile.

"Yes, I suppose we will," replied Maximus happily.

One way or another, Violet was a superior student. Whatever he taught her, she caught on quickly and efficiently. In truth, she was the ideal student. And apart from archery, hunting, sparring and now, love making, Violet gradually transitioned from amateur student to acclaimed master.

"Shall I do the feather plucking or will you?" she dared to ask him.

"That depends," he responded. "Perhaps, we should engage in another duel to solve this dilemma. Winner gets to relax and sleep in, while the other has to prep, cook and clean. What do you say?"

Another dare, another bet. But regardless, it was a challenge that Violet wasn't willing to back down from. Not now, not ever.

"I'll tell you what," she answered, "I think I've got a better idea."

"Oh, really? And pray tell, what is it?"

"If I win, then you'll have to teach me about that new move that you promised to show me before. You might have neglected to demonstrate it to me last night in our bedroom, but I'd like to bring this matter back onto the negotiating table."

And by *that*, Violet was referring to another erotic lover's position that Maximus had previously mentioned to her only but a day ago. By now, Ruby was absent from the cottage for about an entire week or so. And in that time, Violet and Maximus made love each and every night, in practically every possible space... corner... table... and then... some...

"You know, let's just go ahead and skip that conversation altogether," he said with a huge grin painted across his handsome face.

"What do you mean?" she asked in confusion.

"Instead of discussing it, I believe that I'll just show it to you, right now. Really, it's the perfect day. All sunny and bright outside. Shall we give it a go?" he asked her in the slyest of manners.

"Now? Right here, out in the woods?" she cried. "But I'm wearing my buttoned-up dress!"

"Not to worry," Maximus reassured her. "That's why I always carry a spare dagger in my pocket."

And before Violet knew it, Maximus quickly reached over to her side and swiftly pulled her up-close to his chest. Afterwards, he took hold of his dagger and just as he promised her, he began to rip open the seams to her dress... one button at a time!

Within the blink of an eye, Violet's dress quickly fell down onto the dirt ground, leaving her standing exposed and completely stark naked in front of him, with only her long and loose red hair flowing down her back. Plus, given the limited amount of time that she spent dressing up earlier this morning, Violet neglected to wear a proper corset; let alone any undergarments or a brassiere.

"Turn around," he commanded.

Following his lead, Violet did just that. Since she was standing in front of a tree, she decided to lean against it, while she pressed her palms and chest against its bark. Meanwhile, Maximus quickly moved to undress himself, until he, too, was left completely naked from top to bottom.

"Now, spread your legs far and wide apart," he instructed her.

Instantly, a shiver went down her back. Already, this new position of theirs felt both wicked and delightful!

With her bosom pressed up against an apple tree, Violet took in a deep breath, as she welcomed Maximus into her. And much to his great pleasure, she was indeed ready for him. Deliciously wet and inviting.

"And now, my love," he whispered into her ear, as he gently bit down onto it. "I'm going to take you out here, right now. My love, we're going to *fuck* like wild animals and make music in front of all of nature. Are you ready?"

Silently, she nodded in agreement. Indeed, Violet was excited. And eager, too. Her appetite for him was entirely addictive. Really, she couldn't be any hungrier for his touch. Truly, it was desire. Lust. Passion. Overall, it was riveting madness!

Seconds later, Maximus grabbed a hold of his thick, long and hardened cock and gradually, made his way into her. Slowly, he nudged himself into her opening and in one swift and hard thrust, he slid into her completely and thereby, instantly sending shockwaves of blissful pleasure and utter joy throughout her entire body. From this angle, it felt oh so different! Refreshing! Thrilling! Joyful!

"Aaaahhhh...," she moaned, as he plunged further into her womb.

*Deep. Slow.* And *hard.*

And then, he slowly pulled out, only to do it all over again in one swift move. Grabbing hold of her hips tightly, Maximus gently lifted her body up into the air and brought her rear closer to him. With her buttock facing him, he placed her at an alleviated inclined angle. And then, much to both of their extreme pleasures, he plunged himself deeper into her, once more. Again, she moaned. But this time, she also cried. Tears of total pleasure. Ecstasy at its finest!

"Are you enjoying this, my love? Do you enjoy *fucking me*?" he asked her, with a cocky grin. "Because, I enjoy *fucking you*."

However, judging by her reaction, Maximus already knew Violet's answer. She was loving every last inch of him. And he, too, was loving every last inch of her.

"Yes!!!" she screamed.

"Yes, what?" he teased her.

"I enjoy *fucking you*, too!" Violet shouted at the top of her lungs, as her wild red hair floated across the howling wind.

Alas, Violet's screams of pleasure only further pleased him. Excited him. Encouraged him. Truly, their love making really was music to his ears. Nature's finest musical melodies shared between him and her. And so, determined to keep their momentum going strong, he thrusted into her once more.

But going slow with Violet was a crime. If he wanted to make this moment memorable for her, then he needed to pick up speed. He needed to make her desire him, just as much as he desired her.

And so, Maximus did just that. Forward, he plunged himself deeper into her behind, as he began to establish his rhythm. Back and forth, he thrusted himself *deeper* and *harder*... and *faster* into her. *Over* and *over*... *again*... and *again*... he continued to pump into her. Sending wave… after wave… after wave… of pleasure…

Afterwards, Maximus grabbed a hold of her loose fiery red hair with his fist on one hand and used his other to rest alongside her slender hip. And then, he thrusted his muscular hips forward and *pounded*... and he *pounded*... and he *pounded* into her soft body... ingraining his erect cock into her stretched womb. *Fucking her* with all his might. With the sounds of flesh, flapping together loudly, as Maximus' balls slapped against her wet behind. All the while, his fingers dug deep into her skin... marking himself with his imprint onto her as if she was his very own...

Meanwhile, Violet held onto dear life, as she wrapped her arms tightly around the tree's trunk. And as Maximus continued to *fuck her*, Violet closed her eyes shut and enjoyed every last passing second. Thrust after thrust of pure ecstasy. And while he claimed her body over and over again, the tree began to shake and tremble along the way. In fact, the tree shook so much that a generous handful of apples actually fell down onto the ground!

Happily, Maximus roared out like a mighty thunder god, desperately seeking to release his overwhelming inner pleasure. Shortly thereafter, both he and Violet climaxed at the same exact time. Afterwards, he pulled her towards him and buried her into his warm chest.

"Forever and ever," he whispered into her ear. "Violet Galloway, I love you from here to the moon."

And as Violet lifted up her chin to face him, she swore, "Me, too. Maximus, I love you from here to the moon. Now, and forever."

* * *

Later on, that evening, while Maximus retired early to sleep in their bed, Violet allocated some time to focus on her studies. In truth, Ruby's latest homework assignment, aka the ancient spell book, was an unusual item. For starters, it wasn't anything like the normal books found back in the libraries of her family's estates or at her former university.

In contrast to other modern-day texts printed onto paper, this particular spell book, with its brightly golden cover and thick solid binding, appeared to be hundreds of years old. Furthermore, the book was written in handwritten form, using all cursive font and jet-black ink, documented on what appeared to be centuries old papyrus. Indeed, with its crimpled-up edges and smeared text, this really was an ancient manuscript. Probably as old as time herself.

Upon opening the book, there were roughly around a thousand pages or so of text, with each page dedicated to a specific spell or enchantment. Casually flipping through its pages, Violet concluded that most of the chapters were primarily focused on simple remedies to various common ailments. Some of them included the following: Remedies for a Good Night's Rest; Cures to Persistent Hair Loss; and Secrets to Aleve a Pestering Headache— to name a few.

But there were also more magical types of spells as well, such as: Transforming Oneself into a Ravishing Beauty; Teleporting to Another Magical Realm; Body Shifting into a Slimy Toad; Turning into Gold; Freezing One's Heart; etc. Overall, the spell book functioned more like a vast collection of apothecary remedies, primarily aimed to cure common everyday human-like illnesses, with the exception of a few chapters that were entirely dedicated to the magical occult.

But even after reviewing about a hundred pages or so of text, Violet still didn't discover the answer to what she was searching for. However, her lack of findings didn't discourage her.  Somehow, deep within her heart, Violet knew that the answer to her dilemma was lurking within the pages of this ancient spell book. One way or another, the solution to defeating Vera was secretly hidden within this sacred text.

Growing up, Violet's mother, Kassie, used to frequently explain to her daughter that the answers to all of life's mysterious pursuits were almost always guaranteed to be hidden somewhere within the pages of a book. According to the Countess of Galloway, a viable solution to any worldly problem(s) existed with the written text(s) of authors, who were far more experienced and knowledgeable than their readers. And as readers, it just required a bit of patience and efforts on our parts to discover it. After all, all good scholars must dedicate the proper time to thoroughly research their quests for answers directly. And in this special case, Violet decided to take her mother's long held advice to heart.

But with that being said, what could the actual solution be?  After all, in most fairy tales, the villains are usually defeated by either succumbing to death or are saved through the act of unconditional true love. However, in Vera's case, these routes didn't seem to apply to her.

Unfortunately, a witch unwilling to accept her doomful fate, could never die a natural or a violent death. And as far as Violet knew, Vera had never loved anyone before. Sadly, she was the one person in the world who truly seemed incapable of love. Therefore, true love didn't seem to apply to Vera's unique case. Hence, what was the answer to this hopeless riddle?

Suddenly, an excerpt caught the corner of Violet's wandering eye. It was a chapter that was ironically bookmarked with a dried-up violet, hidden underneath its old and worn pages. It read as the following:

*"Kings may rise or fall, while kingdoms might flourish or crumble; worlds may begin or end, while honor and riches might come or go; but your sisterhood will outlast them all. While romantic love might be fickle in nature, sisterly love is the truest form of everlasting love. Unlike romantic love, this love is born not out of attraction or admiration or even, affection; but by blood. And blood, is thicker than anything."*

For some odd reason, this passage resonated with her. Strangely enough, this excerpt felt like the answer. A solution to Vera's ongoing reign of terror. But why was that? In truth, Violet hardly knew much about the evil queen; let alone, her past history. And maybe, *that* was the real problem.

If Violet was ever going to defeat Vera, then she needed to learn everything that she possibly could about her sworn enemy; including her past history and personal characteristics. Apart from being her father's evil stepmother and the wicked witch, Violet really didn't know anything else about the evil queen's mysterious past. Even her own great-grandmother, Maureen, who always seemed to have the answers to just about everything in life, really didn't know much about Vera, either. Just who exactly was the evil queen and what precisely made her tick?

Turning her attention over to Maximus, Violet observed him peacefully sleep in their bed. After spending the past two hours concentrating on her book, Violet decided to call it a night and go to bed. Closing her spell book shut, Violet walked over to a nearby closet to keep it.

And so, as Violet opened the closet's door and placed her spell book down above the shelf, she noticed a portrait hiding in the far corner. Curious as to what this mysterious portrait was, Violet bent down and shined her candlelight towards the painting. And to her amazement, she got the shock of her life.

There before her, was a portrait of a young mother in the center, holding two adolescence girls, each at her sides. One had short blonde locks and the other had long and thick dark hair. Naturally, Violet concluded that the girls must have been the woman's daughters. Sisters.

And as Violet shined her candlelight closer to the faces of these two girls, she instantly gasped at its sight. Lo and behold, the daughters were each wearing a unique piece of jewelry. The blonde daughter wore an amethyst heart-shaped necklace around her neck, while the darker haired girl wore an identical pair in the form of a bracelet around her wrist.

Furthermore, as Violet squinted her eyes, she recognized the blonde little girl from the portraits back at Galloway Manor. That blonde youth was her own grandmother, Sarah! And the very necklace worn around her grandmother's neck, that was the same identical necklace that she was currently wearing around her neck, too!

"This must be a portrait of my grandmother with her sister and mother!" Violet excitingly noted.

"But why would Ruby have a portrait of my grandmother and her family hidden away within a random closet inside of her cottage?" she asked herself out loud.

While Violet didn't recognize the other sister in the portrait, she decided to revert her attention back over to the mother. There, seated in the center, was a young woman, wearing a dark burgundy gown and a ruby stone necklace. She had long raven dark hair and emerald green eyes that shined brightly. A unique pair of eyes that were identical to herself. Eyes of her father, sister and brother. *Galloway eyes.*

And as she gazed closer upon the young woman's smile, it strangely felt so oddly familiar. She'd seen that smile before. And not long ago, too. And then, Violet gasped yet again. Suddenly, it all snapped together and made perfect sense.

"Ruby *is* the mother," she finally acknowledged. "Which means... Ruby is *my* great-grandmother!"

At long last, the pieces were starting to all fit together. That's why Ruby previously wanted Violet to call her granny back at Castle Hope. It wasn't just her being polite as her teacher, but it was because she *really was* her granny!

But now, that Violet knew the truth, she also needed more answers. For example, why did Ruby neglect to tell her about all of this earlier? Why did she keep this portrait hidden away in a closet and not publicly out on display? Was she ashamed of her past? Was she trying to conceal something wicked or foul? And most importantly, who was the second daughter in that portrait? Sarah's estranged sister? Her long-lost aunt?

At this point, Violet was just going to have to wait, until Ruby eventually returned back to the cottage to get the answers that she now, so desperately needed. And hopefully, she'd come back soon. The quicker, the better.

# CHAPTER 21

The next morning, Maximus decided to take Violet out for a picnic by the lake. Conveniently, the cottage was not only hidden deep inside of the dark and murky woods, but it was also walking distance away from a medium sized saltwater lake. Luckily, given the protective enchantment that shielded the cottage and its surrounding lands, the lake was also fortunately, a part of that extended protective territory, too.

And so, come morning after breakfast, Maximus and Violet packed a light lunch, consisting of roasted pheasant sandwiches, cinnamon apple spiced muffins and mint flavored lemonade. Once all of their edible goodies were neatly packed and stored inside of their straw basket, the happy couple headed off to enjoy their day by the lake.

Much to Violet's delight, the lake and its surrounding territory was a breathtaking scenic and stunning view. The cool blue body of water was pristine and crystal clear. In fact, the lake was so transparent that it accurately reflected the surrounding majestic mountains, ancient trees, turquoise blue sky, fluffy white clouds, traveling blackbirds and other wildlife and its surrounding landscape within its clear blue waters, just like a reflection in the mirror. Truly, it was like a serene picturesque scene, coming straight out from a watercolor painting or a classical fairy tale.

Given its own namesake, the Land of Eternal Autumn, the lake was surrounded by colorful foliage all around. With fallen leaves in the shades of tangerine orange, scarlet and crimson red, golden brown with a hint of faded forest green alongside its edges, the vast open fields surrounding the saltwater lake were covered in layers upon layers of warm toned foliage. Honestly, they were just like scattered jewels, all out on public display.

But apart from the enchanting foliage, the fields were also home to hundreds of marigold flowers, all in bloom. Even in the Land of Eternal Autumn, there was still one notable flower that bloomed in the heart of autumn. And while the rest of the surrounding flowers all withered away, the one that maintained its blooming form all year round was reserved to the precious golden petaled marigold. An official flower and color that honored and represented the Kingdom of the West.

"I can see why marigolds are the official flower to your kingdom," Violet remarked, as she admired its golden sunlike petals.

"They're only grown out here in the west," Maximus explained, as he threw a red and white gingham patterned cloth down onto the field. "It's why it's our signature flower. In fact, our own flag is colored scarlet, along with a bright marigold flower placed right in the center of it."

Afterwards, Maximus placed their picnic basket down and pulled her to his side. Before either of them knew it, they both tumbled down onto the ground with Violet landing right on top of him.

"Well, this is convenient," she laughed.

And then, Violet leaned down and placed a gentle kiss alongside his lips. Afterwards, Maximus pulled her closer to him and wrapped his arms around her waist.

"If there wasn't a war, then I'd have taken you out to the town square for a proper date," he told her. "But for now, I think a picnic by the lake will have to suffice. This, my darling, is the world that I want to introduce you to. Welcome to the Kingdom of the West, my love."

"And what a world it is, too," she noted. "It really is quite breathtaking."

With the sun shining high above them and the wind blowing across their faces, life at the Kingdom of the West was serene and peaceful. It was like a small piece of heaven, hidden right behind in their backdoor.

"Once this war is over, I'm going to take you back here again," he vowed.

A promise, Maximus intended to keep. At all costs.

"I'd like that," she admitted.

"Does that mean... you're considering staying here... *with me*?" he hesitated to ask.

Even though they were still a new couple, Maximus already envisioned a future with Violet. Hopefully, she felt the same way as him.

"I think so," replied Violet, in earnest. "Honestly, after spending all this time together, I can't seem to imagine myself anywhere else other than by your side."

And those very words of hers felt like a beaming light shining right through his heart. Whether or not Maximus was looking for love, lo and behold, he found it.

"Violet, I love you," he confessed, as he placed a gentle kiss above her forehead.

"Maximus, I love you, too," she admitted, with a warm smile.

And then, as Maximus reached over to pull Violet even closer to him, she suddenly backed away. Her reaction was certainly unexpected!

"Wait," she said, forcefully.

"Wait?" he asked in surprise. Was something wrong between them?

"I want us to try something new," she explained. "Well... new on my part."

"What do you mean?" he asked in confusion.

"Just watch," she answered.

And then, to his surprise, her hands traveled down below his waist and over to his groin. Before he knew it, she began to unbutton his trousers and within the blink of an eye, she quickly pulled his cock from out of his breeches.

"Violet—" he yelled.

"Shush," she said. "Please, allow me."

Witnessing the sheer determination shining through within her emerald green eyes, Maximus decided to allow her to work her magic. After all, anything that Violet did, never disappointed him. And so, following her command, Maximus rested his head against the ground and surrendered his body over to Violet's custody.

Carefully, Violet took hold of his cock and held it softly within the clutch of her hands. Gently, she began to caress him by moving her fingers up and down against his long and thick shaft. Instantly, he flinched. Every touch and stroke of hers, made his heart flutter with excitement and desire.

Seeing his reaction, Violet smiled to herself. One way or another, she always discovered new and brilliant ways to please him. And so, following the momentum, she bent down and took one slow and long lick of his cock against her wet tongue. Again, he flinched. But this time, he let out a pleasurable sound, too.

"Aaaahhhh....," Maximus moaned, as he closed his silver eyes and ran his hands through his chestnut brown hair.

And if Maximus couldn't imagine more pleasure, Violet shocked him even more. Better than all of his wildest fantasies, Violet placed her entire mouth against his cock and swallowed it whole. Lo and behold, she was sucking him in all of his glory!

"Violet!" he roared, as his body thrusted his erect cock forward into her mouth, hitting the back of her throat.

While it was never his intention to *fuck* her mouth; however, his body naturally reacted in that way, simply by her determination to consume him. And so, as she licked and sucked against his long and thick shaft, Maximus thrusted back and forth into her mouth and released his inner juice, along the way. And as much as Violet thoroughly enjoyed tasting and feasting upon him, Maximus felt equally the same way, too.

But alas, having her serve him wasn't enough for him. He wanted to please her, too. Oh, so desperately. And so, with a great sense of urgency, Maximus reached over and ripped off the buttons to Violet's dress. Yesterday, he might have needed a dagger to do the job; but today, he was eager to use his bare hands. One way or another, he was going to remove her dress, even if he had to tear it apart himself! Which is precisely what he did, too!

"Next time, no more button-downed dresses," Maximus ordered, as he peeled down the tattered remains of her once-beloved dress and quickly discarded it down onto the ground.

Luckily, for him, she wasn't wearing any undergarments nor a brassiere underneath. Just like yesterday, she was left completely naked and exposed. Much to his approval.

"Now, my love," he instructed, "Help me to remove my clothes."

Following his command, Violet did just that. One by one, she removed his clothes. Starting from his blouse and all the way down to his trousers and then, his breeches. Afterwards, Violet tried to climb back up, but before she had a chance to move, he quickly grabbed a hold of her. Within the blink of an eye, she was directly seated right above him, in-between his inner thighs.

"This is going to be another new position for us," he began to explain, "If you're interested, then I'd like us to explore this option next."

"What do I need to do?" she asked him, with her heart rapidly beating in excitement. Already, she felt breathless.

"It's just like riding a horse," he answered, with a sly grin. "Except, this time it's *me*. Just follow my lead. Are you ready to give it a try?"

Silently, she nodded in agreement. Whatever he wanted to try, she was open and ready for it.

"Alright, that's a good girl," he wickedly smiled. "Okay, my love, have at it. *Fuck me hard* and make me proud."

And then, he moved her to his center, stretched her inner thighs as far and as wide apart as possible. Once he felt that she was perfectly secure and comfortably seated on top of him, he grabbed a hold of his cock and slid it inside of her womb. Instantly, she moaned in pleasure.

"Aaaahhhh...," Violet sighed, as she closed her eyes shut and threw her head back.

With him still inside her, Maximus said, "Now, start rocking back and forth. Take me, just like you'd do when riding a horse."

Following his command, Violet did just that. Back and forth, she rocked against him, as his cock plunged deeper into her body, penetrating all of her inner most sensitive nerves, along the way. From this angle, it felt oh so different! Friction at its finest point! And dare she admit it, this new position felt better than anything else that she'd previously experienced with him up until now!

"Are you enjoying this, my love? Do you take pleasure on riding my cock?" he asked her, with a playful smile.

"Yes!!!" Violet shouted, as she continued to ride him in full force.

"Yes, what?" he teased her.

"*Yes, I enjoy riding your cock!!!*" she yelled at him. "*I love fucking you!!!*"

Meanwhile, as her plump breasts jiggled back and forth with each one of her swings, Maximus grabbed a hold of her hips to keep her at balance. With each of her thrusts against him, Maximus lifted up his own hips and plunged himself forward into her. Back and forth, they established their mutual rhythms. And the more she rode him, the faster she went. And as he plunged *deeper* into her, she rode him *faster* and *harder* than ever before... *over...* and... *over...* and *over... again...*

Just as she was right about to climax and collapse down onto his chest, Maximus swiftly took hold of her and within the blink of an eye, he rolled her underneath him, placing himself back on top. At this point, Violet was breathless. And to be fair, so was he. However, Maximus was determined to make this moment last.

And so, as he kissed her passionately with his tongue dancing and gliding inside of her welcoming mouth, he pushed her thighs further apart.

And then, in one swift move, he plunged his cock right back into her. Instantly, she moaned, yet again.

"Aaaahhhh....oh.... Maximus!" she cried his name out loud. Worshiping the god-like-prince inside of her.

But her screams of joy only further encouraged him. And so, Maximus plunged forward, pushing his long and hard erect cock *deeper* and *deeper* into her womb, further inserting himself into her precious body. And as he licked and sucked on her hardened nipples, he continued to thrust *hard* and *fast* in-between her thighs... *over...* and *over...* and *over...* *again...* sending wave... after wave... of pleasure...

Until finally, as their grand finale, he withdrew his cock, only to plunge it back in one last and final time. A few minutes later, they both climaxed together and then, eventually, they collapsed down to their sides.

Afterwards, Maximus rolled over and climbed himself back up. As he made his way over to the picnic basket, Violet stared at him in disbelief.

"Are we done already?" she asked, fearful that their most recent sexual encounter was now over and done with.

Even though it was one of the most blissful experiences of her entire life, Violet couldn't help but feel a bit disappointed with their abrupt ending. If she had a choice in the matter, then she'd have wanted them to go at it again, right afterwards.

"My love, I do believe it's time for lunch now," he answered with a rakish grin. "After all, I need you fully energized and ready for round two."

Without saying another word, Violet quickly joined his side and grabbed a hold of one of the pheasant sandwiches. With the sandwich secured in her hand, she bit down and began to chew.

# CHAPTER 22

While glancing down at her fresh bouquet of violets, Vera sighed to herself. Since conquering the Kingdom of the West and crowning herself as the new queen, she had already gone through at least a dozen or so bouquets. And even though she had the magical ability to enchant them all to last forever, it was the one thing that she neglected to do simply because she didn't have the heart to do so.

In truth, everything around her might have been false and fabricated, but the violets were the only thing that remained true. The one object that reminded Vera of her distant past. Long before she became the wicked witch and the evil queen. A time, when she was still an innocent youth, with a promising future ahead and living back at home in her once beloved and cherished cottage, alongside her mother and sister. Ah, happier times those had certainly once been.

But unfortunately, that was a long time ago and a lot had changed from then to now. Really, it was a whole another lifetime ago. An entirely alternative version to her current hermit-like self. A former version of herself that still possessed the capacity to love. A girl who foolishly believed in true love and clung onto the false power of hope. A Vera, that once owned a pure and untarnished *heart*.

Once upon a time, her late sister, Sarah, used to tease her about her name. As children, Sarah would often say that she wished Vera could have been named Violet, instead. That way, whenever Sarah told others that she loved violets, then it wouldn't be limited to just the flower alone but of her sister as well. Ah, if only it could have been. Perhaps, if she'd been named Violet and not Vera at birth, then fate would have dealt her with a much different path in life. A path of *goodness*. Of *righteousness*. Of *happiness*.

But sadly, *this sister* was ultimately destined for evil. After all, wickedness was her second nature. If Vera wrote an autobiography of herself today, then it'd be called *The Rise of the Tyrannical Queen*.

Sadly, that was the truth. Vera was indeed, a tyrant. An evil queen of the highest order. Her reign of terror would easily go down in the history books for centuries to come. And whenever anyone, now or in the future, heard the sound of her name, then they'd shiver and tremble by the mere mention of it. In fact, she was almost convinced that hence, from this day forth, no child in their land would come to bear her name, Vera, ever again. Alas, she was the *last* of her namesake. After all, what sane person would dare to permit their child to share the same name as a ruthless tyrant and brutal dictator?

Alas, Vera *came*, she *conquered*, and she *devoured*. Only to do it, all over again… *repeatedly*. One way or another, there were always more villages to burn, or rebels to behead. Lives to crush. Dreams to smash. Properties to confiscate. Enemies to destroy. Sadly, it seemed that Vera had more enemies than she did of actual allies. But she supposed that's just how the business of running a monarchy was. Tedious, gruesome and deadly. At least, this was the reality of her reign. *Her reign of terror.*

Ever since Vera was a young girl, she knew the reality of ruling an empire. Sometimes, there were victors and at other times, losers. However, with that said, if Vera decided to run her kingdom down into ruins, then so be it! As far as she was concerned, her kingdom was already in crumbles. But that didn't bother her in the very least. After all, all monarchs and kingdoms were designed to eventually crumble and fall. That was a reflection of true history. An inevitable and unavoidable fact.

Whether or not the Kingdom of the West survived to see another day of light by the end of the month, Vera could care less. She already had her throne. And if she lost all of her citizens to a mass graveyard and be deemed as the sole survivor, then so be it! She could easily be happy as the queen of *none* than a good and righteous queen to *all*. After all, this was her quest for *revenge*. Of *vengeance*. Of *terror*.

Whatever her fate was at this point onwards, Vera no longer cared. Nothing else in this world mattered to her anymore. She might have worn a shiny golden crown above her precious head, but her heart was permanently blackened underneath. After all, she already *lost* everything that truly mattered. Her sister. Her mother. Her son. Her lover. *Everything.*

But alas, with all of this free time spent loathing away in this pathetically empty and lonesome throne room, Vera couldn't help but wonder if all that she had sacrificed for in exchange for the crown, really came to amount to nothing, after all?

Was her lifelong quest for vengeance truly worth forsaking her own soul and the last ounce of humanity left in her, in the end? Did it bring her happiness? Joy? Accomplishment? Contentment? Honestly, she no longer was certain; for truth be told, her heart no longer clung onto anything real anymore. Both of good and... of *evil.*

Over time, Vera's heart grew into cold stone and eventually, she became desensitized to all those around her. By then, any ounce of humanity in her was long gone and as a result, her soul was darkened overnight. Vera might have been alive and breathing, but she also transformed into a walking and talking decorative object. No different from another clay statue or even, a wooden marionette. She might have been the queen, but she was an *unhappy* one.

Death upon death, murder upon murder; it was just another standard day at the kingdom of ruins. Once upon a time, the Kingdom of the West was a happy, thriving and prosperous land; that is, until Vera single-handedly ran it straight down into the ground... just like she had always wanted to do so. After all, if Vera couldn't have her happily ever after, then neither could they. It truly was just as simple as that.

Perhaps, Vera wasn't meant to be a ruler, but a conqueror. In truth, conquering more clans and territories brought her great satisfaction; for it allowed her to claim her vengeance. However, once the battles were all fought and won, and when it came time to rule, Vera felt... well... *unsatisfied*. And dare she admit it... but rather... she felt *bored...*

After burning and destroying most of the western villages down into the ground, and watching these once thriving and prosperous town squares turn into nothing more but piles of ash and dust, Vera continued on with her march of terror. Once these villages were destroyed, she moved on to arrest and execute the rogue rebels. And then, afterwards, she went after her fellow witches and sorcerers and slaughtered those amongst them who refused to aid in her cause. And for anyone else who was reluctant to bow down and accept her reign, then she murdered them on the spot, without so much as a second thought. And most importantly, without any remorse, either.

But after sitting on her golden throne for the past few weeks, Vera came to the bitter conclusion that she *still* wasn't happy. Her quest for vengeance didn't bring her any solace to her stone heart. Perhaps, it really had all been for *nothing*.

And as Vera admired her bouquet of violets, she also took a moment to glance down at her amethyst heart-shaped stone bracelet. Ever since she was a young girl, Vera often gazed upon her cherished bracelet. It was the one and only gift that she still had left from her estranged mother.

And after all of the evil deeds that Vera committed during her troublesome existence, her bracelet was a last reminder of her old life. A time, when she was nothing more than another fair maiden living out in the woods, alongside her beloved sister and mother. A forgotten time when she was still *innocent*.

If Vera could turn back the clocks, then she gladly would. If given a second chance, then she'd have easily renounced her throne and return back to her youth. To once again, be reunited with her beloved sister. Before she left her to get married. Before she met the godforsaken Earl of Galloway!

But unfortunately, Vera already made a sworn enemy with time, herself. As part of King Elryk's order of decree pertaining to her former exile, Vera was forbidden to return back to the Great Kingdom during the course of her lifetime. And while she might have fooled death with her return, she couldn't fool time. And time was not at all pleased with her unannounced *and* unwelcomed arrival back to her native homeland.

Therefore, by returning to the Great Kingdom after her previous exile to Earth, Vera's selfish actions inadvertently set the clocks backwards. Prior to her arrival, the two realms were previously equal to each other in terms of their timelines. However, by traveling in-between these two realms via the enchanted forest without time's blessing, Vera inadvertently created a time loop; in which a single day in their kingdom was equivalent to one hundred years in the lands of Earth. Thus, the only way to end this time loop was if the sole cause to this anomaly ceased to exist in the first place. And in this case: *Vera*. Hence, if Vera were to die, then her death would ultimately, set the clocks back on track and end this faulty time loop shared between the two worlds, once and for all.

Suddenly, the doors burst wide open and two black knights from her imperial dark army entered into the throne room. While all members of the queen's army were previously ordered not to disturb her unannounced at all times, Vera concluded that if these knights chose to risk their ranks *and* lives to seek her out without having her prior permission, then their reasons for doing so must have been urgent, indeed.

"Well... what is it?" Vera asked them, as she stared away at her blackened chipped nails, looking *and* sounding as bored as ever.

"We... have some... news...," spoke the first knight to her right, in hesitation.

"News? We'll be out with it," Vera commanded.

Already, she was beginning to lose her patience by his inexcusable delay.

"Your Highness," spoke the second knight, sounding a bit calmer and more confident than the first.

"Yes?" she asked, turning her gaze over towards him.

"There's been word circulating in town that the crown prince escaped the latest siege," he informed her, as he bowed his head down in both shame and disappointment.

"Oh, is that so?"

In truth, Vera could have easily turned a blind eye to this rather pitiful and useless news. Whether or not the crown prince lived or died, it was of little consequence to her. After all, that brute was harmless. She was already crowned as the queen. Even if he tried to use his fractured army to attempt an invasion into her royal palace, then she was already well prepared to easily defeat them all by using her black magic. With minimal effort, too.

But because, Vera was feeling a bit bored and happily ready to put on a show, she decided to humor these two knights of hers. In her normal state, Vera appeared to be a regular mortal woman. With her long dark hair flowing down her back, she was wearing her signature black dress that was a contrast to her pale complexion and emerald green eyes. In reality, she only transformed into her wicked witch persona, whenever she used her magic or simply wanted to install fear amongst her subjects. And right now, Vera was ready to put some fear into her knights' unsuspecting hearts.

"So, basically... you're telling me that you *all failed*. Am I correct?"

Meanwhile, her eyes shined in bright yellow, while her complexion shifted from pale white to dark green. Immediately, both men gulped in fear.

"I suppose... yes," answered the second knight.

"You *suppose*?" Vera laughed mockingly. "Do you honestly *suppose* that I won't actually decide to kill you, right here and now? Especially, after delivering me with such pitiful and pathetic news? Tell me, dear sirs, give me *one* damn good reason as to why I shouldn't transform you two into slimy toads to make an example of you both!"

Instantly, the first knight dropped his sword down onto the ground and began to tremble. Alas, Vera's harsh methods for installing fear into her men worked. Most tragically, too.

"Wait," cried the second knight. "I... we... have other news... too..."

"Well, then, speak up and tell me!" she snapped.

"The crown prince not only fled the castle, but he was also seen escaping into the woods alive and well. He was accompanied by a fair maiden by his side, too."

"A fair maiden? And why should I care about another lady of his court? Really knight, do stop wasting my time."

"But my queen, she's no ordinary maiden. They call her the savior," he revealed.

"And she's been trained by Ruby, the Great Teacher, herself," added the other knight.

"A savior? Trained by Ruby?" asked Vera, now curious as ever about this latest development. If Ruby had her dirty hands on this, then this maiden was no ordinary girl.

"I see that even after all these years, Ruby still likes to meddle in other peoples' affairs. Especially, *mine*," she huffed in annoyance. "Okay, tell me more about this savior. Who is she and where did she come from?"

"They say she's not from here, but from another realm called Earth."

"Earth?" Vera repeated, in surprise.

But how was that possible? With the time loop still in effect, no one else from Earth was permitted to enter into this magical realm. Apart from the previous spell that Vera placed years ago to ensure that an immortal army of archers permanently guarded the magical cave secretly hidden away within the enchanted forest, it just wasn't logically possible for anyone else to defeat that powerful army and gain access to freely crossover into her world. In fact, she personally made sure of it.

"Yes, Earth," confirmed the second knight. "They call her the savior. And ever since the latest siege that recently took place at Castle Hope, she's been secretly hiding with the crown prince in a cottage located deep within the woods. On protective territory."

Unfortunately, that protective territory just-so-happened to be Vera's own childhood home. Not only was Vera also banned from returning there as punishment for her previous exile, but she also didn't have the *heart* to return there either. After all, there were too many memories of her past still lingering in there. Both happy and *painful* ones, too.

"And they've been there ever since?" Vera asked them, as her complexion returned back to her normal pale self.

"Yes," answered the second knight.

"And who is she? Does she have a name? Who are her parents? Is she of royal blood?" inquired the queen.

"They call her Lady Galloway," he said. "And apparently, she's the daughter of the Earl of Galloway."

"Henry's daughter?" Vera repeated in amazement.

Now, that was the *real shocker* if ever she heard one. Alas, all this time spent away from Earth, one way or another, Vera had long forgotten about her cursed nephew. Ironically, the very nephew that she, herself, had previously cursed.

But apparently, if he had a daughter, then he probably wasn't cursed anymore. However, with that said, why was she here, right now? What business did the girl have crossing over into her realm? In her kingdom? And how? Why?

"I don't know of any Henry," spoke the knight, in earnest. "But they also call her by her given name, Violet."

Upon hearing the name *Violet*, Vera instantly flinched. If ever a name had the power to compel her, then that was *it*.

"Violet, is that what you said?" she asked.

"Yes, Violet," he replied. "Violet, the Savior."

"Violet, the Savior," Vera repeated in amusement.

For the past several days, Vera previously found herself utterly bored and unamused. But now, this war suddenly got interesting. A lot *more interesting*.

"As a reward for this vital information, I've decided that I won't turn either of you into toads, after all," she began, "As you've both, surprisingly, proved yourselves useful to me."

"Thank you," both knights sighed with great relief.

"However," she added, "Your safety is still not guaranteed. Find and bring me this savior. I want to meet her, and see her with my own two eyes. This is a direct order."

"Yes, your Highness," both men vowed, as they proudly saluted her.

"Then, why are you both still standing there, like statues? Go and get her! Right *now*!" she roared.

And within the blink of an eye, the two black knights were gone.

Alas, Queen Vera was once again, left alone in the solitude and comfort of her golden throne room. Walking over to her bouquet of violets, she bent down and took a sniff. Instantly she sneezed, while her eyes grew watery with tears.

"Ah, you pesky violets," she mockingly laughed. "You really are going to be the death of me, after all!"

# CHAPTER 23

On one bright and sunny afternoon, Ruby finally decided to make a formal appearance back at the cottage. Luckily, it was during lunchtime, so Violet and Maximus were thankfully, fully clothed and enjoying a warm meal consisting of rabbit stew. After traveling to visit her trusted allies in the neighboring kingdoms, Ruby returned to her old country cottage to check on how the young happy couple were faring.

"My, my, you two have certainly managed to keep yourselves busy, now, haven't you?" she teased them, fully aware of their most recent love affair.

Although Ruby had been gone for about a week or so; however, just one look at their happy faces and instantly, she recognized their loving expressions. Together, Maximus and Violet were the spitting image of a youthful pair who were madly in love. A familiar love-stricken look that she once shared with her own late husband from many, many years ago.

"And where have *you* been all this time?" asked Violet, as she paused from eating the rest of her meal. Already, her voice sounding both annoyed and relieved at the same exact time.

"As I told you before, I needed to gather some ingredients," she answered calmly and nonchalant.

"And pray tell, where are they? From the looks of it, you seem to be empty handed," Violet made sure to point this vital fact out to her.

"It's in safe keeping, my dear."

And *that*, was all that Violet needed to know. Needless to say, secrets were also a part of Ruby's many ongoing side businesses, too. In fact, one could even argue that secrets were considered to be Ruby's primary signature currency at play, known to many insiders residing within the Great Kingdom.

"Either way," Maximus interjected. "Welcome back, Ruby. Won't you please take a seat and join us in a helping of rabbit stew?"

"Thank you, my crown prince," replied Ruby, happily. "I believe I shall."

"Ah," Violet interrupted, "But before you do, I need to show you something, first."

Instantly, Violet quickly excused herself from the table and ran over into the bedroom. A second later, she returned back into the main living quarters and presented them with a large painting. A secret family portrait that was previously hidden away, inside of the bedroom's closet.

"Care to explain about this mysterious portrait?" Violet dared to ask her.

While Maximus appeared entirely confused by this conversation; Ruby, on the other hand, sighed. Unlike the crown prince, Ruby knew precisely as to what Violet had alluded to by posing this question. One way or another, she'd been discovered.

"It's *you* painted right smack in the center, isn't it?" she asked her in an accusing manner.

"Yes," Ruby sighed, once more. "It is."

"What's going on here?" asked Maximus, this time. "Ruby, is there something that you've neglected to share with us?"

"I promise to reveal everything," Ruby stated coolly. "But first, Violet, please make your granny a nice warm cup of mint tea. I'm going to need some extra energy to try and explain everything to you *both*."

"Very well, *Granny*," replied Violet, with a wryly smile.

Even though it felt strange to refer to Ruby as such, but what else could she say? In the end, she really was her *granny*!

* * *

"**W**ait, do you honestly mean to tell us, that Vera is *your daughter*???" Violet gasped to Ruby's startling revelation.

"Yes, which also makes her your great-aunt, too," Ruby added.

"And according to your version of this story, Vera was *also* the former mistress to my late father?" asked Maximus, equally stunned by this surprising confession. "But why didn't I recognize her from before? If Vera was truly my father's former mistress, then surely, I would have seen her at the palace, right?"

"Your mother, the late Queen Yesinia, God bless her soul, ensured that neither your brother nor yourself, ever crossed paths with Vera," Ruby explained. "In truth, it was a part of the mutual agreement shared between your parents. Honestly, it was the one and only thing that the late king and queen actually agreed upon, during their turbulent marriage."

"You know, I always suspected that my parents' marriage was loveless. But now, I finally have my confirmation," admitted Maximus, with a heavy heart. "But to be perfectly honest, it doesn't surprise me. After all, my late father was a heartless bastard."

"The late king was a great many things," Ruby chimed in. "But the one thing that I do know with absolute certainty, is that he truly loved your brother and yourself. He loved his sons a great lot."

"But unlike my mother, my father apparently loved Vera, too," spoke Maximus, spitefully. "My mother might have been the queen, but she was an unhappy one. Even though my mother died while I was still a young boy, but in my vague childhood memories of her, I do recall her always sporting a melancholy expression painted across her lovely face. I suppose that after I was born, my father most likely cut off all marital relations with her."

"That I cannot answer for certain. After all, the true nature to their private relationship behind closed doors is known only to them," Ruby told him. "While your father might have loved Vera, he also greatly respected your mother, Yesinia, too. In fact, as our queen, we all did."

"Damn him to hell!" shouted Maximus angrily, as he clenched his hands into fists and pounded forcefully against the wooden table.

Although Violet desperately wanted to learn the truth concerning the portrait and the relationship it held to her own family, she never in a million years ever suspected that the truth was also connect to Maximus' family as well.

"Maximus, it's all right. Please don't get upset," Violet spoke gently, while trying her best to help calm his temper back down.

Taking in a deep breath, he said, "It's alright. I'll be okay. Ruby, please do go on."

"Yes, Ruby—"

"Violet, from now on, I do have one request from you," Ruby quickly interjected.

"And that is?" she asked.

"The crown prince may call me by my given name," Ruby clarified. "But *you*, shall call me *Granny*. And that is *not* up for negotiation, either."

"Very well, *Granny*," replied Violet, as she mockingly emphasized the usage of that word, with the vowels slowly lingering on her spoken tongue.

"Very good," Ruby complemented her, with a beaming smile. "Now, go ahead and ask away. I promise to answer all of your questions."

"Alright," Violet began, "I recognize that Vera was your daughter, my grandmother's sister and Maximus' father's mistress. But with that established, how in the world, did Vera end up in all of this mess? Why was she exiled to Earth, all those many years ago?"

"Because she was pregnant with King Elryk's illegitimate child, that's why," Ruby revealed.

"What???" gasped both Violet and Maximus simultaneously.

"Wait, are you saying that my Uncle Phillip—"

"Is *not your* Uncle Phillip, but the crown prince's younger half-brother," Ruby corrected.

"What? Do you mean to tell me that my father had another child out of wedlock with this... this... wicked witch?" asked Maximus, both stunned and disgusted by this unnerving truth.

"Yes. And to be perfectly fair, this happened well before Vera became the wicked witch and the evil queen," replied Ruby. "Once upon a time, my daughter had a soul. She was a good sister and a decent daughter. But unfortunately, this all took place before her heart turned completely into stone."

"But why would Vera's pregnancy force her to flee into exile? Surely, she could have stayed behind and remained at the royal palace, alongside with her child?" Violet asked. "As difficult as this might sound, but plenty of illegitimate children throughout known history have grown up in palaces. Mistresses and concubines are not foreign or new concepts. Therefore, why was Vera made to serve as the exception?"

 "Because unlike other kingdoms, an illegitimate son born into our world would have always served as the potential seed for a civil war," Ruby answered in earnest. "And your father, my dear crown prince, always knew that. He sent Vera away to protect the crown. Ultimately, it was his sworn duty to the throne and his heir, your late brother, King Leopold, to preserve the longevity and stability of our kingdom."

"So perhaps, Vera was a victim in all of this, too," Maximus somberly reflected. "But regardless, she might have started out as the victim in this story, but overtime, she became the true villainess. No matter the injustices fate inflicted upon her in the past, there's still no excuse to the current atrocities that she's recently committed. Unspeakable and unforgivable crimes against humanity."

"You're absolutely correct," Ruby sternly agreed. "All of Vera's cruel and heartless deeds are inexcusable. Even as my daughter, I cannot accept her evil doings. She's slaughtered and killed thousands, out of her own free will. As much as I might have loved her before as her mother; however, the daughter that I once knew and loved is long gone. Which is the *real reason* as to why, I'm willing to do *everything* in my power to stop her, at all costs."

"As her mother, can you honestly say with absolute certainty, that you truly possess the heart to see her undoing?" asked Maximus, in all seriousness.

"Without a shadow of a doubt," replied Ruby, firmly and confidently. "After all, it's my sworn duty to protect every single one of her victims; all past, present and future. I take full responsibility for my family's atonement on her behalf. Especially, as the mother who bore the monster. This is *my final act of penance* for the unholy sins committed by my daughter. A child born out of my own flesh and blood."

Ruby's words struck a deep chord within Violet's heart. How difficult it must have been for her granny to help aid in the destruction of her only living daughter. A person, whom she birthed and once loved, cherished and treasured. No matter her past mistakes, Violet could never imagine her own mother, Kassie, ever hurting herself or any one of her younger siblings. And yet, Ruby was faced with the most impossible task. A heart-wrenching burden that no mother should ever have to come to bear: sacrificing your child's life to protect the rest of humanity.

"Then, there must be a way for us to stop her," Violet spoke up.

"I really do hope so, my dear," Ruby said to her. "After all, we're all counting on you. You are the savior, Violet."

"But what pushed Vera to go so dark? Was it solely due to the late king's betrayal? Or was it before that?"

"What do you mean?" Maximus asked, most curiously.

"I mean, all villains have an origin story. At least, that's the case in all of the famous classical fairy tales," Violet clarified. "There's always a vital turning point, that often sends a character onto the path of darkness."

"You're right," Ruby agreed. "Truth be told, Vera's path to darkness happened long before she met the late King Elryk. Now, looking back at it all, I suppose that I first saw a significant change in her, when your grandmother, Sarah, left us to marry your grandfather, the late Earl of Galloway."

"So, Sarah and Vera were close sisters before then?" asked Violet.

"Yes. They were inseparable," Ruby sighed. "Growing up in this secluded cottage, they only had each other to lean on. And so, when Sarah got married to Henrick and moved over into your world, Vera didn't take it all too well. Slowly, but surely, her white magic started to turn dark."

"Abandonment can sometimes bring out the ugliness in a person's character," Maximus chimed in.

"I agree, my crown prince," spoke Ruby. "Sometimes, the person we hate the most can also be the same person whom we once loved most of all."

Suddenly, Violet recalled the mysterious passage that she previously read in her golden spell book:

*"Kings may rise or fall, while kingdoms might flourish or crumble; worlds may begin or end, while honor and riches might come or go; but your sisterhood will outlast them all. While romantic love might be fickle in nature, sisterly love is the truest form of everlasting love. Unlike romantic love, this love is born not out of attraction or admiration or even, affection; but by blood. And blood, is thicker than anything."*

After hearing Ruby's story, it now started to all make sense. Long ago, before Vera was the infamous evil queen... even before she was the mistress to the late king and the wicked witch... she was a fair young maiden, just like her own grandmother, Sarah. Once upon a time, Vera had a loving heart. And with that heart, she loved her sister. Their sisterly love was stronger than anything... even romantic love.

Instantly, Violet got a bold idea. What if, in Vera's special case, true love wasn't in the form of a romantic love; but instead, it was related to a lost love? The love of a late sister? And what if, their sisterly bond was strong enough to triumph over Vera's current evil emotions? What if that same enduring sisterly love and sacred bond was sufficient enough to help remind Vera of whom, she once was? Before all of this tragedy. That once upon a time, Vera wasn't always so heartless, wicked and evil. That once, she did actually *love someone*.

Maybe, just maybe, if Vera could remember her past lost love, then somehow it could miraculously save her. Free her from her evil worldly pursuits of murder, terror and revenge. Perhaps, by reminding Vera of who she was prior to becoming the corrupted tyrant and evil villainess, then maybe it could make all the difference. Save both herself and their kingdom.

And then, Violet had her answer: the necklace. Alas, she had Sarah's necklace worn around her neck. Which meant, that Vera most likely, still had the matching bracelet. If only she could unite the two pairs, then perhaps, there was still a way to get through to her and help convince her to stop this war altogether.

But in order to make this happen, Violet needed to somehow come face-to-face with Vera at her royal palace. Which could only mean...

"Maximus and Granny," Violet spoke, with much determination. "I think I finally know how to stop Vera, once and for all. Now, you might not like my chosen method; however, can you both please promise me that whatever I ask, you'll come to agree to it, without any hesitations nor questions? No matter how outrageous or dangerous it might sound, at first?"

"Whatever it is, I already don't like the sound of it," Maximus remarked, as he folded his arms against his chest.

But much to Violet's surprise, Ruby replied, "But of course, we will. After all, you're the savior. Violet, whatever you suggest, we'll follow it, no matter what."

And with that, Violet happily smiled on, as she began to secretly plot away...

# CHAPTER 24

"**V**iolet, this isn't a good idea," Maximus muttered underneath his breath.

"Oh hush," she scolded him. "Simply put on your helmet and do just like we planned."

"Oh, really? You want me to put on my helmet?" he asked, mockingly. "And pray tell, what about yourself? Aren't you going to put on your helmet, too?"

"Ah, you're impossible!" Violet exclaimed.

But lo and behold, he had a valid point. If she was going to *order him*, he, the *crown prince*, and request that he wear his helmet to match their uniforms, then she needed to do the same, too. To set the prime example in which to follow. After all, they came together in disguised as black knights to the queen's imperial dark and ruthless army. It was only proper that they fit the roles, in which they came here to play.

"Fine," Violet reluctantly sighed, as she finally put her helmet back on.

"Okay, are you happy now?" Violet asked him, as she placed her hands alongside her hips.

"I'll be happy once this ridiculous plan of yours is over and done with. After *you're* deemed perfectly safe and sound, and not a single moment before," Maximus clarified.

"Whatever happens, stay by my side," he ordered. "At *all* times. Violet, can you at least promise me that?"

"Very well, I promise."

"Okay, that wasn't so hard now, was it?" he asked, as he placed his helmet back on.

Violet might have been the love of his life, but she certainly wasn't an easy one to tame.

"The hardest decision of my entire life," she replied, mockingly.

"You're impossible," he sighed.

"No, my prince. I believe I'm the savior," Violet boldly declared, with a beaming smile.

"Unfortunately, yes. Which is the *only* reason why I agreed to come here, in the first place. Much to my dismay."

"Enough complaining, Maximus. It's showtime."

"Ah, wait," he quickly grabbed a hold of her arm. "Did you bring your dagger?"

"No, why? Isn't a sword enough?"

"No," he growled. "Swords can be lost in a battle. You always need a spare. Here, take mine."

And then, he reached into his sash and handed over to her his dagger.

"Take this. And if we get separated, then don't hesitate to use it, if needed."

"I promise," she vowed. "But first, my love, show me your handsome face one last time."

Following her request, Maximus removed his bevor, revealing his bare lips and all the way down to his chin. Afterwards, Violet did the same. And once they were both exposed, she leaned in and planted one last gentle kiss alongside his tender lips.

But right as Violet was about to pull away from him, Maximus grabbed her tightly and brought her right back to his side. Without saying another word, he kissed her again and this time around, it wasn't gentle. Instead, it was fierce and passionate, filled with such longing, desire and dare we admit it... *fear*. If this was going to be their last kiss before their upcoming battle, then Maximus intended to make their kiss last as long as possible.

And as their tongues danced the forbidden tango of their desires, Violet finally pulled herself away and told him, "This won't be our last, just so you know."

"Good," Maximus happily noted, as he flipped his bevor back on.

"Now, my love," he added. "Let's do this."

*  *  *

Sneaking into Vera's *stolen* imperial palace was surprisingly, a lot easier than what Violet initially anticipated. After spending last night plotting away until the early hours of dawn, Violet, Maximus and Ruby all agreed that entering into the royal palace in disguised as black knights in the queen's imperial dark army was probably the best approach of all.

Although Maximus suggested that they use a glamour spell to alter their physical appearances; Ruby, instead, promptly advised against it. According to her, any form of foreign magic exercised around Vera's vicinity, would ultimately prove to be dangerous. Apparently, with Vera seated on the golden throne, her black magic was at its zenith in terms of her power. As a

254

result, the evil queen possessed the heightened ability to sniff away and detect any forms of foreign enchantments that were lurking within her castle. Magic that wasn't of her own branding.

Therefore, they all agreed that if Violet was to safely reach Vera's side to enact her mission, then the best approach was to sneak into the palace directly in disguised as knights. Luckily, for them, Ruby had just-so-conveniently managed to collect two extra spares of the official black knights' uniforms. Apparently, these highly sought-after coats of armor were *the special ingredients* that Ruby had previously collected during her prolonged absence. Somehow, Violet couldn't help but wonder if Ruby had already foreseen the future well in advance, and that this was always going to be the end game for them. A form of strategic calculations on her part, or a matter of destiny.

Originally, Violet wanted to travel solo for this dangerous mission, but Maximus instantly objected to her idea. Instead, he rejected her reckless plan and instead, insisted that he join her side to serve as both her protector and as her guide. After all, Maximus grew up inside of the royal imperial palace. It was his childhood home. And up until Vera's recent conquest, the castle was always *his*.

And because of these reasons, Maximus knew all of the secret passages, exits and hidden doors. Things that no other black knight serving in the imperial dark army could have ever have known. Plus, as a blood royal prince, Maximus was privy to all of the classified secret royal escape routes in the castle that only the royal family had information on. Passages that most palace courtiers were entirely ignorant about. Therefore, having him by her side proved to be an invaluable asset.

"What do you plan on saying to her, once you cross her path?" Maximus asked her, once they approached the front gates.

"Right now, I can't explain it to you. Instead, I just need you to trust in me," Violet told him.

"So, you're just going to try to negotiate with her on the kingdom's behalf and hope for the best?"

"It's my way of being diplomatic," she replied. "But trust me, this will work."

"For our sakes, I hope you're right," he sighed. "Diplomacy might be a hopeful wish to us dreamers, but for tyrants like her, it's just another excuse to unleash more havoc out into the world."

"Don't worry, my love. No matter what happens, I'll protect you," she promised him.

And then, before he could say another word, Violet knocked at the front gate. Bang… bang… bang… she pounded away. Eventually, the doors cracked open and a young knight appeared, answering their call.

"You two are late," he growled in annoyance, as he flung the entrance doors wide open.

Without saying another word, Violet and Maximus took their first steps onto the palace's grounds. Alas, with phase one of their covert operations, now complete.

* * *

After spending an hour aimlessly wandering through the castle, Violet and Maximus failed to locate Vera's whereabouts. Unfortunately, she wasn't in the throne room or in the royal courtyard and gardens, and neither in her bedchamber or study, either. Apparently, all of the typical locations that a queen would normally have traveled to on a daily basis, Vera was completely absent from.

And so, with an unlucky bad streak, our heroes now found themselves seated down by a wooden and broken-down table, located in the far corner of the servants' dinning quarters and spying on the local knights. As the men enjoyed their rounds of pumpkin broth soups and gossiped about court politics, Violet and Maximus listened in on their conversations, while they pretended to sharpen their swords.

"The queen is planning to attack the Harvest Hollow's district come tomorrow," spoke the first knight.

"Oh really? The farming plots?" asked the second knight. "From what I've heard, our queen plans to sack the apple orchard, instead.”

Instantly, both men disgustingly laughed on. The sheer joy in their merciless voices, simply sickened Violet to her stomach. Who could honestly laugh at the face of death? Of human suffering? It truly was cruel and disheartening to say the least.

“Does it really matter?” asked the third knight, seated in-between the two other men.

“No, I suppose it doesn’t matter,” sighed the first knight. “As long as I have a roof over my head, a pretty wife to fuck and food in my belly, then I could care less about which one of these poor villagers lives or dies. Unfortunately, that’s life, regardless, of who sits on the throne. Poverty and misery are just a constant reality to us all.”

“True, but Harold, you’ve got to also admit that there’s been more deaths under the new queen’s reign than with either King Leopold or his father, King Elryk, combined. Under their reigns, we did have lasting peace,” the third knight politely pointed out.

“Jonas is right,” spoke the second knight. “Our previous kings did not run the kingdom down into ashes. I’m afraid that if more villages fall into ruin, then it’s only a matter of time before the queen’s rage eventually redirects towards *us*.”

“Roderick, as long as we are loyal to the queen and continue to do her biddings, then there’s nothing for us to fear,” replied Harold, the first knight. “Besides, at least with Queen Vera, she means business. She’s a conqueror. She’ll go down in the history books of the future as Vera, the Mighty. In a few years, I predict that she’ll conquer the neighboring kingdoms and establish an empire throughout the continent. Honestly, I highly doubt that former brute of a prince would have ever had the balls to do that. I mean, if that loser prince can ever pick up a sword in the first place.”

“Yeah, what a joke of a king he would have made. He’d have gambled away the entire kingdom between his whores and his mead. All he’s good for is just fucking around and nothing more,” Jonas added.

And then, all three men laughed their hearts out.

Meanwhile, Violet looked directly over towards Maximus. Even though his face was hidden away underneath his iron helmet, she immediately recognized his hands clenched into tight fists. He was angry to be sure and rightfully so, too. Not only was his good name and honor being insulted right in front of them, but these knights also had the nerve to openly support a ruthless queen who wanted nothing more but to bring more havoc and deaths upon the world.

Attempting to console him, Violet reached over and gently placed her armored gauntlet over his. Even though she couldn't see his physical reaction to her gesture, Violet felt like she had already helped to lift his spirits back up. That had she removed his helmet right there on the spot, then she would have witnessed a heartfelt smile form right in the center of his handsome face.

"We'll get through this," she whispered over to him, as he took a breath in and refocused his attention back to sharpening his sword.

"Anyways," Harold continued on, "I'll be on my merry way. My turn to guard the queen is soon approaching."

"Back to the throne room, then?" asked Jonas. "If that's the case, then I'll come join you. I'm supposed to switch places with Paul anyways."

"No, not the throne room," replied Harold. "Today, the queen insisted on visiting the library."

"Really? What for?" asked Roderick.

"I'm not sure. Maybe, to study more spells or review new strategies on warfare," he answered.

"Spells or warfare, who cares," spoke Jonas. "As her knights, it's none of our concern."

"True," Harold agreed. "Now, Roderick, I bid you adieu."

Facing Jonas, he asked, "Are you coming?"

And then, a second later, the two knights left. Meanwhile, Violet looked over to Maximus. After searching for Vera's location for the past hour, they finally had their long-awaited lead. Apparently, this evil queen preferred the company of dusty old books, instead of her prized golden throne.

"Come on," Violet hissed to Maximus. "We've got a library to visit."

And before Maximus knew it, Violet quickly grabbed a hold of his hand and then, they were off.

* * *

The library was far grander in scale than what Violet had previously anticipated. While she had visited many wonderous libraries in her lifetime shared between her family's ancestral estates and at her former university; however, the library found at the imperial royal palace was like none other. The library itself, was enormous. A city of its very own, stretching for miles on end. The room was probably as big as the entire ground levels of both Wiltshire Hall and Galloway Manor combined!

However, apart from its sheer enormous size, the library was also filled with thousands upon thousands of reading materials. Books with bindings and covers consisting in various colors, sizes and textures. Many looked ancient, as if they rightfully belonged on display inside of a glass curiosity cabinet as showcased at a prestigious cosmopolitan museum; while others, appeared more recent, with books reflecting modern style covers that appeared freshly printed. Even the smell of the room was inviting. With its unique scent of ink, pressed against the pages of ancient papyrus and molded paper.

Taking in a deep breath, Violet took a moment to cherish this intoxicating aroma that surrounded her. Had they not been searching for Vera in the middle of a war, then she would have gladly taken a break and dedicate her entire day to just lounging away inside the comfort of this spectacular library. No wonder Vera preferred this library to her throne room!

But apart from the endless shelves of books, the room was pure white, with white marbled floors and matching ceilings, along with bright glass windows in the place of walls. As a result of its unique architectural design and layout, the library was brightly lit and reflected a capsule of light. Just like a shining lamp. Honestly, it truly was the most perfect room to read a book in during the daytime. Meanwhile, the center of the room included endless rows of tables and chairs, fit for all types of readers. Judging by the view from the entrance alone, there appeared to be at least a million tables spread out. Just how large was this palace to begin with?

"I didn't realize just how wealthy you really are," Violet whispered over to Maximus.

"Because of the library?" he asked in surprise.

"Well, yes," she told him. "This is *the* biggest library that I've ever seen in my entire life."

"Huh, I never considered it be so," Maximus remarked, with her words capturing his attention.

"Never? Maximus, this place is a magical wonder!" she happily exclaimed.

"Do you really like it all that much?" he asked her directly.

"Why, yes, of course. Who wouldn't?"

"Fine," he said. "Once this all settled and done, it's yours."

"What?" Violet cried out, almost tripping over her own moving feet.

By now, Violet and Maximus were standing alone at the library's front entrance, with no other knight in sight. Currently, they were still on the lookout for Vera; who, at this moment, was nowhere to be seen. After all, this library was a maze and the evil queen could have easily been hidden just about anywhere.

"The library. You want it, it's yours. Consider it my gift to you," he answered.

"Isn't that sort of gift… a bit too… *generous*? After all, shouldn't a royal library belong to another royal?" she pointed out.

"*Exactly*," he proudly proclaimed.

And even though they were still wearing their helmets, Violet could already tell that Maximus was beamingly smiling by that answer. And to her credit, she, in return, was blushing bright red, underneath her mighty iron armor, too.

"Should we split up?" Violet asked him this time, hoping to revert their discussion back to their mission.

"No, we stick together at all times, remember?"

"Very well," she agreed. "Where should we start, then?"

"Father used to meet with his scribes and advisors in the war wing."

"A war wing? What's that?"

"It's another secret chamber hidden within this library. It's primarily used for meetings to discuss about the palace's strategies pertaining to war and conquest."

"But why build a separate war wing inside of a library?"

"Well, why not? After all, in this room alone, there's an endless supply of books concerning the subject of war and battle," he replied. "It's certainly a hell of a lot easier to pull these reading materials down from off their shelves and discuss them locally, rather than burdening the palace courtiers with the tedious task of transporting these heavy encyclopedias elsewhere within the palace's grounds."

"Ah, that's a good point," Violet agreed with him. "I never thought about it like that before."

"Anyways, if Vera is here in this library, then I suspect that she's more likely stationed there."

"Good idea. Let's head towards that direction then."

Following his suggestion, Violet and Maximus traveled down the library. After passing through the hallway and turning a corner, they arrived to what appeared to be a lounge area.

"We're almost there," Maximus stated. "A few more turns and then, we should reach the—"

"Who goes there?"

Unfortunately, they were interrupted by another knight. A black knight who refused to let them pass, without him questioning them first.

"I said, who goes there," he demanded.

With their helmets still on, Maximus calmly turned around to face him and said, "We're here to take over the previous knights' shifts. We're Jonas and Harold."

"Oh, I see," said the knight.

And for a whole second, Violet sighed a breath of relief. However, it was sadly, short lived.

"Well, Jonas and Harold," he spoke in a mocking tone. "Since when were members of the queen's imperial dark army allowed to use swords that are clearly designed for the former royal family?"

Glancing at Maximus' side, Violet noticed that his sword, just like hers, were different from the other knights at the castle. Unlike their black swords, theirs were silver plated, along with a collection of amber and ruby stones found along their handles, forming a perfect circle resembling the marigold flower. *A royal crest.* The official symbol of the House West. Damn it, they were caught red-handed!

"Either you're another royal, which personally, I doubt," expressed the knight. "Or, you've stolen it from the queen's personal collection and are therefore, a thief. Correction, *thieves*, as the both of you have it."

For a second, Violet just stood there frozen. They were caught and now, they had only one other choice: *fight.*

"Are you ready, my love?" Maximus asked her, as he got into position.

"Yes," she said.

As soon as she gave him permission, Maximus pushed her behind him and pulled out his sword and began to duel with the knight.

"Guards!!!" the knight desperately screamed for help. Unfortunately, the knight quickly discovered that he was battling against a strange man who was clearly much more skilled with the sword than he.

"Seize these criminals!" he screamed, once more.

Afterwards, ten more knights rushed over to the scene from out of nowhere.

And even though Maximus fought hard and bravely, he wasn't a match for an army of that high number. Much to their grave disappointments, they were captured.

With their hands pulled behind their backs, the angered knight ordered for the removal of their helmets. Alas, the damage was done.

"What do we have here," spoke the knight, with much amusement.

"I believe that's the former crown prince and his lady," answered his partner.

"Well, the queen is certainly going to have a field day with this!"

"What should we do?"

"Take them to the dungeons," the leading knight ordered. "I'll inform the queen. I doubt they'll live to see daylight ever again."

And with that, Violet and Maximus were immediately escorted down into the palace's dungeons to await their fates.

# CHAPTER 25

"This isn't how I imagined us spending our first night together in my palace," Maximus sighed, out of frustration.

"What? Being held captive together in a dark and gloomy prison cell, isn't your way of having fun?" she sarcastically asked him.

Naturally, our heroes were referring to their latest adventure: forcibly trapped inside of a tight and enclosed space, having recently been branded as petty criminals. After all, they were currently held in the palace's dungeon. A place, where light ceased to exist. A room where only darkness, dust, mold and creepy creatures of the night lurked at all hours, alongside the cold and grey stone walls and floors that stretched for miles on end. A blackened and godforsaken part of the imperial royal palace, where only the most vile and ruthless villains were sent to dwell in.

But ironically, Violet and Maximus were the only two souls still left in here. Apparently, the evil queen's reign of terror executed more captives, than she did of keeping them held as prisoners... *alive.* And so, as a result, the dungeon was empty, while the kingdom's graveyard was in full bloom.

"Of course not, my love," he answered. "I'd much rather have you held captive in my bedchamber, with me as your personal guard."

"Ah, I see," she blushed. "Perhaps, next time, we can try to make that fantasy a reality."

"Yes, if there is…"

"A next time?" Violet couldn't help but to address the white elephant lurking within the room.

After all, they were caught and now held captive, with their fates unknown. By sunrise, they could either be executed in their sleep or worse.

"Listen, we're going to get through this," Violet promised him. "We will live to see another day."

"I hope you're right, Violet. For your sake."

"What do you mean by that?"

"Just that, as long as you're okay, then I'm content."

"What about you?" she asked him.

"I could care less about me," he replied. "But you, on the other hand, are far more precious."

"But you're the crown prince!" she exclaimed. "How can you say such a thing?"

"Crown prince or not, I don't give a shit about myself," he cursed. "As long as you survive, then that's all that matters. So, if Vera should summon you, then please don't be afraid to do whatever she tells you to do. Even if…"

"Even if?" she repeated.

"Even if you have to throw me under the bus to accomplish your goals."

"What???" she choked.

"Listen, Violet," he spoke up, with his expression as serious as ever. "If Vera offers you a deal, my life in exchange for yours, then take it."

"You can't seriously mean that?"

"Oh, but I do," he proclaimed. "Between the two of us, I'm the greater threat to the legitimacy of her throne. As long as I live, then there will always be a question mark directed to her reign."

"Maximus, what are you saying exactly? That I should offer Vera your life, in exchange for mine? A safe passage back to home?"

"Precisely," Maximus admitted, with a heavy sigh.

"But... what about your people? What about Ruby? And all of the innocent citizens in your kingdom?"

"They can flee as refuges to the neighboring kingdoms. I'm sure the east will gladly take them. After all, their crown prince is a good friend of mine."

"And what about the remaining folks who don't want to flee? What about them?"

"We'll deal with it. But you, on the other hand, need to do what's best for *you*. Violet, if you love me, then you'll do whatever's necessary to ensure your safety."

"Maximus, you're talking utter nonsense," she scowled. "I will *never* do such a thing. I'm not going to leave this palace without you. You're my partner, my ally, my..."

"You're...?" he asked.

"My *everything*."

"Ah, Violet," he closed his eyes in despair. "This can only end *badly* for us."

"The fight's not over yet, my love," she told him. "We will win this war. Trust me."

"I'm afraid that's just the problem," he sighed.

"What is?" she asked.

"That I trust you. Even when everything else around us seems impossible."

And then, without saying another word, Violet reached over and stretched her hand through the opening found in-between the metal bars to her cell, which was located adjacent from his. In return, Maximus did likewise.

And as their hands intertwined with each other from their separating cells, Violet swore to set everything right.

"That's enough, you two love birds," said the knight, who recently arrived onto the scene.

"The queen requests an audience. Right *now*," he announced.

Instantly, both Maximus and Violet proudly rose-up from the bottom pits of their darkened and gloomy prison cells, with their chins held up high. Together, standing tall and proud at the front of their iron cell doors. Ready to face their fates, whatever they might be. Doom or glory.

"Not so fast, Romeo," the knight addressed Maximus. "Just *her*."

"Me?" Violet cried, in surprise.

"Yeah, you," he said. "Apparently, the queen wants to meet with the savior, after all."

A second later, the knight retrieved a set of keys from his pocket and then, he quickly yanked Violet from out of her cell. Afterwards, he briefly set the keys down, while he worked to place a tight rope around her wrists, secured as firmly as possible. And as Violet took her first step onto the cold and grey stone floor outside of her former prison's cell, Maximus cried out to her.

"Remember Violet," he cried. "Do whatever you must do to protect yourself. Don't worry about me."

Within the blink of an eye, Violet swiftly turned around and gave him a light kiss on his lips through the bars of his cell. And then, she leaned down and whispered into his ear, "Use this when you can," as she slipped something cold and metallic into his hand.

Meanwhile, after Violet exited the dungeon, Maximus opened his hand and saw a bright and shiny key. Somehow, in the midst of the knight freeing Violet, she secretly managed to steal an extra spare key with her sneaky fingers!

"Ah, Violet, I'm coming for you. Just you wait," Maximus breathed, as he waited for the coast to clear, before he unlocked the door to his cell.

# CHAPTER 26

"So, you're the savior?" Vera couldn't help but laugh at the mere sight of her.

After all, it was silly. Armies had challenged her. Strong men, with brutal and deadly weapons, fought her on a daily basis. Along with a string of assassins. Not to mention, her fellow witches and sorcerers. All of them, tried to defeat her *and* lost. And now, she was faced with the unlikeliest of heroes. A young maiden who wasn't even a native to their kingdom. Let alone, their realm.

In truth, she couldn't be more than twenty at best. Early twenties at worst. Really, it was all laughable. A young girl... *no* a mere *child*... with an innocent and youthful face... a fair maiden, who was considered to be a *savior*. A *saint*. Someone strong enough to stand up to injustice. To tempt fate. To challenge *her*.

Of course, Vera was no fool. If Violet was deemed as the savior, then it could only mean one thing: this girl was destined to be her *undoing*. Because in their world, that's what saviors did. They undid the mass injustices inflicted upon by the villains. A source of good to combat past evils. And to Vera's credit, she knew that her long-list of deeds were both cruel and evil. Alas, her lifelong pursuit of vengeance was a painful quest that came at a great cost: her heartless soul.

"I suppose this is just time's revenge aimed at me, for inadvertently causing the time loop upon my return back home," Vera sighed. "I guess that it was only my foolish and wishful thinking to presume that I could simply sit back and enjoy my throne, without a savior having to pop-up from out of nowhere. A girl destined to destroy all of my wicked fun."

"I highly doubt that mass murder and torturing innocent souls, should ever count as *fun*," Violet made sure to point this important fact out to her.

"Perhaps, for *some*," Vera retorted back. "But for others, it can be. What might be considered to be good by you, might be dreadful to me."

"Somehow, I find that hard to believe," said Violet.

Patiently, the young lady stood in front of her, while wearing a knight's suit of armor; albeit, absent of a helmet and gauntlets. Meanwhile, her long red hair was flowing loose and wildly stretching behind her back. Violet might have had the face and eyes of her father and grandmother, but that signature red hair clearly belonged to Maureen. From the looks of it, Violet must have been one of her descendants. Evidently, Henry's bride was a relative of her dear old former nanny.

"I'll admit, you do look like her," Vera acknowledged. "The same face and eyes. Of course, minus the hair."

"My hair is like my mother's."

"So, I've gathered," Vera remarked, underneath her breath.

And as Vera gazed upon Violet, *this so-called-savior*, she couldn't help but notice and admire as to just how calm she appeared to be in the face of danger. Really, her reaction was surprising, even to her. After all, most people... *no*... *everyone*... men and women... knights and palace courtiers alike... anyone around her vicinity... they all trembled in absolute fear, whenever in her presence. In fact, this golden throne room of hers, wasn't exactly a warm and inviting place. Although it might have been so under the previous kings' rules; but now, that certainly, wasn't the case anymore. At least, not under her reign.

Even with the golden walls, ceiling and floor that shined and sparkled a warm bronze and honey tone, few found peace and contentment inside of this room... including Vera, herself. Everything in this throne room might have been expensive, exquisite and beautiful; but sadly, it was also so incredibly insincere and fake. Gold, it seemed, might have been the heart and currency of men, but that wasn't the same case for Vera. For her, it was never about the treasures of conquest but the merits behind it.

"Tell me something, savior," Vera began, "Do I not frighten you? You do seem awfully calm in the presence of a fierce queen, whom many consider to be evil. After all, they do call me the evil queen for a reason. A title, I might add, that I consider to be a real badge of honor."

"On the contrary, *Aunt*, I am not afraid of you," she emphasized.

Ah, so the girl knew who she was, after all. Apparently, Vera miscalculated her. Violet was clever and apparently, fearless, too.

"So, you, unlike your father, knows who I am? Don't you?" she asked with a wicked smile.

"Yes, I know the truth," Violet answered. "Which is why I'm here. It's why I snuck into the royal palace in the first place. I wanted to meet with you, face-to-face."

"Let me guess, to assassinate me?" asked Vera, mockingly. "Consider this to be a kind warning, *niece*, that any attempts on my life will prove to be disastrous. A reckless and foolish mistake on your part. Trust me, when I say, that under the ill advisement of my own advisors, I chose the contrary. Instead of executing you on the spot, I decided to summon you here to my throne room. A rare honor that's seldom exercised. But be that as it may, I can still change my mind. Execution is still not off the table, just so you know."

"It's never been my intention to hurt you," Violet confirmed.

*Interesting.* Vera had heard many tall tales in her life, but this was certainly a true first. And judging by the earnest expression painted across her face, this girl truly looked sincere. Alas, she was telling the truth. But why?

"Well, out with it, girl," Vera demanded. "Why are you here? And not just at my palace, but in this realm? Why did you crossover into the Kingdom of the

West? And how?"

"The how part isn't important," Violet answered. "But my reasoning for seeing you is. I've come to help you to remember who you once were. Before your tragic fate."

"Help me to remember? Child, have you gone mad?" Vera cried, as she pounded her golden scepter loudly against the floor.

"Aunt, I'm not mad," she emphasized, once more.

"Once upon a time," Violet continued on, "Before you were the evil queen and the wicked witch, prior to being the late king's mistress, you were a young maiden, like me. You had a home, a mother, a sister... a family. A sister, whom you loved and cherished. And I know that my late grandmother, Sarah, loved you, too. It's why she kept this."

And then, Violet removed her metal gorget to reveal the amethyst heart stone necklace worn around her neck. Looking straight into Vera's direction, Violet saw the matching bracelet around her aunt's wrist. Apparently, after all these years, the evil queen still kept it close by with her at all times. Happily, Violet smiled on. If Vera still had the bracelet, then there was still hope.

"Kings may rise or fall, while kingdoms might flourish or crumble; worlds may begin or end, while honor and riches might come or go; but your sisterhood will outlast them all," Violet began to chant. "While romantic love might be fickle in nature, sisterly love is the truest form of everlasting love. Unlike romantic love, this love is born not out of attraction or admiration or even, affection; but by blood. And blood, is thicker than anything."

"Where did you hear that...?" asked Vera in surprise.

Honestly, it had been ages... *no*... *several lifetimes ago*... when she last heard those words spoken to her by another. Not since her mother and sister...

"I think you've been spending too much time in my mother's company," Vera sighed. "Obviously, she must have taught you that."

"Actually, no," replied Violet, sternly. "It's something that I picked up, all by myself. For you see, I, too, have a sister. A sister that I'd do anything for.

Especially, with I, being her older sister."

"Huh, so you've got a sister, too," Vera remarked. "Tell me, savior—"

"Violet," she stopped her. "Please, call me Violet."

"Very well, *Violet*," Vera repeated, with her heart beating strongly... a first... in a *really, really long time.*

Alas, even saying her name out loud, struck a chord with her. How precious her name really was.

"Aunt Vera," she said, "It's still not too late to change your fate. You don't have to be the evil queen anymore. I'll help you. If my grandmother could love you, then I believe that I can, too."

"You, love *me*?" asked Vera, in complete astonishment. "Are you honestly telling me that a savior, such as yourself, can ever love the likes of me? The same woman who cursed your father? Murdered hundreds... no, thousands of innocent souls? And still, you propose to love me? Me, the villainess to your heroic tale?"

"I believe that we are all the authors to our own destinies," Violet spoke directly from her heart. "And if my grandmother isn't around to offer you her love, then I can serve in her place as a replacement. Aunt, you don't have to continue on with this quest for revenge. It's okay to let go. To close this chapter of your life and begin a new one."

"And you think that's so easy?" she asked her, laughingly. "Tell me, Violet, why do all of the history books reference your crown prince's brother as Leopold, the Great? Or him, Maximus, the Brute? Heck, for the longest time, I was Vera, the Wicked Witch. And before that, King Elryk's whore. And now, the Evil Queen. In fact, even you, yourself, you're known as Violet, the Savior. The Saint. Unfortunately, my dear niece, we've *all* been marked by society. Now tell me, my dearest child, are each of our given titles not already a self-fulfilling prophecy? Unfortunately, our fates have already been sealed. Just or unjustly. Therefore, we might as well give them a show for it, am I right?"

"No, I don't believe that," Violet contested, standing firm in her beliefs.

"Really? Is that so?" Vera challenged her.

"It's never too late to change our fates. The very fact alone, that I'm standing here right now in front of you, should already be a testimony to that. Like you said before, I, technically, shouldn't have been able to crossover into your realm with that time loop still in effect. But yet, here I am. And whether or not you choose to accept me, I've already decided to love you, Aunt. And if my grandmother was alive, then I know that she'd still choose to love you, too. And no matter our current circumstances or even our pasts, we can still move on. To let go. To love. To forgive. After all, we're family. In the end, blood is thicker than anything."

"Powerful choice of words," Vera acknowledged. "And while you proclaim to love me; Ruby, instead, seeks to destroy me?"

"I cannot speak for Ruby, but I can speak for myself. And if you let me, then I can help you to turn your life around," Violet offered.

"You're a lot like her, you know," Vera sighed.

"Like my grandmother?" Violet asked in surprise.

"Yes, like Sarah," Vera confirmed. "Even as children, the world might have despised me, but she never did. Violet, I do, believe that you've inherited her loving heart. And that is the greatest gift above all else. A heart filled with unconditional and endless love is worth more than all the gold and riches in the entire universe."

"You know," Vera continued on, "I'll admit, I've grown a bit tired and restless this past month. No... *years*. As it turns out, my quest for revenge took a toll on me. Looking back on it all now, I probably should have just retired and rode off into the sunset during my exile. But alas, that option is no longer available. It's far too late."

Shifting her attention back to Violet, she asked, "But what shall become of your dear crown prince? Doesn't he want his throne back?"

"I cannot speak for him. But perhaps, that's a conversation that you and him need to discuss together," Violet answered.

"I see," Vera spoke somberly. "In that case, I think it's time for this evil queen to finally call it an end."

"An end? What do you mean?" asked Violet, nervously.

"Nothing for you to worry about," Vera promised her. "Alright, Violet, the Savior, I agree to your proposal. I accept your love."

"You do?" Violet gasped in amazement, with her eyes widened.

"Yes," Vera sighed, at long last. "I can't believe that I'm even admitting this, but I was always more of a conqueror than I was as an actual ruler. Whether or not this kingdom fails or succeeds, it needs a ruler who's willing to do it justice. And truth be told, it's simply not for me. I guess in the end, I'm ready to abandon my lifelong quest for revenge and finally accept my fate."

At long last, Vera was ready to move on with her life. Ready to embark upon her next voyage to whichever path was made available to her.

"Violet, please do me a favor. Please bring me that bouquet of violets over there at the window."

Following her command, Violet did just that. Handing the bouquet over to her aunt, Vera looked on and proceeded to give her some very strict instructions.

"Now, Violet, listen to me very carefully," she began, "After my departure, I want you to enjoin your necklace with my bracelet. Can you promise me this?"

"Yes, I can," replied Violet. "But where are you going?"

"Violet, I've lived a long and fulfilling life," she spoke. "And now, I'm ready to join my sister on the other side. After all, she was my one true love."

"Wait, you don't mean—"

But before Violet could stop her, Vera tore a piece of the flower's petal and quickly threw it into her mouth. Almost instantly, she began to cough and choke. And as Violet swiftly ran over to her side, she watched as her aunt's eyes grew consumed with endless tears. Meanwhile, her face instantly swelled up and turned into a dark shade of... well... *violet*...

"What can I say, love. I've always been attracted to toxic things," Vera admitted, speaking with her last ounce of breath.

"Aunt, what do you mean?" Violet cried, as she rocked Vera's weakening body within her shaky arms.

"Isn't it obvious? I'm allergic to violets."

A moment later, Vera was gone. In the end, violets *really* were the death of her.

# CHAPTER 27

A minute later, Maximus stormed into the throne room, only to find Violet lying down on the floor and rocking the late queen's dead body within her arms.

"Are you okay?" Maximus asked Violet, as he quickly ran over to the scene.

"As safe as I can ever be," she answered.

"What happened?" Maximus inquired, as he stared down at the deceased body of his former enemy.

"I think she took her own life."

"She did what???" he blurted out in shock by this astonishing revelation. "Willingly???" he pressed on.

"Yes," Violet replied coolly.

Glancing across to the golden throne room, Maximus didn't see any traces of a weapon. Or even blood, for that matter. If Vera was dead, then what in the hell killed her?

"What did it?" he finally asked.

"The violets," she whispered. "Apparently, she was allergic to them."

And then, he saw it. A bouquet of purple violets located facedown by her side, along with a single floral petal protruding out from Vera's swollen mouth. How fucking *ironic*.

"Well, I certainly didn't see *that* one coming," he admitted.

"Neither did I," Violet agreed.

"As much as I resented her in life, I'm afraid that the only honorable thing to do now is to bury her."

"I agree."

"I wonder what possessed her to eat them. It's not exactly a go-to-snack," he pointed out.

"I think she did it, because of our last conversation," Violet reflected.

"What did you say to her?" Maximus asked.

"I told her that I loved her."

"You did what???"

Now, *that* was certainly news to him. Never in a million years, did Maximus consider the possibility that his beloved Violet would ever dare to sprout those three precious words to his greatest of foes. And yet, she *did*.

"I told her that it wasn't too late to change her fate," Violet explained to him. "That once upon a time, my grandmother loved her, unconditionally. And if my grandmother wasn't around to love her, then I could love her in her place."

And then, Violet got up, looked directly into his silvery eyes and said, "Because Maximus, the cure to everything is *love. In all of its forms*. Romantic, sisterly... even nieces. A loving heart can cure even the worst of heartbreaks. No matter how painful or devastating they might be. Love is the answer. *Love is the cure*."

"Violet, my love," he spoke, with a warm smile. "You cease to amaze me. No matter what happens in the future, please don't ever change."

"I don't think I can, even if I wanted to," Violet admitted.

A few steps later, Maximus was right by her side. But before he could embrace her, she briefly pulled away from him.

"There's one last thing that I need to do," she told him.

Carefully, Violet retrieved the bracelet from off her late aunt's cold wrist. Afterwards, she removed her own necklace and following Vera's previous instructions, Violet united the two pieces of jewelry and pressed them together. And upon doing so, magic was immediately released straight into the air.

Instantly, a golden cloud of smoke appeared, followed by a bright lilac light. A second later, Violet and Maximus stared straight ahead and in front of them laid a pair of two crowns. They were plated in pure gold and were adorned with several sparkling and shimmering diamonds all around. And in the center on each pair, was a perfectly shaped amethyst heart stone pendant. A matching set fit for royalty.

"I believe this belongs to the next king and queen," Maximus said with a sly smile, as he bent down to pick them up.

"One for me," he said, as he placed the first crown above his head.

"And the second for my queen," Maximus proudly declared, as he placed the second crown above Violet's head.

"Does this mean... what... I think... it means?" she hesitated to ask him.

"Darling," Maximus began, as he pulled Violet up to his chest. "We're way past all of that by now. There's no need to be shy. Obviously, I intend to marry you. From the moment I first laid eyes upon you, it was already a done deal. Violet, whether you like it or not, my love, I do believe that you're stuck with me now, *for life.*"

"Marriage, another form of a life sentence, huh?" she teased him. "You know, before I came here, I was looking for a life's purpose. Truth be told, I even considered becoming a doctor."

"You can still be a doctor, should you choose. I'll never stop you," Maximus made sure to clarify this important fact to his bride-to-be. "As my wife and queen, you'll be my equal. You'll always be free to make your own decisions. And whatever you decide, I will always support you."

"I know, it's why I love you," she sighed. "But truth be told, I'm over the whole medicine thing."

"Really? Why?" he asked, surprised by her sudden declaration.

"Well, after studying magic under Ruby's guidance, I can now safely say, that it's not for me. Honestly, magic is more like studying another form of science than anything else. I guess I just wasn't meant to be a witch... or a doctor... for that matter."

"It's okay," he reassured her. "You've got that grand library now to look after. I'm sure you'll figure out something else to do."

And then, he leaned in and together, they locked in a heartfelt kiss. But unfortunately, their kiss didn't last too long; for at that precise moment, Ruby just-so-conveniently arrived onto the scene and now, she was standing right in front of them.

"Ahem," Ruby alerted them, as she entered into the throne room.

"Why is it that every time that I need to speak with either one of you," she pointed out, "I always seem to be interrupting *something* between the two of you."

"I...," they both stuttered.

"Never mind," Ruby spoke. "Now, that you've defeated Vera, the king's army has safely returned back to the palace. Meanwhile, most of the queen's former black knights have either surrendered or have chosen to flee the castle, altogether."

"Already? But how's that possible?" asked Violet, in surprise.

"I've been monitoring the situation from afar," she explained. "Once I saw you with the late queen, then I knew that it was my time to act."

"Thank you, Ruby," said Maximus.

"But, what about..."

And then, Violet noticed that lo and behold, Vera's body had suddenly disappeared without a trace. Her remains had simply vanished into literal thin air. All traces of her former self were completely gone. All except, for her now smashed bouquet of violets that were left behind.

"Don't worry, her body has passed onto the next life," Ruby clarified.

"Does it mean that she isn't yet dead?" asked Maximus, this time. His voice filled with worry and fear.

"No, she's dead. She won't be coming back to our world again. After all, a witch who's willing to accept her fate, can't be reanimated. Not like the last time."

"Then, what did you mean by saying the next life?" Violet inquired, curiously.

"Her soul, my dear. By now, I'm sure she's somewhere out there in this universe, reunited with Sarah in the hereafter."

"Are you okay with all of this?" asked Violet, in all seriousness. "As her mother, shouldn't you be saddened by her death?"

"It's complicated," Ruby sighed. "On the one hand, *yes*. Of course, I wish that it all could have turned out so differently. But on the other hand, I've already known how this war was going to end from the very beginning. Unfortunately, I've come to accept both of my daughters' fates long ago."

"What do you mean?" Violet and Maximus both asked.

"Years ago, when I pregnant with my first born, Vera, I visited a high priestess," Ruby began to explain. "At that time, I was a student studying magic at the academy. It was there at the convent, that I was foretold about a prophecy concerning my future daughters. I was told that my first born was fated for evil, while my second born was destined for good."

"That's horrible," Violet gasped.

"I agree, that is a bit difficult to swallow," Maximus concurred.

"Sadly, it was what it was," Ruby reflected. "Even though I tried my best to change their fates; in the end, I couldn't. It's why I gifted them with those pieces of jewelry. I wanted them to always remember their love for one another, while also not falling victim to their circumstances. It's why I never stopped my daughters from exercising their free wills. I didn't want either one of them blaming me later on, for what their destined paths led them down to."

"That's why you didn't stop my grandmother from marrying my grandfather? Or Vera from becoming the king's mistress?" asked Violet.

"Precisely," replied Ruby. "And now, it's time for you and the crown prince to lead this kingdom into the next era."

"Thank you," they both told her.

"One last thing," said Ruby. "Now, with Vera gone, the time loop has been restored."

"What does that mean?" asked Maximus.

"It means that the time shared between Earth and our world are now equal," she answered. "Your absence has been only but a single day in your world."

"Wow, a single day," Violet repeated. "It honestly feels like an entire lifetime ago."

"I know," Ruby agreed. "Which also means, my dearest Violet, that after your celebration with the crown prince, then you must return back home to tell your family about your future plans. They deserve to hear about their eldest daughter's decision about her chosen path straight from the source. You owe it to them."

Her granny was right. Violet's parents deserved to hear about her recent engagement straight from her own two lips. Plus, she wanted them here to bear witness to her upcoming nuptials. Including her own sister, Daphne, whom she also needed to make peace with, too.

"Very well," Maximus spoke. "Come tomorrow, I'll personally escort my bride-to-be back to her family's home, myself."

Happily, Ruby nodded in approval. Afterwards, she promptly exited the throne room, leaving Violet alone in her new fiancé's company.

"So, what's next for business?" Violet playfully asked him. "What's on the agenda for my new king?"

"Oh, Violet, I do believe that I'm well overdue, for a trip to my old bedchamber," he said with a sly and wicked grin. "Care to join me, my new queen?"

And before Violet could bat an eyelash, Maximus swiftly scooped her up in his arms and carried her off into his royal bedchamber. With her first night at the imperial royal palace spent entirely within the new-soon-to-be-king's bed!

# CHAPTER 28

L ove. Passion. Desire. There were no perfect words to accurately describe as to just how spectacularly wonderful it felt to finally be alone with the crown prince inside of his royal bedchamber. As it turns out, spending your first night as a newly engaged princess inside of your fiancé's bedroom, who also just-so-happens to be the future king, was quite thrilling and luxurious. It certainly was a grand adventure in the making!

After stripping down their armors, Maximus and Violet enjoyed a warm bath together, before eventually retiring off into his large and spacious bed.

"This is certainly an upgrade from the cottage," Violet laughed on.

"Yes. And unlike there, we won't experience any fears about being so rudely interrupted," he said with a wicked smile. "If I want to spread you across on my bed or bend you over backwards on my chair, then I can. Because, my love, I intend to ravish you until morning. To *fuck you* in my bed, against the wall and beyond. Shall we give it a go?"

"Yes, let's," she agreed, excitingly. "I'm most eager to celebrate."

And with that, Maximus lifted Violet up and carried her over to his bed.

Gently, he placed her down onto his mattress and afterwards, he crawled up beside her. As Maximus bent down, he began to lick and suck on her pink and hardened nipples. Instantly, she moaned upon his contact.

"Aaaahhhh....," Violet cried aloud, which only further excited him.

And so, Maximus sucked on her some more, as his hands traveled across her body.

Meanwhile, her own curious hands did the same. As he touched her, she touched him. While his hands caressed her thighs, hers wandered all the way down until she found his thick, large and hardened cock. With it nestled against her soft hands, Violet slowly began to lightly stroke it upwards. Starting from his tip and all the way up to his base, she stroked his shaft with a great sense of longing and desire. Instantly, he, too, moaned.

"Aaaahhhh... Violet... its feels *so good!*" he roared, as he closed his eyes shut.

His pleasure only excited her even more. And so, Violet increased her speed and proceeded to move up and down his shaft, hard and fast. Pumping him with her hand, while also accelerating her speed with each passing second. Meanwhile, her second hand rubbed against his thigh, making its way to play with his balls.

Pulling his mouth away from her breast, he cried, "I can't take it anymore! I need to feel myself *inside* of you!"

"Then, have at it," she told him with a wicked smile. Acting like the wonton that she was.

And so, he did just that. With a great sense of urgency, Maximus swiftly pushed her thighs apart, stretching them as wide and as far apart as he possibly could. Afterwards, he repositioned himself to align his body directly above her opening.

With her opening left wide open for him, Maximus took a peek in. Upon seeing just how wet and juicy she was, he instantly smiled from ear-to-ear. Regardless of their location, one way or another, Maximus could always find a way to excite her. To please her. Lucky, for him.

Without a moment's notice, Maximus swiftly plunged right into her, smashing through her inner walls and sending her body into flames. Instantly, she cried tears of joy, while moaning in pure pleasure.

Once he was inside of her, Maximus quickly picked up speed. Tonight, he wasn't going to go gentle with her. He wasn't going to hold back. Instead, he intended to give into his burning desires and conquer her. Tonight, she was *his*.

And so, Maximus plunged forward and then, he withdrew... and then... he plunged in once more... picking up speed along the way. A few seconds later, he thrusted straight and hard into her, as his hands tightly squeezed her hips, branding his mark onto her naked body. The body of his queen.

And as his erect cock delved deeper inside of her, Violet closed her eyes shut and surrendered her body over to his custody. Meanwhile, Maximus continued to pump into her... *over*... and *over*... and *over again*... thrusting *deeper* and *harder* into her womb, sending her waves of blissful orgasms.

A few minutes later, Maximus pulled Violet from off their bed and carried her off and leaned her against the wall. With her back pushed up against the wallpaper, Maximus wrapped her legs around his hips and then, he plunged his hard and thick cock deep inside of her. Eagerly, he moved his hips forward, as he thrusted into her body. Instantly, Violet moaned upon his entrance, as she grabbed a firm hold of his muscular shoulders for support. Meanwhile, as he savagely pounded into her flesh, the walls in his room vibrated and the portraits came crashing down onto the floor. It was a mess, but a glorious one at that!

"Who is *your king*?" he wickedly teased her.

"You are," Violet answered him, as she threw her head back against the wall.

"Good answer." *Thrust.*

Instantly, Violet moaned, once more.

"And who is *my queen*?"

"I am," she declared proudly.

"Exactly." A second *thrust*. But this time, it was much *harder* and *deeper* than before.

"Aaaahhhh…," Violet blissfully moaned.

"And good kings *fuck* their queens," Maximus whispered into her ear, as he plunged himself even deeper into her. "They *fuck* their queens, until they can't see or walk straight anymore. Shall I continue on, Violet? Shall I *fuck you*, until kingdom come? Until you are left seeing nothing else but stars?"

"Yes!" she screamed at the top of her lungs.

"Yes, what, Violet?" he teased her. "Tell me now, or I won't do it."

"Yes, Maximus!" she yelled. "Go on, and *fuck me*! Pound my pussy and make me yours!"

"That's what I like to hear," he said with a devious smile, followed by another deep *thrust*.

"Aaaahhhh…," Violet instantly moaned, as her hands and nails dug deeper into his shoulders.

"And while we're at it. Let's get one thing straight about our marriage," he whispered into her ear, biting down onto her lower lid. "At court, you may present yourself as a lady. My queen, my equal. But here…"

"Hmmm…," she moaned, already anticipating his filthy words. Words that literally sent her over the edge with dangerous excitement.

"In the privacy of our bedchamber, you shall be *mine*. And I, *yours*. No holding back, *ever*. Tell me your needs, and I promise to deliver. There shall be no others. Is that understood?"

"Yes," she sighed, accepting her inevitable fate with her lover. Her soon-to-be husband and king.

"Yes, what Violet?" he pressed on.

"Yes, I shall *always be yours*. And you, *mine*. Faithful, until the very end."

"Exactly," he said, followed by another deep and hard *thrust*.

"Now, Violet," Maximus added on. "Shall I go on? After all, I did promise to send you seeing stars."

"Yes," she breathed.

And with that request, Maximus carried Violet over to his chair, bent her over backwards and had his way with her. Savagely *fucking her* like a barbarian king, as he rapidly pounded into her swollen flesh, sending shock waves of pleasure… after pleasure… after pleasure. Happily, she cried tears of joy, as he continued to thrust into her. Pounding her flesh into melted butter, while marking his fingers onto her slender hips. Branding his imprint over to her. *Harder… faster…* he thrusted deeper into her naked body. Claiming her… *over* and… *over… again…*

Afterwards, he pulled her up towards his chest, as he took a seat down. With Violet standing in front of him, he slowly lowered her back down onto his lap. Meanwhile, his hands were squeezing the life out of her plump breasts.

"Now, Violet," he whispered into her ear. "This might not be my throne, but for the moment, it will do."

"But next time," he warned her, using his deep and seductive voice, "I plan to *fuck you* there, too."

And then, without any warning, Maximus brought Violet further down onto him, until she felt his large and erect cock sliding in-between her thighs and entering into her dripping wet womb.

"Now, my queen, it's time to ride your king," he commanded.

His words were like music to her ears. Instantly, Violet shuddered from excitement. After spending all these past several weeks together, this was a brand-new position for them to try out. And in all fairness, she was willing to do almost everything in her power to please him, too. *Her mighty king.*

Following her instincts, Violet let her body run wild. With his cock filling her up whole inside of her, she rocked back and forth against his wet thigh. With his hands resting alongside her sides, Violet rolled her hips against his, relishing on the friction taking place between them. From this position, it felt oh so wonderful!

At first, Violet went slowly, but the more she rocked against his cock, the faster she began to go. Eventually, her speed picked up, until she was riding him at full force.

"That's it, Violet," he roared in pleasure. "That's a good girl. Keep going. *Fuck me hard.* Ride my cock, like the queen that you are."

His words only further encouraged her. And so, Violet did just that. She rode her fiancé, her lover and her king, in full force. Slamming against his muscular thighs, as she grinded herself against his hardened cock. A glorious cock that sent her body into shock waves of pleasure. *Fucking him* with all her might. And as her breasts jiggled along the way, Maximus tugged at her long red hair and rolled his own hips against hers.

A few minutes later, Violet found herself out of breath. But their celebratory sex journey still wasn't over. Far from it. Instead, Maximus brought her back and over to his bed and continued with their epic dance of love. Flipping her over with her hands held tight against the headboard, as he entered her even deeper from her behind. Meanwhile, his hands were digging into the flesh of her hips, as he buried his cock deep inside of her, determined to release his juice from within her. All the while, pounding her to kingdom come. With each one of her screams of pleasure, forever branding his heart.

Afterwards, they both climaxed and collapsed onto their sides. After spending the past twenty-four hours in disguise as knights, then captured and held as prisoners, and then, defeating the evil queen… by now, the crown prince and crown princess were officially exhausted. At long last, they finally dozed off to sleep, wrapped together safely in each other's arms.

And in the end, Violet was really left seeing nothing else but stars. It was a true miracle that she could even walk the next day, too!

❊ ❊ ❊

The next morning, outside on their balcony, Violet and Maximus watched as the sun rose over the Kingdom of the West. A land that they together, were about to jointly rule as the next king and queen.

Its enchanting beauty was unparallel. With its rolling emerald hills, bright tangerine pumpkin patches and scarlet red apple trees that stretched for miles on end; that, along with the endless fields of amber daisies and golden marigolds all sprouting throughout, this land and all of its inhabitants were truly a gift sent directly from heaven above.

Alas, this was Violet's future. This was her new life. This was the land, where her children... and their children's children... and their children's children... would all grow up in. A place to call *home*. For many, many generations to come.

"My darling, I do hope that you won't feel too disappointed by remaining as a princess for no more but a single week," Maximus gently whispered into her ear, as he held her tightly within his arms.

"What do you mean? A princess for a week?" she asked him in confusion.

"Because that's how long I'm willing to wait, before I claim you as my bride," he clarified. "And once I do, we'll be officially crowned as the next King and Queen of the West."

"An engagement for a week? Isn't that a bit too short of a notice to plan a proper royal wedding?"

"*A week*," he emphasized, "Is all than I'm willing to spare. Be glad that I didn't order for our wedding to take place today. I could have, just so you know."

"I take it, that as the new king, that would have been your first order by royal decree?" Violet asked him, with a beaming smile.

"Yes," Maximus replied. "But, like I told Ruby yesterday, your family deserves to be here for our special day. It's the only reason as to why I'm agreeing to delay our marriage in the first place."

"Then, shall we get going?" she asked him. "After all, the magic mirror is still at Castle Hope. And the way I see it, the sooner we get there, then the quicker we'll return back home to the palace."

"One step ahead of you, my love," he said. "I've already got a magic mirror in my possession, here at the palace. Ruby's mirror isn't the only magic mirror in this realm either, just so you know."

"Really?" asked Violet. That was certainly a surprise.

"Who else owns a magic mirror?" she pressed on.

"Oh, a few other royals and magicians. Really, they aren't so uncommon in this part of the world," he shrugged.

"Okay, but apart from you and Ruby, who else is a member to this prestigious club?"

"A few folks, including my good friend, Prince Florian of the East," he replied. "He's another crown prince from the neighboring Kingdom of the East, the Land of Eternal Spring. By the way, he'll be at our wedding. Perhaps, you can meet him then."

"Alright, then, shall we get going?"

"My darling, Violet, I thought you'd never ask."

And then, before Violet knew it, Maximus grabbed a hold of her hand and together, they were off to embark upon their next grand adventure.

# CHAPTER 29

Outside in the gardens of Wiltshire Hall, Daphne was enjoying a morning stroll through the park, when she was unexpectedly met by her elder sister. It had only been but a day since she last saw Violet, but their parting wasn't a particularly good one.

In fact, it was Daphne's own selfish desire to take what didn't belong to her, that inadvertently caused their great fallout during Violet's birthday party. A day that should have been filled with joy, happiness and celebration, instead of argument, anger and resentment. Had Daphne conducted herself in a more regal and princess-like manner, then perhaps, their unfortunate altercation could have been avoided, altogether. If only she had acted more respectful and mature, just like a true *princess*.

But now, with Violet's arrival, Daphne needed to atone for her past misdoings and seek her sister's forgiveness. After all, she was wrong to take Violet's pearl earrings without her permission. And no matter what happened between them in the past, her sister still deserved a proper apology.

"Violet," spoke Daphne, as she took her first step towards her sister.

"Daphne, just the person I was looking for!" Violet happily exclaimed; accompanied by a surprisingly warm smile to go along with her joyful facial expression, too.

Her positive reaction wasn't something that Daphne was anticipating or even, prepared to see. Was it possible that her sister was already in a jolly good mood? Open and ready to possibly forgive her, too?

"Daphne, we need to talk," Violet told her, as she quickly grabbed a hold of her hand.

And before Daphne knew it, the sisters were off and walking towards the direction of the gazebo. A serene place in the garden, where the lilies were surprisingly, magically in full bloom. Even in the midst of the autumn season.

* * *

# A Few Minutes Later...

"**Y**ou're getting married???!!!" cried Daphne, in shock. Equally, she was happily stunned and surprised by this joyful, yet unexpected news.

Truly, she couldn't have been any happier for her sister. But yet, this special news was still rather alarmingly shocking. Especially, given the fact that as of yesterday, her sister was very much single and most importantly, *un*engaged.

"Yes, it's true," Violet confirmed. "Plus, I've already taken the liberty to speak with Mother already. And I can happily say that she approves of my engagement and gives her full blessing to our union. In fact, Mother even plans to write to Father this very afternoon to inform him about Maximus and I."

"But will Father approve, too?" asked Daphne, with suspicion.

"According to Mother, yes, Father will approve," Violet answered. "Apparently, Mother believes that so long as I am happy, then Father will have no objections. I guess in the end, our parents really do want us to be happy, after all."

"That's comforting to know," Daphne remarked, while also secretly thinking about her own future, too.

"Anyways, the wedding will take place next week. And as I've already mentioned before, he's the crown prince—"

"Which makes you the new crown princess and the next future queen," Daphne finished her sentence.

"Precisely," Violet replied, with a proud smile.

"But, more than anything," she added, "Regardless of his royal status, I love Maximus for *who* he is. Whether he's a brute or a king, I love him either way."

"I suppose that's awfully romantic of you," Daphne interjected. "But still, I'm rather surprised as to how quickly this all came to be. Especially, considering that only just yesterday, you were single, unattached and most importantly, contemplating about the direction of your own future."

"Like I said before, time operated differently between the Great Kingdom and our world," Violet pointed out.

"And now, with Vera's demise, it's since been fixed? Time is truly equal between our two realms?" asked Daphne.

"Yes, Vera's death undid the time loop," Violet answered. "Everything is essentially, back to normal."

"And in a week, you'll be married and gone, while I'll be forced to stay behind at home and suffer the dreaded wrath of Adrian," Daphne sighed in despair.

In the past, having Violet around also meant that she, too, was forced to share on some of the burdens associated with their younger brother's pestering antics and endless pranks. But sadly, with Violet married and gone, Daphne was now left all alone. And as a result, she was fearful about her own future as the only Galloway sibling left to endure Adrian's ongoing fury.

"You shouldn't worry about Adrian," Violet reassured her. "Besides, Daphne, soon enough, he's going to be moving far away to attend military academy. I highly doubt that Adrian will be visiting home anytime soon. In fact, the majority of the time, he'll be elsewhere. Well, apart from the holidays."

"Trust me, Violet, I already fear and dread about those upcoming holidays. Even within the span of a single week, Adrian's return visit can easily cause enough havoc and damage to last an entire lifetime," Daphne explained. "When left alone, Adrian is simply too much to bear. Especially, for *me*."

"Ah," Violet sighed. "Our younger brother really is a nuisance, isn't he?"

"Yes," breathed Daphne, in frustration.

"But regardless, Daphne, you've got to learn to be more patient with him. Just like I've been patient with *you*," Violet reminded her.

"You're right," Daphne reluctantly agreed. "So, does this mean, that you forgive me? Because, Violet, I truly am sorry. With all of my heart, please accept my sincerest apologies for disrupting your birthday. It was wrong of me to selfishly take your earrings and again, I'm sorry."

Seeing the apologetic expression written across her sweet face, Violet couldn't help but to also feel sorry for her younger sister, too. After all, in a week's time, she wasn't going to see her daily anymore, like she used to. Unfortunately, their time spent together in each other's constant company was slowly drawing to an end.

"Of course, I forgive you," she said.

"You do?" Daphne asked.

"Yes. Plus, Daphne, in case you've forgotten, you're also my only sister," Violet explained. "And no matter what happens next, both now and in the future, please always remember that I love you, unconditionally. And even though I'll be moving far away, that doesn't mean that we can't keep in touch anymore. In fact, our separation will only serve as another excuse for you to come and visit me. Besides, if Adrian becomes too much of a burden for you later on, then you can always travel to my new kingdom to escape."

"You know, that's not such a bad idea," Daphne seriously contemplated. "Any reason to escape from Adrian, honestly, I welcome it wholeheartedly.

Besides, your new kingdom has princes' and other royals, too, right?"

"Yes, as a matter-of-fact, it does," Violet confirmed. "In fact, there's a crown prince from the Kingdom of the East that's expected to attend the wedding. I believe he's a close friend of Maximus. Prince Florian, is his name. From what I've heard thus far, he's rumored to be quite charming and handsome. Perhaps, you can meet him at the ceremony?"

"Well, that does sound promising," Daphne smiled on.

"Oh, and before I forget," Violet reminded her. "Those pearl earrings, they're yours. Consider it as my parting gift to you."

"Wait, what do you mean?" asked Daphne, in surprise. "I'm the one who took them from you. Why should they be mine?"

And then, Daphne proceeded to remove the earrings from off her ears. However, Violet stopped her midway.

"No, Daphne," she spoke firmly. "They're my gift to you. Something to remember me by. If anything, wear them to the wedding. Perhaps, they'll bring you some luck."

"Oh Violet, are you sure?" Daphne hesitated to ask. "After all, they were one of your favorite pieces. A gift from Father. Besides, I was wrong to take them before in the first place."

"Wrong or not, I don't care," Violet answered. "You're my sister, and I love you. I want you to have them. Plus, I want us to have a clean start. I don't want what happened between Sarah and Vera to happen to us, too. I refuse to allow history to repeat itself again. Please, promise me, Daphne, that if there's ever a problem lingering between us, that you won't neglect to tell me the truth? Remember, good communication is the key to a lasting relationship."

"What happened between our grandmother and our great aunt, it will never happen to us," Daphne told her sternly. "Violet, we are *not* like them. And might I also add, unlike our Aunt Vera, I'm not afraid to speak up. Trust me, Violet, the day that you stop responding back to my letters, then that will be *the day* when I storm into that fancy royal palace of yours to let you know, myself!"

"Promise?" asked Violet playfully, with a raised brow.

"Promise," Daphne vowed.

And then, together, the two sisters had a much-needed heartfelt laugh.

Meanwhile, as the Galloway sisters stood inside of the gazebo, Violet walked over to the far edge of the enclosure to an area in which the lilies were in full bloom. Carefully, Violet proceeded to pluck one of its buds from off its stems. Afterwards, she approached Daphne's side and gently tucked the bright pink flower behind her ear.

"Daphne, this lily suits you perfectly," Violet complemented her sister with a warm smile. "A pink lily to go along with your emerald green gown and pearl earrings. My dear sister, pink and green are truly your colors. They suit your complexion to absolute perfection."

"Thank you," she said. "Do you really think so?"

"Yes, I do," Violet told her. "Besides, I once read in a book that the color green is often regarded to be a lucky color, too."

"I see," Daphne reflected. "Then, perhaps, in the future, I'll make it my signature color. After all, I could use all the luck in the world to win the heart of a future prince."

And with that, the two sisters happily walked together side by side, making their ways back towards the direction of the estate, having finally made peace with each other.

# CHAPTER 30

On the eve before Violet's wedding, there was a sudden knock at her door. Ever since she moved into the royal palace, she shared her primary bedchamber with her betrothed, Maximus. However, given her family's recent arrival to the castle, Violet and Maximus decided that it was for the best that they kept a safe distance apart and thereby, slept in different bedchambers. Separate wings, to be precise. And located on the opposite ends of the castle, too. As much as Maximus resented leaving Violet's bedside alone, he also acknowledged that it was the only honorable thing to do as her husband-to-be. Especially, with respect to her family and his future in-laws.

After all, this *special request of separation* was also a premarital requirement made specifically by Violet's own father, Henry. As an old-fashioned gentleman, the earl expected his eldest daughter to follow in this sacred tradition of chastity, upheld by the gentile class. Regardless, if she was a virginal bride or not. But to Henry's credit, he remained completely ignorant to Violet's and Maximus' already intense and highly sexual relationship. As far as the earl was concerned, his daughter was expected to remain as a young and innocent maiden up until her expected wedding night.

"Please do come in," Violet answered the call.

A moment later, her parents entered into her bedchamber. Now in their matured ages, Henry was no longer the same youthful gentleman from the days of his curse. Now, as a mortal resembling a man at the ripe age of fifty, his hair was now colored salt and pepper, along with a few wrinkles formed around the far corners of his eyes and on the sides of his mouth. However, Henry still maintained his famously tall, fit and muscular figure. Regardless of his slightly aged appearance, Henry Galloway was still one of the most dashing and handsomest men in all of England.

Meanwhile, her mother, Kassie, remained the ever-stunning and graceful beauty. Just like her own daughters, Kassie's hair remained long, wild, thick and fiery red as ever. The years had certainly been kind to her.

Luckily, for Kassie, the countess possessed no traces of visible wrinkles found around her soft porcelain face. In fact, had her age remained unknown, then most folks would have failed to guess Kassie's true age. Even well into her forties, Kassie remained as flawless as ever. And because of this fact, Violet only wished that as she matured, that she'd also gracefully age well, just like her mother before her.

"Mother, Father," Violet cried out loud.

"We just couldn't wait until tomorrow to speak with you," Kassie admitted to her eldest daughter. "Your Father and I are most eager to wish you a proper farewell, before the upcoming festivities."

"Especially, given the fact that this will be our very last night spent together as a family, with you being our special little girl," Henry told her, while showcasing a warm smile.

And then, both of her parents came to Violet's side and each of them, gave her a heartfelt hug.

Pulling away, Violet said, "This doesn't have to be farewell. Mother and Father, you're always welcome to visit me and stay for however long as you both like."

"Ah yes, but that wouldn't be fair to either you or your new husband," Kassie replied.

"No, that simply wouldn't do," Henry agreed.

"Over these past twenty-one years, Violet, you've been nothing short but a wonderful daughter to us," her mother proudly declared. "And regardless of the past minor disagreements that you've shared with yourself and your younger siblings, you've always been a good role model to them all. You are the best sister, Violet Galloway. And an even better daughter to us, too."

"We both couldn't be any prouder of you and all of your many accomplishments," her father gushed. "Since that blessed day of your birth, Violet, you were always my perfect, sweet and charming little girl."

With tears in his eyes, the earl confessed, "Why, the very first moment that I held you within my arms, my life forever changed. I might have discovered true love with your mother, but with you, I found my heart. My dearest and sweetest daughter. A piece of me to live on forever. Seeing you for the first time, it made me realize that eternity is not measured by one's years, but by the legacy of one's children."

"And you, Violet, changed me, too," Kassie joined in. "You made me a mother. I remember staring at you for the first time and noticing your perfect smile. It was there, at that moment, when I realized just how truly special you were and still are. It's why I named you Violet. It's because at first sight, I already knew that you were just as magical and wonderful as those blessed flowers."

"And we both couldn't possibly love you anymore than we already do," Henry added.

And then, the Earl and the Countess of Galloway gave their daughter one last and final hug for the night.

"Get some rest, my darling girl," spoke her mother. "Tomorrow, you'll be crowned as the next queen."

"But," added her father, "King or no king, if that boy ever makes you feel unhappy, then you let me know right away. I'll drag you back to England, if it's the last thing I do. Either way, you're still *my* daughter, before his wife. Royalty or not."

And with that, Henry and Kassie kissed their daughter's forehead goodbye and exited her bedchamber. Afterwards, Violet blew out the flickering flame to her candle and went straight to bed. With a beaming smile on her face, she closed her eyes and went to sleep. Sleeping like a real beauty and a princess, with a bright new future as queen ahead of her.

# CHAPTER 31

It was the wedding of the century, or so, that's what her family claimed it to be. All throughout the Great Kingdom, ordinary citizens and royals alike, traveled far and wide to bear witness to the grand royal wedding that united a savior with a crown prince.

And as the joyful crowd gathered around inside of the cathedral to cheer on and happily clap away, Violet gracefully descended down the aisle, ready to meet her fate and marry her prince. Like the fairy tale princess that she was, Violet wore a pure white ballgown style wedding dress that was made from pure silk and adorned with hundreds of sparkling diamonds, shiny opal pearls and strands of gold, each individually hand woven directly onto her exquisite bridal gown.

Overall, it was a magical sight that brought many happy tears to her family's eyes. Meanwhile, her long white lace veil stretched from to the top of her head and all the way down onto the red-carpet floor. In fact, the train to her elongated veil required two full-time dedicated flower girls to help her to carry it, while Violet journeyed down the aisle, ready to embark upon her new and exciting journey as a newly fledged member of the western royal family.

Meanwhile, Maximus was equally dressed just as lovely as his beloved bride. Sporting his royal military uniform, consisting of a white silk shirt, a pair of black trousers and a thick velvet scarlet cape, his uniform was also decorated with several prestigious gold medallions, all proudly out on display. According to Maximus, the medallions represented all of the awards that he previously won and collected from various battles throughout the years.

And much to his credit, Maximus did possess many. Plus, that, along with his handsome face, silvery eyes and silky chestnut brown hair that was currently slicked back, Maximus graciously wore a golden crown above his head. A golden crown that was identical to the same crown that was now worn above the head of his blushing new bride. Crowns that Violet and Maximus had previously inherited from the late Vera upon her death.

And so, with her golden crown, along with a fresh garland of marigolds currently worn above her veil, Violet happily descended down the aisle with her father, Lord Henry, by her side.

However, unbeknownst to the happy crowd surrounding them, was the fact that no more than an hour ago, Maximus and Violet were already secretly married and previously declared as the new king and queen. Prior to their very public wedding ceremony, Maximus and Violet ultimately decided to go against upheld tradition. Instead of having a large audience to witness their heartfelt vows, Maximus and Violet quietly legally married within the comfort of his study. Afterwards, with the blessing of the high court, they were proclaimed as the new King and Queen of the Kingdom of the West through a private coronation.

Given the devastating aftermath associated with the last war that was sparked by the late evil queen, the high court unanimously agreed to move quickly to ascend Maximus and his bride onto the throne, without any further delay. Therefore, they all agreed to the crown prince's special request to hold a private ceremony to declare him as their new king. Furthermore, in their continued efforts to protect and secure the integrity of the monarchy, they all agreed to forgo holding another public event, such as a coronation. Therefore, the wedding ceremony itself would just have to serve as the only public event to celebrate the new royal couple. And celebrate, they most certainly did, too!

In honor of the newly married couple, the wedding took place at the local cathedral and was visited by a large crowd, numbering in the thousands. Keeping true to western culture, the cathedral was decorated with the official colors of the Land of Eternal Autumn. From red carpets to forest green chairs, to amber linen tablecloths to a scarlet red velvet wedding cake, the unique autumn colors of their land were all out on public display.

And apart from the millions of marigolds and other foliage that were scattered across the venue, including at every possible corner, ceiling, table and window; the food also represented their western traditions as well. From red apple pies and green apple spiced tarts, to orange pumpkin stews and red cranberry infused puddings, to roasted pheasants and minty spiced rabbits, the generous wedding feast was offered to all who came.

Meanwhile, in the grand company of her parents, siblings and great-grandmothers, along with the rest of their neighboring royals and all of the many citizens residing within their realm, Violet and Maximus happily exchanged their public vows to one another in front of the entire world. Together, they promised to love, honor and cherish each other, until death, do they part.

Alas, after years of harboring the ruthless title of Maximus, the Brute; today, marked a new milestone for the happy couple. From this day hence forward, not only were they crowned as the new King and Queen of the Kingdom of the West, but they would also be known in the history books as Maximus, the Brave and Violet, the Beloved. A new identity for our heroes.

And for the young maiden who once wished for a knight in shining armor, Violet finally found one in Maximus, the prince, and now the king of her heart. *Her equal.*

In the many years to come, King Maximus and Queen Violet of the West would continue to go on to have many more adventures and celebrations. But no matter the challenges that they endured during their golden reign, they faced it together bravely and courageously. All the while, treating their many subjects with the utmost honor and respect, no matter their circumstances. Important values that they also successfully instilled upon onto their own children, including their sons, the Princes' Leopold and Tristan, and their daughter, Princess Marigold.

And in the end, they all lived *happily ever after.*

# EPILOGUE (PART 1)

## Six Months Later...

On the first day of spring, the twenty-first of March, Daphne Galloway peacefully sat underneath a laurel tree, while reading a chapter from her favorite book, *An Encyclopedia of Fairy Tales*. And within that book, Daphne read her most beloved fairy tale above all else, called *True Love's Kiss*. It was a story about a young maiden who fell madly in love with a cursed prince. But to break his spell, it required a kiss from his beloved maiden. His one true love.

Ever since Daphne was a young girl, she always dreamed about growing up and marrying a prince. And just like her elder sister, Violet; she, too, wanted to find her own knight in shining armor. A real-life prince. And thereby, becoming a future princess in her own right.

Meanwhile, as Daphne happily sat underneath her laurel tree, with her fiery red hair adorned with a bright pink lily flower that was carefully tucked right behind her ear and sporting an emerald green velvet dress, she peacefully sat down and curiously pondered about her own impending future.

Now, with her sister married and gone from the nest, Daphne was left with the sweet memories of Violet, along with the set of pearl earrings that she previously gifted to her before her departure. While the earrings might not have been a royal crown or a tiara; in the end, Daphne was still grateful to have them.

And with Violet gone, Daphne now considered this piece of fine jewelry as a personal and sentimental keepsake, in remembrance of their cherished sisterhood. No matter how far apart they were in this universe, Daphne would always keep Violet's fond memories nearby and locked closely within the chambers of her heart.

"Hello Daphne," suddenly, spoke her younger brother, Adrian.

Much to Daphne's dismay, the young Lord Adrian Galloway, the only son of the Earl and the Countess of Galloway and the sole heir to the Galloway title, fortune and estates, was currently standing before her. While Adrian might have been the pearl to their parents' adoring eyes, Daphne was no fool to his true devious personality. Behind that sinister and wicked smile of his, was a naughty adolescent. A scoundrel who had most recently returned back home to Galloway Manor, after spending the majority of the school year attending an all-boys preparatory military academy in London.

As a notorious troublemaker, her younger brother was *forced* to enroll in England's strictest military academy that was famously known throughout the entire European continent to *rehabilitate* naughty young boys into becoming more refined and well-behaved gentlemen. Ha, a mockery if ever one existed!

But even though their mother, Kassie, publicly claimed that his enrollment was purely *voluntary* on Adrian's part; however, Daphne, on the other hand, knew better. In truth, she was his elder sister. Therefore, she knew the *real him*. After all, Daphne grew up alongside with him. Much to her great disappointment.

Needless to say, Adrian was only meant to stay here temporarily. At least, for the remainder of his spring break holiday. Afterwards, he'd be forced to return back to London to complete the remainder of his studies at the academy. And as much as Daphne tried her best to avoid him, it simply wasn't possible. Even hidden underneath the laurel tree found within Galloway Manor's private garden, Daphne still failed to escape from him. Unfortunately, her laurel tree wasn't far enough away from the likes of troublesome Adrian.

"Hello Adrian," Daphne sighed, as she closed her book shut. "Why have you come? Haven't you already bothered me enough since this morning?"

And by *that*, Daphne was referring to Adrian's persistent rounds of silly and mindless pranks. With Violet gone, Daphne was now left to suffer as the sole victim to their younger brother's constant and highly annoying petty little games. Endlessly, too. In fact, just an hour ago at breakfast, Adrian had the nerve to switch her glass of freshly-squeezed orange juice with actual paint! Needless to say, the *mess* resulting from that sticky situation already forced Daphne to change into a second pair of clothing— all before noon!

"Oh, Daphne, I'm never done with pestering you," Adrian laughed on hysterically.

Of which, Daphne had absolutely *no* patience for! Really, his rudeness and childish antics were simply too much to bear! Had he *not* been her brother, then Daphne would have gladly pushed him down into the bottom of a steep and darkened well!

"Well, if you're going to just stand there and laughingly mock at me, then I'll just get on with reading the rest of my book!" Daphne retaliated by flipping open the pages to her book and promptly, returned back to her reading.

Instantly, Adrian stopped laughing.

"Come now, sister. Don't be so serious," he told her. "In fact, if you take a moment to pause from your reading, then I've got a nice present to give to you."

"A present?" asked Daphne in surprise, as she lowered her prized storybook away from her face.

Closing her book shut for a second time, she asked, "Alright, you've got my full attention. Go on, tell me now. Be out with it."

"Well...," began Adrian, "Since Violet was kind enough to give you those pretty pearl earrings, I, too, have a present just for you."

While Daphne generally loved to welcome all gifts, regardless of their givers; however, when it came to Adrian, she was skeptical. And for good reason, too. One way or another, her brother's gifts *always* seemed to come with a catch. Usually, a catch that resulted in her grave misfortune.

"Okay, Adrian, and what pray tell, is your gift?" she asked him.

It then occurred to Daphne that Adrian's hands were conveniently placed behind his back. Whatever his gift to her was, he must have been hiding it from his rear behind.

"Very well, since you asked," he said.

Slowly, Adrian brought forth his hands over to his chest. And as he opened up his palms, he revealed a small and slimy green frog lying on top of his hands.

"What's this?" cried Daphne, in disgust.

If there was one thing that Daphne hated most in this world, it was frogs. Second, came flies. And third, every other insect known to mankind.

"My gift to you, of course," replied Adrian, with a beaming smile. "Here you go, Daphne. Enjoy your new pet!"

Suddenly, the little frog leaped up high into the air and landed straight down onto Daphne's lap. Instantly, Daphne blinked her eyes several times in pure shock. The worst possible thing imaginable just happened. One way or another, she came face-to-face with her greatest of foes: *frogs*!

Within the blink of an eye, Daphne jumped up high into the air and quickly ran for her dear life. As she fled the scene, she also managed to leave her favorite storybook behind. And as the pages to her fairy tale, *True Love's Kiss*, opened back up, the little emerald green frog found his way over and sat himself down on top of it. Just like a bookmark.

"I guess, she won't be needing you anymore," Adrian remarked to both the frog and the storybook.

And as Daphne disappeared into the garden, Adrian sat himself down onto her vacant old spot underneath the laurel tree and pulled a red juicy apple from out of his pocket. Meanwhile, as the frog leaped off the pages of the storybook, Adrian took a bite of his apple and flipped through its pages, until he finally stumbled upon a fairy tale called *The Archer*.

"Perhaps, while I'm here, I'll take up archery as a new hobby," Adrian said to himself, as he continued munching away on his juicy red apple.

Meanwhile, his sister was nowhere to be found.  Alas, she escaped from the company of the infamous slimy green frog!

But little does Daphne Galloway know that in a few years' time, she'll cross paths with another similar green creature. A curious emerald green frog, who will one day make all of her wildest dreams come true in the most unexpected of ways... ah... if only she had but known... but that, dear reader, is another tale... for perhaps, a later time...

# EPILOGUE (PART 2)

A bright white light shined against Vera's face, as she opened her eyes. A moment ago, she was surrounded by pure darkness. And now, it was replaced by an all-consuming light. A bright and white majestic light, which left her with a calm and serene sensation growing deep within her chest. For once, she no longer felt anger. Hatred. Heartbreak. Suffering. *Pain.*

Instead, this time around, she surprisingly felt... *happy.* At *peace.* And in truth, she hadn't felt this way in a very... very... very *long time.*

"Where am I?" she asked, as her eyes adjusted to her new environment.

Around her was nothing but magical light. But as her eyes grew accustomed to this new world, Vera realized that she was standing out in a meadow. A garden that was filled with endless flowers, found in every possible shape, size and color. Above her was the clear sky, except it wasn't blue. Instead, it was pure white, along with twinkling yellow stars shining high above.

Across from her were orange monarch butterflies flying about, while white rabbits hopped alongside the grassy fields. Wherever she was, Vera was at a safe place. And for once, she felt at blissful ease.

"Welcome home," spoke a familiar female voice.

Instantly, Vera turned around and there, standing before her was her estranged sister. Her *deceased* sister. And if she was here, then it could mean only one thing…

"Whatever you're thinking, the answer is yes," spoke Sarah.

Just as she last remembered her, Sarah stood before her with her long blonde hair gracefully flowing against the howling wind, while dressed in all white, along with her emerald green eyes sparkling like a pair of jewels. It had been ages since she last saw her. No, several lifetimes ago.

"I'll admit, I always wished to reunite with you again," Vera confessed. "Although, I know I'm not deserving of such a reward. Honestly, for all of my past crimes and evil deeds, I half expected to be welcomed by the devil, himself. But somehow, God must have made a mistake, because you're here, instead."

"God did not make a mistake," Sarah corrected her. "Our God is a merciful lord. He knows of your past pain and suffering. And because of this, he has forgiven you. Like all of mankind, we are sinners. We all make mistakes. And as a result, we are all gifted with the chance to achieve redemption. But the most important lesson to learn in one's life is to *let go. To forgive. To move on. To accept love, in all of its forms.* And that, my dear sister, is a painful truth that you finally came to learn the hard way. Albeit, it took some extra time. Longer than most folks."

"Indeed," she sighed.

"Shall we continue on?" Sarah asked her. "There's someone who's been eagerly waiting to meet with you."

"Someone other than yourself, actually cared enough to greet me? Here, in the hereafter?" she asked in surprise.

But before Sarah could respond to her question, a young man suddenly appeared beside her. And in that instant, Vera's heart nearly stopped beating altogether.

No longer was he the old king, whom she last saw. Instead, he, like her, was a youthful soul. Resembling the same boy, whom she recalled back from the past days of their youth. With his brown chestnut hair shining against the bright starry lights and his silvery eyes focused directly upon her, Elryk was the spitting image of his son and the new king, Maximus.

"Elryk?" she cried.

"It's been a long time," he told her, as he grabbed a hold of her hand. "Oh, how've I've missed you."

"I… I… can't believe it," she burst into tears.

After everything that she endured in her past life, Vera was finally reunited with the two people whom she loved most of all, in the entire universe: her sister and her long lost love. Her heart and her soul.

"There are more happier times in store ahead of us," spoke Sarah.

"Happier times for us all," Elryk added.

And then, with her right-hand laced with Sarah's hand and her left-hand interlinked with Elryk's, Vera followed them deep into the woods of the hereafter.

And after a lifetime of heartbreak, at long last, in the gardens of heaven, Vera was finally blessed with her long awaited *happily ever after.*

# AFTERWORD

To all my readers, thank you for taking this wonderous journey with me through the Enchanted Forest.

And this saga continues on with our next heroine, Lady Daphne Galloway, in…

### The Emerald Prince

# About the Author

Kristina Stangl is an American author. She was born and raised in San Francisco, California, USA. She holds a Master's degree in Public Administration, MPA; a Bachelor of Arts in International Relations, with a minor in Middle East and Islamic Studies from San Francisco State University; along with Teaching English as a Foreign Language (TEFL) credentials from the University of Toronto, Ontario Institute for Studies in Education. Before writing her first novel, Kristina previously worked in both the public and private sectors, having served in the United States federal government for nine years. In addition to writing, Kristina enjoys traveling across the globe and visiting famous and historical sites, which she documents on her social media accounts. To date, she has traveled to over thirteen countries, three continents, and speaks three languages. When Kristina is not traveling or writing, she's at home experimenting with baking new desserts, pies and other sweet treats.